GREAT LAKES

GREAT LAKES

Love Stretches Her Hand

Across Rough Waters

in Three Historical Novellas

ANDREA BOESHAAR & SUSANNAH HAYDEN

BARBOUR

PUBLISHING

An Uncertain Heart © 1996 by Andrea Boeshaar
An Unexpected Love © 1998 by Andrea Boeshaar
Tend the Light © 1997 by Susannah Hayden

ISBN 1-59310-901-6

Cover art by IndexStock and PhotoDisc

Scripture quotations are taken from the King James Version of the Bible.

Published by Barbour Publishing, Inc., P.O. Box 719, Uhrichsville, Ohio 44683, www.barbourbooks.com

Our mission is to publish and distribute inspirational products offering exceptional value and biblical encouragement to the masses.

 Member of the
Evangelical Christian
Publishers Association

Printed in the United States of America.
5 4 3

An Uncertain Heart

Andrea Boeshaar

For my mother, Janice Kuhn,
who encouraged me in writing this book. . .
and who hates typing as much as I do. I love you.

Chapter 1

U nion Depot was a flurry of activity as porters hauled luggage and shouted orders to each other. Reunited families and friends hugged while well-dressed businessmen walked along briskly, wearing serious expressions.

Just outside the train station things were bustling as well, what with all the carriages and horse-pulled streetcars coming and going on Reed Street. Sarah McCabe had all she could do just to stay out of the way. And yet she rejoiced in the discovery that Milwaukee was not the small farm town she'd assumed. In fact, it wasn't all that different from Chicago where she had spent the last nine months teaching music. The only difference she could see right off was that Milwaukee's main streets were cobbled, whereas most of Chicago's were paved with wooden blocks.

Looking down the street now, Sarah squinted into the morning sunshine. She wondered which of the carriages lining the curb belonged to Kyle Sinclair. In his letter, Mr. Sinclair had said he would meet her train. Sarah glanced at her small locket-watch. It was 9:30, and a half hour later than Mr. Sinclair had said he'd meet her. Sarah's train was on time. Had she missed him somehow?

My carriage will be parked along Reed Street, Mr. Sinclair had written in his last letter, the one in which he'd offered Sarah the governess position. *I shall arrive the same time as your train: 9:00 a.m.* The letter had then been signed: *Kyle Sinclair.*

Sarah let out a sigh and tried to imagine just what she would say to her new employer once he finally came for her. Then she tried to imagine what the man looked like. *Older. Distinguished. Balding and round through the middle. Yes, that's what he probably looks like.* She eyed the crowd, searching for someone who matched the description. Several did, although none of them proved to be Mr. Sinclair. With another sigh, Sarah resigned herself to the waiting. Her mind drifted back to last August when she had left her home in rural Missouri for the excitement of the big city: Chicago. As the youngest McCabe, she had grown tired of being pampered and protected by her parents as well as her three older brothers, Benjamin, Jacob, and Luke, and her one older sister, Leah. Sarah thought they all had nearly suffocated her. Oh, they loved her, of course, but Sarah felt restless and longed to be out on her own.

So she'd obtained a position at a fine music academy in Chicago—one of which her parents approved—and began her travels, enjoying every minute of her newly found freedom. She had made good friends in Chicago, friends she was sorry to leave for the summer months. However, the academy was closed during June, July, and August. Therefore, Sarah had been forced to seek other employment for the summer. Either that, or return to Missouri—a fate worse than death as far as Sarah McCabe was concerned!

Then she had seen a newspaper advertisement. A widower by the name of Kyle Sinclair was looking for a governess to care for his four children. Sarah answered the ad; she and Mr. Sinclair corresponded numerous times; she'd obtained permission from her parents—which had taken a heavy amount of persuasion—and then she had accepted the governess position. She didn't have to go home. She would work in Milwaukee for the summer. *Another adventure!*

Now, if only Mr. Sinclair would arrive.

In his letter of introduction he explained that he owned and operated a business called *Sinclair & Company: Ship-chandlers and Sail-makers.* He had written that it was located on the corner of Water and Erie Streets. Sarah wondered if perhaps Mr. Sinclair had been detained by his business. Next she wondered if she ought to make her way to his company and announce herself, if, indeed, that was the case.

An hour later, Sarah felt certain that was, indeed, the case!

Re-entering the depot, she told the baggage man behind the counter that she'd return shortly for her trunk of belongings and, after asking directions, her reticule in hand, Sarah set out for Mr. Sinclair's place of business.

As instructed, she walked down Reed Street (or South Second Street, as it was also called) and crossed a bridge over the Milwaukee River. Then two blocks east, and she was on Water Street. From there she continued to walk the distance to Sinclair & Company, which she found with little effort. Squinting in the sunshine, she scrutinized the building from where she stood across the street. It was three stories high, square in shape, and constructed of red brick.

Crossing the busy thoroughfare, which was not cobbled at all but full of mud holes, Sarah lifted her hems and walked up the few stairs leading to the front door. She let herself in, and a tiny bell above the door signaled her entrance.

"Over here. What can I do for you?" a young man asked, sounding quite automatic about it, for his gaze hadn't left his ledgers. Sarah noted his neatly parted straight blond hair—as blond as her own—and his round wire spectacles.

Sarah cleared her throat. "Yes, I'm looking for Mr. Sinclair."

The young man looked up now and, seeing Sarah standing before his desk, he immediately removed his spectacles and stood. He was quite tall, she noticed, and he wore a crisp white dress shirt and black tie, although his dress jacket was nowhere in sight and his shirt-sleeves had been rolled to the elbow.

"Forgive me," he said apologetically, looking a bit surprised. "I thought you were one of the regulars. They come in, holler their orders at me, and help themselves."

Sarah gave him a slight smile.

"I'm Richard Navis," he said, extending his hand. "And you are. . ."

"Sarah McCabe," she replied politely as she placed her hand in his, "formerly of Maplewood, Missouri, but most recently of Chicago."

"I see." Richard grinned in a mischievous way. "A pleasure, Mrs. McCabe."

"Miss," she corrected.

"Ahh. . ." His deep blue eyes twinkled. "Then more's the pleasure, *Miss* McCabe."

The young man bowed over her hand regally, and Sarah yanked it free as he chuckled.

"That was very amusing," she said dryly, for he'd obviously done that on purpose in order to check her marital status. *The cad.* But worse, she'd fallen for it! The oldest trick in the book, according to her three brothers!

Richard chuckled again but then put on a very businesslike demeanor.

"And how can I help you, Miss McCabe?"

"I'm looking for Mr. Sinclair, if you please." Sarah noticed the young man's dimples had disappeared with his smile.

"You mean the captain? Captain Sinclair?"

"Captain?" Sarah frowned. "Well, I don't know. . . ."

"Well, I do." Richard grinned and once again his dimples winked at her. "He manned a gunboat on the Mississippi during the war and earned his captain's bars. When he returned from service, we all continued to call him Captain out of respect."

"I see." Sarah felt rather bemused. "All right. . .then I'm looking for Captain Sinclair, if you please."

"Captain Sinclair is unavailable," Richard stated with a twinkle in his eyes, and Sarah realized he'd been leading her on by the nose since she'd walked through the door. "I'm afraid you'll have to do with the likes of me."

She rolled her eyes in exasperation. "Mr. Navis," she began, "you will not do at all. I need to see the captain. It's quite important, I assure you. I wouldn't bother him otherwise."

"Miss McCabe," he countered, "the captain is not here. Now, how can I help you?"

"You can't!"

The young man raised his brows and looked taken aback by Sarah's sudden tone of impatience, but she didn't care. She crossed her arms and took several deep breaths, wondering what on earth she should do now. She gave it several moments of thought.

"Will the captain be back soon, do you think?" She tried to lighten her voice a bit.

Richard shook his head. "I don't expect him until this evening. He has the day off and took a friend on a lake excursion to Green Bay. However, he usually stops in to check on things, day off or not. . . . Miss McCabe? Are you all right? You look absolutely stricken."

Sarah snapped her mouth shut, realizing she'd been fairly gaping. *Mr. Sinclair—that is, the captain—not here?*

Then she reached into the inside pocket of her jacket and pulled out the captain's last letter—the one in which he stated he would meet her train. She looked at the date. . .today's. So it wasn't her who was off, but him!

"It seems that Captain Sinclair has forgotten me." She felt a heavy frown crease her brow as she handed the letter to Richard.

He read it and looked up with an expression of deep regret. "It seems you're right."

Folding the letter carefully, he gave it back to Sarah. She accepted it, fretting over her lower lip, wondering what she should do next.

"I'm the captain's steward," Richard offered. "Allow me to fetch you a cool glass of water while I think of an appropriate solution."

"Thank you." Sarah began to relax. She felt as though he truly meant to help her now instead of baiting her as he had before.

Sitting down at a long table by the enormous plate window, Sarah pulled off her gloves and waited for Richard to return. *He's something of a clown* she decided, and she couldn't help but compare him to her brother Luke. However, just now, before he'd gone to fetch the water, he had seemed very sweet and thoughtful. . .like Benjamin, her favorite big brother. But Richard's clean-cut, boyish good looks and sun-bronzed complexion. . . now they were definitely like Jacob, her other older brother.

Sarah smiled and let her gaze wander about the shop. She was curious over all the shipping paraphernalia. But before she could really get a good look at the place, Richard returned with two glasses of water. He set one before Sarah, took the other for himself, and then sat down across the table from her.

He took a long drink. "I believe the thing to do," he began, "is to take you to the captain's residence. I know his housekeeper, Gretchen."

Sarah nodded. It seemed the perfect solution.

"I do appreciate it, Mr. Navis, although I hate to pull you away from your work." She gave a concerned glance toward his books, piled on the desk.

Richard just chuckled. "Believe it or not, Miss McCabe, you are a godsend. I had just sent a quick dart of a prayer to the Lord, telling Him that I would much rather work outside on this fine day than be trapped in here with my ledgers. And then you walked in." He grinned. "Your predicament, Miss McCabe, will have me working out-of-doors yet!"

Sarah smiled, heartened that he was a believer. "But what will the captain have to say about your abandonment of his books?" She raised a brow in a teasing manner.

Richard responded with a sheepish look. "Well, seeing this whole mess is *his* fault, I suspect the captain won't say too much at all."

Sarah laughed, as did Richard. However, when their eyes met. . . sky-blue and sea-blue. . .an uncomfortable silence settled down around them.

Sarah was the first to turn away. She forced herself to look around the shop and then remembered her curiosity. "What exactly do you sell here?" she asked, eager to break the sudden awkwardness.

"Well, *exactly*," Richard said, appearing amused, "we are ship-chandlers and sail-makers and manufacturers of flags, banners, canvas belting, brewers' sacks, paulins of all kinds, waterproof horse and wagon covers, sails, awnings, and tents." He paused for a breath, acting quite dramatic about it, and Sarah laughed. "We are dealers in manilla, hemp and cotton cordage, lath yarns, duck of all widths, oakum, tar, pitch, paints, oars, tackle, and purchase blocks. . .*exactly!*"

Sarah swallowed her giggles. "That's it?"

Richard grinned. "Yes, well," he conceded, "I might have forgotten the glass of water."

Smiling, Sarah took a sip of hers. And in that moment she decided that she knew how to handle the likes of Richard Navis—tease him right back, that's how! After all, she'd had enough practice with her big brothers!

They finished up their cool spring water, and then Richard hitched up the captain's horse and buggy. He unrolled his shirt-sleeves and, finding his dress jacket, he put it on. Next he let one of the other employees know he was leaving by shouting up a steep flight of stairs, "Hey there, Joe, I'm leaving for a while! Mind the shop, would you?" Finally, Richard announced he was ready to go.

"Do you know the Lord Jesus, Miss McCabe?" Richard asked after they had picked up her baggage from the train station. They were now heading for the captain's home.

Sarah was momentarily stunned by the blunt inquisition but replied nevertheless. "Yes, I'm a Christian. I asked Jesus into my heart when I was just a little girl. Why do you ask?"

"I always ask."

A smile tugged at the corners of her mouth. "Good for you!" In his present state, Richard reminded her of her brother Luke. He was a serious Christian, too. "My father is a pastor in Missouri," Sarah offered, "and two of my three brothers are missionaries out West."

"And the third brother?"

"Benjamin. He's a photographer in St. Louis. He and his wife, Valerie, are expecting their third baby in just a couple of months."

"How nice for them."

Nodding, Sarah felt a blush creep into her cheeks. She really hadn't meant to share such intimacies about her family with a man she'd just met. But Richard seemed so easy to talk to. Like a friend already. However, Sarah soon recalled her sister Leah's words of advice: *"Outgrow your garrulousness, lest you give the impression of a silly schoolgirl! You're a young lady now. A teacher. . ."*

Sarah promptly remembered herself and held her tongue—until they reached the captain's residence, anyway.

"What a beautiful home!" she exclaimed as Richard helped her down from the buggy.

"Yes, it's quite a sight."

Walking toward it, Sarah gazed up at the enormous brick mansion. It had three stories of windows which were each trimmed in white, and a "widow's walk" at the very top gave the structure a somewhat square design. The house was situated on a quiet street across from a small park which overlooked Lake Michigan. But it wasn't the view which impressed Sarah. It was the house itself.

Richard seemed to sense her fascination. "Notice the brick walls which are lavishly ornamented with terra-cotta. The porch," he said as they climbed its stairs, "is cased entirely with terra cotta. And these massive front doors are composed of complex oak millwork, hand-carved details, and wrought iron. The lead glass panels," he informed her as he knocked three times, "hinge inward to allow conversation through the grillwork."

"Goodness!" Sarah felt awestruck. Then, with a glance at Richard, she grinned impishly. "You are something of a walking textbook, aren't you?"

Before he could reply, a panel suddenly opened and Sarah found herself looking into the stern countenance of a woman who was perhaps in her late forties.

"Hello, Gretchen," Richard said in a neighborly way.

"Mr. Navis." She gave him a curt nod. "Vhat can I do for you?" Sarah immediately noticed the housekeeper's thick German accent.

"I've brought the captain's new governess," Richard announced. "This is Sarah McCabe." He turned. "Sarah, this is Mrs. Gretchen Schlyterhaus."

"A pleasure to meet you, ma'am," Sarah said, trying to sound as pleasant as possible, for the woman looked quite annoyed at the moment.

"The captain said nussing about a new governess," she told Richard, fairly ignoring Sarah altogether. "I know nussing about it."

Richard grimaced. "I was afraid of that."

Sarah gave him a quizzical look.

"Let's show Gretchen that letter. . .the one from the captain."

Sarah pulled it from her inside pocket and handed it over. Richard opened it and read its contents. Yet, in spite of what she heard, Gretchen still maintained that she knew "nussing" about a new governess.

Finally the crusty older woman closed the door on the both of them, and together Sarah and Richard walked back to the carriage.

Chapter 2

S o now what?" Sarah asked.

Richard helped her climb aboard the buggy. "You'll have to stay with me this afternoon."

Sarah noted that he appeared none too disappointed. She tossed a glance heavenward.

"We'll have some lunch; I'll show you around town; and—"

"And you won't have to look at your ledgers for the rest of the day," Sarah finished for him with a little laugh.

"My, my, Miss McCabe, you're quite astute." With that quip, he climbed into the carriage.

"And you're quite a stinker. I've got an older brother just like you, too. His name is Luke. He can be quite fun. . .unless I get myself into trouble. There's no persuading Luke when I'm in trouble!"

"You? In trouble? I can hardly believe it!" Richard grinned and flicked the reins. The buggy jerked forward. "Is Luke the photographer or the missionary?"

"Missionary. Benjamin is the photographer."

"Oh, yes, that's right." With a sidelong glance in her direction, Richard gave her a "stinker's" grin.

Sarah just shook her head at him.

"Did you say you're from Chicago?"

Sarah nodded. "I've been teaching music there for the past year. I came to Milwaukee because I saw Mr.—I mean, Captain—Sinclair's advertisement for a governess. I needed summer employment, so here I am."

Richard frowned. "The captain knows this is only temporary?"

"I presume so. Why do you ask?"

"Well, you see, several governesses have come and gone at the Sinclair household, and I got the impression the captain wanted to hire someone. . .well, more permanent. Then, again, the captain is growing

15

more desperate with each passing day."

"Desperate!"

"No insult intended. But with a business to run and four children—"

"Yes, I see what you mean." Sarah's blond head bobbed as the carriage bumped along the rutty street. " 'Desperate' is likely a fitting word."

Richard smiled. He enjoyed listening to Sarah's chatter.

"Personally," she continued, "I believe the reason Captain Sinclair agreed to take me on *temporarily* is because I promised to give his children piano lessons at no extra charge. However, I also made it clear that I must be back in Chicago by the first of September."

But more than he liked to listen to her sweet chatter, he liked tease her—in fact, he liked that most of all.

"Are you saying," Richard began, feigning a shocked expression, "that I have only until the first of September to steal your heart?"

Sarah raised a brow, though she didn't appear shocked by his comment in the least. "Mr. Navis, the man who intends to 'steal my heart' will have to contend with my father and four brothers first. I highly doubt you're in a position for such an undertaking."

"You're quite right about that." Richard couldn't conceal his grin. "A father and four brothers are enough to deter any man."

"Yes. . .a sad chapter in my life's story." Sarah shook her head, and Richard chuckled for a good thirty seconds.

"You know, you do remind me of one of my brothers. His name is Luke. He teases me incessantly. The day he left to go West was a day to rejoice for me!"

Richard smiled. "Yes, well, I wonder how many young ladies wished that I'd go West on account of my wit. In fact, I know of several who would gladly buy my ticket!" Richard thought that most women these days didn't have a sense of humor. Such a tragedy. Except for his mother. Now, there was a woman who appreciated a good laugh!

"I must confess," Sarah was saying, "I do miss Luke now that he's gone. But he's doing very well out there, and I believe he'll be back in the fall. He started a church in Arizona—in just a little nothing town. He needs a schoolteacher, and I wanted to be the one; however, my father said it was out of the question."

"Good for your father!" Richard drew his brows together in consternation; he had never known a young lady willing to venture into the untamed West. He'd heard the journey was laborious, even dangerous, and once they arrived, settlers found deplorable conditions—especially in the "little nothing towns" of the Arizona Territory. It certainly wasn't a place for sweet Sarah the music teacher.

Richard drove the buggy to Grand Avenue, and they ate at a small establishment by the Milwaukee River. They watched the boats and barges sailing in the sunshine as they enjoyed their meal.

"My goodness," Sarah said, realizing she'd behaved "garrulously" again. "I have been talking up a lather, haven't I?"

Richard dabbed the corners of his mouth with the white linen napkin. "I don't mind."

"You're very gracious. But I've been quite rude. Imagine, monopolizing our entire conversation! Please forgive me, Mr. Navis."

Richard chuckled. "You're forgiven. . .and it's Richard. I insist. I equate Mr. Navis with my father." He shook his head. "I only wish Gretchen would call me by my first name. She, however, doesn't feel it's in line with her position—even though she has always been 'Gretchen' to me."

Sarah nodded, thinking it over. "All right, then, Richard. Tell me about yourself." She pushed out a smile as embarrassment gnawed at her. "I certainly have talked enough about me."

Richard smiled. "Fair enough."

Sitting back in his chair, he began to tell Sarah the basics. He lived with his parents in their home which was about five miles northwest of the city. He had no siblings to grow up with, just farm animals. He'd completed his education in May of last year, which earned him a certificate in accounting.

"But I hate accounting more than words can tell," he admitted.

"Then why continue to work in that capacity?"

"Because I still owe the captain several more months of service." Richard obviously took note of Sarah's bemused expression and explained further. "Captain Sinclair paid for my education." He leaned forward. "A friend of my father's initially got me the job. . .doing dock work. But as soon as the captain discovered I had a 'talent for figuring,' as he put it, he sent me to school."

"What a wonderful opportunity!" Sarah felt the smile slip from her lips. "But you hate it? The book work?"

"Yes, I hate it. . .although I'm grateful for the education. Knowledge is never lost. That's the way I see it."

Sarah agreed. "But does the captain know you hate your work?"

"Yes, though he constantly encourages me. I believe he'd like me to stay on after my service is up. . .but that's a decision I'll make when I have to. I'm indentured until the end of December. So for now, I leave my fate in the Lord's hands."

With the meal finished, they walked out of the little eating establishment and went back to the captain's store on Water Street.

"Captain Sinclair will be arriving shortly," Richard informed her. "But now I, unfortunately, must get back to my books. I do apologize. . . ."

"Please don't." Sarah shook her head. "You've done over and above in seeing to my welfare. But can I browse a bit?"

Richard inclined his blond head. "Most certainly."

Sarah walked up and down the wide aisles of the store. In the back, she discovered the manufacturing part of the business. Upstairs, she found the chandlery office; its purpose was contracting for the shipping and receiving of various goods.

Finally bored with her wandering, Sarah sat down near Richard, promising not to babble while he was busy at work.

At precisely five-fifteen, Captain Sinclair walked in. He was tall, suntanned, and darkly handsome—and looked nothing like the distinguished, heavy-set, older man Sarah had imagined. He had thick, black, curling hair and black eyes. Sarah was fairly mesmerized; she'd never seen a man with black eyes before, nor had she ever seen one so handsome!

"Minding my business, are you, Richard?" the captain asked with a chuckle. He gave a quizzical look in Sarah's direction and then turned back to Richard expectantly.

"Captain, this is Sarah McCabe," Richard said. "I'm afraid she's been waiting for you since early this morning."

The captain froze, and his expression registered the shock of his error. "Oh, no. . .it's Wednesday." He narrowed his gaze at Richard. "Why didn't you tell me it was Wednesday?"

"Thought you knew that, sir. After Tuesday comes Wednesday. . . happens every week."

Sarah was aghast at the flip reply; however, the captain didn't seem bothered by it in the least. In fact, a hint of a grin pulled at the right side of his mouth.

Then the captain fixed his dark gaze on her. "Miss McCabe," he began in earnest, "I am terribly sorry about this. . .er. . .mixup."

Sarah forced a polite smile, feeling suddenly shy in the captain's presence. "It's quite all right." After clearing her throat, she found a more steady voice. "Richard has been a wonderful host."

"Good." Captain Sinclair eyed Richard. "My steward can be quite useful when he puts his mind to it."

"Aye, aye, sir."

Sarah pressed her lips together to prevent a smile. But the urge vanished as Captain Sinclair searched her face. Sarah thought her knees might buckle under his scrutiny, for she had never met a man quite so handsome as the captain!

Richard cleared his throat. "I took Sarah to your residence, Captain, but there was a problem with Gretchen. . . ."

"Hmm. . ." The captain pursed his lips in thought and glanced at Richard. "Is she acting ferociously again?" Looking back at Sarah, he sent her a good-natured wink.

Sarah decided to sit down, lest her lower extremities give way.

Richard, however, didn't seem to notice her odd response. "Gretchen was more than ferocious, sir, and apparently she had no idea that Sarah was arriving today."

"Oh, I'm certain I told her." With his black eyes still on Sarah, he added, "I gave Gretchen your name and read your letter of qualifications to her. . . ." He paused, momentarily pensive. "Or was that the last governess? Well, no matter. I'll take care of Gretchen when I get home." He smiled at Sarah then, in a way that threatened to stop her heart.

Then all at once his expression changed to one of irritation. "Oh, blast! I forgot. I have a dinner engagement tonight." He glanced at Richard, then back at Sarah, considering her at great length. Finally, he turned and faced Richard once more. "Why don't *you* take Sarah to dinner?" he suggested. "Eat slowly, perhaps take a ride, and I'll make sure Gretchen has Sarah's room prepared by the time you return her to my house later."

Richard appeared to think it over.

"Captain Sinclair," Sarah put in, feeling like a burden that neither man wished to bear, "I really can't impose on Richard. . .again."

"Well, of course you can. Richard doesn't mind, do you?"

He shook his head.

"Perhaps there's a hotel," Sarah persisted.

"No, no, it's quite all right," Richard told her. "I'd consider it a privilege to take you to dinner."

"Of course you would. See, Miss McCabe? This matter is now under control." The captain's smile exuded confidence.

Sarah tried to return the gesture, but, truth to tell, she was tired. She wanted to change her traveling clothes, and she'd absolutely love a bath!

"And don't worry about transportation home tonight, Richard," the captain said. "You may use my horse and carriage."

"Thank you, sir."

"And put dinner and everything else on my tab."

"As you wish," Richard replied, wearing a mischievous grin.

The captain noticed. "But don't overdo it!"

"Not to worry, sir."

Captain Sinclair looked worried nevertheless.

Finally, he turned to Sarah. "I'm terribly sorry about all this, my dear. But tomorrow morning will be soon enough for us to get further acquainted."

She managed a weak nod, and her ideas about settling in for the night were all but forgotten. When Captain Sinclair looked at her with his black eyes shining like polished stones, she completely forgot herself.

"Now then," he declared, with a clap of his hands, "everything's settled!"

He gave Richard a few more instructions, asked about the day's business, then whistled his way out the door.

After he'd gone, Richard turned to Sarah. "There is a small room upstairs where we keep a cot. You might like to rest a bit and then freshen up or even change your clothes. The room is very private, so you needn't worry, and, seeing as your trunk of belongings is still in back of the buggy. . ."

A sense of calm returned to Sarah's being. "Thank you, Richard. You are most thoughtful."

Suddenly all seemed right in the world again.

Chapter 3

Richard and Sarah dined at the Kirby House, a hotel on the corner of Mason and Water Streets. Abner Kirby, Richard said, had been the mayor of Milwaukee in 1864. Now, however, he was the owner of a fine hotel and known for his peculiar sense of humor. One suite in the hotel was named "Heaven"—the bridal suite. Another was called "Hell." That room, Richard told Sarah, was usually assigned to "inebriates."

"Oh, my!" Sarah replied, aghast, and Richard chuckled.

After dinner, Richard took Sarah for a ride through town, pointing out several sites of interest. He showed her the bridges, many of which were under construction. A flood back in April had washed five of them away into the Milwaukee River. The flood had also caused quite a stir among the "wards" which, Richard explained, were sections of the city—mostly ethnic: Irish, German, Italian, and so forth. However, only memories of the old "bridge wars" surfaced during this time of reconstruction and, thankfully, not the wars themselves.

"Years ago," Richard told Sarah now, "there were terrible fights concerning the location of certain bridges and which roadways would be connected. Those days were known as the 'bridge wars.'"

Sarah mentally digested the information. She was interested in the history of this city since it would be her home for the next few months, but she was also amazed at the extent of Richard's knowledge.

He must read an awful lot of history books, she thought. *But he's so entertaining. . .what a marvelous teacher he'd make!*

"So, you're twenty-one years old and not married yet? I can't believe it!" Richard said, wearing a wry grin.

Sarah shot him a stern look from where she sat next to him in the carriage. "If I hear one old maid comment out of you, Richard Navis, I'll—"

"No, no, that's not what I find funny." He gave her a side glance. "What's funny," he said in softer tones, "is that no man has succeeded in claiming you for his bride."

"I have my big brothers to thank for that."

Richard laughed, but moments later turned thoughtful. He wondered if she had a love interest back in Missouri. Or maybe Chicago. Or perhaps she'd lost her true love, as so many had, during the Civil War a few years back. Whatever the scenario, he found it hard to believe that pretty Sarah McCabe didn't have a special *someone*.

Richard cleared his throat. "I realize it's none of my business," he began, "but you, Sarah, are much too pretty to be twenty-one and without a husband."

She stifled a laugh. If she had a nickel for every time she'd heard that "you're much too pretty to be without a husband" line, she would be a very rich woman! And, although hearing the comment had been aggravating at first, Sarah now thought it was quite amusing.

Feigning seriousness, she turned to Richard. "You think I need a husband, do you? Are you proposing?"

At that, Richard gasped and sent himself into a fit of coughing. Sarah gave him a few good whacks between the shoulder blades.

"Touché, Sarah!"

His coughing now resolved, Richard had to marvel at what had just transpired. *Bested.* And never in all his twenty-three years of life had anyone ever gotten the best of him. His cronies called him "the king of wry retorts." But Sarah McCabe had undoubtedly out-witted him.

"I suppose that's what I get for prying into your affairs."

"Oh, that's all right. Actually, I'm rather used to it. I guess it's not very natural for a woman to *choose* to remain unmarried. However, I do. I like my independence."

"Independence, huh?" Richard cocked a brow. "You're not one of those woman suffragettes, are you?"

"Hardly." Sarah laughed again.

Listening to her, Richard smiled. He liked the sound of Sarah's laughter. If a tickle had a sound, her laughter would be exactly it.

They exchanged several more glib comments. Then, as they turned around and headed toward the captain's residence, they both seemed content to ride in an amicable silence.

"Thank you for a most pleasant evening," Sarah said as Richard slowed the buggy to a halt.

"It was entirely my pleasure—especially since the captain paid for all of it."

Sarah smiled, and Richard jumped down from his perch. After helping Sarah alight, they made their way up to the porch where Richard banged the large, brass knocker against the front door.

Suddenly Sarah was curious. "With no governess, where have the children been all day? Who has been taking care of them?"

"I believe Captain Sinclair's mother, Mrs. Aurora Reil, or simply Aurora, as she prefers, has the children on Wednesdays. She cared for them today and then, as it usually happens, they'll stay overnight at her house which is about a half hour's drive north of here. Aurora will return them in the morning."

"Oh. Then I take it Wednesdays are to be my day off?"

"Yes, or at least that's how it's been in the past. As for governesses, in the last two weeks there have been four of them."

"Four governesses? You're joking!"

Richard pursed his lips but didn't reply. He hadn't been kidding, but he certainly didn't want to discourage Sarah either.

The front door suddenly swung open, and Gretchen met them with a frowning countenance.

"Good evening, Gretchen," Richard said cheerfully. "I'm returning the captain's new governess."

The housekeeper replied with an indignant toss of her graying hair, and Sarah shifted uncomfortably.

"I trust Sarah's trunk of belongings has arrived by now," Richard continued, undaunted by the older woman's scowl. "I sent it on before Sarah and I went to dinner this evening."

"Yes, it arrived," she stated irritably.

"Good. Good."

Richard took a step forward, and Gretchen opened the door to them, albeit reluctantly. Taking hold of Sarah's elbow, Richard ushered her into the foyer.

"What a lovely hallway." Sarah's gaze took in the floor made up of various shades of brown terrazzo. Next she glanced at the goldenrod papered walls. "How absolutely lovely."

Gretchen donned a bored expression as she lit another lamp and set it upon a marble-top table. "Your room is on the second floor," she told Sarah. "Next to the nursery vhich is in the far hallvay, first door to the right vhen you come up the back stairs. . .and that's another thing: Be sure you use the servants' stairvell and not this vun," She inclined her head, indicating to the grand, curving staircase at the end of the foyer.

Then she strode off into the darkness.

When Gretchen was out of earshot, Richard said, "Listen, Sarah, if something doesn't seem right. . ." He paused as if groping for words. "Well, please let me know if you're uncomfortable in any way."

"Thank you, Richard, but—"

"Anything at all, Sarah, I mean it."

She smiled, though she was taken aback by his vehemence. "Well, all right. And, thank you again, Richard. For everything."

His expression relaxed, and he sent her a nod of goodnight.

From where she stood in the center of the foyer, Sarah watched him leave and close the massive front door after him. She expelled a sigh. *Now to finally get myself settled!*

Taking the lamp which Gretchen had set on the table, Sarah walked through the foyer to the kitchen. It was a large room, tiled in white and yellow and scrubbed clean for the night. There appeared to be a breakfast nook at one end of the room, and Sarah noted the children's chairs pushed in neatly around the table.

This must be where the children dine. She was counting the hours till their meeting. And she absolutely loved this house! Why, it seemed like the very house in which she had always dreamed of living, with beautiful rooms and beautiful things. This house was nothing like the small, wood-framed house in which she'd grown up. Three small bedrooms for two parents and five children—Sarah had always felt crowded in her family home. But one could never feel crowded in a house of this magnitude!

Beyond the kitchen was another hallway, dark and imposing. Sarah realized this was the "servants' stairwell." Climbing the steps, she reached the second floor and found her bedroom. As she stepped inside, she gaped at her surroundings. Had she made a mistake? This seemed too lovely and spacious a chamber for a governess. But, it must be her room. . . . Sarah had entered the first door to her right, just as Mrs.

Schlyterhaus had said. This was it.

Setting the lamp upon a desk in the far corner, Sarah did as much exploring as possible, given the poor lighting. Afterward, she felt one thing was sure: She was going to enjoy living here for the summer!

"Good heavens, Richard! Where have you been? I've been worried sick!"

Standing in the kitchen of the farmhouse that his father had built some fifteen years ago, Richard grinned as his mother strode toward him. Her thick auburn hair was tied in rags for the night, and traces of cold cream could be seen like patches on her face, while her white cotton nightgown billowed around her ankles as she moved.

"Mama, you're a vision of loveliness," Richard crooned.

Beatrice Navis stopped short, sensing that she was about to be the object of a joke. "The Lord commands that you respect your mother. . . even when she's not looking her best!"

Richard chuckled nevertheless as Bea smoothed the cream on her face and patted her hair.

"Well, I suppose I do look a sight, don't I?" she admitted.

"A sight for sore eyes, Mama."

"Oh, you just hush!"

Richard laughed while his mother shook her head at him. "You are so much like your father," she said. "Always finding something funny in every situation. Sometimes I truly wonder if I'm the only one in this house with any lick of sense."

Richard cut off a thick slice of bread. "Now, Mama, I know you love Pops and me anyhow."

"I do. So where were you tonight, Richard?" she asked again. "I've been concerned."

"I'm sorry." Richard turned serious. "Captain Sinclair's governess arrived today and, of course, he forgot about her."

"Is the governess for him or the children?" Bea asked tartly, fully aware of the captain's absentmindedness.

Richard smirked. "As far as I know, she came for the children."

"That man needs a wife."

"Well, all he's got is a governess at this point. . .and quite a pretty one, I might add."

His mother perked up. "Oh? Is that so? She's pretty?"

Richard nodded. "And I took her to dinner on the captain's orders. We had a very nice time."

Richard knew his mother was eating every word. She'd love nothing better than for her only son to settle down with a pretty wife and produce some grandchildren. So he decided to have a little fun with her.

"We get along very well, Mama," Richard said with a grin. "Did I say she was pretty?"

"Yes—yes, you did."

"And she's a believer."

"Is that right?"

"Her father is a preacher in Missouri, and Sarah teaches music in Chicago. She's only in Milwaukee for the summer."

"And you like her, huh?"

"Oh, yes," Richard replied, fighting to keep a straight face. "Such a pity she's as wide as a house, though." He shook his head, feigning a look of remorse.

In truth, Sarah had a very comely figure, but Richard couldn't resist the prank on his mother.

"Mama, you should have seen her putting the food away at the dinner table tonight. She would have shamed any lumberjack!"

Bea paled beneath her patches of cold cream. "Heaven above!"

"Yes, it is," Richard said with a mischievous grin. He kissed his mother's petal-soft cheek. "And I'm teasing you. Sarah isn't really as wide as a house."

"Richard Andrew Navis!"

"But she is ninety-four. I don't know how she'll ever keep up with those children! However, she uses a cane. . .I suppose that'll come in handy."

Beatrice gave her son a level look. "You have five seconds to get up to your bedroom before I thrash you within an inch of your life!"

Richard's eyes widened in mock terror and, after grabbing another hunk of his mother's fresh bread, he took the steps up, two-by-two.

Chapter 4

S arah awoke early and had her prayer time. Afterward, she washed and dressed in a blue and white striped dress with a white apron. For working, she thought the apron was perfect, both for a governess or a music teacher, because it sported two large pockets in the front and it fit nicely over the crinoline underneath the skirt. Moreover, the apron protected her dress. How glad she was that her mother had suggested making several of the aprons.

With a final pat of inspection to her braided and coiled blond hair, Sarah left her room and ambled downstairs. She entered the kitchen with trepidation, fearing she would encounter the stern housekeeper. Instead, she was pleasantly surprised to find the cook, a plump, smiling, talkative woman.

"I'm Isabelle," she told Sarah while serving her breakfast. "I take care of the cooking, but I leave for my own home at three o'clock or so. Don't board here in the house like Gretchen. And I've got dinner started by the time I go. Just needs to be served, and Gretchen takes care of that."

"I see." Sarah forked another bite of hot cakes and syrup into her mouth. "This is delicious, Isabelle."

The cook smiled with satisfaction and went back to her work at the stove.

Sarah finished eating and then walked around the house, awaiting the captain's presence. Unfortunately, it was the children who showed up first. Any introductions and explanations, Sarah realized, were mere wishes at this point; she was left on her own. . .again.

"Well, well, well, who have we here?" asked the beautiful woman accompanying the children. Since she bore a decided resemblance to the captain, except for a lighter complexion, Sarah assumed this must be his sister.

"I'm Sarah McCabe."

"And I'm Aurora Reil," the woman replied. "These urchins," she said, her gloved hands indicating the children, "are my—my—my—"

"Grandchildren," put in the tallest boy. He was obviously the oldest. Then he looked to Sarah with a frown. "Aurora hates the words 'grandmother' and 'grandchildren.'"

"Oh, Gabriel, I don't *hate* those words." The regal-looking lady lifted her chin. "At least not always. I only hate those words when they apply to me."

"You're—you're the captain's mother?" Sarah blinked. "But you look so young."

Aurora smiled. "I can see you and I are going to get along famously—just never, never, never refer to me as a—a. . ."

"Grandmother!" the children declared in unison. Giggles immediately followed.

However, Sarah felt stunned. Every grandmother she had ever known wore the title proudly, feeling truly blessed by her grandchildren. How could it be that Aurora was so different?

"I must be off," Aurora declared with a dramatic flare. Her chestnut-brown hair was swept up and pinned in an elegant chignon, and she wore a lovely hunter-green felt hat which matched the silk of her skirt.

Because of the woman's attire, Sarah wondered if she were "off" to an important affair. But then Aurora stated that she was going home to rest after her "duty day" with the children, and Sarah had to wonder. Back in Missouri they called dressing up like that their "Sunday-go-to-meetin' best." And here it was only Thursday! Sarah was in awe.

"Ta, ta, my darlings," Aurora said, allowing each child to place a perfunctory kiss on her smooth, powdered cheek. "Be kind to your new governess, and I shall see you next duty day!"

With that, she was gone.

In the foyer, Sarah surveyed the children. Four of them. Two boys—the older ones—and two little girls. Oddly, they didn't look the least bit upset to have been left by their grandmother. And left with a complete stranger, at that! Not even the youngest, who didn't look any older than three years old, seemed tearful.

"Come," Sarah told them, leading the way into the magnificent reception parlor. "Let's get acquainted."

The children followed, albeit reluctantly. Sarah sat down and smoothed out her skirts; however, the children continued to stand, and Sarah wondered why. "All right, let's start with you." She pointed to the oldest boy.

"I'm Gabriel. And if you're wondering why we're standing it's 'cause we're not allowed to sit on the furniture in here."

"Oh. . ." Sarah wondered if the rule applied to her as well.

"But sometimes we sit on it anyway," said the older of the two girls. "We sat on it lots when Mama was alive."

Sarah's heart filled with pity. So young to have lost their mother. "You poor, dear child." But as she considered each young face standing before her, she saw all dry eyes and very little emotion.

She cleared the sudden awkwardness from her throat. "How long ago did your mama die?" She figured it was a long time passing—so long the children could barely remember her.

"Um. . .it was awhile ago," Gabriel answered in a nonchalant tone.

Curious, Sarah wondered how long "awhile" was, but she decided not to pursue the matter.

Then the little girl beside her offered the information. "Our mama died at Easter time, but she was terrible sick ever since Rachel was born."

"How sad. I'm truly sorry for your loss."

The youngest girl suddenly climbed into Sarah's lap, regarding her all the while.

"You must be Rachel."

The little darling nodded.

Turning back to the other girl, Sarah searched her eyes. They were like her father's, black as coal. Her features resembled his as well, especially the color of her black hair which hung in one fat braid down her back. So like the captain's, so black the hair looked blue.

"What's your name?" Sarah asked gently.

"Libby."

"Her given name is Elizabeth."

Sarah looked at Gabriel, nodding her thanks for his input.

"And this is Michael, my brother." As if to prove the point, the older gave the younger a brotherly shove.

Michael returned the gesture.

"Now, now, I'll have no roughhousing in here. Surely if you can't sit on the furniture, you can't roughhouse either."

The boys ceased their antics.

Sarah's gaze rested on Gabriel. He was fairer than the captain, similar in coloring to his grandmother. His eyes were hazel and his hair dark brown. The other children, except for Libby, were of the same skin tones, although Michael's eyes were dark brown like his hair.

"How old are you, Gabriel?"

"Twelve. . .and I don't need a governess, either!" he said, looking quite resentful.

"I'm sure that's right," Sarah replied. "Twelve years old is quite mature. However, I've never been to Milwaukee before, and I'm going to need you, Gabriel, to show me around the city. Why, I'm also going to need you to let me know how things are done around here at home. Would you help me?"

He shrugged. "I suppose."

"I'll help you, too, Miss—Miss. . ."

Sarah looked at Michael. "My name is Sarah McCabe, but you can call me Miss Sarah."

"All right, well, I'll help you, Miss Sarah." Michael gave her a wide grin. "I'm eleven, but I know more than Gabe does."

"You do not!"

"Do so!"

"Do not!"

"Boys! Boys! Boys!" Sarah exclaimed while trying to hide a smile. "I'm quite sure I'll need both of you," she added diplomatically. "Gabriel? Michael? Is the matter settled?"

Gabriel shrugged and Michael nodded while Libby said that she'd like to help "Miss Sarah," too.

"You can't," Gabriel told his little sister. "You're just a baby."

"I am not! I'm six!" Libby retorted. "Rachel is the baby. Aurora even said so!"

"Really, Libby," Sarah said with furrowed brows, "you don't actually call your grandmother by her given name, do you?"

"If we call her 'Grandmother,'" Gabriel said in a matter-of-fact tone of voice, "she'll take the switch to us. She even said so."

"I'm sure she was joking." Sarah could hardly believe her ears. But all of the children were nodding.

"Do you have a grandmother?" Libby asked, leaning closer to Sarah now.

"Well, yes I do, and I call her 'Granny.'"

"You do?"

Sarah nodded.

"I think Aurora would kill us if we called her 'Granny,'" said Michael. Then he and Gabriel snickered together over the thought. It was the first time Sarah had seen Gabriel's expression change since she met him.

"Well, I see you children are getting along with your new governess."

Sarah turned suddenly at the sound of the male voice coming from over her shoulder. She found Richard standing there, wearing a huge grin.

"Mr. Navis!" The children cried happily. Even little Rachel squirmed off Sarah's lap to greet him.

Richard rewarded her with a candy stick and then proceeded to treat the other children. He had brought one for Sarah, too, which made her smile.

"What do we say to Mr. Navis, children?" she prompted.

"Thank you!" they answered at once.

Sarah led the children outside where they sat on the front stoop and ate their candy. Sarah, however, pocketed hers for later.

Standing on the porch, Richard told her the captain had sent him. "Captain Sinclair had an early appointment, but he'll be home at lunchtime to give you a bit of an orientation. He sends his apologies."

"It couldn't be helped," Sarah replied, her feelings teetering between disappointment and frustration. Seeing the captain again would be something of a thrill, for she had never met a man so captivatingly handsome. And yet, handsome or not, she simply *had* to see him—to speak with him. It was disturbing to be on her own with these children and to be unaware of what their father expected of her.

"It would seem you have everything under control," Richard stated.

Sarah smiled, watching the children as they enjoyed the candy. She looked up into the sunshine, now well above the lake.

"And it would seem you, Richard Navis, have gotten away from your books and out-of-doors once more."

"Hmm. . ." He pretended to think about it. "Well, what do you know? I did get away, didn't I?"

He laughed while Sarah shook her head at him.

Then, on a more serious note, he said, "There's a concert tomorrow night at the Shubert Theatre, also known as the Academy of Music. It opened last year, and it's quite a popular place. Would you like to go?"

"I—I. . .don't know. . . ."

"We will be well chaperoned," he added quickly. "I had originally made plans to attend the concert with friends."

"*You* have friends?" Sarah couldn't help teasing him.

Richard answered with an indignant "Humpf!" Then, feigning a lofty brow, he declared, "Just for that, I shall arrive at precisely seven o'clock tomorrow evening, and I will not tolerate any tardiness, Sarah McCabe!"

Richard bounded down the brick stairs, wishing the children a good day.

Sarah watched as he unhitched his horse, mounted, and gave her a grand salute before riding off down the street.

Chapter 5

Captain Sinclair arrived just before noon, and Sarah and the children joined him in the dining room for lunch. Isabelle had prepared plates of sliced beef and cheese which were served on chunks of freshly baked bread. For dessert, she brought out a jar of her "famous" canned pears. The boys ate so fast and so much that Sarah wondered if they'd ever be full.

After lunch, the captain summoned Gretchen and asked her to watch the children while he and Sarah held a brief meeting in his study. Gretchen agreed, but not without sending Sarah a scathing look. Once more Sarah wondered why she was the recipient of such contempt. Was Mrs. Schlyterhaus unhappy in her position? And what did she, Sarah, have to do with it?

"Sit down, my dear," the captain told her after they'd entered his study.

Sarah chose one of the two black leather chairs situated in front of the captain's large oak desk. Nervously taking her place, Sarah nearly jumped out of her skin when the captain closed the door to his study.

"Relax, Sarah," he crooned with a chuckle. "Do you think I'll bite?"

"No—no, of course not," she replied, although she wished she could sound more convincing. What was wrong with her anyway? Ever since Captain Sinclair came home for lunch, she had felt awkward and unsure of herself. Furthering her discomfort, the captain took the chair beside her instead of sitting behind his desk as she'd expected.

"Now, about the children and the household situation as a whole. . ."

Sarah watched the captain stretch out his long legs. Tapered black pants were tucked snugly into black boots. His tall frame looked as though it had been poured into the chair, for he seemed so relaxed. Sarah thought it was unfair that he should be so comfortable while she was so tense!

"As you know from our correspondence," Captain Sinclair began, "I am a widower. My wife, Louisa, died just over three months ago. She was very sick for a very long time." He sighed. "Her death was almost a relief."

"I see," Sarah said, noting the same dispassionate expression on the captain that she'd seen on his children's faces earlier.

"The children saw Louisa very seldom. So did I, for that matter," he added on a sarcastic note. "She was very beautiful and very. . .busy with her social schedule, as much as her health allowed."

Sarah hid her shock and surprise by lowering her head and momentarily studying her folded hands.

"Louisa and my mother were the best of friends, despite their age difference. They shared a kindred spirit, I suppose." The captain pursed his lips in momentary thought. "Did you meet Aurora this morning, Sarah?"

She nodded. "I must admit, I was a bit surprised that the children addressed their grandmother by her first name. It seems. . ." She caught herself before she used the word "disrespectful." *That might be too strong*. Clearing her throat, she began again. "Well, I guess it doesn't seem conventional, that's all."

Captain Sinclair chuckled. "There isn't anything *conventional* about Aurora. And Louisa was the same way."

Sarah's eyes widened. "Did the children call their mother by her first name also?"

"No, no. Only Aurora gets away with that offense, as it were."

Again he paused, and it seemed as if he contemplated whether to continue—as if he were debating whether to let Sarah in on some great secret. Finally he said, "It's my intent that my children have some sense of family unity. I never did. Aurora acted more like my sibling than my mother, a fact which she freely admits. A fact of which she seems most proud."

Sarah lowered her gaze once more, this time staring at the plush imported carpet. Her heart was suddenly burdened for the captain and his children.

"I will do whatever I can to further your intent, Captain," she told him, looking up at him now.

"I know you will, Sarah. From your letters, I had a feeling you were both caring and competent."

"Thank you, sir."

The captain went on to describe the past for Sarah so she would fully understand the situation.

"We have had governesses come and go in the last years. I can't understand it, either. No one will stay. I suppose it's our lifestyles. . .that is, Louisa's and mine. When she was alive neither one of us was here very much—and, of course, I was at war." He heaved a sigh. "Too big of a load for a mere governess to bear, am I right?"

Sarah lifted her shoulders in a helpless gesture. She thought the problem might have more to do with a certain housekeeper's "ferociousness" than the children being too big of a load.

"The only one of my staff who has stayed on is Gretchen," the captain continued. "She and her husband had been in service with my in-laws—both of whom are dead now, along with Gretchen's husband. But back fifteen years ago, upon my marriage to Louisa, I acquired both Gretchen and Ernest as household help. Gretchen has been faithful ever since." The captain's mouth curved into a sardonic grin. "Of course, I do pay her very well to stay and put up with all of us."

Sarah just nodded.

Captain Sinclair went on to give Sarah a few instructions, none of which were beyond reason. Her evenings were her own, and Wednesdays were to be her day off. She would earn five dollars a week, and Sarah nearly gasped at the gracious allotment. Her teaching position in Chicago paid less than that!

"You see," he said, leaning toward her now, "I'm hoping to convince you to stay longer than the summer."

Before Sarah could even think how to respond, the captain asked, "Is everything to your satisfaction? Your accommodations? Your salary? And how about the children? Isn't Rachel a darling?"

"O–oh, y–yes, she certainly is."

Just then a knock sounded on the door, and upon the captain's, "Come in," Gretchen appeared.

"Mr. Navis has sent a message: You are late for your two o'clock appointment."

The captain frowned. "Did I have a two o'clock appointment?"

Gretchen shrugged. "Apparently."

After a sigh, the captain looked back at Sarah. "It's a good thing I have Richard and Gretchen. . .and now you also. . .to look after me."

With that, he rose and strode from the room, leaving Sarah to wonder whose governess he really intended her to be!

Richard awoke at dawn. After dressing, he took to the stairs and found his mother in the kitchen, cooking breakfast.

"Your father couldn't wait for you this morning," she said over her shoulder while stirring the mixture on the stove. "He's already out in the barn. But even though you're late this morning, don't take it to heart, dear. Your father was up early anyway. His legs. . ."

Bea didn't say anymore. She didn't have to. Richard understood.

Opening the back door, Richard left the family's large kitchen and walked down the wooden ramp which had been built after his father's return from the war. Martin Navis had been wounded in battle. A Rebel's bullet had caught him in the back, and the damage caused by removing it had rendered his legs useless. He rode about the house and property in a wooden chair that had two large wheels on each side. Richard had been able to obtain the chair for his father at a good price, too, thanks to Captain Sinclair and all his contacts. And, although his father was confined to the thing, Marty Navis's disposition was as good-natured as the day he'd left for war.

" 'Mornin', Pops," Richard said as he entered the barn. He grabbed a pail and proceeded to milk Lyla, one of the family's Guernsey cows.

Marty wheeled up beside him. "I've milked two cows already."

"Sorry, I'm late, Pops. I overslept."

"Been keeping late hours, there, haven't you, son?"

Richard grinned, then shrugged. "Business is booming."

"Right-o," his father replied, albeit on a sarcastic note. " 'Course I don't imagine your coming in after dark has anything to do with this new governess your mother has been telling me about."

Richard didn't answer right away. Embarrassment got a hold of his tongue. His father's comment was only half true, however. The captain had been keeping him very busy at the store.

"Sarah has only been in Milwaukee for two days—"

"And you've been seeing to her comfort."

"Yes. . .I mean, no. . .I mean. . ." Richard groped for words. "What I mean is, I've been helping her out because the captain is gone a lot. I haven't been making a pest of myself."

Marty just laughed. "Listen, I'm proud of you for taking care of things for the captain like you do. You're a good son."

Richard's heart warmed. "Thanks, Pops."

Marty wheeled off, and nothing more was said as both men went about their early morning chores. Then, being late as he was, Richard went upstairs, washed and changed into a fresh shirt. He donned his tie, grabbed his suit coat, and ran back down to the kitchen where he gobbled his breakfast—much to his mother's consternation. Lastly, he saddled his horse.

"I'm staying at Aunt Ruth and Uncle Jesse's tonight," he told his father as he put his foot into the stirrup. "I won't see you until tomorrow night."

"Ah, yes, it's Friday," Marty said with a nod of understanding. "Don't suppose you've invited your Sarah to the theater with your friends."

Richard had to chuckle. "Pops, you've got it over on me."

"Well, I was young once, too, you know."

"You sure about that?" Richard laughed at his father's feigned scowl. Then, as he was about to ride away, his mother beckoned to him from the back door.

"Ask Sarah to church on Sunday," she called, "and Sunday dinner. The Staffords are coming, too."

Richard swallowed the reply that both his parents were getting more serious about Sarah than he was. But the truth in his heart ran contrary to that. He felt more for Sarah than he had felt for any young lady he'd ever known. She was different in a refreshing sort of way—in a way that made him long to be around her.

"Sarah will most likely have the captain's brood with her," he warned his mother. "Four pistols, you know."

"Oh, I just love those children," Bea said with a sparkle in her eye. "Tell Sarah to bring them. They're invited, too."

"Orders from Headquarters," Marty said with a guffaw.

Richard smiled, then bade his parents good-bye and rode the three miles into the city, and to the captain's store on Water Street.

Chapter 6

On her third day in Milwaukee, Sarah took a walk in the warm summer air while the children ate breakfast with their father. As much as he was not a family man, Sarah thought that he was certainly trying. And his children seemed to adore him, especially the little girls. *Better to give them some time together,* she decided as she slowed her pace. A cool breeze blew off the lake and, taking the stairs down to the beach, Sarah walked for over a half hour. All the while she plotted and planned the day ahead of her.

When she finally arrived back at the Sinclair residence, the captain was just getting ready to leave for the day.

"Good morning, Sarah. Out for some air?"

"Yes, sir. It seemed to get my blood moving."

He smiled. "The lake breezes do that for a body." His smile grew. "So what are your plans for today?"

"We're going fishing!" Gabriel exclaimed, joining in the conversation. "Miss Sarah says she knows how to bait a hook just the way the fish like it."

Sarah felt her face flame with embarrassment. While the boy meant it as a compliment, Sarah didn't want the captain to think she wasn't ladylike.

The captain, however, didn't seem to notice. "I take it we'll have fish for dinner this evening."

"Oh, you bet we will!" Michael declared while Gabriel nodded.

Libby wrinkled her little nose. "I hate to fish. They smell!"

"I wholeheartedly agree!" Sarah replied. "But I thought you and Rachel could collect precious stones while the boys fish. I have an idea for a special project, and it will take lots of beautiful stones and paste."

"Goody!" Libby cried, dancing around her father's knees.

Captain Sinclair laughed. "Sounds like a fun day."

He kissed his children good-bye before waving farewell to Sarah. She smiled and wished him a good day as he left the house.

An hour later, she was back down at the beach, but with the children this time. Libby and Rachel had taken off their shoes and stockings and now had their skirts hiked to their knees as they searched for "diamond rocks." Each girl carried a pail, and they walked through the wet sand at the water's edge, looking quite serious about their work.

Sarah sat on the long brick pier, showing the boys how to bait a hook. "You've got to fold up the worm onto the hook. . .like so."

Gabriel was fascinated. "I never knew a lady that wasn't ascared of worms."

"Afraid, Gabriel," Sarah corrected. "And, no, I'm not afraid of worms."

"How 'bout snakes?" Michael asked.

"What kind of snakes?" she countered.

"All kinds. . .but mostly really slimy, slithery ones."

"Oh, those are the best kind," Sarah said, fighting the urge to giggle. No doubt these two stinkers were up to something, what with all their questions.

"Our last governess didn't like any kind of snakes," Michael blurted. "She especially didn't like them in her bed."

Sarah gasped. "Mercy! You little rascal! You didn't really put a snake in your last governess's bed, did you?"

"Nope. Gabe did it."

"Gabriel!"

"We didn't like her," he said simply, as if that was all the reason he needed to do such a dastardly deed.

"For shame," Sarah admonished him.

"Well, she was mean," Gabriel said.

"But don't worry," Michael added with his heart in his eyes, "we like you, Miss Sarah. You're not mean. Right, Gabe?"

Gabriel raised one shoulder in utter nonchalance, and Sarah took that as an affirmative, coming from him.

"Well, I'm very fond of both you boys," she told them honestly. "Now, let's get busy and catch some fish!"

Richard couldn't resist. When Captain Sinclair announced that Sarah had taken the boys fishing, he just had to see it. Sarah, the sweet music teacher from sophisticated Chicago, was fishing? That would be a sight to behold for sure!

He balanced the morning's figures, then, just to get out of the store, he volunteered to run the day's errands. With his tasks completed, he headed straight for the beach. And there she was. . .bare feet dangling in the water, her blond hair tousled by the lake breeze, her bonnet blown backward, and a fishing pole in hand.

"If I hadn't seen it, I never would have believed it," he muttered to himself. Then he chuckled as he walked toward the pier.

"Hi, Mr. Navis," Libby shouted from several feet away.

"Good morning, ladies," Richard called back to Libby and her sister.

"Hey, Mr. Navis!" Gabriel called.

Sarah gasped and spun around. "What are you doing here?" she asked with wide and guilty eyes.

Richard thought she looked as though she'd just been caught in some scandalous act—probably because of her lack of attire. But, of course, having her shoes and stockings off was hardly scandalous, considering this part of the beach was seldom occupied. Most people opted for the public beach closer to the busier section of the city.

He grinned. "I came to see the refined music teacher fishing like an old seaman."

Sarah gave him a quelling look. "Oh, fine. Well, now you've seen me, so go on back to your books where you belong."

Richard laughed.

"And I'm hardly an 'old seaman.' "

"I'll say. But if you're not careful, you'll have a fine sunburn."

Sarah gasped again and nearly lost her pole to Lake Michigan as her hands leapt to secure her bonnet on top of her head. Richard chuckled all the while.

"Why can't Miss Sarah get a sunburn?" Michael wanted to know.

"Because it will smart," Richard replied.

"More so because it will tan and then I'll look like the farmer's daughter." She released an exasperated sigh. "I just hope my face and hands aren't already brown from this outing. How uncouth I'll seem to the captain."

"What's so bad about looking like the farmer's daughter?" Gabriel asked, turning away from his fishing pole to peer up at Sarah.

"Yeah, what's so bad about it?" Richard added. After all, he had been born and raised on a farm. His mother never complained about the sun tanning her skin, and she looked healthy with that little bit of brown.

"A *real* lady," Sarah began, "shades her skin from the sun. In Chicago, all the women whiten their skin with powder. It's stylish."

"So, what you're saying," Richard said, "is that sophisticated city women think it's stylish to look sickly."

"Like Aurora," Michael said, looking proud of himself because he thought he understood.

"And Mrs. Craighue," Gabriel interjected.

"Who is Mrs. Craighue?" Sarah asked.

"She's one of the ladies who visits Father sometimes. She has white skin like you said and wears her dresses so low you can see clear down to her—"

"That's quite enough, Gabriel, thank you!"

Sarah turned a shocked expression on Richard who had the good sense not to laugh but changed the subject instead.

"How many fish have ye caught, men?" he asked, imitating a rugged sea-faring man.

Sarah glared at him for including her as one of the "men."

"We caught three, mate," said Michael, playing his part. "But Miss Sarah is the one who caught 'em, so I guess they don't count."

"Now, see here!" she cried indignantly.

"Besides, they're puny," Gabriel added.

Sarah clicked her tongue. "That does it! I'm going to help Libby and Rachel collect diamond rocks!"

Richard laughed and laughed. What fun she was!

"You're not *really* angry, are you, Miss Sarah?" A worried little frown stretched across Michael's brow.

"You bet I am!"

But then she turned and gave the boy her sweetest smile. Michael smiled back, looking relieved.

"I wish you were my governess," Richard teased as they walked side-by-side along the pier.

"You, sir, *need* a governess. . .to keep you at your books!"

Richard chuckled at the comeback while Sarah sat down beneath the sun-shade she'd brought along.

"I thought you were going to help Libby and Rachel."

"I changed my mind." She sounded tired. "I need a rest."

Richard sat down beside her while Sarah removed her bonnet. He thought she smelled of fresh air, and her feet were covered with sand—so was the hem of her skirts, but she didn't seem to care. In fact, she looked comfortable, completely natural, in this environment.

"Is everything going well at the captain's house?" Richard asked. "I mean, with Gretchen?"

"Everything is fine, although I try to stay out of Mrs. Schlyter-haus's way."

Richard nodded. "That's probably wise. At least until Gretchen gets used to having you around."

Shifting slightly, he cleared his throat. "My parents asked me to invite you and the children to the farm for Sunday dinner after church. Would you come?"

Sarah appeared a bit surprised by the invitation, or perhaps it was curiosity that heightened the blue of her eyes. At any rate, Richard felt chagrined. How could he say he'd told his parents about her without seeming like a lovesick fool?

"Actually, Richard, I'm glad for the invitation. I've been wondering what to do about church and the children on Sunday." She paused a few seconds, seeming deep in thought, and Richard wondered if she'd refuse his offer.

He held his breath.

"Richard, I get the impression that the Sinclairs aren't Christians. The captain won't mind me taking his children to church, will he?"

He expelled a relieved sigh. "No. The children have been to church and our farm before. My mother is very fond of them. The captain won't mind, I assure you."

"Oh, well, that's good." Sarah gave him a smile that rivaled the sunshine. "Then, yes, with the captain's permission, I'd love to come on Sunday."

Richard matched her smile. He thought Sarah was the prettiest young lady he'd ever met. And, not only was she pretty, but she had a heart for the Lord and a sense of humor that even he, Richard, could appreciate.

Oh, Lord, he silently prayed, *is it possible for a man to fall in love in less than three days? If it is, then I believe I've succumbed!*

Richard had never been interested in any one woman, not seriously, anyway. Then again, no one woman he'd met was like Sarah McCabe.

"Well, I'd best get back to work," he said, knowing he couldn't put off the inevitable for much longer. "But I'll see you this evening. . . ." Then he just couldn't help teasing her. "Unless, of course, you're too. . . *sunburned*!"

"I will not be sunburned!" Sarah retorted. Next she hastily arranged her skirts so they covered her feet and fixed the sun-shade so it protected her arms and face.

Richard chuckled as he left the beach.

Chapter 7

The concert at the Shubert Theatre proved delightful. Sarah, being a music teacher, considered herself a tough critic. But the ensemble played without a flaw. Then once the concert ended, she and Richard and his friends walked over to the ice cream parlor.

Sarah decided Richard's companions were nice enough people, at least the majority of them were nice. Nickolina, or "Lina" as she preferred, was Richard's cousin, and she and Sarah got along well from the beginning since Lina taught at a local elementary school. Sarah then learned that Lina was betrothed to a dashing young man named Timothy Barnes who was in attendance that night as well. Mr. Barnes was an expressman who delivered packages, parcels, and mail. Mr. Barnes's younger brother, Lionel, also came along for the concert, but he was unlike his brother, and Sarah found him to be rather obnoxious.

And then there was Bethany Stafford.

Bethany was a quiet and melancholy young woman of seventeen years. She had gray eyes and what Sarah thought was nondescript brown hair. It was soon quite apparent that Bethany had designs on Richard who'd chosen to center his attentions on Sarah. This earned her some chilling stares that belied pleasant conversation.

"It was nice of you to walk me back to the captain's home, Richard," Sarah said later.

In the shadows, she saw him grin. "Well, I wasn't about to let Lionel take you."

"Thank you for that." Sarah smiled and gazed at him askance. "I just hope Bethany won't be upset. . .that you're walking me home, I mean."

Richard seemed to think about it for a moment before he shrugged. However, he didn't say anything else about her, so Sarah didn't press the matter.

"How's your sunburn?"

She stifled a groan. "It smarts, all right." Her forearms were pink where she'd rolled up her sleeves. The bridge of her nose was candy-apple red, along with her cheeks, and the back of her neck. Sarah had applied a good amount of cold cream on the areas in hopes they wouldn't tan.

"It looks uncomfortable."

"It is, but I suppose it was worth it since Gabriel eventually caught a fish. It was really something of a beast, too. You should have seen it! Gabriel was so pleased. I think he wanted to impress his father."

"And? Was the captain impressed?"

Sarah's heart sank as she recalled the disappointment on Gabriel's face. "The captain didn't come home when he said he would, and Isabelle had to fillet and cook his fine catch before she left. It would have spoiled by tomorrow, since the thing didn't fit into the ice box. So the captain won't get to see the fish—whole, anyway."

"Captain Sinclair is a hard one to keep on a schedule," Richard said with a note of weariness. "It's miraculous when it happens. However, I will defend him by saying that he does love his children very much."

A little smile tugged at Sarah's mouth. "And who knows better than you, his faithful steward!"

Richard returned the compliment with a smile of his own. They reached the captain's residence, and he walked Sarah up to the porch.

"I had a very nice evening, Richard. Thank you."

"It was entirely my pleasure," he said, bowing slightly.

Sarah had to suppress a giggle. Even when he wasn't trying to be funny, he was funny.

"I'll come for you after breakfast on Sunday," he stated on a more serious note. "About eight o'clock. All right?"

Sarah nodded. "Captain Sinclair has given his approval, so the children and I will be waiting."

She let herself into the house, dark now except for a single lamp shining from the hallway. She made a move to extinguish it, but then Gretchen caught her with a shout.

Sarah jumped.

"Leave it on! Captain Sinclair will be home late. I always leave a light on for him. Don't touch it!"

"Yes, ma'am." Sarah willed her heart to cease its pounding as she made her way upstairs, using the servant's stairwell. She was only too glad that she had remembered. Unfortunately, she was having trouble in that regard, since she wasn't accustomed to being a "servant."

In her room, she prepared for bed and decided to write to her parents before extinguishing the lamp. Sitting at the lovely desk, she told them about the captain and his children. She mentioned Richard and Lina and the concert tonight. She wrote about Gretchen and asked for prayers. But, later, as she closed her eyes for sleep, Bethany Stafford was who came to mind.

What's her story? Sarah wondered. *And why, like Mrs. Schlyterhaus, did she seem to take an immediate dislike to me?* It made her angry, and she wanted to dislike both Bethany and Mrs. Schlyterhaus right back!

But then Sarah recalled a passage of scripture where Jesus said, "Love your enemies, bless them that curse you, do good to them that hate you, and pray for them which despitefully use you, and persecute you. . . ."

Turning over in her soft, fluffy bed, Sarah sighed and whispered. "All right, Lord. I will do my best to obey Your Word. . .no matter what the cost."

A loud clap of thunder awoke Sarah early the next morning. She crawled out of bed and padded to the enormous closet. *My! Even this closet is grand!* she thought. Pulling on a warm robe against the damp chill in her bedroom, Sarah took her Bible in hand and began her morning devotions.

Later, after she had washed and dressed, she went down to the kitchen. Isabelle was there cooking breakfast. They bid each other a good morning as Sarah poured herself a glass of freshly squeezed orange juice. However, she would wait for the captain and the children before eating breakfast.

"This is such a beautiful house," she said, looking around the room. "Even this kitchen is beautiful."

"Sure it is," Isabelle replied with a broad smile. "I'm glad to work here."

"Me, too." After only a few days, Sarah was beginning to think she'd like to stay here the rest of her life.

The children woke up, and Sarah supervised their dressing. The three older ones managed almost completely on their own, but little Rachel needed assistance each step of the way. When at last they came downstairs, the captain was already at the table. He chatted with his children while Isabelle served the food. Then Sarah announced that she would begin piano lessons today.

"It seems a good day for it," she added.

"I'll say!" The captain replied as thunder reverberated over the house.

Rachel, sitting up in her junior chair, covered her ears. "I don't yike dat noise!"

"Well, now, thunder can't hurt you, darling," the captain said tenderly. "Don't be afraid."

Sarah's heart fairly skipped a beat. *What would it be like to have Kyle Sinclair call me "darling,"* she couldn't help but wonder. His voice had been so low and soft just now when he'd spoken to little Rachel.

Embarrassed by her thoughts, Sarah immediately concentrated on her breakfast.

"If you learn to play a whole piece on the piano by the end of the summer," the captain promised his children as the conversation returned to their lessons, "and if I can *recognize* the piece," he added with a grin, "then I'll throw a party for you—a recital. And I'll invite all my friends to come and hear you play."

The children heartily accepted the challenge and seemed quite impressed that their father's friends would come just to hear them play the piano. Even Gabriel looked somewhat enthused.

After breakfast, the captain went about his business while Sarah situated the children in the music room. It was located at the end of the hallway between the ladies' parlor and the men's parlor—not to be confused with the reception parlor. And Sarah was again amazed at the home's enormity.

Opening up several sheets of music that she'd brought with her from the academy in Chicago, Sarah began the piano lessons. But, before the children could actually play, they had to learn to read the notes. Much to Sarah's delight, they learned quickly. By lunchtime, Gabriel, Michael, and Libby could play one of the primary tunes.

"Can we have the party now?" Libby asked.

"Not quite yet," Sarah replied. She was sure that the captain expected to hear more than a basic four-note piece.

"Father! Father! Listen to what I can play!" Libby shouted, running down the stairs to meet the captain as he arrived home later that night.

The child was in her nightgown, and Sarah was embarrassed that she hadn't been able to contain her upstairs in the nursery.

"I'm sorry, Captain."

He waved a hand in the air. "Quite all right." Scooping Libby into his arms, he carried her toward the music room. "I would be happy to hear what you can play."

As Sarah stood at the doorway, Libby played her little song. When she finished, the captain applauded with vigor.

"Such talent!" he exclaimed, with a wink at Sarah. "I'm so proud of you, Libby!"

The little girl beamed and ran into her father's lap.

Sarah reveled in the sight and recalled the days when, as a little girl, she found love and security in her daddy's lap.

"Sarah, why don't you call the other children, and then you play for us?" Captain Sinclair suggested. "A bedtime melody."

"Oh, yes!" cried Libby.

Sarah felt embarrassed, but agreed. Exiting the music room, she collected the boys. Rachel was already asleep for the night. Returning, she made her way to the piano. She began to play. Her long, slender fingers danced above the ivory keys in practiced motions. First a piece from Chopin. Then Mozart. A Brahms lullaby next. And, finally, one of her favorite hymns: "Be Still, My Soul."

When Sarah finished playing, she sighed. That last piece never failed to stir her heart. In the next moment, however, she remembered her audience. Turning around, her eyes met the captain's.

"That was beautiful, Sarah," he said quietly. His black eyes shone beneath the pale glow of the lamplight.

"Thank you." Her reply was but a whisper, and Sarah found she could barely pull her gaze away from his stare. Was that admiration in his eyes?

Then suddenly the captain grinned. "But now look what you've done."

Noticing all of the children had fallen fast asleep, Sarah smiled. What a touching photograph they'd make—a father and his children. Such a pity her brother Benjamin wasn't here with his camera.

Captain Sinclair stood and scooped Libby into his arms. "I'll carry her, if you'll wake the boys. They're old enough to stumble up to bed."

Sarah set to task, gently shaking Michael first, then Gabriel. They moaned and groaned and stomped up the front staircase, angry to have been awakened.

With the task completed, and the children all in their beds now, Sarah met the captain in the hallway.

"I've made a decision tonight," he announced.

"A decision?" Sarah tipped her head. "And what might that be, sir?" She had a hunch a new rule was about to be instated—something, perhaps, about the children being down in the music room, dressed in their bed clothes well after their bedtime.

"I've decided," the captain said softly, "that I'm going to do whatever it takes to keep you here, Sarah McCabe. You're good for my children, I can see that already. And, tonight, for the first time ever, I felt like a family man instead of a businessman. I have you to thank for that."

Stunned, she didn't know what to say.

But the captain didn't seem to expect a reply. He merely smiled and bade her a good night. Then he turned and descended the stairs.

Alone in the large hallway, Sarah experienced a tumult of emotions. She would love to live in this house forever, and she couldn't help but wonder at the look in the captain's eyes when he said he had decided to "keep her here." Could that have been a romantic gleam shining from their dark depths?

Hardly! I'm imagining things! Didn't Leah always tell me I have a runaway imagination? Sarah sighed heavily. *I should have never read the Bronte sisters' books!*

To serve as something of a reality check, Sarah decided to mention the incident to Richard the following day after the worship service. She felt she could trust Richard. He was practical, and they were friends.

Richard, of course, was amused. "He said that? That he's going to do 'whatever it takes'?"

Sarah nodded, looking down at Rachel in her lap. Gabriel, Michael, and Libby were in the back of the wagon as they rode to the Navis' home. "What do you think about it, Richard?" she ventured.

He grinned rather sheepishly. "I think maybe I'll help him. . .keep you here, that is."

He chuckled when Sarah lifted her eyes heavenward, shaking her head.

"I should have known better than to ask you a serious question!" she charged.

Richard only chuckled again. "Aw, Sarah, I'm just kidding." Then he put on his best, most serious, expression. "Captain Sinclair has hired many governesses in the last few years. Personally, I think Gretchen scares them away."

Could be the snakes, Sarah thought, remembering what Gabriel and Michael had confessed.

"Anyway," Richard continued, "I suppose the captain has seen how well you manage the children. . .and Gretchen. . .and he doesn't want to lose you. That only seems logical."

Turning to Sarah, he raised his brows as if waiting for her to agree.

She did. And of course she had imagined that look in the captain's eyes last night; it wasn't a romantic gleam at all, but a look of—of desperation! The poor man. He couldn't afford to lose another governess!

Richard continued to drive the wagon west on Lisbon Plank toll road.

"How much farther?" Sarah wanted to know.

"Less than a mile."

Farm fields now stretched out as far as the eye could see. They had left the city behind, though they were still in Milwaukee. Out here, Richard informed her, near Western Avenue, it was all rural area. Moreover, the temperature was a good ten degrees warmer than it had been closer to Lake Michigan.

"Once you cross the river," Richard explained, "it's hotter. And, in the winter, it's colder. However, nearer to the lake, you never can escape the humidity."

Sarah well understood the statement. "St. Louis is that way, too. Except, we have both during the summer months—the heat and humidity. It's ghastly!"

"I imagine so."

Minutes later, Richard turned the wagon onto a neat gravel driveway which split in half to form a large circle that passed in front of his house. There, he halted the wagon and jumped down.

Sarah took his hand as she alighted, noticing that this section of the driveway was all brick, like the house. Once her feet touched the ground, she surveyed the rest of her surroundings. To her right was an apple orchard next to a small pond. To her left was another orchard, but it stood behind rows of flowers.

"What a lovely place," she murmured.

Richard smiled at her comment. "The house is quite unique. However, we're just average folks, and this is a typical farm."

"But it doesn't seem 'typical.' And this house looks like a country mansion! Why, it's much larger than any farm house I've ever seen!"

A pleased expression crossed Richard's face. "My father inherited a good sum of money and used it to build this house. His 'dream house' you might call it. He patterned it after his aunt's villa in Germany, where he had spent some time as a child. He loved it there, so when she left my father money, he decided to honor her in this way. With this." He made a great sweeping gesture toward the house. "My father finished building it in 1851."

"How fascinating!" Sarah had never been to another country before, and she was in awe of anyone who had.

"The actual farm is out back," Richard continued. "We've got hogs, cows, sheep, chickens, a vegetable garden, a corn field, a wheat field, and a grove of pear trees."

"I see." Sarah tried to cover her sudden disinterest. She'd grown up around farms and fields. What appealed to her now was the genteel city life.

Richard's parents' wagon pulled into the circle drive, drawing their attention. Sarah gathered the captain's children while Richard helped his father down from the wagon and into his wheelchair. Sarah had already met Mr. and Mrs. Navis at church, and the children were well acquainted with them from previous visits. Mrs. Navis asked Sarah inside while Richard and his father took the children out back to the barn to see the kittens.

"The Staffords should be arriving soon." Bea removed her bonnet. "Richard told us you met Bethany on Friday evening."

"Yes, I did," Sarah replied, and she had been praying for Bethany ever since.

"Can I show you around?"

Sarah nodded and followed Richard's mother through one room after another. The furnishings weren't elegant at all, like they were in the captain's home. Here, the furniture was large and sturdy and everywhere handmade quilts and knitted blankets covered faded upholstery. Sarah was reminded of her parents' home in Missouri.

"Can I help you prepare dinner?" Sarah asked Mrs. Navis after they'd entered the large kitchen.

"Sure can. I'm roasting a couple of chickens."

In this heat? Sarah thought.

"Then I'll bake up some biscuits and set out some of the pickles I canned last year. How does that sound?"

"Sounds hot," Sarah replied in all honesty. "Except for the pickles."

Bea only laughed and waved her into the cellar. "I've got a summer kitchen down here."

Sarah glanced around at the white-washed walls, cupboards, and large wood-burning stove and oven. It was nearly fifteen degrees cooler down here. Then Bea led her into the fruit cellar where numerous glass jars stood on paper-lined shelves.

"We'll have some applesauce, too," she stated, grabbing a few jars.

Minutes later, Richard brought in two freshly butchered chickens. "I had the boys help me pluck and clean 'em, and would you believe Gabe and Michael squawked louder than the hens? Such complaining!"

"Good jobs for those boys," Bea replied.

"Not to worry. We all put on aprons." Richard glanced at Sarah. "The boys haven't ruined their good clothes. . .but give them time."

Sarah smiled. "Where are Libby and Rachel?"

"They're with Pops on the back porch, holding the kittens."

"Pops?" Sarah found the word humorous. "You don't really call your father *Pops*, do you?"

"Sure, I do," Richard replied while his mother nodded, feigning a helpless expression. "He's Pops and she's. . .Mops. Mops and Pops."

He chuckled, while Mrs. Navis raised an annoyed brow. "Mops, you say?"

Sarah shook her head. "You poor, poor woman," she teased, "having to put up with his bad jokes."

He brought his chin back, as if insulted. "That wasn't a bad joke, Sarah."

"The worst I've heard," she retorted.

Bea laughed with shoulders shaking. Richard was now the one wearing the annoyed expression.

"An ally!" Bea declared, putting an arm around Sarah. "At last I have an ally!"

Chapter 8

Shortly after Mrs. Navis got the chickens into the oven, the Staffords arrived with their eight children. Bethany, who was the oldest of them, looked surprised to see Sarah. Then she chose to ignore Sarah's existence altogether. Sarah tried not to feel hurt and stayed out of Bethany's way. Minutes later, Richard's Aunt Ruth and Uncle Jesse showed up. Lina was with them, along with her fiancé Tim.

"Oh, Sarah, it's good to see you again," Lina said, giving her a quick hug that made up for Bethany's lack of friendliness.

When dinner was ready, they ate out on the lawn with their plates in their laps. It reminded Sarah of the annual church picnic in Missouri; they ate with plates in their laps then, too.

Once they'd finished, Richard helped Sarah carry dishes into the kitchen. "I promised all the children cow rides," he said with a grin.

"Cow rides?"

Richard nodded. "Last time the captain's children were here, I gave them a ride on Lyla's back. She's one of our Guernsey cows, and the children had so much fun that they have requested to do it again."

Sarah smiled. "How fast does Lyla go?"

"About as fast as I can pull her."

They shared a chuckle, walking back outside. Sarah watched from the back porch as first Libby, then Rachel took a ride on poor Lyla. When their turns came, Gabriel and Michael bounced and shouted, "Giddyup!" However, the cow wasn't very cooperative.

From her place near the kitchen door, Sarah could hear the rattling of pans and dishes. She called to Richard, telling him she was going to help clean up inside. He nodded.

Entering the house, Sarah was surprised to find only Bethany in the kitchen. She was washing the dinner dishes from a large basin of water on a counter with wooden cupboards underneath it.

"Here, let me help you." Sarah grabbed a dish towel. Bethany didn't reply, but she began drying dishes anyway. After a few minutes of uncomfortable silence, Sarah decided to clear the air once and for all.

"Bethany," she began carefully, "have I said or done something to offend you?"

Bethany paused in her washing. "No," she replied at last.

Sarah sighed in a dramatic fashion. "Well, that's good. Nevertheless, I'm under the impression that you dislike me, and I believe it's because of my friendship with Richard. Is that right?"

Bethany stopped washing the plate in her hands. "Your *friendship* with Richard?" Her lips curved upward into a cynical smile. "Is that what you call it? *A friendship?*"

Setting down the towel, Sarah put her hands on her hips and lifted a defiant chin. "Yes. *Friendship* is most exactly the word I would use! Richard has been very good to me since I arrived in Milwaukee. We both work for Captain Sinclair, and I believe Richard and I are what Charles Dickens referred to in his novel *Great Expectations*. . ." Sarah cleared her throat. "We are 'fellow sufferers.' "

"Oh, hardly!" Bethany retorted.

"Well, we are, too!" Sarah replied, even though she was joking. She very much appreciated her job, but she couldn't help teasing Bethany. "The captain is a very forgetful man, you know, and that places a great burden on Richard and me."

"Yes, I'm sure it does." Sarcasm dripped from the reply.

"Well, anyway," Sarah continued, "I think Richard has just been kind to me because he wants me to feel comfortable here and make some friends. That's all."

Bethany laughed. "Richard is not that gallant. Trust me. I've known him practically all my life. Besides, Captain Sinclair has had dozens of governesses, and Richard never took one of them to the theater or home to meet his family."

Sarah paused to think about this. Perhaps Richard was, indeed, interested in her romantically, though she hadn't thought so until now that Bethany suggested it. Sarah had merely assumed that Richard's attentions were due to politeness and loyalty to the captain—and, maybe even pity toward her as a new governess in a strange city.

And how do I feel about that?

In truth, Sarah didn't know. Richard was considerate and witty, and she enjoyed his company; however, he didn't make her heart pound or her knees weak. . .and that was the sort of love Sarah was waiting for. Heart-pounding, knee-weakening love! Like the kind in Longfellow's *Evangeline* or one of Sir Walter Scott's books.

Oh, well, I'll think about love and Richard later, Sarah decided, realizing that there was still this matter of Bethany Stafford to contend with for the moment.

Then suddenly, an idea struck. . . .

"Bethany, are you and Richard betrothed?"

The other girl's head shot up with surprise at such a blatant question. Finally she answered, "No."

"Has he spoken to you of marriage?"

Bethany considered Sarah and then shook her head. "No."

"Well, then," Sarah said practically, "he's fair game, so to speak. . .not that I'm interested, of course. I'm merely trying to make a point."

"Who's fair game?"

Sarah's eyes widened at the sound of Richard's voice, coming suddenly from right behind her. She looked over at Bethany who was blushing profusely. *Not much help there!* she decided.

"The chickens!" Sarah finally managed, donning an innocent grin and turning to face Richard. "Wouldn't you agree? The chickens are *fair game.*"

"Oh, yes," Bethany blurted from over the basin of water. "Chickens. Fair game."

Through a narrowed, speculative gaze, Richard looked from Sarah to Bethany and then back to Sarah. He nodded slowly before a grin split his face. "Sure. That's what I thought. The chickens."

Sarah lowered her chin in an effort to conceal a smirk, and beside her, she noticed Bethany doing the same. Richard must have noticed for he mumbled something about Sarah being an instigator as he left the kitchen. She let the comment go since she knew full well that she could get even with Richard later. Then, picking up the next plate from the wooden rack beside the basin, Sarah resumed her job of drying. She sensed her relationship with Bethany had changed for the better.

Once the dishes were washed and put away, Sarah and Bethany joined everyone else in the yard. Cool evening breezes began to blow, rustling the branches of the apple trees overhead. Gabriel and Michael were at the pond, trying to catch a frog or two, and the little girls were playing hide and seek in the orchard. Bethany no longer ignored Sarah and struck up a friendly conversation. She pointed out their neighboring farm and talked of the concert they had heard two nights ago.

Awhile later, Mrs. Navis discovered the kitchen had been cleaned when she went inside to make coffee. And when she learned Sarah and Bethany had cleaned it, she chided them, saying, "No guests of mine clean up the kitchen!"

"But we wanted to help," Sarah told her.

"Nonsense! Now you'll both have to come back next week so I can be a proper hostess!"

"Yes, ma'am," Bethany replied with a tiny smile that almost reached her sad gray eyes. Once Bea ambled away, she leaned over and whispered to Sarah, "Mrs. Navis says that every Sunday, because every Sunday I clean up for her."

Sarah smiled. "So, why do you do it, Beth?"

She lifted her shoulders in a quick up and down motion. "I guess I just feel that Mrs. Navis has so much to do since Mr. Navis was maimed in the war."

Sarah nodded her understanding and sensed Bethany had a real heart for this family.

But where is Richard's heart? she couldn't help but wonder. She supposed it wasn't any of her business. What Richard said or did shouldn't concern her one bit. After all, she reveled in her freedom. She had her independence, and Richard could have Bethany!

"My aunt and uncle have offered to take you home," Richard said later, as the sun began to set. He stood on the lawn, near the front porch, and Sarah thought he looked quite handsome with the orange sky in the background.

And I shouldn't even care! she told herself.

"Are you listening to me?" Richard said with a grin.

"Yes, of course I am." Sarah cleared her throat to cover her discomfort.

"I said my aunt and uncle—"

"I heard that." Sarah lowered her lashes, softening her tone of voice. "And that's very kind of them."

"Well, they don't live far from the captain, so it's no trouble." He nodded to where the children were playing. "The 'trouble' will be rounding up those four rascals."

Sarah had to agree.

And it took awhile, but finally the children were gathered up and loaded into the large buggy.

"I'll see you tomorrow," Richard said.

Sarah nodded and couldn't help but notice the light of promise in his blue eyes.

Then, riding back to the captain's residence, she wondered whether Richard was truly interested in her romantically, as Bethany presumed, or if this, like her thoughts of Captain Sinclair, were mere imaginings.

Wednesday was Sarah's first day off and, after Aurora arrived and collected the captain's children, she sat down and made note of all she had to do today. She had, among other tasks, her clothes to wash, and Gretchen was a help in telling her of a woman whose fees were reasonable. She explained to Sarah that when a working woman has but one day off, it should not be spent doing laundry.

"You'll be no good to anyone," Gretchen said sternly, "if you don't have something of a rest."

Sarah smiled, glad that Mrs. Schlyterhaus wasn't berating her as usual.

"Even God took a rest," the woman added in a thick German accent, "after He made the vorld."

Sarah's smile broadened. "Are you a Christian, Mrs. Schlyterhaus?"

At the question, a heavy frown settled on Gretchen's brow. "It is none of your business vhat I am or vhat I am not!"

Sarah gasped. "Oh, but I didn't mean. . .what I meant was. . ."

The older woman scowled. "Irish!" she fairly spat at Sarah before walking away.

Stunned, Sarah could only wonder at that last comment.

Later, she asked Richard when he "happened" to stop by. "What did Mrs. Schlyterhaus mean by calling me 'Irish'? That is to say, I am of Irish decent, but—"

After giving the matter some thought, Richard replied, "It's not you, personally, Sarah. It's just that. . .well, it seems Gretchen isn't a very forgiving person, and your being Irish just gives her an excuse not to be friendly. I believe Gretchen knows the Lord, but she refuses to exercise forgiveness toward others."

As they sat together on the front porch, Richard continued to explain. "About ten or fifteen years ago, the Germans and the Irish were at war with each other here in Milwaukee. Each had claimed its own section of the city and, if one wandered into the other's area, there was a bloody fight—or sometimes a riot. Gretchen's husband was killed in one of those riots."

"How awful!"

Richard agreed. "Later, when a law was proposed to ban alcohol here in Milwaukee, the Germans and the Irish—both known to like their beer—joined forces and rallied, or perhaps I should say *rioted*, against the proposed law."

"They must have won, too," Sarah murmured, "for I've noticed that there's a tavern on practically every corner of this city!"

Richard chuckled. "That there is, my dear Sarah McCabe. However, sometimes I wonder if Gretchen still believes she's at war with the Irish." He smiled. "But please don't be too concerned about it. You're perfectly safe. I'll make sure of it."

Richard searched her face in a way that gave Sarah yet another indication he might be interested in her. She felt herself blush and quickly lowered her gaze.

"Will you allow me to take you to dinner tonight?" he asked.

Sarah looked up to find a very solemn expression on his face. A moment later, he glanced at his pocket watch. "I have some time. . . before I need to be home. . . ."

Curious, Sarah asked, "Do you have an appointment tonight, Richard?"

He smiled and shook his head. "No. Only chores."

"Chores? You mean that after working all day for the captain, you go home and work on the farm?"

Richard bobbed his head to the affirmative. "My father can't manage many tasks anymore, so I do most of the work. But we've hired planters this year."

"But still. . .you must be exhausted!"

He grinned. "Not too exhausted to take you to dinner. Will you come?"

Sarah thought about it, wondering if she should encourage Richard this way. She didn't want to give him false hopes, and yet she liked his company. He made her lonesome for her brothers.

"What do you say, Sarah?"

"Well, I don't know. . . ."

"We can ask Lina and Tim to join us if that will make you feel more comfortable."

"That's not necessary."

Richard lifted a teasing brow. "You're not afraid of me?"

Sarah swallowed a giggle. "Not in the least!"

Richard shrugged, indicating that perhaps she ought to be, and this time Sarah laughed aloud. Oh, how he could make her laugh with a mere facial expression or a simple shrug of his broad shoulders.

"Will you dine with me or not?" he asked in mock irritation. "I'm hungry."

"Ten minutes to freshen up?" she pleaded, donning one of her sweetest smiles.

Richard glanced at his watch again. "Ten minutes."

Sarah scurried into the house. She only took five minutes to splash water onto her face and check the pins in her hair. Leaving her bedroom, she grabbed a light wrapper, just in case the wind shifted abruptly as it was known to do here in Milwaukee.

"Ready?" Richard asked, meeting her in the foyer under Gretchen's scowling countenance.

"Ready." Sarah chanced a look at the housekeeper. "Good night, Mrs. Schlyterhaus."

"I lock the doors at eight o'clock on Vednesdays," she stated firmly. "If you're not home by then, I vill lock you out!"

When Sarah gasped, Richard gave her elbow a squeeze and whispered, "I have a key. Don't worry." He smiled at Gretchen then and wished her a good night.

Laughing softly at Richard's cleverness, the two left Captain Sinclair's residence for a riverside cafe. What Sarah learned about Richard that night amazed her. First of all, he knew almost everyone at the restaurant. Several businessmen greeted him by name.

"Did you take me here to impress me?" Sarah asked impishly when the proprietor seated them at one of his best tables.

"Sure I did," Richard replied with a grin.

Secondly, he was honest. And he was a hard worker—Sarah saw the telltale signs worn into his hands. They were the hands of a working man. A farmer. And yet, there was an air of sophistication about him, a manner that came from education.

But what impressed Sarah the most was Richard's generosity. Not only with his money, for the meal was surely a costly one, but he gave of himself. Like the way he helped his father and the captain; the way he managed Mrs. Schlyterhaus by not getting in her way, but around her instead. He seemed to strive to appease and accommodate, but never to the extent of compromising his faith.

My father would like him, Sarah found herself thinking. So would my brothers—especially Luke, that rascal!

"What are you thinking about?" Richard suddenly asked. "You're smiling."

Sarah's smile broadened. "I was thinking of my brother Luke. You remind me of him."

Richard lifted a brow. "If I remember correctly, that's not always good."

"It's only *not* good when I'm in trouble." Sarah had to laugh, hearing Richard's chuckle.

After supper, they decided against the hackney and walked back to the captain's home. The evening temperature was mild, even with the Lake Michigan breezes, so their stroll was enjoyable.

"I'll have to take you roller skating some time," Richard remarked. "It's quite the rage in Milwaukee right now. We have several brand-new rinks, in fact."

"Really?" Sarah had heard of roller skates. The wooden-wheeled toys had been invented in New York several years ago. "Well, that would be fun, Richard."

Finally they reached the captain's house. On the side porch, Richard turned the knob. The door opened.

"Not quite eight o'clock." A sheepish expression crossed his face.

Then suddenly, he became serious. He leaned forward and placed a gentle kiss on Sarah's cheek. His expression, as he told her good night, made Sarah realize that he meant business. The courtship sort of business. The whole business Sarah tried to avoid. Why couldn't she and Richard just be friends?

Oh, dear Lord, she prayed, forgetting herself and climbing the front stairwell. *Now what do I do?*

Chapter 9

"C aptain, may I enroll the children in swimming lessons?"

Captain Sinclair lifted his dark gaze from the papers on his desk. "Swimming lessons?" He frowned slightly. "They already know how to swim."

"Yes, I know. I've seen them at the lake. However, the boys are so energetic. . ."

The captain laughed. "You're seeking to take the, uh, wind out of their sails, are you?"

Sarah smiled. "Yes, exactly."

He chuckled once more.

"The swimming lessons would be perfect. They begin at eight o'clock every weekday morning and go until noon. The swimming school, as it's called, is right on the river."

"Yes. I know the one. It's north of here."

"That's it, Captain."

He nodded. "All right. You may enroll the children, Sarah."

"Thank you, sir."

Exiting the captain's office, Sarah congratulated herself on contriving the perfect solution to the boys' exuberance and Richard's mid-morning visits. She had decided to put some distance between them. Hopefully out of sight would mean out of mind. For both of them!

However, as the days passed, Sarah discovered such was not the case. Richard soon began visiting her at the swimming school since he couldn't catch her at the captain's home. Then he always drove Sarah and the children back in the Owensboro wagon or sleek black buggy— whichever of the captain's vehicles he had that day. And he obtained the captain's permission to make these visits. Obviously Captain Sinclair valued Richard greatly to grant him such allowances, and that fact spoke volumes about Richard's character.

Sarah couldn't help but grow fonder of him by the hour. Richard was quick-witted, and he made her laugh. The children adored him, and he added more fun to their days. Like stopping for ice cream or candy sticks. Or telling Bible stories in the most interesting, most amusing way as they picnicked on the front lawn of the prestigious Sinclair home—in spite of Gretchen's disapproving frowns at their "cluttering up the captain's yard."

Finally Sarah gave up. There was no point in trying to avoid Richard; he was unavoidable. Besides, when he wasn't around, because the captain's business kept him away, Sarah actually found herself missing his company!

Then one Sunday, when he came to get them for church, Sarah noticed a change in him. There was suddenly a seriousness about him, and it caused Sarah a measure of alarm. All too soon, however, she learned what he was up to.

"Sarah, I know you said you enjoy your independence," Richard began. "I know you said that you've chosen to be unmarried. But I was thinking. . ."

"Don't, Richard!" Sarah held up her gloved hand in warning. She sensed what was coming, and she didn't want to hurt him.

"But it's not proper for us to be such good friends. . .not without some sort of commitment."

Sarah lowered her gaze to her gloved hands, folded in her lap. "Yes. I suppose you're right."

They rode for a few minutes in silence, both busy with their thoughts. Then, after they'd arrived at the church, Richard spoke again.

"Will you think about it, Sarah? About allowing me to court you? I'll write to your father and ask his permission." With that, he helped her down from the wagon.

"I'll think about it." The reply was halfhearted as she gathered the captain's brood and marched them into the sanctuary.

Later that day, after they'd eaten supper, Richard managed to persuade Sarah into taking a walk around the farm. Again the discussion of courtship came up.

"I like you very much, Richard," Sarah told him. "In fact, I was looking forward to your company today. . .at least until—"

"Until I had to ruin everything just before church."

Sarah had to suppress a giggle in spite of the seriousness of the moment. "Yes. That's right. You ruined everything," she replied teasingly.

Richard grinned. "Well, it couldn't be helped. As I said, I've been thinking."

"Richard, you don't know what you're getting into," Sarah stated earnestly. "We've known each other just a short time. . .and you don't know my family. My brothers. I always felt sorry for my suitors; my brothers gave them such a terrible time. And then my father, being a pastor, drilled them mercilessly." She shook her head. "It's a wonder my sister Leah managed to get married. My brothers did the same to her, although not to the same extent."

Richard was smiling nevertheless. "Something tells me I'll be able to handle your brothers, Sarah."

She smiled right back. "You probably will. . . ."

Raising his brows, Richard asked, "Does that mean yes?"

"No!" she replied impishly.

He laughed as they walked near the cornfield.

"Richard. . ." Searching for the perfect words, she took his arm and pulled him to a halt. "I don't know how to say this except to just come out and say it." She sighed. "Richard, I don't think I love you. . .I don't know if I ever will."

Much to her surprise, he didn't seem hurt. He merely smiled and said, "What do you think a courtship is for? It gives a couple permission to get to know each other. . .to fall in love."

Sarah sighed once more and shook her head. "I don't know. When my father hears of your interest in me—and that I *allowed* you to write to him—he'll tell my mother, who will immediately begin wedding preparations. She'll tell my brothers, of course, which will bring Luke home, and then you'll be sorry, Richard, because if Luke comes home, he'll be expecting a wedding!

"And then there are all my cousins. When they find out, particularly my cousin Brian, who resembles Luke in thought, word, and mischievous deed, they'll—"

Richard quieted Sarah's ramblings by touching a finger to her lips. "Perhaps we should worry about all that at the precise moment each crisis arises."

Sarah rolled her eyes heavenward. "You sound like my brother

Benjamin. He can be so very practical."

"Thank you." Wearing a grin, he pulled a folded piece of paper from his shirt pocket and handed it to Sarah. "This is the letter I wrote to your father. I'd like you to read it and, if you agree and accept its terms, I'll post it tomorrow. Will you do that? Will you read it and think over everything I've said?"

"Oh, I suppose so." Sarah took the letter. "I'll do as you ask."

"Good."

They turned and, as they headed for the house again, Sarah spotted Bethany sitting on the front porch. She could see Bethany watching them intently. If Sarah had won her friendship last week, she had surely lost it now.

"Perhaps you should talk with her," Sarah suggested, inclining her head toward Bethany. "I think she's going to be hurt if you start courting me."

"I wish Bethany's father wouldn't have put ideas into her head in the first place." At Sarah's questioning gaze, he explained. "Paul Stafford owns the neighboring farm and long ago, when Bethany and I were still children, he got this notion that it would be great to combine the properties via a marriage between Bethany and me." Richard looked into Sarah's deep blue eyes. "Only problem with that idea is. . .I don't love Bethany."

His gaze locked with hers in what Richard hoped was a meaningful gaze. Sarah didn't turn away, as if meeting his challenge.

"So you'll talk to her then?" she asked softly.

Richard nodded. "I'll talk to her."

Later that evening, after Sarah and the children had left with Lina and Tim, Richard asked Bethany if he could walk her home.

"I need to speak with you," he said.

"Certainly, Richard."

They took the long, winding path that went around the vegetable garden. "It's about Sarah. I've written to her father and asked permission to court her. I thought you should know."

Bethany said nothing for several steps.

"I've prayed about this," Richard added. "I think Sarah is the one God has chosen for me."

Bethany stopped short. "She's going to break your heart! She's a. . . a flirt!"

"No, she's not." Richard wondered where on earth Beth got that idea.

She stood with arms akimbo. "Well, she's certainly very comfortable talking to men. Even my brother Billy noticed. . .and he's only fifteen!"

"Sarah is comfortable talking to men because she has three older brothers, and she's the youngest in the family." Taking a hold of Bethany's elbow, Richard urged her to continue their walk. "You know," he said gently, "sometimes I think younger children have an advantage in that they get to see how things work by observing their siblings. Whereas you and I usually have to experience life by trial and error."

"You're making a mistake," Bethany maintained, in spite of what he'd just said. "Sarah doesn't love you."

"It may not be love yet. But there is something between us." *And it was there from the beginning*, Richard added silently.

"You're making a mistake," Bethany repeated. "She doesn't. . .she can't. . .love you. . .like I do."

Richard hid his shock over her candid admission. But then, as they reached the back door of the Staffords' home, he said, "I'm sorry, Beth. I really am. But it's not meant to be for us. I'm sure about that much. And I love you, too—but as a sister in Christ."

"That could be enough—enough to start," Bethany replied with tears rimming her eyes.

"That would *never* be enough. And someday you'll thank me for my honesty. Someday when the right man comes along. . ."

But Bethany wouldn't hear any more. With tears spilling down her cheeks, she ran into the house. The tightly sprung door slammed behind her, and Richard decided he never felt so awful in his life. He hated to hurt her.

Please, Lord. . .please give Bethany a sense of understanding. Please free her from these unrealistic thoughts of marriage to me. It's as You said, "The truth shall make you free." Lord, I had to tell her the truth.

Up in her bedroom, once her duties were completed for the day, Sarah unfolded the letter Richard had written to her father. The first page was mostly introduction and some background information about Richard and his family—things he had already told her. Not until Sarah got to the middle of the second page was her full attention captured.

> *While I've only known Sarah a short time,* Richard wrote, *I believe I love her.*

Love? Sarah was stunned. She, of course, understood that Richard was interested in her. But love?

She read on. . .

> *This love is not based upon physical attractiveness, although Sarah is a beautiful young lady.*

Beautiful? Shaking her head in wonder, she continued.

> *This love is based upon the Light I see shining from within her. Her concern for others, namely Captain Sinclair's children, is remarkable. Her ability to play the piano and sing are gifts from God, to be sure! Just last Tuesday I heard her singing an old Sunday school hymn to the children, and it moved my soul. . . .*

Sarah inhaled sharply, feeling somewhat embarrassed. She had no idea that Richard heard her playing last Tuesday! He should have made his presence known, the sneak!

Forcing her attention back to the letter once more, Sarah finished reading the remainder of its contents. When finished, she carefully folded it up. *He loves me,* she thought. *After only three and a half weeks, he loves me. And he's terribly romantic. He thinks I'm beautiful—and not just on the outside, but on the inside, too!*

Sarah wasn't sure if she'd ever had a man love her before, other than family members. No one, that she knew of, had ever considered her "beautiful," although her brothers called her "pretty." That is, pretty silly, pretty sassy, and pretty much a pain in their necks!

Sarah smiled at the memory and then strolled to her bedroom window. She brushed the lovely ivory-laced curtain aside and gazed out into the blackness of the backyard. She'd had plenty of suitors who asked to court her. But they had seemed rather insignificant, so her father refused them because of Sarah's lack of interest. She had been taught that courtship was the first step toward marriage. She hadn't wanted to marry any of her past suitors. But did she want to marry Richard?

No. Not now, her heart seemed to reply. *But, perhaps, in the future. . .*

With a heavy sigh, Sarah flounced on her bed. The thick crazy quilt, made of silk, satin, and brocade swatches, enveloped her like a soft hug. She thought about Richard for a good long time. Round and round she went. Did she? Didn't she? Should she? Shouldn't she? Would she? Wouldn't she? And out of all her thoughts and questions, one thing was sure: Next to her brothers, Richard was probably the best friend she would ever know.

In that moment, Sarah knew what she must do.

The next morning before leaving with the children for their swimming lessons, Sarah left a note for Richard. She put it in an envelope along with the letter he'd written to her father. The note for Richard was two words long. It said, "Post it."

Richard read Sarah's note and couldn't believe his eyes. *Post it! Post the letter to her father! Glory hallelujah!*

He had prayed himself to sleep last night, asking for God's will in this situation and for help to accept the plan for his life, whether it be with Sarah, or without her. This was exactly the answer he'd hoped for; he had been given his heart's desire!

Going about his business routine that day, Richard did every chore with renewed enthusiasm. Some of his coworkers noticed and teasingly asked if he were trying to minimize their efforts by working twice as hard.

"Just feel especially good today," Richard replied with a grin.

One of the customers chuckled. "Seems a mite late for spring fever, hey boy? It's nearly July!"

"This isn't spring fever," Richard retorted, wearing a secret little smile. "Can't you see I'm in love?"

Everyone in the shop hooted. Richard Navis in love? Never!

"There ain't a woman alive who'd have you," teased another coworker.

"Well, I didn't say she loved me back," Richard replied good-naturedly.

They laughed again and had more fun doing their jobs that afternoon since Otis Lazinski spilled a barrel of crude oil and they all skied off the loading dock while trying to help him clean it up!

That evening, as he saddled his horse and then headed for home, Richard allowed his imagination to wander. He had ideas. Big ideas. He'd been thinking about quitting his job with the captain at the end of the year and then buying his father's farm.

Pops will be pleased. After all, that's what he's wanted—his only son to carry on the family farm. To work the land as he did before the war disabled him.

And Richard loved his animals and the field work. He loved being outside amidst all that God had created. True, the hours of back-breaking labor were long; however, the fruits of that labor were awfully sweet! To take a seed, plant it, and watch it grow into something life sustaining was utterly rewarding for Richard. Much more rewarding than the captain's book work, that's for sure!

And Mama—Mama will faint with happiness, Richard decided with a smile. *Sarah will fill that farmhouse with her music and her laughter and, God willing, there will be children. Lots of children. Mama always wanted lots of grandchildren. . . .*

Richard smiled. He had big ideas, all right. Now all he had to do was win Sarah's heart!

Chapter 10

This is the most beautiful room I've ever seen!" Sarah exclaimed, glancing at the sculptured plaster work on the ceiling, the two crystal chandeliers which hung from it, and finally the matching crystal wall sconces. This was the first time Sarah had been up on the third floor of this house, inside the formal ballroom.

Captain Sinclair turned from the windows. "Do you like it, Sarah?"

"I should say I do!"

He chuckled softly, and his deep voice echoed through the room. The hardwood parquet floor gleamed beneath its new coat of wax, and the tables lining the walls were covered with freshly washed and starched linen cloths.

"I see Gretchen has already begun to prepare for the party on Friday night," the captain observed. His dark gaze came to rest on Sarah. "I'd like the children dressed formally so they can make an appearance." He grinned. "I enjoy showing off my children."

"Yes, Captain," Sarah replied with a smile.

"And you, too."

Sarah raised questioning brows, and the captain laughed.

"Plan on making an appearance," he said between chuckles. "I didn't mean to imply that I'd enjoy showing you off, although—" The captain raised a dark brow as he considered Sarah in two sweeping glances. "I may enjoy it at that."

Sarah felt a deep blush creeping up her neck and face, but she chose to laugh off the remark and treat it as though the captain were teasing. However, when he said things like that or scrutinized her with those black eyes, Sarah felt weak-kneed and nervous.

Uncomfortable, she continued to survey the ballroom. There was a stage at one end prepared for musicians. And a piano. . .

Goodness! she thought. *Imagine two pianos in one household!*

Sarah turned back to the captain. "Is Richard coming on Friday night?"

"Yes. He'll be here in case I need him to explain my books." Captain Sinclair rubbed his palms together. "Hopefully Friday night we will secure several new shipping deals." A wry grin curved his lips. "Elise Kingsley will be here—her late husband owned Great Lakes Shipping. The poor woman has no idea how to run the business, so I've been trying to help her out." He lifted his brows as if to emphasize the latter.

Sarah frowned in confusion.

"You don't understand, do you, Sarah? You're much too sweet and innocent. The truth is, I want Elise's business for myself—at any price, and that's why Richard's attendance is required."

"I see." She really didn't; business dealings weren't Sarah's strong point.

"On Friday night," the captain continued, waving his hand in two quick sweeps, "this room will be filled with Milwaukee's biggest beer barons."

"Beer barons, sir?"

Captain Sinclair nodded. "Frederick Miller; Jacob Best's son, Phillip; Captain Fred Pabst; and Valentine Blatz, to name a few. It ought to be very interesting."

"And all those men make beer?" Sarah asked.

"They do," the captain replied. "And they're rich, Sarah. Very, very rich." He smiled indulgently. "Have you ever tasted beer, Sarah?"

She shook her head. Her father preached against partaking of strong drink such as beer.

"Well, perhaps you can have a small glass on Friday night after the children are asleep. Just to taste it."

"Well, thank you, sir, but that's quite all right. . . ."

"Do you know how to waltz?" the captain asked her next.

"I know the basics." Sarah's mother had wanted all the McCabe children to know how to dance as part of their education. However, Sarah had never actually done any dancing, except with Leah as her partner.

"Come here," the captain said, holding his arms out to her.

Sarah froze, hearing her mother's voice warning her never to dance with a man unless she was sure of his intentions. *It's best to wait until you're betrothed,* her mother had said. *Dancing is a very intimate thing. . . .*

"Captain Sinclair, I don't think—"

"Oh, come here," he said with an amused grin. "I'm not going to devour you in a single gulp."

Sarah forced a smile. "Well, yes, I know, but—"

The captain chuckled and came forward in two great strides. "Here," he said, putting an arm around Sarah's waist. Then he took her right hand in his left. He smiled down into her face. "Let's waltz."

Against her better judgment, Sarah didn't protest. *This won't last long,* she told herself. *Leah always said I was a terrible dancer; I stepped on her toes constantly.* Feeling awkward, Sarah looked down.

"Ah-ah-ah," the captain said on a note of admonition. "Don't look at your feet. Look at me. Your partner. And follow my lead."

Sarah tried to relax in the captain's embrace, and she nearly lost herself in his deep dark eyes as they slowly waltzed down one length of the ballroom.

"Very good," he said with a smile. "Now pick up the speed a bit."

They danced back to the other side of the room and then around in a full circle. At last the captain released her waist and spun her in a *pirouette.* Sarah laughed.

"See? There's nothing to it."

"I guess that wasn't so bad." Sarah replied.

Captain Sinclair held on to her hand. "You'll have to save a dance for me on Friday night."

Sarah's legs almost gave way, but she managed a smile. "Yes, sir, Captain."

Days later, on Wednesday, her one day off, Sarah met Richard for lunch.

"I don't expect we'll hear from your father for at least a month," he said, cutting the slice of roast beef on his plate.

Sarah nodded, feeling a bit guilty over not being more excited. Ever since she'd danced with the captain, she was having second thoughts about a courtship with Richard. And yet she had looked forward to this luncheon engagement with him.

"So what are your plans for this afternoon?" Richard asked, bringing Sarah out of her thoughts.

"Oh, Lina and I are going to do some shopping."

A teasing gleam heightened the hue of Richard's blue eyes. "That sounds dangerous. . .you and Lina, cut loose on the streets of Milwaukee."

"We're a dangerous pair to be sure." Sarah smiled and took a sip of her tea. "Lina tells me it's your birthday next week."

Richard grimaced.

"She said you hate to make a big deal of your birthday. She said it embarrasses you no end."

"Sarah, please don't. . ."

She merely shrugged, but her mind was humming with plans for a celebration.

"I've been known to disappear on my birthday," Richard informed her, cocking an eyebrow.

Again, Sarah shrugged, trying to appear nonchalant.

"Tell you what, Sarah, if it's that important to you, I'll bear the embarrassment of a surprise party."

"Who said anything about a surprise party?"

Richard smiled indulgently. "My mother and Lina try to surprise me every year, and every year I guess what they're up to."

"Well, this year will be different." Sarah graced him with a grin. "This year I'm in town."

After lunch, they left the eating establishment and Richard went back to his books. Sarah walked a few blocks to where a row of shops lined the busy street. Lina was already waiting for her. Since school was closed for the summer months, Lina had her days free, although much of her time was spent planning for her upcoming fall wedding.

Strolling down Wisconsin Street, Sarah and Lina peered into shop windows and marveled at the new fashions in the clothing stores. They stopped at the apothecary, and Lina picked up some items for her mother and then they continued their walk.

"What can I buy Richard for his birthday?" Sarah asked after a couple hours of shopping. They had decided on a treat at the ice cream parlor.

"You want to buy Richard a gift?" Lina replied with an incredulous expression. "I don't think that's necessary."

Sarah licked her frozen treat. "I know, but Richard has been very good to me since my arrival, so I'd like to buy him something special."

Lina laughed softly. "My cousin has ulterior motives, Sarah."

This time Sarah laughed. "Yes, I know." At Lina's second look of surprise, she added, "Richard and I have discussed his 'ulterior motives' in great length."

"Sarah. . . !"

She rolled her eyes at Lina's sudden expression of delight. "Don't start making wedding plans just yet."

"But, Sarah. . . !"

"Oh, will you stop it!"

Lina placed a gloved hand over her mouth to cover her mirth. Regaining her composure, she said, "Richard has never been interested in any particular young lady. That's why I'm so tickled. It's a family joke that Richard will be our lifelong bachelor. It started when he was just a boy. He used to tease all the girls and make them cry, so they avoided him—right up until last year, I believe."

They laughed together, and Sarah said she could well imagine.

With their ice cream now finished and thoroughly enjoyed, Sarah and Lina left the shop. The day was sunny and bright, and the streets of Milwaukee were busy. The remaining afternoon was spent dawdling in and out of every kind of shop the city had to offer; however, except for a few necessities, Sarah returned to the captain's residence empty-handed. She would have to continue to search for a small birthday gift for Richard.

Up in the quiet of her bedroom that evening, Sarah wrote to her parents. She wanted a letter to follow Richard's so that her parents could make the appropriate decision. She prayed God's Holy Spirit would work in their hearts and minds, and out of that, Sarah thought she, too, might come to some conclusion regarding her feelings for Richard.

I like him very much, she wrote. *However. . .*

Concerning her heart, there always seemed to be a "however." Sarah thought her parents would not be surprised.

Sarah also thought of writing about the captain and her feelings toward him, although she knew her parents would not approve. Most likely they would make her come home, especially if she confessed to the dancing.

The unfortunate thing was, a part of Sarah—the adventurous part —wanted to dance with him again!

"How long do we have to stand here?" Gabriel whined.

Sarah smiled at the boy. He looked so handsome, all dressed up for his father's party, although he'd rather be fishing—and he had been making his feelings known for the last half hour.

"I'm sure your father will dismiss us shortly," she told him.

"I'm sure he's forgotten all about us," Gabriel retorted. "He always forgets. Can't we just leave?"

"No. And let's remember to be respectful at all times. He is your father, whether he forgets or not."

The boy merely shrugged his shoulders.

Libby was tugging on Sarah's skirt. "Miss Sarah! Miss Sarah!"

"Yes, dear," she replied, giving the girl her full attention.

"There's Mrs. Kingsley—the one who came to Aurora's house when we were there. Look!"

Glancing across the crowded ballroom, Sarah spied the woman. "Don't point your finger that way, Libby," she chided softly. "It's not polite." However, Sarah had to will herself not to openly gape.

The widow Elise Kingsley was, by far, the belle of the ball. She was a tall, slim brunette, wearing a red silk gown trimmed with black lace. She was dancing with the captain in a most intimate way, and suddenly Sarah felt foolish for ever imagining herself matched with Captain Sinclair. He was much too sophisticated for a little country bumpkin such as herself.

No! Sarah thought. *I will not succumb to self-pity. I will have to watch and learn. Then I'll be just as sophisticated as anyone here in this room.*

A half hour passed, then an hour, and Gabriel began to complain again. "Can't we go now? I hate this stuffy party!"

"I believe your father wants you, Michael, and Libby to play your songs on the piano," Sarah replied. "He said you were good enough. He said you wouldn't have to wait until the end of the summer."

"I don't want to play my song," Michael whined. "I'm hungry and tired."

"And I'm hungry, too, Miss Sarah," Libby said with a pout.

"Me, too!" cried little Rachel.

"Father forgot us, anyway," said Gabriel, "so let's go."

Sarah let another twenty minutes pass before deciding that the captain really had forgotten them. His eyes, it seemed, were only on the Widow Kingsley tonight, and Sarah had the odd feeling that the captain was purposely ignoring them. Was it that Mrs. Kingsley didn't like children? Was that why he pretended they didn't exist—because he wanted to impress the rich woman? But he said he enjoyed showing off his children.

Sarah felt both disgusted and confused. She was half tempted to stay here all night just to annoy Captain Sinclair and let him know they would *not* be ignored! But then she noticed several guests eyeing the tired children speculatively, and she made the decision to leave the party. It wouldn't do, she reasoned, to have the captain's friends think his children were unruly because they were hungry and crabby. They were *children,* after all!

And when they paraded out of the ballroom, the captain didn't even notice.

Down in the kitchen, after the children were done with their supper and cake, Sarah took them for a walk—a "promenade" really, for they were still all dressed up in their Sunday best. Sarah felt a little sorry for them, being ignored by their father, but the captain's mind was obviously elsewhere.

Upstairs, preparing the children for bed, Sarah tried to make up for their father's neglect by telling them stories. Bible stories, stories of hope and victory through trusting God. First David and Goliath for the boys, next Deborah for the girls.

"She was the fourth and only female judge of Israel," Sarah told them. "So you see, God uses women, too. And for important reasons."

Libby's eyes were wide with wonder, and Sarah thought even Gabriel looked impressed.

Once the children were asleep, Sarah retired to her bedroom. She could hear muffled voices from above in the ballroom. She could hear the violins playing beautiful melodies, accompanied by the piano. How tempted she was to join that elite crowd; after all, the captain had invited her. But when Sarah had asked Gretchen if she was going to the party, Gretchen said it was not appropriate for her station. "And it's not appropriate for yours, either, Irish!"

Sarah had frowned at the remark, but gradually concluded Gretchen was only reminding her of her proper place. She was only the governess here. She was not a guest.

But someday, Sarah promised herself, *someday I'll have a governess for my children. . .and a big house just like this one. Perhaps the captain will give Richard a promotion. . .a partnership, even! Then I'll be glad to marry him, and we'll never ignore and neglect our children. But we'll teach them proper manners and how to be sophisticated.*

Suddenly, Sarah heard a sound at her window pane. It came again. And again. *Ping. Ping. Ping.*

"Richard Navis!" she said, opening the window and leaning over the sill. She could see him standing in the yard. "What do you think you're doing?"

Beneath the moon's glow, Sarah saw him grin. "I'm throwing gooseberries at your window," he replied. "I was going to throw a brick, but I decided that might be too conspicuous."

Sarah laughed.

"Come down," he beckoned. "Let's go for a stroll."

"I've been for a stroll."

"Then come for another."

"With no chaperon?" she teased.

"I could ask Gretchen," he countered.

"Never mind."

Richard chuckled.

"All right. I'll come down."

Grabbing a light wrap, Sarah left her room. She met Richard on the back patio.

"You look lovely tonight," he said with a smile. "I think blue is your color."

"Thank you," Sarah murmured, smoothing the silk of her skirt. It was the best dress she owned. Store bought, too, in Chicago.

Richard held his hand out to her. "Shall we?"

Sarah hesitated for a moment before taking his hand; however, Richard held hers only long enough for her to fall into step beside him. Then he released it, acting the proper gentleman as always.

They walked down a moonlit path along the steep cliffs which overlooked Lake Michigan. Overhead, the sky twinkled with stars. *Such a lovely evening,* Sarah thought, inhaling the scent of summer blooms along the walkway. *And to think, God created it all!*

As if divining her thoughts, Richard began quoting the Psalms.

" 'When I consider thy heavens, the work of thy fingers, the moon and the stars, which thou hast ordained; What is man, that thou art mindful of him?' " He turned to Sarah. "An awesome thought, isn't it?"

"Yes. We truly have an awesome God." Solemnly, she added, "I wish Captain Sinclair would come to know Him."

Richard paused. "I've tried, Sarah. I've explained God's plan of salvation to him, and we've talked about it. But I'm afraid the captain refuses to acknowledge that he's a sinner, separated from God, and that the only way to God is through His Son, Jesus Christ. The captain doesn't see—or doesn't want to see—the immediacy of the moment; eternity could be just a heartbeat away. For any of us."

"Very true." Sarah felt the sting of rebuke. She hadn't once spoken to the captain about Jesus, even though the Bible so clearly warned in the book of James that life is "a vapour, that appeareth for a little time, and then vanisheth away."

"We'll keep praying for him," Richard said, taking Sarah's hand and slipping it around his elbow. "All right?"

She nodded, feeling reassured. After all, as her older brother Benjamin liked to say, prayer is what moved mountains and parted seas!

Chapter 11

I forgot all about Richard's birthday!" Captain Sinclair exclaimed the following week. He had just walked into the kitchen where Sarah and the children were cutting and pasting colored paper together, creating birthday cards for Richard.

"His birfday was really yesterday, Papa," Libby announced, "but we're s'prising him tomorrow with a party. . .right after church." She looked to Sarah for confirmation. "That so, Miss Sarah?"

"That's correct, Libby." Sarah glanced at the captain. "I didn't think you'd mind my taking the children, since they've accompanied me to church and then the Navises' farm every week so far."

"I don't mind at all," he stated graciously. "I only wish I would have remembered that Richard's birthday was yesterday." The captain narrowed his gaze at Sarah, feigning irritation. "You should have reminded me."

"Forgive me, Captain," she replied. "I suppose I could have. . .and should have reminded you." *The poor man*, she thought. *He'd forget his head if it weren't attached!*

"Papa, look at my card," Michael said, pushing it into the captain's hand.

"Well, that's a fine one," he replied with pride in his voice, and Sarah recalled how Richard had once said that, despite the captain's shortcomings, he did love his children.

"How 'bout mine, Papa?" Libby asked. "Do you like it?"

Captain Sinclair studied it. "Very good," he finally pronounced.

"Wook! Wook!" cried Rachel.

Captain Sinclair praised his younger daughter for her efforts. "What about yours, Gabriel?" he asked. "Can I see it?"

The boy grudgingly handed it to his father.

The captain studied it. "Why, this is very good." He looked over at his son with approval shining in his dark eyes. "I should say you're a talented young man."

"You've seen the pictures in his bedroom, haven't you, Captain?" Sarah asked.

He frowned. "No, I haven't."

Sarah turned to Gabriel. "You'll have to show your father your. . . your *gallery*."

"You really want to see my pictures?" Gabe asked, looking at his father.

"Of course I want to see them!" Captain Sinclair tousled Gabriel's hair and went about his way.

"He'll forget," Gabriel murmured as he finished his card for Richard. "He always forgets."

Sarah's heart went out to him. "Perhaps this time your father will remember. We'll pray. . . ."

Gabriel looked up at her with questions clouding his light green eyes. But he didn't ask, not yet.

Sarah smiled. *It won't be long,* she thought. Gabriel was interested in God and His ways; and Sarah sensed that the young man would soon be ready to accept God's gift of salvation.

The children finished making their birthday cards and then Sarah helped serve their supper. Afterward, she instructed the children individually at the piano.

Later that evening, after the children were in bed, Sarah encountered Gretchen in the hallway upstairs. "Give this to Mr. Navis!" the housekeeper demanded in her thick German accent.

Sarah examined the basket covered with a checkered linen cloth. "Whatever it is," she said, "it smells delicious."

"It's apple kuchen," Gretchen stated quickly. "Mr. Navis loves my apple kuchen. I made him a dish for his birthday."

Sarah smiled. "That was very thoughtful."

The older woman bobbed out a curt reply. "You will give it to Mr. Navis, then?"

The question sounded more like a command, but Sarah nodded anyway. Then she had a question of her own to ask. "Why don't you address Richard by his first name instead of calling him Mr. Navis? I heard him specifically tell you to call him Richard."

"It is not my place, Irish!" Gretchen replied sternly.

Sarah's raised her chin. Gretchen might try to insult her, but Sarah was proud of her heritage.

"Mr. Navis has a higher position than I do," Gretchen continued. "Higher than yours, too!"

"But he asked me to call him Richard."

"And I know he has asked you more than that also!"

At the remark, true as it was, Sarah felt her cheeks grow warm with embarrassment. Gretchen, however, didn't seem impressed by her reaction one way or another.

"The children address their grandmother as Aurora," Gretchen continued. "Is that proper? I should say not! But the captain allows it anyhow, and it is hardly my place to tell the captain his business."

"Well, somebody has to. . .and you've been in the captain's employment for a very long time. Why, you're practically part of the family!"

"Ha! If a better housekeeper came along, I vould be gone in a minute!" Gretchen exclaimed. She narrowed her gaze at Sarah. "Ve are guaranteed nussing in this lifetime! In minutes, life can change and that vhich ve loved can instantly be gone." She snapped her capable fingers. "Just like that."

Sarah frowned in momentary puzzlement, but then the pieces of Gretchen's past seemed to fall into line. Gretchen Schlyterhaus was angry, hurt, and bitter, Sarah realized, because of her husband's death. And now she was trying desperately to hold onto the only thing she thought she had left: her position with Captain Sinclair. How obvious it suddenly became!

Sarah's heart began to ache for the older woman. *She needs the Lord Jesus,* she thought. *Jesus is all she'll ever need to get her through this lifetime. . . .*

"In any case, you just make sure to give the apple kuchen to Mr. Navis."

"Yes, of course I will."

As Gretchen sauntered off, an idea formed. "Mrs. Schlyterhaus, would you like to come with us tomorrow? To church and then to the Navises' for Richard's birthday party?"

"Sunday is my day off," the housekeeper replied gruffly over her shoulder.

"Well, yes, I know and that's why I wondered—"

"Of course I vould like to come!" Turning, Gretchen marched the few steps back to Sarah and retrieved the apple kuchen. "I vill give this to Mr. Navis myself!"

With that she stomped away, leaving Sarah gaping in her wake.

Then, on an afterthought, Sarah called, "Be ready by eight o'clock. Richard's cousin Lina is coming for us."

No response; however, Sarah knew Gretchen had heard. Moreover, she was certain that Gretchen would be ready right on time!

Lina and her fiancé Timothy arrived in his carriage shortly after breakfast. Sarah made the appropriate introductions and then climbed in after the children. From the front door, Captain Sinclair waved and called, "Have fun." Sarah wished he was coming to church with them, and she prayed that someday he would.

When they arrived at the little country church, Gretchen walked in with the children as Lina held Sarah back by the elbow.

"What happened on Friday?" she whispered.

"Just as you suspected," Sarah whispered back. "Richard asked me to dinner and the theater, but I told him I couldn't go because of—of a previous commitment."

Lina giggled. "Oh, that's just grand! Richard probably stewed all weekend!"

Sarah frowned slightly, remembering his expression two days ago. The usual shine in Richard's bright blue eyes had disappeared like the sun behind thunderclouds.

"Lina, I think I hurt his feelings, turning him down on his birthday."

"Well, you can make it up to him today," she replied. "And Richard will laugh about it when he finds out why you turned him down. He loves a good prank. Here he thinks all his friends forgot his birthday, when we've really been planning a party all along. . . ."

Sarah smiled, and Lina laughed softly as they walked into the sanctuary and found their places. Richard and his parents were seated in the pew in front of them. After she had sat down and settled the children between herself and Lina, with Gretchen at the other end, Richard turned around. He narrowed his gaze speculatively, first at Lina, then at Sarah.

"What are you two up to?" he finally asked. "I saw you whispering outside."

"None of your business," Lina answered.

He glanced at Sarah, who merely shrugged. Then, after giving her an I-know-that-you're-up-to-something look, Richard turned back around. Sarah and Lina exchanged amused and knowing smiles.

The service began with hymns of praise. Sarah watched curiously as Gretchen opened the hymnal and followed along. She didn't sing, although she seemed to be looking at the words. Then it occurred to Sarah that perhaps Mrs. Schlyterhaus couldn't read English. She was, after all, from Germany. Returning her gaze to her own song book now, Sarah decided she would have to do something about that. She would ask Richard about getting a German hymnal.

After church, Sarah ushered the Sinclair children outside to the waiting carriage. Gretchen suggested that she keep the two little girls with her and ride with Lina and Timothy while Sarah take the boys and ride with Richard and his parents.

"*Ve* will not be so cramped," she added, fanning herself with her white gloves.

Sarah nodded and had to agree that it was certainly a hot day!

Richard, of course, was all for the idea. He helped Sarah up into the wagon, after which he boosted the two boys into the back. He had already helped his father aboard, which was no simple task because of Marty Navis's paralyzed legs. However, Sarah had noticed that Mr. Navis helped himself by using his arms which, since his accident, had grown thick and muscular—a result of having to constantly lift his own weight.

"How did you manage to get Gretchen to church this morning, Sarah?" Richard flicked the reins, and the wagon jerked forward.

"I just invited her."

"Well, I've been inviting her for years!" Richard exclaimed. "So has my mother."

"Really?" The idea gave Sarah pause. "Well, perhaps Mrs. Schlyterhaus doesn't dislike me after all."

Richard grinned. "I'd wager that it's impossible to dislike you, Sarah." He chuckled. "Why, you've even managed to win Gabriel and Michael, and they disliked every governess the captain ever hired!"

"Yes, so I've heard in great detail." Sarah chuckled. "Those two can be mischief-makers." She looked into the back of the wagon and found the boys preoccupied with something Michael was holding in his palm. Some sort of insect, no doubt.

"I'm so pleased you're spending Sundays with us," Mrs. Navis said from where she sat on the other side of Sarah. The two men were in front, Richard with the reins.

"I am also pleased, Sarah," Richard said. He glanced over his shoulder, wearing a mischievous smile, and Sarah shook her head at him.

"Must you always state the obvious?"

He nodded. "Uh-huh."

Sarah laughed. She enjoyed Richard's humor more than she cared to admit, and she was very glad to spend Sundays with him and his family. The Navises made her feel right at home with their relaxed and unpretentious ways. They weren't out to impress her or win her; they just loved her—Richard's feelings being quite different from his parents', of course. In any case, Sarah knew they were genuine, earthy folks around whom she could freely share her heart and enjoy the goodness of the Lord.

"Sometimes I get homesick when I spend time with your family," she confided to Richard hours later as they took a walk around the potato field. The stroll was actually a diversion of sorts, as Lina and Mrs. Navis wanted to get things in order for Richard's surprise birthday party—without him around.

Richard smiled at her statement. "What is it exactly that makes you homesick?"

"Well, sometimes all the activity at your house on Sundays reminds me of home in Missouri. Ben and Valerie bring their two little boys. . ." Sarah shrugged, feeling misty-eyed all of a sudden.

"I thought you were glad to be away from Missouri."

"I am, I guess. I mean, for the most part, yes, I'm glad to be on my own. I value my independence, you know. I just miss my family sometimes."

Walking around the property, they ended up on the far side of the apple orchard.

"So, you value your independence, do you?" Richard asked rhetorically as they sat down beneath a large tree.

Sarah nodded and, reaching up, she removed her bonnet and then patted several pins back into place.

Richard chuckled. "Sarah, how independent do you really think you are? You don't have to cook, launder clothes, clean house, concern yourself with finances, a roof over your head, clothes on your back. . ."

"I am, too, concerned about the clothes on my back!"

Richard laughed again. "That's not my point. Sarah, don't you see? Everyone takes care of you. The captain. Gretchen. Isabelle. Me."

"You're wrong. If you haven't noticed, I work for my living. Taking care of four children isn't exactly complete luxury."

"I'll say!" Richard was quiet for a long while. "Sarah, you know what I think? I think you're not independent. You're spoiled!"

"What?" She turned sharply, studying his face. She couldn't tell if Richard was teasing or if he'd meant that last remark. In any case, Sarah thought she deserved to be a little spoiled. Hadn't she worked—and worked hard!—back in Missouri? She knew very well what it was like to do all those things Richard had mentioned. . .and then some! It wasn't until she'd met her sister-in-law Valerie that she'd begun to hunger for a different way of life. The kind of life Valerie had had as a socialite in a big city like New Orleans before she married Benjamin. And, although Valerie maintained that she was happier in love and doing all those mundane household chores, Sarah had grown tired of them and had longed to be on her own. And now she was!

Richard suddenly stood and held his hand out to Sarah. She refused to take it and pushed to her feet on her own.

"And you're stubborn, too."

"Well, I can think of plenty choice words to describe you, Richard Navis."

"Oh, now, Sarah. . ."

She whirled around, intending to head for the house, but before Sarah took even one step forward, Richard grabbed her hand and pulled her into his arms. Slowly, he lowered his mouth to hers.

Sarah's first impulse was to push him away, but curiosity allowed her to relax. As if sensing her acquiescence, Richard deepened his kiss until Sarah felt herself responding.

Finally, Richard tore himself away. His deep blue eyes held such tenderness that Sarah thought she might like to drown in them. Slipping her arms around Richard's neck, she leaned forward for another sweet kiss.

"No more, Sarah," he said hoarsely, pushing her arms away gently. "I was wrong to even initiate the first." He closed his eyes in what seemed like a mixture of remorse and agony. "Please forgive me." Looking at her once more, he added, "I just love you so much. . .I love everything about you, your talents and your faults. Can't you see that?" He sighed. "I'm sorry I said you're spoiled and stubborn. It's just that. . .well. . .I've been smarting all weekend because you chose a 'previous commitment' over me on my birthday—and I hope I don't know him."

"Richard!" Sarah took a step backward. "How dare you imply that I'm some sort of hussy, accepting an invitation from another man when you're courting me."

He looked immediately contrite. "No, Sarah, I didn't mean that you were anything of the sort." Richard groaned and raked his fingers through his hair. "Sarah, forgive me, please. All these emotions are new to me. I never suspected I had a single jealous bone in my body. But I do."

Lifting her bonnet off the grass, she whacked him across the chest with it.

"I suppose I deserved that."

"Yes, you did, you beast!" With that, Sarah stomped out of the apple orchard and toward the house.

Chapter 12

Hours later, Richard watched as his uncle's carriage pulled out of the circle drive, heading toward Lisbon Plank Road. The evening sun was just beginning to set, casting long shadows across the lawn. Richard waved to Sarah who returned the gesture with a smile. They had long since resolved things between them. And once Richard learned Sarah had purposely fibbed about her "previous commitment" on Friday night in order to surprise him today with the most memorable birthday party he'd ever had, Richard felt ashamed of himself. But in the end, he and Sarah were able to laugh about it.

Richard inhaled the fragrant summer air. The afternoon had been delightful, and he would treasure its memory for a long, long time. Gretchen's gift would certainly be a delicious reminder; the handkerchief, on which Bethany had embroidered his initials, would be useful, and Lina and Tim's generous birthday gift of two theater tickets was more than appreciated. However, Sarah's gift—the handsome set of pens—bothered Richard. A farmer would have no use for pens of that magnitude! Sleek and black, trimmed with gold, they must have cost Sarah plenty. Moreover, she had said she'd searched and searched for the "perfect birthday gift."

Was there to be more trouble between them?

"Did you tell her, son?"

Richard turned to find that his father had wheeled his chair onto the large front porch.

"Did you tell her about the decision you made last night?"

Slowly, Richard shook his head.

"I thought you would have taken the time while you two strolled this afternoon."

"I should have, Pops. But Sarah and I got into a discussion on a whole nother topic." He didn't admit they'd argued, and he didn't tell his father that he'd made the mistake of kissing Sarah. Richard was sorry enough as it was, and he'd asked for God's forgiveness. That kiss was sin in his mind; Sarah didn't belong to him. . .yet.

Marty expelled a long sigh. "Well, if you want to change your mind about the farm—"

"I don't. I won't," Richard stated. "A farmer is who I'm called to be, Pops. I want to work the land, marry Sarah, and live here. . .and raise my family here."

His father laughed. "Well, I know you've always loved this place, Richard, but to hear you talk about marriage. . ." He chuckled again. "Until you met that pretty little gal from Missouri, you were singing a bachelor-for-life tune."

Richard grinned. "I guess that's right."

Marty squinted speculatively. "Do you think Miss Sarah will want the same? She seems awfully city-minded. Told me she was tired of country living, and she told your mother that she likes being in the captain's fancy house."

Now it was Richard's turn to sigh. He had suspected that's how Sarah felt, and yet he was praying she'd come to love him enough to live anywhere on God's green earth. . .including his farm!

"I don't know, Pops." Richard sat in a porch chair next to his father's wheelchair. "I suppose we'll just have to see."

"It may be, son, that you'll have to choose—this farm, or Sarah." His father looked him square in the eye. "Then what?"

Richard didn't answer right away, thinking the question through. Finally he said, "Pops, I refuse to decide on one or the other. I want Sarah for my wife, and I want this farm. And I believe, because I've taken this matter to God, that He intends to bless me with both."

Looking across the acreage, Richard's gaze stopped at the small pond. "A good amount of my sweat and an equal amount of my tears may have to be shed, Pops, but, with God as my witness, I'm going to work this land as best I'm able. . .and I'm going to marry Sarah McCabe!"

The month of July continued, hot and sticky, and finally a letter from Reverend McCabe arrived. Tim delivered it to the captain's shop, wearing a grin.

"Open it," he urged. "The suspense is killin' me."

Richard could barely muster a smile as he tore into the envelope and read the letter.

Dear Mr. Navis (May I call you Richard?):

My wife and I were quite surprised by your letter. The fact that Sarah gave you consent to post it, coupled by her subsequent note in which she told us of your interest as well, astounded us no end!

But, having recovered from the shock, I do hereby give you my permission to court Sarah. I do, however, expect her to return to Chicago and to her teaching position in the fall. The two of you will just have to correspond until the Christmas holiday. At that time, I want Sarah to return home, here to Missouri, but she may bring you and your parents along.

My wife and I are very eager to meet you, Richard. We think it'll be a very merry Christmas, indeed!

Smiling, Richard looked up. "Thank You, Jesus!" he shouted, causing several of his coworkers to cast curious looks in his direction. But Richard was too happy to care what others thought. Looking at Tim, he said, "The courtship of Sarah McCabe has just begun!"

"Amen!" Tim declared.

That very evening, Richard read the letter to Sarah as they walked along the cliffs. His grin seemed permanently affixed on his face, causing Sarah to feel both pleased and embarrassed—and more than a tad concerned.

"You've done it now, Richard Navis. My father will interrogate you the entire Christmas holiday and so will my brothers."

"I'm not worried," he replied, chuckling.

"You ought to be," she murmured.

Richard laughed all the harder. Then, folding Reverend McCabe's letter, he tucked it back in his shirt pocket before taking Sarah's hand and wrapping it around his elbow. As they strolled amicably toward the downtown area, a gnawing conviction swelled inside of him. He had to tell Sarah about his decision to farm. . .and it seemed the Lord was prompting him to be honest with her right now.

"Sarah, let's sit and talk awhile." He nodded toward a bench on the walk that overlooked Lake Michigan.

"What do you want to talk about—and why do you look so serious?"

Lowering herself onto the bench, Sarah wished Richard would say something to make her laugh. Having taken the children to their swimming lessons, taught them their piano lessons, then seen to their supper and baths, she felt wilted. She closed her eyes as a cool breeze wafted off Lake Michigan, and she thought it felt wonderful after the heat of the day. This walk was doing wonders for her disposition.

Richard cleared his throat. "Sarah, you know I'm very pleased that your father has given me permission to court you."

"Really? I would have never guessed." She giggled.

"Sarah, please. This is important."

"Oh, all right." She cast aside her mirth and sat up a little straighter.

Richard wetted his lips. "Let's just imagine for a moment that you fall madly in love with me and we get married. Where do you see us making our home?"

Sarah thought a moment and then shrugged. "Right here in Milwaukee, I suppose."

"Good! I had thought the same."

Sarah watched as a frown furrowed his brows. "What is it, Richard?"

"It's. . .well, oh, I guess I should come right out and tell you. It's good news, really. . ." His gaze met hers before he lifted one of her hands, holding it between both of his. "The transfer has been legally made—I've purchased my father's home, and I plan to farm the land. I'm going to give my notice to Captain Sinclair tomorrow, but I wanted you to know first. When my service is up, which will be at the end of the year, I will resign and take up farming full time."

"What?" Sarah's jaw dropped at the incredible news. "A farmer? You are planning to be a farmer?"

Richard didn't flinch. "Yes, I am."

"But you have such a promising future with the captain!"

"Perhaps in a sense, yes. But I'm unhappy in my current position, and I've known for quite some time now that it's not for me."

Sarah yanked her hand free and stood, then considered the matter for several long minutes as she gazed out over the lake. "So what you're telling me is. . .if I marry you, Richard, I will be a farmer's wife."

"That's right."

She whirled around to face him. "No! Never! I care for you, Richard, but not *that* much."

Richard swallowed his sudden hurt. "Sarah, won't you even think about it—pray about it?"

"I have prayed about it. I know where my life is heading, and it is not to your farm. I'm sorry, Richard."

He stood, wondering what he could say to change her mind. The words "I love you" were obviously not enough.

"I think it's best we end our courtship."

"Sarah. . ."

"No, Richard. If I wanted to marry a farmer, I could have stayed in Missouri!" With that, she strode in the direction of the captain's house.

Too stunned to even follow her back to the captain's home, he let Sarah walk the short distance alone. Her reaction was one he feared all along, but he hadn't been prepared for the pain that followed her rejection. Sarah's words had pierced his heart with an indescribable sorrow.

Sitting back down on the bench, Richard clasped his hands together and lowered his head to pray. . . .

And then the tears began to fall.

Entering the captain's home, Sarah couldn't believe what she'd heard. A farmer? Had Richard gone mad? Well, perhaps he'd have a change of heart. Things had been going so well. In fact, sometimes Sarah thought she even loved Richard. But marry a farmer? No! No! No!

As she came around the back stairwell, someone caught her arm. Turning suddenly, she found herself looking up at Captain Sinclair.

He donned an amused little smile. "Why on earth are you frowning so? You're lucky Aurora didn't see you. She'd give you an hour's lecture on how a frown ages a young lady's face!"

Sarah realized the captain was teasing her. She forced a smile. "Forgive me, sir, but I've just heard some disturbing news."

The captain frowned. "And what is that?"

Gently pulling her arm free of his grasp, Sarah groped for an explanation. "I believe you'll hear it tomorrow, Captain."

His dark gaze narrowed as he considered her with pursed lips. *Now why can't Richard be more like the captain?* Sarah wondered as she looked into his handsome face. *Why can't Richard be more ambitious, business minded, serious, and mature?*

"Sarah, tell me what you've heard."

"I'm afraid I can't, Captain Sinclair. It's not my place to tell you."

"I see." He folded his arms across his chest. "Has this anything to do with my steward, Richard Navis, with whom you have been spending a good deal of time lately?"

Sarah didn't need a looking glass to know her cheeks were aflame. She could feel the heat of her chagrin right up to the tip of her nose.

The captain smiled. "By your expression, I can tell that it does. May I assume that your short affair with him is now over?"

"Affair?" Sarah wondered if that's what sophisticated people termed a courtship: an "affair."

"Sarah, my dear," the captain continued, "I could have saved both of you time and heartache—that is, I could have saved Richard the heartache and you the time. You are hardly a match for him. I can tell. You want more from this life than Richard could ever give you."

He paused, putting a booted foot up on a stair and leaning a powerful-looking forearm against his leg. If Sarah hadn't taken a step back, their noses would be touching.

Captain Sinclair considered her long and hard with a slight smile curving his handsome mouth. "If I weren't such a gentleman, Sarah, and you weren't quite so young, I should say I'd like to kiss you."

Her eyes widened, and her heart fairly flew into her throat.

"Moreover," the captain continued, "I expect that you'd enjoy it."

"Captain Sinclair!" she gasped, feeling horrified now. "I am not that kind of a—a. . ."

"Of course you're not," he agreed. "And I didn't mean to imply that you are anything less than a proper young woman. However, you have a passionate nature, Sarah, and that's quite obvious."

"Oh, dear!" She cupped her face with gloved hands, wondering what her mother would say if she discovered this "passionate nature." Then Sarah recalled how she had enjoyed Richard's kiss, and the memory added a feeling of shame to her current discomfort.

But Captain Sinclair just laughed. "Sarah, what I mean is that you would never be happy with a man like Richard. He's too—too dependable.

You want to live life to its fullest. You want adventure and the finer things this world has to offer. Richard, on the other hand, could care less for finery and, matched with him, you would be miserable. And so would he, because he could never please you."

Sarah thought the captain had spoken exactly what was in her heart, and yet, once verbalized, the words made her feel like a haughty and shallow person. And that, Sarah decided, was more disturbing than the captain's remark about how he'd like to kiss her.

However, she was unwilling to pursue these conflicting emotions. In a swirl of skirts, Sarah turned and ran up the stairs, leaving the captain chuckling in her wake.

Chapter 13

For the next few days, Richard pursued Sarah in spite of the hurtful words she'd hurled at him. He couldn't believe she really meant them, nor was he about to give up. Not yet. He even managed to overcome the captain's words of discouragement.

"Why don't you forget this farm idea?" the captain suggested. "Perhaps Sarah would consider you then. You'd have a good future working for me; you would be successful and could afford a young woman like Sarah McCabe. She desires fine things and a life in the city. To tell you the truth, I can't blame her."

Richard gritted his teeth. "Money isn't everything, Captain. I can't buy Sarah."

"Come now, Richard, I'm not talking about buying anyone or anything. I'm talking about a way of life. A comfortable way of life."

"I know what you're talking about," Richard said, softening his tone, "and I thank you for your concern. But either Sarah loves me for who I am, or she doesn't love me at all!"

Captain Sinclair shook his head sadly. "Such a romantic."

Richard, however, didn't think he was more romantic than any other man. He was just in love. . .in love with Sarah McCabe. What's more, he had a feeling that, worldly things aside, she loved him, too.

So Richard prayed often and fervently, desperately wanting God's will for both their lives—and hoping he could live with the outcome.

Sarah, on the other hand, was both amazed and irritated at Richard's perseverance. She allowed him a few visits but finally refused him altogether until, at last, he agreed to put some distance between them.

"So you can come to your senses," Richard said.

"So you can come to yours!" Sarah retorted.

And for the weeks following, as the hot summer days passed into the sultry month of August, Richard didn't come around. Likewise, Sarah and the children refrained from going to the Navises' farm on Sunday afternoons. However, they continued to attend church services since Lina and Tim insisted upon driving them, despite Sarah and Richard's "misunderstanding," as Lina called it. And there, at church, Sarah caught glimpses of Richard, although they only exchanged polite greetings.

The only problem was, now that Richard had given Sarah her way, she was miserable! She found herself remembering his laughter and how blue his eyes would become when he was up to some kind of mischief. She thought her days were longer and more tedious now, without Richard spicing them up. Yes, she missed him; however, she didn't know what to do about it. She wished they could at least be friends, but Richard said he didn't want to be her friend; he wanted to be her husband!

To make matters worse, each week the children begged to go to the farm after church, and each week Sarah had to tell them no.

"But why?" Gabriel cried this week—just as he had last week. "Why can't we go to the Navises' farm?"

"I have explained this to you already, young man." Sarah pulled on her gloves with a vengeance. "We no longer have a standing invitation there."

"But Mr. Navis said we were invited if you'd say yes!" Michael declared.

"I will not say yes to Mr. Navis's offer." Sarah wasn't stupid. She knew the *offer* went well beyond a visit to the farm. And yet she, too, missed Sunday afternoons with the Navis family—and yes, with Richard, too! *If only he weren't so intent upon being a farmer,* she mused. *And he once called me stubborn! Ha!*

"Please, Sarah," Gabriel continued to plead, "it's the only thing that makes me happy—going to that farm on Sunday afternoons."

Sarah swung around from where she had been examining her appearance in the foyer's looking glass. "Why, Gabriel," she said, astounded, "we do plenty of fun things."

"But they're not like being on the farm."

Considering the boy, Sarah tilted her head. "Why not?"

" 'Cuz I'm free there," Gabriel replied simply. "It's not like here or at Aurora's house. I'm not free here or there. I have to sit up straight and not slurp my soup, and I have to wear fancy jackets that make me feel sweaty. But on the farm, I can just be me, and if I accidentally slurp my soup, nobody cares."

Sarah sighed, thinking the whole matter trivial. "Nobody cares here either, Gabe, if you accidentally slurp your soup—"

"You don't understand!" he shouted. "You're just like them! My father. . .and Aurora!"

Sarah gasped at the outburst.

"I thought you were different!" With that, Gabe turned on his heel and ran up the front staircase just as the captain entered the foyer.

"What's going on here?" He sent Sarah a quizzical look.

Quickly, she scooted Michael, Libby, and Rachel onto the front porch to wait for Lina and Tim.

"It was nothing, Captain. Really."

"But the shouting—was that Gabriel?"

Sarah hesitated in her reply. She didn't want to get the boy in trouble with his father.

"Sarah? Was Gabriel shouting at you?"

"Actually, we were discussing something that Gabriel feels very strongly about, sir. But I'll fetch him now, and everything will be fine."

Forgetting herself, as she often did, Sarah ran up the front stairs. She passed Gretchen in the upstairs hallway.

"Vill you ever learn to use the servants' stairvell?"

"Yes, ma'am, I will," Sarah promised over her shoulder. "I'll try not to forget again."

Gretchen clucked her tongue but said no more. Ever since Sarah had purchased a German hymnal for her, Gretchen's outward disdain had faded.

Sarah reached Gabriel's bedroom and knocked on the door. "Come on, Gabe," she called, "open up. Everyone is ready for church. Even Mrs. Schlyterhaus."

Slowly, the door opened, and Sarah had to force herself not to react when she saw Gabriel's tear-streaked face. The sight was enough to bring tears to her own eyes, for Gabriel Sinclair was not a boy easily moved to emotion.

"It's that important to you?" she asked him softly. "Visiting the farm?"

Gabriel just stood there, staring back at her.

"You know," Sarah began, "freedom really starts in the heart of a person. It's not a place. And only Jesus can make us free."

Gabriel shook his head. "You don't understand. I can't explain it. . .

it's like I'm happy there at the farm. But I'm not happy here."

"Perhaps that's because the Navis family knows Jesus and you can sense that. Perhaps the reason you experience happiness there is because you're experiencing the Navises' freedom. Freedom from sin and guilt and shame—because of what Jesus did on the cross."

Gabriel appeared to be taking in her explanation.

"And if you ask Jesus to forgive you for your sins, and if you ask Him into your heart," she continued, "then I believe you'll find happiness anywhere."

Gabriel regarded her askance. "Have you asked Jesus into your heart?"

Sarah nodded. "Jesus saved me when I was a little girl."

"Then how come you can't be happy anywhere?" he countered. "How come you can't be happy on a farm?"

Sarah gasped. "Why, Gabriel! How in the world—"

"I heard you," he continued. "I heard you talking to Miss Lina. You said you couldn't possibly marry Mr. Navis 'cuz you'd never be happy on a farm."

Sarah drew back her chin. "I was speaking of a different kind of happiness!" she declared, sounding defensive to her own ears. "And you can't understand because you're a child. Now, come along, Gabriel, we're going to church!"

Sarah marched back down the hallway and then down the front staircase. At the bottom, she found Captain Sinclair leaning against the banister, smiling.

"Oh, my, I forgot again," she murmured.

The captain chuckled. "It's a good thing Gretchen didn't see you. . . again. I escorted her out to the carriage and saved you another tongue lashing!"

Sarah smiled. "I'm very grateful, Captain."

"And what about Gabriel?"

"He's coming, sir."

"Very good."

"And what about you, Captain?" Sarah asked, suddenly feeling bold. "Will you come to church with us today?"

He laughed heartily. "I think not, my dear. I am not interested in hearing anything a long-winded preacher has to say." Looping Sarah's gloved hand around his elbow, Captain Sinclair ushered her toward the front door. "Besides, I won't hear anything at your church that Richard hasn't already told me. Sitting in a pew won't do me a bit of good!"

"But, Captain—"

"Now, Sarah," he chided her gently, "I'll hear no more of it. The fact is, I can't go to church. . .even if I wanted to. I have an engagement. I'm taking Elise Kingsley, Aurora, and her escort, John St. Martin, on a lake excursion today. We'll set sail mid-morning. Aurora has already sent a messenger so I won't forget."

Captain Sinclair suddenly grinned. "Why don't you and the children join us, Sarah? Come sailing with me out on beautiful Lake Michigan instead of perspiring in a stuffy chapel. It'll be so refreshing. . .sailing does a body wonders. And Aurora is very fond of you. She says you have 'possibilities.' And the boys can fish. What do you say?"

Sarah faltered, but only momentarily. She wouldn't feel right about skipping church to go sailing. Her father had taught her that one misses church only if one is at death's door.

"Thank you, Captain, but I think it would please God more if I went to church."

"Are you certain, Sarah?" the captain asked with a handsome grin. "You look like you might be persuaded—"

She hesitated, wondering what it would be like to go on a lake excursion with a man like Captain Kyle Sinclair and his affluent friends.

But Jesus sacrificed His life for her—couldn't she spare a few hours this morning for Him?

"Sarah?"

"No, thank you, sir," she said with some determination this time. "This is the Lord's day, and He has commanded that we set it aside to worship Him."

"Worship your God out on the lake. During the war, soldiers worshipped on the battlefield. There wasn't a church for miles."

"I'm sure that's true, but. . ." Sarah swallowed down her desire to go with him as well as her timidity to tell him why she couldn't. *Help me, Lord*, she pleaded. Then to the captain she said, "Please forgive me if I'm out of line, but you and your friends, Captain, are not believers, nor do you care to be. You said as much yourself. Therefore, I highly doubt that your excursion will be conducive to worshipping God Almighty!"

A slow, sardonic grin curved the captain's mouth. "You've got a point there, my dear. My friends and I have very little use for God. I guess you might say we have our own religion."

Sarah found the captain's comments very sad.

"So you won't come?"

"No, Captain."

"Very well." He exhaled a sigh of resignation. "You and the children go to church. I suppose it is better for my children anyway."

Sarah nodded her agreement as Gabriel came down the stairs, all shined up and ready to go.

The captain walked Sarah out to the awaiting carriage.

"I'm going to pray for you, Captain Sinclair," she stated in a final act of daring.

He gave her a patient grin. "And I shall think of you, dear Sarah, while I'm cooling myself in the middle of Lake Michigan with two of the wealthiest people in Milwaukee: Elise Kingsley and John St. Martin."

He saluted her then, and Sarah knew he was mocking her. But as he chuckled and helped her up into the carriage, Sarah promised herself that she wouldn't give up praying for his salvation.

When the carriage pulled onto the dusty gravel drive in front of the little church, Sarah was hot, sticky, and withered. The children, too, were miserable from the heat, and Sarah half wished she had taken the captain's offer of a lake excursion. Cool Lake Michigan. . .how refreshing it would feel. Unfortunately, the only available supply was not that of a vast body of water, but of a little spring-fed well.

Sarah led the children around back to the pump where they splashed their faces and took long, thirst-quenching gulps. Afterward, Sarah gathered the children, and together they entered the church building. Richard was standing at the doorway; he appeared to be waiting for them, and a little thrill passed through Sarah. He looked so handsome in his fashionable matching suit, and Sarah tumultuously decided it wasn't fair that a farmer should look so good!

"Good morning, Richard," she said in her formal best as the children descended upon him.

He lifted Rachel into his arms. "Hello, Sarah." He greeted Gabe, Michael, and Libby next. "I saw Gretchen come in behind Lina and

Tim, but I didn't see you or the children."

"The heat slowed us down, I'm afraid."

Richard's expression said he understood. "Well, when I didn't see you I began to worry. . .that is, I became concerned. I think worry might be a sin."

Sarah smiled at the glib remark and, despite the "distance" she had agreed to—even insisted upon—she couldn't help but feel cheered just seeing Richard again. *Oh, why can't I just fall in love with him and be done with it?* she wondered. *If only Richard's ambition weren't farming. If only he were more like Captain Sinclair. . . .*

They walked into the cool sanctuary and sat down in the back pew. Sarah had been taking this same spot for weeks in case Rachel got fussy during the services. But seeing they had arrived early today, the children were allowed to get the talking and squirming out of their systems while the rest of the congregation was scattered about chatting.

"How have you been, Richard? I haven't spoken more than three sentences to you in weeks," Sarah ventured. "How are your parents?"

Richard shifted in his place beside her. He seemed suddenly uncomfortable. "Sarah, I think. . .well, I mean, I need to talk to you about something. . . ."

At that exact moment, Bethany Stafford plopped down excitedly in the next pew in front of them. Her smile was so brilliant that Sarah had to wonder why she'd ever thought Bethany was a plain young woman. Today her soft brown hair was carefully pulled back, and her cheeks were flushed prettily. "Hello, Sarah. I have something to show you. Look!" Bethany fingered an ivory locket which hung on a delicate golden chain around her neck. "I'm betrothed!"

"Betrothed?" For a moment Sarah thought all the breath had left her lungs, she was so stunned. Bethany? Bethany was to marry—marry. . . *Richard?* Was that why he seemed so uncomfortable just now?

As if divining her thoughts, Richard leaned forward. "Beth, you may want to inform Sarah who it is you're betrothed to before she faints dead away!"

Sarah forced herself to inhale.

Two pink spots heightened Bethany's color. "I'm betrothed to Lionel Barnes. Mr. Timothy Barnes's younger brother. Remember him, Sarah? We all went to the theater together."

Sarah nodded. She remembered Lionel, all right.

"My parents have insisted that we wait for at least a year to get married," Bethany babbled on happily. "Papa says Lionel is a good fellow, but he's got some rough edges that need smoothing."

"Well. . .my goodness. . .congratulations." Sarah chanced a look at Richard, relieved that Bethany wasn't marrying him, although her betrothal to Lionel did seem a bit hasty. On the other hand, a year's time would surely tell.

Bethany stood to show her locket to another friend, and Richard began chuckling.

"You should have seen your face, Sarah. Could have knocked you over with a feather after Bethany announced her betrothal."

"Oh, quiet," Sarah replied irritably. She wished she'd done better at hiding her reaction.

"You know what I think?" Richard whispered, leaning over slightly. "I think you're in love with me, and I think you ought to do yourself—and me—a favor and admit it!"

"Go sit somewhere else," Sarah retorted. "I've got enough to manage with the captain's children, let alone you!"

Richard sobered. "Do you really want me to go, Sarah?"

She folded her arms, feeling like a fly caught in a spider's web. Richard was so much like her brother Luke. Their wills and determination barely gave a person a chance to think.

"Sarah? I'm waiting for an answer. Shall I go?"

Her tongue felt pasted to the roof of her mouth. She didn't want Richard to sit somewhere else either. Not really. She missed him, it was true. And perhaps she did love him. But to admit that would mean spending the rest of her life on a farm.

A farm! No! No! No! She had dreams, that was all. Ambitions. Why couldn't Richard understand that?

Then slowly, and without another word, Richard rose from the pew and walked forward to where his parents were sitting. Sarah watched as they moved to make room for him, and then Richard sat down. Smoothing her skirt, Sarah willed back the tears which threatened; she had made her decision, and now she had to live with it.

Chapter 14

Two hours later, Sarah stood in the shade by the wooden wagon, waiting for Lina and Tim and the captain's children. The service had long ago ended, but many of the congregation, including Lina and Tim, were still partaking in some fellowship. The Sinclair brood, along with several other children, chased about in the adjacent field and splashed in a nearby stream. Sarah was glad she had remembered to pack the children's play clothes. Now they would be much cooler on the ride back home.

She sighed as a faint breeze touched her cheek, causing her to long for much more. *Oh, for a hearty breeze,* she thought, *I think I'd do anything, Lord,* she prayed now, looking skyward. *Please send just a bit of a wind. . . .*

Right then Richard came strolling toward her. He looked as uncomfortable as she felt, although he had long since removed his suit jacket. But on his face he wore a mischievous grin, and Sarah was irked that he could smile while she felt so hot and miserable.

Then she thought of the captain and his friends, cool and comfortable and sailing away on Lake Michigan. She nearly groaned aloud.

"Waning by the wagon, are you, Sarah, my lovely?"

"Waning and lovely are words that don't belong in the same sentence."

"A matter of opinion. You're always lovely in my eyes—even when you're waning."

Sarah gave him a grin before removing her gloves. The heat didn't leave much room for propriety. The gloves were off now and, as soon as they left the church yard, Sarah was determined to remove her waist jacket with its stylish three-quarter-length sleeves.

"The heat is ghastly, isn't it?"

Sarah nodded. "Seems we agree on that much, anyway."

A wry grin curved Richard's mouth. Then for the next few moments, neither of them spoke. Richard leaned against the wagon beside her.

"Sarah, I wrote to your father again." All traces of humor were gone from his face now. "I told him of the problems we've been experiencing during our, uh, courtship."

Sarah didn't know what to say. Her family, of course, would not be surprised. Disappointed, perhaps, but not surprised.

"You do realize," Richard continued, "that your father wants you to return to your teaching position in September. That's two weeks away."

She nodded.

Richard turned sideways now to face Sarah. He propped his elbow on the side of the wagon. He wished he could force her into changing her mind, but he knew he couldn't. Only God could change Sarah's heart. But once she left for Chicago, Richard feared he'd lose her forever.

"I wonder," he said slowly, "if you and the children would like to come out to the farm today. The children will have a wonderful time. They can play in the pond. And we can watch them from the front porch. It's shaded for most of the day and stays nice and cool."

"I—I don't know."

"My parents would love to have you visit again."

"Your parents," Sarah said, sounding dejected, "must think I'm a shrew."

Richard laughed. "Hardly. They know who you're dealing with—me, their son!"

Sarah smiled and appeared to consider his offer. Then suddenly she folded her arms stubbornly. "Look, Richard, despite any feelings I may have for you, I don't want to live on a farm!"

"And I don't want to argue with you. It's much too hot."

She pivoted and now they stood face-to-face. "Why don't you change your mind, Richard? I've missed you so! We have such fun together. Can't we just put all this strife behind us? I mean, why must it be your way or my way? Can't we just come to some sort of compromise?"

Looking down at her earnest, pleading face, Richard was tempted, and he thought perhaps he understood now how Adam felt in the Garden. However, he'd stand his ground. He simply could not compromise on what he felt certain was the will of God for his life. He was called to plow and plant; he was called to be a farmer.

But he also loved Sarah, and his relationship with her was slipping through his fingers like rich, black soil.

"Sarah, come to the farm today. We'll talk. We'll get some things settled between us once and for all. I promise."

She fretted over her lower lip for a good thirty seconds as they both gazed at each other.

"We don't have much time left," Richard reminded her. "It'll be more difficult to communicate once you're back in Chicago."

Sarah finally acquiesced. "All right. I'll come to the farm today."

Gabriel was ecstatic at the change of plans, and his enthusiasm spilled over onto the other children. They skipped and hopped back to the wagon, acting as if the temperature wasn't pushing ninety-nine degrees.

Lina and Tim were pleased, too, as they accepted an invitation from the Navises for the afternoon. Then later this evening, they would drive Sarah and the children back to the captain's home. Gretchen, too, was invited, but declined and found a way back to town in a landau with a widower friend who owned a German sausage shop.

Sarah allowed Richard to assist her into Tim's buckboard. Minutes later, they were on their way.

"I do hope you and Richard can come to terms about your relationship," Lina remarked as they rode to the Navis farm. "You make such a handsome pair."

At Lina's hopeful look, Sarah just smiled. But for the remainder of the journey, she prayed and lost herself deep in thought.

She knew this predicament was of her own doing. She initially enjoyed the all the attention Richard paid her—she had even encouraged it. Soon they became friends and Richard fell in love with her. And now it was as plain as the sun in the sky that she loved him, too. This morning in the sanctuary when she incorrectly assumed that he and Bethany were betrothed, an inexpressible heartache took Sarah's breath away.

Yes, she loved Richard. But for years she'd fancied herself married to someone like Captain Sinclair. Love, however, hadn't been a part of that fantasy. Sarah had merely assumed that she'd grow to love whomever she married. But affluence, ambition, a darkly handsome face, and mysterious disposition. . .those were the traits Sarah had longed for in a man. And, in her dreams, that man looked very much like Captain Sinclair.

Sarah shifted uncomfortably now as she admitted the truth to herself. All summer long she had avoided it, but here it was. The truth, like an incessant child, was crying and begging to be reckoned with, and Sarah could ignore it no longer.

She was drawn to the captain. Yes, it was true. And he tempted her to the point where she violated her conscience. . .like when they had waltzed together alone in the ballroom. But Sarah was sometimes uneasy around the captain as well. He was too—too familiar with her. Sarah wasn't accustomed to that sort of behavior. The captain thought nothing of taking her hand in his. Or smiling into her eyes. Or holding her close as they danced that one day. . .

She squirmed. Her conscience still pricked about that incident. She had been raised quite differently in her conservative Christian home. However, the captain was not a Christian, nor was he the slightest bit interested in her faith. No, he was not the man for her; Sarah was suddenly certain about at least that much! She'd been foolish to even consider him, even if only in her dreams.

On the other hand, Richard loved the Lord and lived for Him. And Richard was handsome, though he was more of a rascal than "mysterious." As for affluent and ambitious, those words did not describe him, at least not in the monetary sense. Hard-working and determined were better adjectives. And, except for one stolen kiss—which had been more given than stolen—Richard was a fine gentleman. But, alas, "farmer" said it all!

Lord, help! Sarah silently pleaded as Tim pulled into the Navises' circle drive. *Help me discern my future. Help me know what I should do about Richard.*

Then, suddenly, God replied to her soul. "Trust in the Lord with all thine heart; and lean not unto thine own understanding. In all thy ways acknowledge him, and he shall direct thy paths."

All Sarah could do was give thanks in return. Her Savior was with her always. She only needed to trust Him with her future. He was the One who truly understood her. He knew her heart, as fickle as it was.

She sighed as the peace of God which passes all understanding filled her being. Why should she fret when God was in control?

Richard, too, had been praying on the way back to the farm, Fervently, in fact. He prayed that he'd be able to keep his promise to Sarah and that something would be settled between them. The only problem was, Richard had no idea what that "something" might be.

After a light lunch, Sarah put little Rachel down for a nap. It was only then that Richard got a chance to speak with Sarah privately.

They sat together on the steps of the wide, cement front porch which ran the entire width of the house. It was covered by an overhanging roof, shaded and very cool. Meanwhile, Gabriel, Michael, and Libby splashed happily in the pond near the apple orchard, and somewhere in the fields beyond the cattle were lowing.

"Sarah, I think—"

"No, Richard, let me begin. May I?"

Surprised by her question, he nodded, although not without a twinge of trepidation. He noticed she'd been thoughtful for the last hour and a half. Would what she have to say break his heart forever?

"You're quite a stinker, Richard," she began.

He grinned. "Such flattery, Sarah. Really!"

She laughed before turning serious once more. "I realized on the way here today that I have to be honest with myself. . .and with you." She cleared her throat. "I need to tell you that—that you have succeeded in. . ." She paused, looking Richard square in the eyes. "Well, I love you, Richard. Truly, I do."

He narrowed his gaze. "Don't tease me, Sarah. Not like that."

"I'm not teasing. I did some soul-searching and. . .I love you."

"Sarah, I'm about to break into a few bars of the 'Hallelujah Chorus,' here! Don't tease me!"

She lifted an impish brow. "Will you be singing soprano or alto?"

"Whichever you'd prefer." A wide, happy grin split his face. "I think I could do just about anything right now."

She laughed as Richard, in falsetto, sang a poor rendition of Handel's beloved piece.

"Stop!" she finally cried. "Stop, please! The music teacher in me beseeches you!"

But she was giggling so hard that the children came running from the pond to see what all the ruckus was about.

"I'm afraid it's heat stroke," she told the children. "Perhaps we'll have to throw Mr. Navis in the pond to clear his head."

"Yes, let's!" they cried in unison.

"Oh, now, Miss Sarah is only joking," Richard told the children as he rose from the steps. Then he descended several of them. "But, tell you what: I'll come over in a few minutes and. . .well, maybe I'll let you throw me in after all. This heat is oppressive!"

With a cheer, the children went running back to the pond.

"If I had extra clothes," Sarah said, "I'd let them throw me in the pond, too."

"Extra clothes could easily be arranged," Richard replied with a twinkle in his eye. "Now tell me again that you love me."

"I don't know," Sarah replied, feigning a hesitant tone. "Look what happened the last time I did that!"

Richard grew suddenly serious. "Will you marry me, Sarah?"

"Oh, Richard, I haven't gotten that far yet." A deep frown marred her blond brows. "Can you give me some time? I mean, this farm. . .well, a girl has dreams, you know. I made myself a vow that I would work my way up the social ladder and never settle for the simple country life. But here you are, suddenly the man I love, asking me to do exactly that. In essence, Richard, you're asking me to give up my aspirations!"

For several long moments, Richard considered her words carefully. Then, finally, he nodded. "All right. Fair enough. I'll give you all the time you need. I'll love you forever, Sarah, so I guess I can wait until you change your mind about being a socialite."

She expelled a dramatic sigh. "Oh, why do I feel doomed?"

Richard laughed. "Here," he said, "give me your hand."

"Why?"

"Give me your hand."

Sarah complied, and Richard pulled her to her feet. One good yank and she was in his arms. But now, as he carried her toward the pond, Sarah grew wise to his intentions.

"Don't you dare, Richard Navis!"

He just kept walking and grinning.

"Richard, I mean it! Don't you dare!"

Sarah struggled, but he held on fast.

"Stop, Richard!" she pleaded as they neared the pond. "I can't get wet. I'm supposed to be a lady!"

"Aw, Sarah, I won't tell."

"Richard!"

He chuckled and, heaving her upward, tossed her into the deepest part of the pond—about two feet deep. With a cry of indignation and a sound splash, Sarah hit the water, petticoats, stockings, leather ankle boots with their spool heels, and all. The children squealed with delight.

"Richard Navis, I can't believe you did that!" Sarah cried. She looked from the laughing children to Richard's grinning face, and she shook her wet head at the lot of them. Then she sighed, "Oh, this feels wonderful!"

Grabbing Michael's leg, Sarah pulled the boy down and under the cool water. He came up surprised, but sputtering and laughing all the while.

Next she went after Libby, who did a grand imitation of Sarah's "Don't you dare! Don't you dare!" Warnings ignored, Libby, too, got dunked but came up giggling hysterically.

Then Richard and Gabriel got into it, and both went under, laughing and splashing.

Suddenly Lina appeared and shook her head at them. "I won't even ask who instigated this nonsense," she said, looking pointedly at Richard who was lounging at one end of the pond.

From the other end, Sarah called, "Come on in, the water's fine."

A sudden gleam flashed in Richard's eyes, and he sprang from the pond.

"Oh, no you don't!" Lina cried, and she took off running.

Richard chased his cousin into the orchard, and everyone in the pond could hear Lina screaming. This brought Tim to the rescue.

"What in the world. . . !" he exclaimed, looking horrified.

Richard carried Lina back, kicking and pleading, but try as she might, she couldn't escape. Poor Tim looked too stunned to be of any help, so Lina also ended up in the pond.

"This does feel rather good, doesn't it?" she admitted.

Sarah nodded.

Then suddenly Tim jumped in on his own accord, causing a gigantic splash, and everyone laughed until their sides ached.

Finally Marty Navis wheeled his chair onto the lawn. He laughed at the sight, then called, "I came to tell you there's a storm approaching. Look to the west!"

At once, everyone turned to stare at the great, ominous, black clouds and, in the sudden hush, they heard the distant rumbling of thunder.

"I'd best tend to the animals," Richard said.

"I'll help you, brother," Tim replied.

"I'll get the children into dry clothes," Sarah said, taking Libby's hand.

Lina nodded and followed Sarah. The afternoon's fun in the pond had come to an abrupt end.

Chapter 15

The dark clouds drew closer and the thunder louder. But upstairs, safe inside the Navises' home, Sarah helped Libby into dry clothes while Lina tended to Rachel who had just awakened from her nap. Each little girl wore her cotton chemise from this morning, which could properly suffice as a nightshirt for now. Gabriel and Michael, however, had to change into their good church clothes. Then for Sarah, Lina found a simple calico dress and petticoat, minus the crinoline.

"I hope this will do," Lina said. "I left these items here last year, if I remember correctly. But my mother and I usually keep some clothes here in case of emergencies. And our entire family comes here and spends days at a time," she explained. "So we're always forgetting and leaving things behind."

Sarah gladly accepted the dress and underthings. They weren't very stylish, but they were dry. Lina found dry garments for herself, too, and Sarah noticed that the clothes she and her mother had left at the farm were all as simple as the calico dress Sarah was borrowing. Of course they had no need for fancy attire on a farm. Modest and practical, that was what a farmer's wife needed in the way of a wardrobe. Sarah knew that much from her growing up years in rural Missouri.

"Do you and your family come often?" Sarah asked.

"Twice a year," Lina replied with a grin. "Just think. . .after you marry Richard, you and I will be related. And Tim and I can come stay with you and Richard on holidays!"

Sarah rolled her eyes at Lina's presumption.

Suddenly the room grew dark as night, and a strong gust of wind blew through the treetops outside the open bedroom window.

"I'm scared!" cried Libby.

"Me, too!" Rachel said in her baby voice. "I don't yike the thunder!"

"Oh, don't worry," Sarah told them, closing the window as Lina lit

110

the lamp. "Jesus will take care of us."

Just then, Bea called up the stairs to them. "Come down quickly, girls. Marty thinks it's a twister coming!"

Lina extinguished the lamp she'd just lit, and then she and Sarah each grabbed a little girl. They hurried down the stairs where they met Gabriel, Michael, Tim, and the Navis family. Moving into the cellar, they took cover in the summer kitchen under the house. Marty went first in his wheelchair, accepting help from Richard and Tim. Two oil lamps were lit, and then Richard found some old barrels which served as seats for the men while the ladies took the chairs around the large, square work table.

"Let's play some chess," Marty suggested with a challenging grin.

Gabriel accepted the challenge, and everyone watched as the game commenced.

Outside, the rain pelted the cellar door as the wind raged. Rachel clung to Sarah while Lina held Libby on her lap.

Then all at once, the storm passed, leaving just as quickly as it had come. Richard and Tim lifted the cellar door, and shafts of sunshine lit the entrance. The temperature had cooled at least twenty degrees, and now the angry dark clouds were blowing eastward, over the lake—all very typical, Richard said, of Wisconsin's summer storms.

Marty Navis was carried upstairs, after which Richard, Tim, Gabriel, and Michael walked around the property, looking for damage. They came back nearly an hour later, reporting a few downed trees. But that was all.

"And it looks as though the Staffords' property is fine, too," Richard announced as they all sat down to supper. Now that the oppressive heat was gone, appetites had returned.

Bea smiled as she served up the hastily prepared meal of fried eggs, ham, and sliced homemade bread.

When their meal ended, Marty requested his Bible and read from Isaiah chapter twenty-five: " 'For thou hast been a strength to the poor, a strength to the needy in his distress, a refuge from the storm, a shadow from the heat, when the blast of the terrible ones is as a storm against the wall. . . .' " He looked around the table. "Let's bow our heads and give God thanks for protecting us today."

Sarah lowered her chin as a hush fell over the group. Just then Libby tugged on her skirt.

"Miss Sarah," she whispered, loud enough for all to hear, "Jesus really did keep us safe, didn't He?"

Sarah smiled and nodded. Then she closed her eyes to give thanks.

"Miss Sarah," Libby's voice came again, "can I pray, too? Will you show me?"

After a moment's pause, Sarah realized that Libby was ready to accept Jesus into her heart! Sarah looked at Richard, who winked and nodded encouragingly.

"Come, Libby," Sarah whispered back. She took the child's hand. "Let's go pray together."

"Can I come, too?" Michael asked before Marty even got started with his prayer of thanksgiving.

"Me, too?" Gabriel asked as well.

Richard stood and grinned broadly. "Come on. Let's all of us go pray together."

Bea held Rachel on her lap while Sarah and Richard led the other children into a quiet spot in the front room.

"Before we pray," Richard began, "I want to tell you about four things that God wants you to know. First of all, He wants you to know that you're a sinner. Do you know what sin is?"

The children nodded, but Libby was the one who replied, "Sin is when you do something wrong. Like tell a lie."

"That's right," Richard said. "The Bible says in Romans 3:23, 'For all have sinned, and come short of the glory of God.' You see, I'm a sinner and Miss Sarah is a sinner, too. The only difference is, Sarah and I have been forgiven of our sins by God. But if you aren't forgiven by God, then, like the Bible says, 'The wages of sin is death.' God also says, 'And whosoever was not found written in the book of life was cast into the lake of fire.' " Richard looked at each child. "That's a description of hell—the lake of fire. See, that's the second thing God wants you to know: Sinners who aren't forgiven can't go to heaven."

"Well, I want to go to heaven!" Michael declared. His siblings nodded in agreement.

Richard smiled. "Good. Then here's the third thing God wants you to know: Jesus Christ died for all sinners. 'For God so loved the world, that he gave his only begotten Son, that whosoever believeth in him should not perish, but have everlasting life.'

"You see, Jesus is God and He was perfect. He never sinned, so He was our substitute."

Richard frowned, seeing the children's puzzled faces. *How can I explain it better?* he wondered.

Then Sarah piped in. "Jesus got the spanking that you should have gotten when you sinned. Jesus took your punishment. . .to save you."

"Oh," said the children, nodding in understanding now.

Richard sent a look of gratitude Sarah's way, and she smiled.

"All right, now here's the fourth thing God wants you to know," Richard continued. "Anyone can be saved. The Bible says, 'If thou shalt confess with thy mouth the Lord Jesus, and shalt believe in thine heart that God hath raised him from the dead, thou shalt be saved.' " Richard looked at each of the children. "Jesus died on the cross, but He didn't stay dead. God raised Him up again—brought Him back to life. And that's what God will do for you, too, if you believe what I just told you." Richard smiled gently. "Do you believe what the Bible says about Jesus?"

The children bobbed their heads.

"Well, if you truly believe what the Bible says about sin and about what Jesus did to take away your sin," Richard continued, "then you can pray and ask God to forgive you and ask Jesus into your heart where He'll live forever. Do you want to do that?"

Each of the Sinclair children nodded.

Sarah lowered her head, and Libby followed. Then the boys did the same, and Richard instructed all the children to repeat after him. . .

"Dear God, I know I am a sinner and deserve to go to hell. But I am sorry for my sins, and I ask Your forgiveness. I know Jesus died to save me with His shed blood, and I ask for Him to come into my heart. I here and now accept Your free gift of salvation through Jesus Christ, Your Son. Amen."

"Amen!" Sarah said, looking up and smiling brightly.

"Amen!" Gabriel and Michael said, too.

Then Libby added her own, "Amen!"

It was nightfall before Tim, Lina, Sarah, and the children finally rolled out of the Navises' circle drive. The air was cool and crisp, and the sky was clear; the stars shone like sprinklings of silver on black velvet.

The children fell asleep almost at once, and Sarah was still awed that Gabriel, Michael, and Libby had seen their need for the Savior. Libby had even said later that she "felt happier inside" which made Sarah want to rejoice all the more. What's more, she was reminded that the angels in heaven were rejoicing tonight. Looking heavenward, Sarah breathed deeply and smiled.

"It seems you and Richard have gotten things squared away," Lina remarked.

Sarah continued to smile. "Yes, I suppose we have."

"And?"

"And what?"

"A wedding date?"

On the other side of Lina, Tim's chuckle could be heard.

"What's so funny?" Lina demanded.

"You, my sweet," he replied. "You waste no time in securing wedding plans—including our own."

Lina swatted Tim's arm playfully.

"Not that I mind, of course," Tim added, in an effort to redeem himself.

Sarah smiled at their larking around. But suddenly they quieted, and Sarah knew an answer was expected, all joking aside.

She cleared her throat. "Well, uh, no wedding date. Not yet."

"Oh, what a shame." Lina sounded disappointed.

"Well, marriage is a big step." Sarah felt a need to explain herself. "One has to be certain. And. . .well. . .living on a farm is not what I had planned for my life. I've told you this before, and I mean no personal offense to the Navis family in the least. It's just that I. . .well. . .I had always thought I'd live in a house like Captain Sinclair's house—"

"And marry a man like the captain, too, I presume," said Tim. "He's handsome and rich, and I wouldn't doubt that he turns many a woman's head with his velveteen words."

Sarah couldn't deny it.

"I can't help but think of what the Bible says about men like the captain. 'For what is a man profited, if he shall gain the whole world, and lose his own soul?' "

"The answer is he gains nothing but an eternity apart from God," Sarah replied. She knew that portion of scripture from the book of

Matthew very well. She believed it to be true.

"All the captain's money," Tim said, "will do him little good on judgment day."

"I agree, and I pray for him often."

"That's commendable, but we all sense there's more to it. My opinion is—"

"I don't recall having asked for your opinion," Sarah snapped.

Lina patted her hand, a gentle reminder that Sarah should watch her tongue.

Long and uncomfortable minutes passed as the wagon moved eastward toward the city. Sarah checked on the children, hoping none overheard the heated discussion.

"Are they sleeping?" Lina asked.

"Oh, yes. They've been asleep for quite some time." Nostalgia washed over Sarah. "Look how Rachel has snuggled right up against Gabriel. . .that's just how I used to snuggle against my big brothers."

"I never had any big brothers or any siblings," Lina said. "I'm an only child, just like Richard, although he's as close to me as any brother could be."

So, of course she's on his side, Sarah thought. It was unfortunate Lina couldn't see that Richard was just as stubborn as he accused her of being.

"Richard mentioned that your brothers are missionaries," Tim said, his tone conciliatory.

Sarah tamped down her irritation with Tim long enough to reply. "Yes, that's correct. But only two brothers are missionaries. The other is a photographer in St. Louis."

"And the missionaries. . .are they married?" Tim asked.

"Not yet." Sarah had to smile, thinking of Jacob and Luke. "Both are such rascals! Serious Christians, but rascals all the same. It'll take two special women to tame them, I'm afraid."

Lina giggled. "That's what I always said about Richard, isn't it, Tim?"

"Yes, indeed." He paused. "Well, I'll certainly pray, Sarah, that when your brothers do find women to love, they won't be scorned merely because they're missionaries. I mean, there's not much prestige in missionary work, but there sure is an awful lot of sacrifice involved."

"And persecution," Lina added. "Missionaries have been known to be burned at the stake, pierced with arrows, buried alive. . .stoned to death, like Stephen was in the book of Acts."

"Quite true, Lina," Tim said. "And to be scorned by the woman you love would hurt terribly—another kind of torture, I'd say!"

"All right, that's enough out of you two!" Sarah put her hands over her ears, unwilling to be chastened further. But, try as she might, she couldn't shut out the point her friends had made. Moments later, Sarah viewed her circumstances very differently. She would hate it if a woman refused either of her brothers simply because he was doing what God willed. She would think that kind of woman was unworthy of her brother. Furthermore, she would think of that woman as prideful and haughty.

And yet, wasn't that exactly the way she was behaving toward Richard?

Sarah gulped back the tears. She felt like she'd been snapped in two. She realized, much to her disgrace, how wrong she'd been to allow herself to be tempted by the captain and his influence, his wealth, and all his beautiful things. How ashamed of their youngest daughter her parents would be if they could see how she had tossed her careful upbringing aside.

Forgive me, Lord. Forgive me for not seeking Your will in all of this but, instead, seeking my own. Help me now to right any wrongs that I've done.

Chapter 16

S arah climbed down from the wagon, with Tim's help, and then both he and Lina helped her carry the children upstairs to bed. After seeing Tim and Lina on their way, Sarah retired to her bedroom and wrote to her parents.

Dear Mother and Father:

I need to confess to you, since I have already confessed my sin to God, that I have behaved badly toward Richard. He's a wonderful young man and, Pa, you will like him. I believe I do love him, and I told him so today. I had been hesitant to make any sort of commitment because I didn't want to live on a farm. I thought I was too good for farm life. You see, Richard has chosen farming instead of bookkeeping—but I'm sure he told you all that in his last letter.

Tonight I realized that I have been harboring a haughty spirit and, as the Bible warns, a haughty spirit goes before a fall—I believe mine came tonight.

What I also need for you to know is that I am willing to marry Richard. . .even if he has chosen farming as a way of life. I believe it is God's will for my future; He has shown me many things this summer. Of course, you will have to approve before I can accept Richard's proposal of marriage; however, he has asked. Several times, in fact. Each time I refused him simply and solely because he has chosen to be a farmer.

So now, seeing as I am forgiven by God, I need to ask Richard's forgiveness as well, but I know he will forgive me because he loves me. . . .

Sarah paused to collect her thoughts. Then she continued writing, telling her parents about today's storm and of Gabriel, Michael, and Libby's salvation decisions.

She wrote freely, describing the Navises' farm, its out-buildings, the animals, the gardens, the orchard and. . .the pond.

> *And he threw me in! Why, my fine leather boots will squish and squash for weeks when I walk. That prank was something Luke would enjoy!*

Sarah then wrote that Richard's father had built his home in 1851. She described how unusual it was, not at all a typical farmhouse. Sarah had never relayed the story to her parents, but now, for some reason, she felt compelled to tell them everything about Richard and his family.

Finally, with her letter finished and ready to be posted, Sarah left her bedroom to check on the happenings within the household. It was nearing midnight, and the captain wasn't home yet. Nothing odd about that, although Gretchen's pacing was troublesome.

"Are you all right, Mrs. Schlyterhaus?"

"I'm going up to the vidow's valk, Irish." The housekeeper's tone held no note of malice, just fear and weariness.

"May I come?"

"You may."

Sarah had never been up on the widow's walk before, though she knew the captain enjoyed being up there. He had a large telescope with which one could peer out over Lake Michigan. Gabriel had once told Sarah that he'd been given a chance to look through it on several occasions.

"He is out there somewhere," Gretchen murmured now, staring out over the vast body of water.

"The captain? Out. . .there?" Sarah felt confused. "Where?"

"The lake. The lake. . ." Gretchen heaved a great sigh. "Oh, Irish, it's a terrible thing. This evening, about seven o'clock, a man named Mr. Craine delivered a message. It said that the captain's small schooner, *The Adventuress*, vas discovered in pieces after today's storm. No bodies have been recovered yet, but all on board are presumed dead."

"What? No!" Sarah cried as fingers of horror ran up her spine. The captain? Dead? Aurora? It couldn't be true!

"Mr. Craine said it could be months before the bodies are recovered," Gretchen managed in a strained voice.

"No, they can't be dead!" Sarah cried again. "Let's dwell on the positive. They could be alive. Perhaps they made it safely to shore and we just don't know it yet!"

Gretchen didn't reply, and a long moment passed between the two women who stood gazing out over the murderous waves of Lake Michigan.

"I had to give Mr. Craine the names of those aboard *The Adventuress*, and I vasn't sure. . ."

Sarah thought a moment. "Aurora."

"Yes."

"And the captain, of course. And Mrs. Kingsley."

"Yes, yes. . ."

"And Mr.—oh, what was his name again?"

"St. Martin."

"That's right."

"Any others?" Gretchen asked.

"Not that I know of."

Then it hit Sarah—and the truth, like a thunderbolt, shook her to the very core of her being. *If I had given in to my temptation and gone sailing with the captain today. . .I would have been. . .and the children. . .we would be among those presumed dead!*

Sarah immediately thanked God for His Holy Spirit which had prompted her to obey Him.

Another long moment passed in silence, and Sarah felt more and more sick inside. Heartsick.

"This is like a bad dream," she murmured. "I wish this wasn't happening. I mean, what of the children? I suppose we shouldn't tell them anything until we hear some definite news."

"Yes, I suppose. . ." Gretchen was silent for a while and then finally she said, "I have a feeling it's all over, Irish. The captain is dead and my life's vork has drowned in that lake vith him." She shook her head. "Life can be so unkind!"

Before Sarah had a chance to reply, Gretchen swung around and strode quickly into the house.

The night passed fretfully for Sarah. She didn't sleep a wink. She prayed as hard as she knew how that the captain, his mother, and their friends had somehow survived the storm. But such seemed not to be God's will. Richard arrived the next morning with the bad news.

"Two bodies have been recovered," he told Sarah and Gretchen. "I've been asked, as the captain's steward, to go and identify them right now." He sucked in a breath, raking a troubled hand through his blond hair. "This is not something I relish doing!"

"Would it help if I went along?" Sarah asked. She really didn't want to go, but she would do it for Richard.

He shook his head. "It's not a sight any woman should have to see, I think. You and Gretchen stay here. Try not to upset yourselves overmuch. I'll be back in a couple of hours."

Once Richard left, Sarah wished she could tell him of her decision last night. She was willing to marry him, farm and all. Right now he seemed so gallant and brave. But this other business was more important; she would have to wait until later to talk to him.

"You could do a lot vorse than Richard Navis," Gretchen said tersely.

Sarah turned and faced the cantankerous housekeeper. "Actually, Mrs. Schlyterhaus, I believe I couldn't do better than Richard Navis."

With that, Sarah ran up the front stairs to check on the children.

"The servant's stairvell, Irish!" Gretchen called. "Vill you ever learn?"

Richard was back by suppertime, looking somber and distressed. As the children ate under the cook's supervision, he told Sarah and Gretchen that he had identified Elise Kingsley and Aurora.

Immediate tears stung Sarah's eyes as she sat down heavily on a chair in the main reception hall. *Aurora. Dead. The children's grandmother. Gone.*

"They're all dead, aren't they?" Gretchen asked, looking forlorn.

"I don't know," Richard replied. "We can only hope and pray. I would really hate to speculate at this point." He turned to Sarah who couldn't contain her tears a moment longer. "Don't cry." He knelt beside her and took her hand.

"What should I tell the children?" she asked, wiping the tears from her cheeks.

"Tell them the truth," Richard told her. "As gently as you can, Sarah, you must tell them the truth."

"I vill help you, Irish," Gretchen announced with her usual stoic expression. "I love them, too, you know."

"I can help as well," Richard said. "And perhaps now's as good a time as any."

When the children finished eating, Sarah, Richard, and Gretchen took them for an evening stroll near the bluffs overlooking Lake Michigan. Richard did all the explaining while Sarah and Gretchen stood by for moral support. Oddly, the children took the news very well. Solemnly, with only a few tears.

They're in shock, the poor dears, Sarah thought because of the little emotion each child showed. *They'll cry their eyes out later.*

"Is Aurora with Jesus?" Libby asked suddenly.

"She could be," Richard told the wide-eyed little girl. "God is the only one who can judge a person's soul. But here on earth we can rejoice in the fact that Jesus is good and allows no one to die without hearing about the gift of eternal life through Him. I know Aurora heard the good news about Jesus—just like you did yesterday."

At that Libby smiled, and the two older boys appeared mollified by Richard's reply.

A few more questions were thrown at him, and he answered them to the best of his ability. When the children seemed all talked out, the three adults walked them back to the house.

"It looks sad, too," Sarah observed.

"What does?" Richard asked.

"The house. It looks sad, somehow. I can't really explain it."

"Maybe it's because you're looking at it through sad eyes."

"Could be."

They climbed the stairs to the entranceway. "I can stay for a while if you want me to."

Sarah nodded. "Yes, I'd like that. Thank you."

He smiled, looking pleased in spite of all the tragedy surrounding them.

Inside, Sarah sent the children upstairs but hung back to speak with Richard in private. "Perhaps this isn't the best time for this, but. . .well, I need for you to know I wrote to my parents last night. It was before I learned about the captain and Aurora. . ."

Sarah gulped down her sadness and pressed on. "You see, I felt compelled to let my parents know what I came to realize last night on the way home. The Lord used Tim and Lina to help me see things more clearly." She turned, producing the letter from where it sat on the hallway table. "I would like for you to read it."

Richard took the proffered envelope and stared at it for several long moments. He looked like he was afraid to read it.

Sarah smiled. "I think the letter will encourage you, Richard; however, I must get the children to sleep now, so no hallelujahs, all right?"

He grinned. "All right."

Sarah walked through the hallway and passed the kitchen, using the servant's stairwell. For once, she actually remembered!

With the children snug in their beds, she was just about to read Libby and Rachel a story when Richard entered the nursery.

"Excuse me, girls," he said to Libby and Rachel, "but I must borrow your governess for a moment." Taking her hand, he led her into the hallway.

"What is it?"

Richard grinned. "You have made me an enormously ecstatic man. Do you really mean what you wrote in this letter?" He waved the envelope at her. "Or was it merely a surge of emotion?"

"I meant every single word."

"And you're really going to post the letter and send it to your parents?"

"Well, of course I am! Why would I write all that and. . .and *not* post it?"

"Just making sure," Richard replied. He drew himself up, taking a large breath. "Sarah, I want to take you in my arms and kiss you until you swoon!"

She couldn't contain her smile. "I think I'd enjoy that very much."

But suddenly Gretchen appeared, wearing a dour expression. She cleared her throat. "The captain may not be here, but you are still on duty, Irish."

"Yes, but only for another fifteen minutes." With that she gave Richard a meaningful look.

"I'll wait for you downstairs," he replied.

She gave him one last smile before reentering the nursery. She marveled at how her heart felt both heavy and happy all at the same time.

Chapter 17

Several days passed and still no word came on Captain Sinclair; however, the body of Mr. St. Martin had surfaced and washed ashore. The news traveled through various social circles within the Milwaukee community until all of the captain's friends, acquaintances, and business associates knew that he was missing. Not a day went by when Sarah, the children, and Gretchen weren't bombarded with concerned and curious neighbors knocking at the front door and asking questions.

The day of Aurora's funeral arrived. Richard had arranged the entire affair, capable man that he was, and, for a funeral, it was very lovely. Held at the Sinclair home, up in the ballroom, people crowded in to pay their respects. Gretchen had decorated the room in somber colors, and large vases of flowers graced every corner.

"I should hope that my wedding day is so grand," Lina whispered as she surveyed her surroundings.

Sarah smiled. "If Aurora were here, I believe she would highly approve."

Lina nodded, and then she and Sarah took their places.

Each of the captain's children read selections from the book of Psalms, and then the pastor of the Navises' church got up and gave a brief message. He spoke on the importance of making decisions that affect eternity. He told of God's free gift of salvation and that, like every gift, one has to *decide* to accept it.

After the message, Sarah played the piano while Lina sang one of William Cowper's beloved hymns:

> *There is a fountain filled with blood*
> *Drawn from Immanuel's veins;*
> *And sinners, plunged beneath that flood,*
> *Lose all their guilty stains.*

The stirring melody touched many hearts. Even Gretchen, despite her rigid exterior, wept openly while Lina sang. The children, too, were teary-eyed, causing several ladies and a few gentlemen to cast long, pitiful glances their way.

Once the service ended, a luncheon was served, and Isabelle outdid herself in preparing the elegant food trays. After eating, friends and neighbors roamed the grounds. Men smoked cigars in the men's parlor, and ladies sipped iced tea in the ladies' parlor. Some people preferred to be outside or sit in the adjacent gazebo. Richard whispered to Sarah that Aurora's funeral, apparently, was a tremendous success socially. But more importantly, he added, it was successful spiritually. Sarah agreed; they'd honored the Lord in every detail of their planning.

Nevertheless, by the end of the day Sarah's nerves were frayed. After the last guest left, she sat down at the kitchen table, put her head in her hands, and cried. Her sobs wracked her body, and she realized she'd harbored her sadness for days, trying to be strong for the children.

Richard managed to console her, and then he made a decision— Sarah, Gretchen, and the children would live at the farm until further notice.

"Oh, I don't know if that's such a good idea, Richard." Sarah dabbed her eyes with a cool wet rag that Gretchen had handed her at some point.

"I think it's the best idea, considering the circumstances. You've worn yourself out answering neighbors' questions and comforting the captain's friends. And I'm so busy right now, what with the captain's business and this mess of him missing, that I can't look after you. But my mother can. . .and will. And I think that's what you need right now. A little bit of mothering. Gretchen could use some reprieve also." He glanced from Sarah to the housekeeper and back to Sarah. "What do you say?"

Unable to speak for fear she'd start sobbing again, Sarah merely nodded.

"Good. I'll send a wire to your parents, letting them know what's happened."

Again, Sarah bobbed her head in agreement. She was only too glad to let Richard handle this and oh how thankful she was that she had him to depend on right now.

Marty and Bea Navis had attended Aurora's funeral also, and they were all for the idea. That very evening, Sarah and the children were packed and ready to go. Gretchen, too, agreed to move to the farm, and Sarah watched as she carefully covered the captain's furniture with white bed sheets to protect it.

A haunting shiver, an oppressive chill, came over Sarah as she thought about the captain and all his beautiful things. His rich, important friends. His money. All he possessed could not save him from the angry waves of Lake Michigan.

"What is a man profited, if he shall gain the whole world, and lose his own soul?"

Gretchen seemed to read Sarah's mind. "The captain didn't share our faith, but he vas a good man. He vas not immoral, nor did he use profanity like some men do. But the captain's fault is that he vould not listen to the truth of the gospel." Gretchen grew bleary-eyed. "Come and help me, Irish!" she demanded, and Sarah sensed the gruffness was to cover her true emotions.

"Of course, I'll help," Sarah said, her throat constricting with a new onset of unshed tears. "What can I do?"

"Take an end and help me cover these things."

Together they covered the grand piano and the coffee tables. In the large dining room, they covered the table and chairs under one huge drape. In the kitchen, they helped Isabelle put everything away in cupboards while Aunt Ruth and Bea tended to the ice box. Outside, Richard, his father, and Uncle Jesse were with the children playing with a ball.

"Come, Irish," Gretchen said, after they'd finished in the kitchen. "Ve have more vork to do."

Sarah followed the housekeeper into the captain's study where she helped cover his desk, papers all askew, just the way the man had left them. Next they draped a sheet over the leather upholstered chairs.

"You know, he may not be dead," Sarah stated at last.

"Oh, he's dead all right," Gretchen said. "Everyone else is dead."

Sarah lifted her shoulders in a helpless shrug. "Can't blame a girl for wishful thinking. I believe in miracles."

Now it was Gretchen's turn to shrug.

Richard appeared outside the doorway, holding little Rachel in his arms. "The wagon is all packed, and we're ready to roll when you are."

"I'm ready!" Sarah said at once. She turned and marched out of the captain's study, pausing in front of Richard. "If someone would have told me when I first came to this house that I'd one day be eager to leave it, I would have laughed at the very idea!"

Richard gave her an understanding grin.

Then Sarah gave one last look around. "I am eager to leave," she reiterated.

Richard took her hand with his free one. "Well then, let's go!"

Richard wired Sarah's parents the following day, and a response came the very next afternoon. Richard brought the telegraph message home with him that evening.

"Oh, no!" A feeling of impending doom settled in the pit of Sarah's stomach as she read it. "Luke is coming to fetch me, and I'm not to return to Chicago on September first!"

Richard frowned. "Your parents are angry?"

"I don't know."

The young couple considered each other speculatively from where they stood in the front yard beneath the colorful evening sky. Splashes of orange and gray were painted on the horizon, but neither Sarah nor Richard could appreciate the scenery at the moment.

"Sarah, honestly, I sent the best, most informative wire I could afford," Richard told her.

"I'm sure you did. It's not your fault. And thank you again for sending it."

He tipped his head, thinking. "Your teaching position, Sarah. . .are you sorry to lose it?"

She sent him a smile. "Not at all. In fact, I had already given it up in my heart when I decided I'd like to marry you."

Now Richard smiled and a love-light shone from the depths of his eyes. Even so, Sarah decided to tease him.

"I imagine that my parents got my last letter, and now Luke is coming to check you out like a prize thoroughbred."

"I guess I'm flattered," Richard replied, wearing a look of uncertainty. He sported a grin nonetheless. "Will your brother examine my teeth as well?"

"No, but you had better memorize the entire Bible!"

Sarah made the remark in jest, but suddenly nothing seemed very funny. Her nerves felt as taut as Bea's clothesline hanging out back, and tears pooled in her eyes from the mounting tension. First the captain, who was probably drowned, then Aurora's funeral, moving to the farm, not to mention trying to be strong for the children's sakes. And now Luke, coming to fetch her and take her home. . . .

She plopped down on the front porch stoop.

"What's wrong, Sarah?" Richard sat beside her and slipped his arm around her shoulders.

She sniffed. "Everything. And you may change your mind about marrying me once you meet my brother."

Richard hung his head back and laughed. "I doubt it."

"I hope you won't," Sarah said.

"I won't." Richard took her hand. "I love you, Sarah. That's for always and forever. And let's not forget that God is in control. 'The king's heart is in the hand of the Lord, as the rivers of water: he turneth it whithersoever he will.' "

Sarah recognized the passage at once, and it brought immediate assurance to her troubled heart. God was still on His throne. He'd take care of everything.

After more than a week on the Navises' farm, coupled with some more extra doses of tender loving care from Bea, Sarah felt rested. What's more, she regained her composure. The stressful weight she'd been carrying grew lighter as she continually gave it over to the Lord in prayer.

The children, too, settled into a comfortable routine and began to push the tragedy concerning their father aside; however, they still had many questions that Sarah and the Navises did their best to answer. Mostly, though, the children stayed busy and seemed happy. They were up early in the mornings and helped milk the cows and feed the pigs and chickens. They each chose a kitten for their very own. Gabriel named his "Killer," while Libby called hers "Fluffy." Michael's kitty was "Jimmie," and Rachel simply called hers "Kiddykiddy."

Sarah, too, kept busy, and she began to meet Bethany in the garden around the same time each day. They talked amicably across the property line as they picked green beans, strawberries, and peas. The boys had been assigned to the cornfield while the little girls napped in the afternoons, and Gretchen occupied herself in the summer kitchen, helping Bea can the vegetables for the winter months.

On this particular day, Bethany came out to the garden and picked and chatted as always. But then she grew quiet, and suddenly Sarah noticed that she was crying.

"Beth, what is it?" Dropping her basket of peas, she ran the short distance through the rows of vegetables to where Bethany stood. "Tell me, what's wrong?"

"Oh, it's Lionel," she finally confessed. "He's broken our engagement."

Sarah put a compassionate arm around her new friend. "I'm sorry to hear that."

"He said he doesn't love me," Bethany eked out.

"What a horrible thing to say!" Sarah locked arms with her. "Say, I have an idea. Why don't you come on over for some lemonade. Mrs. Navis made a pitcher this morning. It's so tart, it'll make you pucker, but it sure tastes good on a hot day."

Bethany acquiesced and the two of them walked through the garden to the house. Once inside the kitchen, Sarah sat Bethany at the table. "You just rest. We'll talk this whole thing out, and you'll feel better."

"There is nothing to discuss, Sarah. I am never giving my heart to another man as long as I live and that's that!"

"Now, now, don't be hasty."

"Lionel is the second man to say he doesn't love me." She gave Sarah an almost guilty look. "Richard was the first."

Sarah felt a twinge of remorse for her, but not pity since she'd had an inkling that Lionel was the wrong man for Bethany from the start.

"I remember my father telling my older sister Leah that she couldn't give her heart to any man until she gave it to Jesus first," Sarah said. "And, from watching my sister, I learned that important lesson without having to experience the heartache she did." Sarah sipped her lemonade. "So, while I can't relate to your feelings in that respect, Beth, I do know that it's far better for you to learn now that Lionel isn't the man whom God has chosen for you than to be locked in an unhappy marriage."

"Yes, that makes sense." Bethany wiped away an errant tear. "But it still hurts."

"I'm sure it does. Here, let me give you a hug." She did, and then Sarah smiled impishly. "Would you like a kitten, too? Did wonders for the children."

Bethany rolled her eyes and shook her light brown head. Freckles were splattered across her nose from the summer sunshine. "We have dozens of kittens on our farm, Sarah McCabe. I think my mother would tan my hide if I came home with another one!"

Sarah laughed, and even Bethany managed a smile. But just a little one.

Chapter 18

The second week of September, Luke McCabe stepped off the train at Union Depot in downtown Milwaukee. Richard recognized him at once from Sarah's description. Tall, blond, and broad-shouldered, he wore a dark suit which contrasted with his light features and bright blue eyes. In one hand, he carried a wide-brimmed hat and in the other, he held his valise.

"Pastor McCabe," Richard called.

"Yes?" He looked surprised. Then he smiled and set down his bags. "You must be Mr. Navis."

He nodded and offered a grin. "Please call me Richard."

"Very well."

The two men clasped hands in a friendly shake.

"Can I help you with your things?"

"Thanks, but I can manage."

Leaving the train station, the two men climbed into one of the captain's carriages. Under the circumstances, Richard didn't think the captain would mind. His estate would be completely liquidated in time, both the house and the business would be sold. Richard was handling it all, with the help, of course, of Captain Sinclair's attorneys. For all his dislike of figures and calculations, Richard seemed to be working at solely that lately. . .until he got home in the evenings. Then the children came running from the yard to greet him with sweet Sarah not far behind. Her welcoming smile was the highlight of Richard's day!

"How is Sarah?" her brother now asked.

"She's well," Richard replied. "This whole ordeal with the captain shook her badly, but I think she is recovering."

"Good. The folks at home have been quite concerned. Me included. The wire you sent was most disturbing."

"I understand and apologize. But there wasn't any good way of conveying the sort of news."

"True enough."

They rode a ways in silence, leaving the city behind them. Finally, Luke spoke again.

"So you want to marry Sarah, huh?"

"I do, indeed." Richard tried to relax, hoping Pastor McCabe would grill him now and get it over with.

"From her last letter, I gather that she wants to marry you, too."

"Yes, sir. And it's a direct answer to prayer. . .for me."

Luke lifted the corners of his mouth in an amused grin. "Well, I need to tell you that I'm planning to talk my baby sister into coming out West with me. We need a schoolteacher in a mighty bad way."

Richard didn't even flinch at the challenge. Sarah had warned him, saying Luke would try to dissuade him. "But don't let him talk you out of marrying me," she'd added with a lovely pout.

Recalling their conversation now, Richard grinned.

"You're not worried?" Luke asked.

"No, sir."

"Hmm. . . So, tell me about yourself, Richard."

He did, for the rest of the ride home. He talked of his parents, his upbringing, his education, his position with the captain, and, finally, his decision to buy his father's farm. Then he told Luke of this summer's events with Sarah, how they had met, how he had come to love her.

"Sarah is very easy to love," Luke stated candidly. "Half the men in our small hometown, just outside of St. Louis, were in love with her at one time or another. The other half are relatives."

Richard chuckled. "Yes, Sarah has told me."

"She prepared you, eh?"

"In most every way she could think of."

Luke found the remark amusing and, a short while later, Richard pulled into the circle drive of his family's home. The children came running around the house, but when they saw the stranger, they came to an abrupt halt.

"This is Pastor McCabe," Richard called to them. "He's Miss Sarah's brother. No need to be afraid. Come and say hello."

Gabriel and Michael came forward and shook Luke's hand, but Libby hung back, and Rachel ran back into the house.

Sarah appeared moments later. "Luke!" she cried with a huge smile.

"Hey, there, baby sister."

Richard watched as he scooped her up and twirled her around. Setting her feet on the ground, he placed a kiss on her forehead. "Well, you look no worse for wear."

"You either. The Arizona Territory must agree with you."

"Sure does."

Richard grinned as he unloaded the buggy.

"And I have a mind to take you back with me, although I'd be challenged daily trying to keep away all the cowboys. You've become a right pretty young lady."

Sarah stepped back. "Take me back with you?" She glanced at Richard, feeling hysteria on the rise.

Meeting her gaze, he sent her a confident wink.

Sarah forced herself to relax. Last night they had talked about this, about Luke's arrival. Richard's mother encouraged the young couple greatly by reminding them that if God intended them to marry, they would. With that wise piece of advice, she had quoted Philippians 4:6.

"We'll talk later, baby sister," Luke promised. "I've got an adventure in mind for you, and I know you're not one to turn down an adventure."

"You may be surprised at my reaction," she replied with a sweet smile. "You may be very surprised. . . ."

After a hearty supper of roast beef, mashed potatoes, fresh spinach, and corn on the cob, Richard showed Luke to his room. It was wide and comfortable and right across the hall from Sarah's bedroom. Libby and Rachel slept in the bedroom at the end of the long hallway, but the boys forfeited their room for Luke's sake and would sleep in the barn with Richard. Mr. and Mrs. Navis had their own bedroom on the first floor. Gretchen slept in the adjacent parlor which had been made over into comfortable sleeping quarters.

"I hate the thought of you, Gabe, and Michael in the hayloft tonight," Luke said. "Sorry to put you out like this."

"We'll be fine. Come on—I'll put your mind at ease."

Richard showed Luke around the property and, when they entered the barn, Luke was surprised to find a bunkhouse built into the side of it.

"In the past," Richard explained, "we've had to hire planters and pickers. We let them bunk in here. But, since Sarah, Gretchen, and the children moved in, I've been sleeping out here. It's quite comfortable, really, and Gabe and Michael feel quite grown up to be allowed to sleep out here, too, while you're visiting."

"Quite appropriate—and fun for the boys, I'm sure." Luke grinned and regarded Richard. "I sure appreciate the way you've taken such good care of my sister."

"It has been entirely my privilege."

"Yes, so I've gathered."

Richard chuckled, and Luke grinned.

They left the barn and walked back to the house. In the living room, Luke sat down and observed some of the goings-on. Sarah was getting the Sinclair kids ready for bed. The little one, Luke noticed, clung to Sarah much of the time.

"Vould you like some good strong coffee, Pastor McCabe?" Gretchen asked.

"Yes, thank you."

She left the room and returned holding a cup and saucer.

"So what will you do, now that you're no longer employed with Captain Sinclair?" Luke asked her, sipping the brew.

Gretchen didn't reply immediately, and Luke thought she intended to ignore his question altogether. But then suddenly she answered. "I think my life is over. Vhat is left for me to do now? Who vould hire an old housekeeper like me?"

Luke grinned. "Well, pardon my boldness, ma'am, but we sure could use you out West. I know plenty of ranchers who would pay dearly for your housekeeping services. Our little church could use your help, too. We've started a Sunday school and a ladies' Bible study group."

"Out Vest!" Horror shadowed Gretchen's features. "I can't move out Vest; I'm almost sixty years old!"

"But you're healthy, aren't you? And Richard told me that you're a believer. Wouldn't you like to be a witness for Christ out in the Arizona Territory?"

Gretchen gaped at him, then slowly the idea registered as a plausible one. "Are you serious?"

"I am," Luke replied before taking another sip of coffee.

"Then I vill consider your offer. . .seriously."

"Very good."

With a curt nod, she strode back into the kitchen, passing Richard on the way. He carried a cup of steaming coffee and, taking a seat across from Luke, he took a drink.

An amicable conversation ensued and, within minutes, Marty joined them in his wheelchair. Bea strolled in minutes later, then Sarah, and finally Gretchen.

"Tell us about Arizona, Pastor McCabe," Marty said.

"I was hoping someone would ask!" Luke chuckled and sat back.

"Are there really savages out there? Ready to scalp every man, woman, and child?" Bea asked with wide eyes.

"Yes and no," He replied. "First off, I don't think of the Indians as *savages*. They are people, like you and me, and they need Jesus Christ, too. Our government has not been fair with the Indians. That's my personal opinion, of course. And the Indians whom I've come in contact with have been anything but savage. On the contrary, they've been very generous, caring, and helpful.

"On the other hand," Luke continued, "some Indians are bitter about their land having been taken from them, and it's those tribes that are murdering white folks. That's where the horror stories begin, I'm afraid, and it's a shame it's mostly the bad news about the Indians that people hear."

"Well, what about these fellows—these *cowboys* I'm hearing about?" Richard asked. "I've heard that they drive cattle all over creation. . .but for what purpose?"

"For the purpose of feeding the entire western half of this nation," Luke said with a patient smile. "Cattle driving has become quite the thing to do lately."

Richard grinned mischievously. "Say, Pops, you and I could do some cattle driving right here."

"Why, sure we could, son," Marty replied with a humorous smirk. "You on your horse and me in my chair."

"Lyla, our fairest Guernsey, leading the way."

The two of them enjoyed a hearty laugh while Sarah and Bea exchanged weary glances. Gretchen, however, was chuckling softly from behind her knitting.

Suddenly a voice could be heard, calling from the kitchen. "Sarah? Sarah, would you care to go for a str—"

Luke watched as the young woman with light brown hair stopped short when she got far enough into the house to see the company. "Oh, my apologies for interrupting," she said quickly. "I forgot. . .your company. . ."

"Quite all right, Beth." Sarah rose from her place on the sofa, next to Richard. "In fact, come on in. Let me introduce you to my brother." She turned to him. "Luke, this is Bethany Stafford. She lives on the neighboring farm. Beth, this is my brother, Luke McCabe."

Luke had stood the moment Bethany entered the room. "Miss Stafford," he said politely. "It's a pleasure to meet you."

"Likewise, Mr. McCabe." Bethany seemed suddenly nervous but mustered a smile.

Sarah continued with the introductions. "My brother is a preacher out West."

"Oh, that's right. I—I should have remembered. . .a pleasure to meet you, *Pastor* McCabe."

Luke gave her a gracious smile. "I answer to 'mister' as well as 'pastor,' Miss Stafford. You're well within the bounds of propriety."

"Well, I must take my leave," Bethany said, looking flustered. "Good night."

"But you just got here, dear." Bea stood. "Why don't you stay for a cup of tea?"

"No—no thank you. I—I think I forgot something at home." With that, she fled the room.

Luke smiled in her wake. *She's one shy young lady,* he thought. And then an idea began to form. Bethany Stafford might be just the kind of woman who would make a perfect schoolteacher in the Arizona Territory. She was plain enough. The men would leave her alone. . . .

"I know what you're thinking, Luke," his sister said with a gleam in her eyes.

One glance at her told him that Sarah had divined his thoughts, all right. "And? What about it?"

"Bethany's qualified, all right." A slow smile curved Sarah's mouth. "And it might be the very thing she needs in her life right now. A change."

Richard suddenly cleared his throat. "Would you two care to let the rest of us in on this conversation?"

Sarah laughed. "Luke thinks he may have found his schoolteacher for out West. Bethany!"

"Bethany Stafford? Well, sakes alive!" Bea exclaimed.

"She'd fit the role perfectly," Sarah added.

"Teacher? Yes, of course. Out West?" Bea shook her head as if uncertain. "I don't know what her papa would say about all of it, though."

Luke grinned. "Well, I guess I'm going to go visit her papa, then." A sense of purpose began to bloom in his heart.

Chapter 19

Eight days later, on a lazy Sunday afternoon, Sarah and Richard sat together on the front porch swing. The September day was fair and mild with a light wind rustling through the leaves. Sarah appreciated the colors around her, the fiery reds and rich golds. She inhaled, enjoying the fresh country air while thinking about so many things. . . .

"Do you think she'll take Luke's offer?" Sarah suddenly had to ask, speaking of Bethany.

Richard just shrugged. "We'll know shortly."

Sarah nodded. Luke had gone over to the Staffords' house this afternoon. After days of much prayer, he felt confident in offering the schoolteacher's position out West to Bethany. . .not Sarah. And what a relief that was for Sarah! At one time, she would have jumped at the chance to experience the Arizona Territory with Luke, but now she'd had quite enough of adventure. She'd come to realize that she was a simple country girl. . .and that there was nothing wrong with it, either!

"Has Luke decided when he'll take you home?" Richard asked.

Sarah shook her head. "He's concerned about the children. He thinks taking me away could be detrimental, especially since they've lost both their parents in such a short period of time."

"I agree. . .and not just because of personal reasons," Richard replied with an affectionate smile. "Libby and Rachel have been looking to you as children look to their own mother."

"Yes, I know. I can't say I mind it, either." Sarah's gaze met his smiling eyes. "You know, Luke had thought of taking the children back to St. Louis with us," she confided, "but they're so comfortable here, and they need some stability in their lives. They've got it right here."

"Ironically," Richard said, gazing out over the orchard, "that's what the captain wanted for his children all along. . .some stability in their lives."

"Yes, that was one of the first things he said to me after I arrived."

Richard shook his head. "Even more amazing is the fact that the captain made no provisions for his orphaned children. Only when they become adults." He took Sarah's hand and held it between both of his. "The captain's will calls for trust accounts to be set up for each child; however, there is no one named their legal guardian. Obviously Captain Sinclair hadn't planned on dying until his children were grown."

"Richard, perhaps he's not really dead," Sarah said hopefully.

He just shrugged. "I suppose it's possible, since his body hasn't surfaced yet. But Lake Michigan doesn't always give up her dead, either. And where could he be all this time if he were still alive?"

Sarah swallowed hard. She would like nothing better than to ignore the entire subject of death. But death was very much a part of life. That fact had only recently hit home with Sarah, even with her father and two brothers in the ministry. Even after attending dozens of funerals throughout the years. . .none seemed quite so tragic as Aurora's death and Captain Sinclair's disappearance.

"Wouldn't it be a miracle, Richard, if the captain really were alive and well somewhere. . .only we don't know it yet?"

"You're a dreamer. That's for sure!"

"Or maybe the captain is alive, and he just *forgot* to send a message and tell us so."

"Now, that I'd believe." After a short chuckle, Richard turned thoughtful. "I must confess, Sarah, that I'm a little angry with Captain Sinclair for leaving such a mess behind—including that of his children's welfare. His intentions may have been fine for the most part, but the captain was irresponsible in so many other ways."

"Yes, I suppose you're right. He promised the children many things and never followed through on them. Case in point, the children never did get their piano recitals and the party he'd promised." Sarah still felt disappointed for Gabe, Michael, and Libby. They'd been diligent about practicing. "I'm afraid to say that and other incidents have caused the children to be somewhat distrustful of adults and their promises."

"A real shame, too, isn't it?"

Sarah nodded.

Several long minutes passed as Richard and Sarah wrangled with their own thoughts.

"So Luke hasn't said anything one way or another, huh?" Richard asked, moving the conversation back to his original question.

Sarah shook off her musings and smiled. "He did post a letter to my parents on Friday. And I know Luke approves of you, Richard."

"Well, I approve of him, too." He laughed. "We had a grand time at the store on Thursday and Friday. I certainly did appreciate all his help. Luke has practically finished all the inventory. . .in spite of a few pranks."

"You two are a lot alike," Sarah said, pleased but concerned at the same time. To think she wanted to marry someone like her brother Luke!

Richard was chuckling now. "Oh, Sarah! You should have been there last week! You see, the men have been rather slothful since the captain's absence, and Luke picked up on it immediately. I, of course, have done the best I can with them; however, they see me as a coworker and not one in position of authority. But Luke—Luke implied to the men—without actually lying, mind you—that he had been appointed overseer and that if they didn't quit loafing on the job, they'd lose their employment!"

Sarah grinned. "So what happened?"

"Well, the men didn't take their habitual two-hour lunch breaks on Thursday and Friday."

"Good," Sarah said, feeling that was just. After all, her poor Richard was lucky if he even got a lunch break at all!

"And as far as I'm concerned," Richard continued, "Luke can be in charge for as long as he wants. We're closing up the business and closing up the house, and all the captain's assets will be in probate until he either returns or the court declares him legally dead. Then, once these matters are all settled, my darling Sarah, I will officially be a farmer!"

Sarah smiled, not minding that latter statement at all. The way she saw it now, she was being courted by the handsomest, most educated farmer in the entire Midwest, maybe even the entire world!

"And if your father allows me to marry you," Richard added, "I believe we're going to be instant parents. . .of the four Sinclair children."

Sarah thought it over and then smiled impishly. "Why, I'm going to have four children on the first day that I'm married, while it took poor Ben and Valerie years to produce only three children! Same with my sister, Leah!"

"But you'll have four children in one day?" Richard grinned. "That's quite a feat, Sarah."

"I'll say," she replied with a dramatic sigh. "I'm exhausted just thinking about it!"

But truth to tell, Sarah had never relished the thought of leaving those children behind. She loved them like they were her very own already!

Richard was smiling over her last declaration. Dropping her hand, then, he put his arm around her shoulders. "You're quite a lot of fun, you know?"

"You're not so bad yourself."

Richard's eyes took on a mischievous gleam. "Do you think your brother would mind terribly if I kiss you?"

"I should say he would!" Sarah exclaimed. "Luke would probably take me home immediately, and I hate to think of what he would do to you."

Richard grinned. "A shotgun wedding, perhaps? I understand those things are quite popular out West."

Sarah rolled her eyes. "Don't get your hopes up now, Richard."

He just laughed.

Luke McCabe watched with interest as an array of emotions played across Miss Bethany Stafford's young face. Shock at his suggestion that she go out West. Suspicion as to why Luke wanted her to go. Trepidation of facing the unknown. Then, finally, consideration of the whole idea.

As Luke regarded her, he questioned his initial judgment. Bethany was quite pretty when she smiled, although perhaps she looked plain when she frowned so hard. In any case, Luke was prepared to protect her in the Arizona Territory where women were a scarcity. He would protect Bethany just as he had been prepared to protect his own sister.

"Well, Pastor McCabe," Mr. Stafford said, rising from his chair, "my wife and I, along with Bethany, of course, will discuss this matter and get back to you."

"Very good," Luke replied, standing to his feet.

"When do you need our decision?" Bethany asked meekly.

"In a week. . .two at the most. If you decide to come West with me, you'll have to buy some supplies and pack. There is, of course, this matter with my sister that I need to settle. I'm waiting for a letter of instruction from my father. I can't leave until I receive it. But I would like to begin my travels back to Arizona before the weather gets bad."

Bethany nodded and gave Luke a timid smile. "I'll pray about it in earnest, Pastor McCabe. But I feel in my heart that this would be. . .well, I. . ." Bethany began to blush a pretty pink. "Well, I think I'd like to go."

Luke barely made out the whispered reply. "You'd like to go?"

She nodded.

He smiled. "Glad to hear it." Turning to Mr. Stafford now, he said, "And I should add that Mrs. Gretchen Schlyterhaus, the captain's former housekeeper, has decided to travel to Arizona with me. She agreed to act as chaperon for the journey if your daughter accepts the teaching position."

With that, Bethany looked at her father expectantly.

"We'll see," he replied, his expression unreadable. He looked back at Luke. "Thank you for the offer, Pastor, and we'll talk again soon."

After another polite nod, Luke left the Stafford home.

Walking back through the field to the Navises' place, Luke reflected on Bethany's last reaction to his idea. While her parents seemed skeptical, Bethany appeared to want to make the trek out West. Sarah had said that Bethany experienced a couple of heartbreaks in the recent past, and Luke couldn't help but wonder over the details. He also wondered if those experiences were what prompted Bethany's interest in Arizona.

In any case, Luke imagined that Bethany would make a fine schoolteacher. She had a quiet disposition and didn't seem given to complaining. Furthermore, she seemed patient with children. Being the oldest of her siblings, who ranged in age from four to fifteen, Bethany had helped raise her brothers and sisters. And she'd been educated. Both Mr. and Mrs. Stafford said they felt education was very important, and Mrs. Stafford taught all her children at home.

Yes, Luke thought now as he reached the Navises' property, *Bethany will make a right fine schoolteacher! Far more than my baby sister, Sarah—who is hardly a baby anymore!*

Luke's train of thought shifted from Bethany to Sarah. He had to admit he found the changes in his sister remarkable. In eighteen months' time she'd become a very beautiful young woman. However, the inward changes, emotionally and spiritually, were what impressed him the most. In a word, Sarah had matured on both accounts.

Even so, she'd always be Luke's "baby sister"—and he'd always love to tease her!

One week later, Sarah and Bethany stood in the kitchen peeling potatoes for their Sunday dinner. The Staffords were there, as well as Richard's aunt and uncle and Lina and Tim. Everyone visited with Luke in the front room, everyone but Sarah and Bethany, that is. They had, out of the kindness of their hearts, volunteered to peel potatoes and help poor Mrs. Navis.

"I love Mrs. Navis dearly," Bethany said now, "but I sure do hate peeling potatoes."

"Amen to that!" Sarah cast a glance at her friend. "But you must admit, Beth, it's better to peel potatoes and suffer together."

"Right. Misery loves company."

Both young women smiled as they peeled several more potatoes.

"Your brother preaches a powerful message," Bethany finally ventured to say. "I enjoyed hearing it this morning, and wasn't it nice of Pastor Thomas to let him be our guest speaker?"

Sarah nodded. "I may be partial, Beth, but I think Luke is one of the best preachers I've ever heard—next to my father, of course!"

Bethany smiled. "Speaking of fathers—mine said I could go out West."

"Really?" Sarah stopped peeling in mid-stroke. Then she smiled. "How exciting! I think it will be a good experience for you. Have you told Luke yet?"

"Not yet. But my father is probably relaying the news to him right now. He said he would." Bethany paused in momentary thought. "Sarah, I think this is the new beginning I've needed. I had been praying. . .for a new. . .well, a new direction in my life. Something to pour my energies into." Bethany smiled. "And here it is: a position as a schoolteacher. Me! Imagine it! Out West!"

"I'm so happy for you."

A blush swept across Bethany's features as she picked up another potato. "You know," she began, sounding overly careful, "I fully expected to marry Richard, raise a family, and live right here all my life. I never would have dreamed of leaving Milwaukee. . .or the state of Wisconsin.

Yet, here I am, preparing to travel out West with a man who is. . .well, he's. . ."

"He's what?" Sarah tipped her head, curious to what Bethany thought about Luke.

"Well, he's so—so. . ."

"Oh, for pity sakes, Beth, just spit it out."

"He's so handsome that he makes me nervous! There, I said it."

"Luke? Handsome?" Sarah frowned slightly, feeling a little surprised to hear her brother described that way. *Captain Sinclair, yes. . .but Luke?*

"It's his eyes, I believe," Bethany continued. "They're the eyes of a kind and gentle man, but they can stare holes right through a person, too—especially when he's intent on delivering the gospel."

"Luke—my brother—with eyes that. . . ?" Sarah shook her head, wondering if they were speaking of the same person.

Then Sarah couldn't help teasing her friend. "Why, Bethany, I thought you were finished with men."

"Oh, I am!" she declared. "I'm more than finished with men. It's just that. . .well, for a pastor, your brother is, um, very pleasing to look at when he's behind the pulpit."

Sarah hooted at the remark. "Bethany Stafford! And here I thought you were listening to the message this morning."

"I was!" She blushed and then tried her best at a careless shrug. "I was merely stating an observation, that's all."

"Of course you were." Sarah giggled.

"Now, Sarah, don't you dare misunderstand me. I am really through with men. Getting my heart broken twice is twice too many times. It won't happen again."

"I should hope not." Sarah paused, thinking everything over. "You know, Beth, I think you just gave your heart away too fast; that's what you did."

"Like I said, it won't happen again." Then she turned toward Sarah. "But I harbor no bitterness toward Richard. . .or you. . .or Lionel. I want you to know that."

"Thank you." Sarah gave her a smile derived from the fondness she felt for Beth.

"I really did love Richard," she confessed in a hushed tone of voice. "I think maybe I still do."

Sarah's heart ached. "Please know neither Richard nor I ever meant to hurt you."

"I know that. And I also know that Richard loves you and. . .I can see you love him, too."

"Yes, I do," Sarah stated. The more she prayed about marrying Richard, the more she knew it was God's will for her life. "But, you know, Bethany, my situation is just the opposite of yours. I never expected to marry a farmer. I wanted to be part of the affluent society, which I have since learned is not all that different from a farming community—not in God's eyes, anyway. We're all people, and people need the saving grace of Jesus Christ. Rich or poor, we all need Him."

"Amen!" said Luke from the doorway. "Sarah, you'd make one fine preacher!"

"Oh, quiet!"

Luke chuckled.

Sarah turned to see her brother leaning against the wooden door frame with his arms folded across his broad chest. He smiled, and his blue eyes twinkled with mischief.

Shaking her head at him, Sarah turned to Bethany. Her friend's face was flushed as bright as Mrs. Navis's red roses.

"So how long were you spying on us, Luke McCabe?" Sarah asked with raised brows. She sensed this was the very question on Bethany's mind just now. She was probably fretting over her comment about Luke being handsome.

But Luke just laughed. "I was spying on you only long enough to hear my baby sister say what would be music to our parents' ears. They've wanted to marry you off for a long time now."

Sarah groaned. "I pity you, Bethany, going out West with the likes of this one." She shot her brother a glance of annoyance; however, when she gazed over at Bethany, Sarah thought she looked relieved. Luke hadn't heard a word Bethany had said about him.

Luke took hold of one of the wooden kitchen chairs, turned it around, and straddled it, leaning his forearms against its back. "I'm glad you mentioned the West," he said. "Miss Stafford, I guess we're on. Your father gave his permission just minutes ago, and I can't tell you how pleased I am. We need a schoolteacher in a mighty bad way!"

Bethany just inclined her head ever so slightly, wearing a tight little smile which caused Luke to frown. Sarah knew her brother well and suspected that he was wondering why Bethany didn't appear more excited. The McCabes were an animated family, quite given to their emotions at times. They hugged and kissed each other and didn't think twice about displaying their affections. Bethany's apparent nonchalance would be a puzzle to Luke, of course, but Sarah wasn't about to divulge any of her friend's secrets. Beth could tell Luke everything she felt he should know.

Suddenly she looked from Luke, at her right, to Bethany, on her left, then to Luke again. Something seemed strange—Luke was studying Bethany like he might study an intense chess game, while Bethany, her chin lowered, was peeling potatoes as fast as her hands would go.

There's something between them, Sarah decided, and she felt caught in the cross fire. And then she realized just what that *something* might be. . .

For days, Luke had been asking vague questions about Bethany. Then, today, Bethany said Luke was "handsome," so handsome that he made her nervous.

Can it be? Sarah wondered. She felt like laughing as she looked from one to the other. *Luke and Bethany? On the brink of a romance?*

Sarah shook off her imaginings. What a ridiculous notion. The worst she'd come up with in months!

However, the atmosphere did not lighten until Richard ambled into the kitchen, and only then did Bethany slow her potato peeling to a comfortable pace.

Chapter 20

S arah took a deep breath and inhaled the fresh country air. The October sunshine streamed through the autumn-colored leaves above her as she stood in the orchard. Sarah smiled at the beauty surrounding her, and then she resumed her apple picking.

The children, too, picked apples. Libby and Rachel carried theirs in their aprons; however, the boys were carelessly tossing the apples they collected and occasionally throwing them at each other. But Sarah didn't reprimand them. Gabriel and Michael were just being boys and, as long as they didn't throw apples at the girls—or her—they weren't doing any harm. Mrs. Navis would just have to make applesauce out of what the boys collected today.

"These apples are the last of the crop," Sarah told Libby and Rachel. "But they'll be good in pies, turnovers, and, of course, applesauce." She gave the boys a pointed look.

"I yike apposauce!" Rachel declared, nodding her head vigorously.

Sarah smiled at the precious child.

Suddenly a great noise could be heard coming from the road. Sarah and the children stopped to look. In surprise, they watched as first one wagon—Richard's—and then buggy after buggy pulled into the circle drive. One, two, three, four, five. . .

"Goodness!" Sarah exclaimed. "It looks like a parade!"

The apples were dumped into a large bushel basket which sat on the edge of the orchard. Then Sarah and the children walked toward the driveway to see who. . .or w*hat* had arrived.

"Mama!" Sarah cried after recognition set in. Next she saw her father alight from the buggy. "Pa!" She ran to greet them, enveloping each parent in a loving embrace.

Much to Sarah's amazement, the next ones out of the buggy were her brother Ben and his wife Valerie, who was holding three-month-old Elaina.

"Why, I haven't even seen this baby yet!" Sarah admired the wee one in her sister-in-law's arms. But then her young nephews, Mark and Joshua, demanded her attention. "Well, just look at you two boys. You sure have grown!"

Leah, Sarah's older sister, suddenly appeared, along with her husband and three children who were near the ages of Gabriel and Michael.

Leah hugged Sarah and then whispered, "I'm expecting a baby myself. After all these years. . .number four!"

Sarah gasped with delight.

Then Aunt Cora and Uncle Marlow emerged from the last two buggies, along with their six children—Cousin Brian being one of them.

"Oh, no, it's you!" Sarah teased, as she and Brian had a long-standing friendly feud going on between them.

"I heard you'd be gettin' hitched," he retorted, "and I came to give your husband-to-be my deepest sympathies." Cousin Brian laughed and then hugged Sarah so hard she thought her ribs would crack.

The commotion brought the Navis family outside. Luke appeared and joined in the welcoming, and introductions were made.

"Well, Sarah," said her father, the Reverend Nathanael McCabe, "a letter just wasn't going to suffice. We all had to come in person."

"So I see," she replied, casting a suspicious glance at her cousin.

"And since we're here," Sarah's mother Hannah said, "we thought we may as well have a wedding!"

"I even brought my wedding dress for you, sis," Leah said with a big smile. "I think it'll fit you just right, too."

Sarah forced a smile, trying to conceal her surprise at the sudden "wedding" plans.

"This is so wonderful!" Bea was saying now. "And how ironic that I was just saying to my sister-in-law Ruth, whose daughter is getting married next week," she explained to Sarah's parents, "why, I was just saying that a double wedding would be so lovely. But I dared not even hope it. . .but here you all are anyway!"

"Next week. . . ?" Sarah's head was spinning from all the activity around her. "You can't mean a double wedding with Lina and Tim. . . ?"

"Well, of course I mean a double wedding with Lina and Tim!" Bea clapped her hands together and beamed with happiness. "And all the families together. . .oh, Sarah, this will be so special!"

Sarah nodded, albeit reluctantly. "But. . .next week, already?"

"I reckon next week will be fine," Nathanael stated on a weary note. "But we'll have time to mull things over later. Right now, I feel dead on my feet from traveling."

"Oh, please forgive my bad manners!" Bea told all her guests. "I just get carried away sometimes. Please—please come inside."

The McCabe family followed Bea and Marty into the house, Bea pushing her husband's wheelchair, while Sarah turned a troubled look on Richard and mouthed, "Next week. . . ?"

He grinned and came toward her, saying, "Tomorrow wouldn't be soon enough for me."

"But I can't plan a wedding in a week!" she cried helplessly. "Look how long Lina and Tim have been planning for their special day."

"They were just making sure, Sarah. All that time had nothing to do with wedding plans." Richard gave her a patient smile. "But we're sure so—so what's the problem?"

Sarah groped for the words but could find none to express her tumult of emotions.

Finally Richard cupped her chin, urging her gaze into his. "What's wrong? You're uncertain?"

The question took her by surprise. "Uncertain?" she repeated. "About what? You? About us?"

Richard nodded.

Smiling, Sarah shook her head. "No, I'm not uncertain about any of that." She folded her hand into his. "I love you, Richard," she said softly. "I am sure about at least that much."

At that moment, Melody and Shelene, two of Sarah's young cousins, came out onto the front porch. When they spied Sarah and Richard together, they fell into a fit of giggles which set Sarah's teeth on edge. Then the girls went running back into the house.

"You see, Richard," Sarah began, "it's not you at all. It's my family that I'm uncertain about!"

Richard chuckled. "Well, you can't imagine my shock and surprise when a message arrived at the captain's store, informing me that the McCabe entourage had arrived at Union Depot."

Sarah grimaced. "My sincere apologies, Richard. I love my family, don't misunderstand me, but there are a lot of them. It's a blessing that only a handful has come."

"There are more coming," Richard told her with a wry grin.

Sarah lifted her fingers to her temples in an effort to stave off an oncoming headache. "Oh, dear. . ."

Over the course of the next few days, more aunts and uncles arrived, bringing with them cousins and more cousins. The only McCabe that Sarah missed was her brother Jacob, who was still in Arizona. However, those who came were all impressed with the Navises' home and hospitality, and when they learned that Richard owned the farm, they approved of the young man all the more.

"It's the fanciest farm I ever did see!" declared one of Sarah's aunts. "And that young man is the best lookin' farmer around. Why, his fingernails ain't even dirty!"

Sarah was given to blushing over her relatives' remarks on more than one occasion.

The house, itself, was packed full of McCabes. The bunkhouse, too. Finally, Sarah gave Richard her entire savings, which she'd earned as the captain's governess, and asked him to see about some hotel accommodations for her relatives. Richard agreed to do it and even put some of his own cash toward the endeavor.

"I love them, Richard, but I haven't had a moment's peace since they arrived."

"I understand completely." He gave her an affectionate wink and a teasing grin. "Your wish is my command."

Richard returned that very evening with the good news: he had secured an entire floor at the Newhall House, a large hotel on Main Street.

"Mr. Daniel Newhall, the owner, is one of America's largest wheat dealers, and he did a lot of business with Captain Sinclair," he explained to the McCabe clan. "Mr. Newhall remembered me as the captain's steward and went out of his way to accommodate us. . .for a very good price, too."

The McCabes were delighted. They, too, were feeling pinched and cramped; however, they were only too grateful for the Navises' hospitality.

"The hotel is close to the train station," Richard added, "so when it's time for you to leave, you won't be inconvenienced by any lengthy traveling."

The offer was too good to pass up, and all except for Sarah's immediate family packed their things and moved downtown. Most had never been in a hotel before. They were simple farming folk who had used all their savings to come to Milwaukee and see Sarah married off. Many had thought they'd never see the day! In any case, Sarah's relatives were of the notion that staying in a big city hotel was something of an adventure, and they went away wearing expressions of anticipation.

With the Navis household suddenly much quieter, the parents were able to get properly acquainted. Then, one evening, Nathanael McCabe went for a long walk with Richard, and Sarah knew poor Richard was being drilled, quizzed, and questioned mercilessly. She waited for his return, feeling edgy and only half listening to her mother and Bea chatting over the hasty wedding plans.

"Are you sure your niece doesn't mind sharing her special day with our Sarah?" Hannah asked. "I realize I've asked before, but I just want to make sure. . . ."

"Oh my, no. Lina doesn't mind a bit. In fact, she's thrilled," Bea said. "Lina and Richard are like siblings, and she's awfully fond of Sarah."

"Well, that's so nice of her. It does make things easier, doesn't it?"

Bea nodded as the conversation turned to flowers and wedding gowns.

"Leah's dress fits Sarah almost perfectly. Just a tuck here and a tuck there. . . . I have it hanging upstairs so the wrinkles fall out."

"And I can certainly heat the iron if that's necessary."

"I'm afraid it might just have to be. . ."

Richard and Reverend McCabe finally returned. Entering the house, Nathanael gave his daughter a stern look. "Sarah, come outside. I'd like a word with you."

"Yes, sir." Pushing to her feet, Sarah followed him outside. The mothers watched her go with raised eyebrows, but Richard wore a little grin which Sarah recognized at once. She thought their talk must have gone well.

"Richard Navis is a fine young man," Pa stated in a no-nonsense tone. "He loves the Lord Jesus Christ, and he's certainly crazy about you."

Sarah forced herself not to smile prematurely. "Can I marry him then?"

"You may." The reverend glanced at his youngest child. "You've grown into a beautiful woman, Sarah," he said. "You could probably marry any man you set your sights on. . . . You sure about this one? Marriage is forever, and forever is a mighty long time."

"I know."

Sarah thought about Captain Sinclair and how she had nearly "set her sights" on him. . .or a man like him. But, no, Richard was the one for her. She was certain about that now!

"Can't come home cryin' and sayin' you made a mistake," Nathanael drawled.

"I won't." Sarah couldn't even imagine such a scenario.

Her father grinned. "I know too well that determined little tilt of your chin, young lady. I reckon you're as sure as you'll ever get." Chuckling, he put an arm around her, and the two walked back toward the house. "Better promise to visit us at least twice a year," he added.

"I promise," Sarah replied. "As long as I'm not in the family way and can't travel."

A broad smile split Reverend McCabe's aging face. His bushy mustache twitched, and his blue eyes twinkled. "Well, knock me over with a feather," he said. "It's love for sure! Never heard you talk about yourself being in the *family way* before! Just the opposite, I'd say!"

He laughed loudly, and Sarah blushed over her father's straightforwardness.

Finally the day arrived, and Sarah dressed carefully with the help of her mother and Leah. Then, after arriving at the church, she nervously stood with Lina in the small, stuffy room behind the vestibule, each awaiting her cue to make her way down the aisle. As she surveyed Lina, who stood just as stiffly as she did, Sarah thought that, to an onlooker, they would seem like two fragile dress-up dollies—like the kind Sarah used to see in the St. Louis shop windows at Christmastime.

"I'm so glad we didn't do this in the summer heat," Lina sighed with flushed cheeks.

"It is rather close in here, isn't it?" Sarah replied with a smile.

Lina nodded. "Between the two of us," she said jokingly, "we could heat all of Milwaukee this winter!"

Sarah laughed and smoothed the silk skirt of her ivory gown. "You know, Lina," she finally said, "once we walk down that aisle, our lives will never be the same."

Lina dabbed her hairline with the lace hankie in her gloved hand. "You sound remorseful, Sarah. Are you?"

"Of course not! I'm only. . .well apprehensive, I guess."

"I certainly share that particular feeling. But at the same time I know Tim will be good to me. And Richard. . ." Lina lifted a warning brow. "Well, he had better be good to you, too, or else he'll have me to contend with!"

"As well as my entire relation!" Sarah giggled, and it helped alleviate those nervous flutters in her stomach.

"Richard said he has arranged for the two of you to stay at the Cross Keys Hotel tonight." Lina sighed, looking envious. "Abraham Lincoln spoke there once, you know. The place is quite famous!"

Sarah smiled. She knew. But she also knew why Richard had chosen that particular hotel. "Richard has a friend working there," Sarah explained, "and this friend has agreed to conceal our identities from my prankster brothers and cousin Brian." She gave Lina a wide-eyed look. "Can you imagine what might occur if those fun-lovin' country boys ever found out where Richard and I were spending our wedding night?"

"I hate to even think about it," Lina replied with an expression of dread.

"Although, my father has threatened all my cousins, not to mention my brothers. They're to leave me alone tonight."

"And, of course, they will obey."

"Of course," Sarah echoed, but she was feeling suddenly skeptical. No doubt those rascals would find some way around her father's instructions. "Yes, but you should have seen what they did to my sister Leah!"

"Now, now, don't fret. You're about to marry the man you love. This is a happy moment."

Sarah's pout changed to a smile.

Just then the pipe organ began to play, and Sarah and Lina exchanged glances.

"That's our signal," Lina said.

Leaving the little dressing room, they met their fathers in the vestibule. Pastor Thomas had again humbly stepped aside so Luke could do the honors of performing his sister's wedding ceremony, and Lina and Tim were gracious enough to allow Luke to perform theirs also.

With knees shaking, Sarah took her father's elbow, and slowly they made their way down the aisle.

Turning slightly to her right, Sarah spotted Gretchen and gave her a smile. The older woman smiled back. It seemed that all barriers, all strongholds between them, had been pulled down and now a friendship existed. Gretchen had asked Sarah's forgiveness, acknowledging her prejudice and insecurities which, in turn, had caused her to feel "mean spirited," as Gretchen deemed it. Then she said that when she renewed her commitment to God this past summer, He had shown her the Irish people were the same as the German people—all people with feelings and a need for Him in their lives. Sarah acknowledged, too, that she had learned something of the same lesson.

Sarah looked forward again. Tim stood on the one side near the altar and Richard on the other. Sarah marveled at how handsome Richard looked. She smiled and he smiled back, and Sarah wondered if he was as nervous inside as she.

The ceremony proceeded without incident, much to Sarah's relief. She had expected Cousin Brian to do. . .well, to do *something*. Lina and Tim said their vows first. Then Richard and Sarah said theirs.

Finally, with a smirk, Luke whispered, "You have my condolences, Richard." He paused then, looking smug. But he didn't move or say another thing.

"Get on with it, man," Richard whispered back. "I want to kiss my wife!"

"Oh, yes, of course. I knew I was forgetting something."

Sarah gave her brother a quelling look.

"By the authority vested in me—"

"C'mon, Luke," Richard hissed, although he sported an ear to ear grin.

"I now pronounce you man and wife and. . ." Luke smiled. "And you may kiss the bride."

"About time," Richard muttered.

Sarah was smarting from her brother's teasing; however, when Richard took her into his arms, she forgot everything but the warm touch of his lips against hers.

"You're mine, Sarah McCabe," Richard whispered as he pulled away slightly. "I mean, Sarah Navis." With that he kissed her once again.

And a heartfelt "Amen!" echoed through the little country church.

An Unexpected Love

Love

Andrea Boeshaar

Chapter 1

D o you think he'll live, Dr. Hamilton?"

The doctor, a gray-haired man with bushy whiskers, had to ponder the question for several moments before he answered. He chewed on his thick lips as he weighed his reply.

"Yes, I think he will," he finally said. " 'Course he's not out of the woods yet, but it seems he's coming around."

Lorrenna Fields, called "Renna" for short, breathed a sigh of relief. It had been almost a week with nary a sign of life from this half-drowned man, but finally. . .finally he showed signs of improvement!

"You've done a good job with this patient, Nurse Fields," the doctor added. "I don't think he'd be alive today if you hadn't given him such extraordinary care."

"Thank you, Dr. Hamilton, but it was the Lord who spared this man and the Lord who gave me the strength and skill to nurse him."

The old physician snorted in disgust. "Yes, well, it might have had something to do with the fact that you've got a brain in your head, Nurse Fields, and the fact that you used it, too, I might add!"

At this Renna smiled inwardly. Dr. Hamilton always disliked it when she gave God the credit for any medical advancement. But especially the miracles. And yet, it was true: Renna was an intelligent woman—and one who made no secret of it.

Suddenly the patient moaned, and his head moved from side to side.

"Easy now, Mr. Blackeyes," Renna crooned. "It's all right." She picked up the fever rag from out of the cold water, wrung it once, and set it on the patient's burning brow.

Dr. Hamilton snorted again, only this time in amusement. "Mr. Black-eyes? How in the world did you come by that name, Nurse Fields?"

Renna blushed, but replied in all honesty. "It's his eyes, Doctor. They're as black as pitch and as shiny as polished stones. And, since we don't know his true identity, I've named him Mr. Blackeyes."

"I see." Dr. Hamilton could barely contain his laughter.

"Well, I had to call him something, now didn't I?" Renna countered, somewhat defensively.

"Ah, yes, I suppose you did." Dr. Hamilton gathered his instruments and put them into his black leather medical bag. "Well, carry on, Nurse Fields," he said with a hint of a tired-sounding sigh. "If your patient's fever doesn't break by morning, send for me at once. However, I think it will, especially since we got some medicine and chicken broth into him tonight."

Renna nodded while the old man waved over his shoulder as he left the hospital room.

Returning her attention to her patient, Renna saw that he was still and sleeping for the moment. His blue-black hair, which had just a slight wave to it, shone beneath the dampness of the fever. The stifling August heat in the room threatened to bring his fever even higher.

Wiping a sleeve across her own sweat-beaded brow, Renna continued to sponge down her patient. Tomorrow would be exactly one week since Mr. Blackeyes was found floating in Lake Michigan after a terrible storm. The crew of the passing ship that found him had thought he was dead at first. But they pulled him aboard anyway. The ship's doctor immediately examined him and detected a heartbeat, so he cared for him until they docked in Chicago's harbor. Then Mr. Blackeyes was deposited at Lakeview Hospital, located on the corner of Wabash Avenue and Congress Street. From there he was admitted to the second floor and into Renna's care and, now finally, he showed some improvement.

Pulling the fever rag from the round porcelain bowl filled with cool water, Renna placed it carefully across Mr. Blackeyes' forehead. She could tell this man was different from the usual "unknowns" that the hospital acquired. His dark, chiseled features implied sophistication—even through a week's worth of beard. And his powerful, broad shoulders and muscular arms indicated the strength of a working man.

"But who are you, Mr. Blackeyes?" Renna murmured, gazing down at him with her hands on her hips.

As if in reply, the man groaned.

Renna settled him once more and then made her way through the sick ward, a large room with white-washed walls and a polished marble floor. Eight beds, four on each side, were neatly lined in rows, leaving a wide area in the center of the ward.

Moving from bed to bed, Renna began checking on her patients, thankful that this ward wasn't full. Mr. Anderson, suffering from a farming accident in which he lost his left arm; Mr. Taylor, who had had pneumonia but had recovered and was soon to be released; and, finally, young John Webster, who had been accidentally shot in the chest by his brother. It appeared he wouldn't live through the night, and his family had gathered around him, his mother weeping.

Taking pity on the Webster family, Renna set up several wooden screens to allow them some privacy. Then she checked on John. She could see death settling in and, even being somewhat accustomed to the sight, as she'd trained in an army hospital during the Civil War, it never got easier. Renna was heartened, however, that the Websters were believers. Young John would soon go home to be with his Savior.

"Can I get anything for you, Mrs. Webster?" Renna asked the boy's mother now.

She shook her head.

Renna asked the same thing of the boy's brother and father, but both declined.

"I didn't mean ter shoot 'im, Ma!" the brother declared. He suddenly began to sob.

"Aw, I know ya didn't mean it, son," Mrs. Webster replied through her own tears. "It was an accident—that anyone can see!"

"Tell it to Jesus, boy," the father said. His eyes were red. "Then give the matter to Jesus, just like we done gave John over to Him."

Renna thought it good advice and gave the family a sympathetic smile before moving away. She respected this family enough to leave them to their privacy.

Walking to the other side of the room now, Renna sponged down Mr. Blackeyes again. Afterward, she checked his head wound. Nearly a three-inch gash above his left ear. It had needed to be sutured, and Dr. Hamilton had seen to that when Mr. Blackeyes was first admitted. "Unknown Male" was the name on his chart. Most "unknowns" didn't survive, so Renna was heartened that Mr. Blackeyes' prognosis seemed promising.

Now if only his fever would break, she thought. *If only he'd regain consciousness and pneumonia didn't set in....*

Momentarily closing her eyes, Renna prayed for God's healing of this man. She had been praying earnestly for the last week. Why she felt so burdened for him, she couldn't say, but she was.

Suddenly an abrupt command broke her thoughts. "Nurse Fields. . . Nurse Fields, you may go. I'm on duty now."

Renna glanced at the doorway where the night nurse, Nurse Ruthledge, stood. She was a large woman with small eyes and a stern disposition.

"As usual, your charts are in order." She sent Renna a crisp smile. "You're excused."

Renna nodded. She didn't dislike the night supervisor. "Thank you, ma'am. I'll just finish up here, and then I'll be on my way."

The older woman came up alongside her. "The first rule in nursing," she said, "is do not get emotionally attached to your patients. You know that."

Renna rinsed the fever rag once more and draped it across Mr. Blackeyes' forehead. "I'm not getting emotionally attached," she said, wishing she felt more vehement about the statement. "I'm just. . .well, I'm burdened for this man. In the spiritual sense."

"Humph! Well, call it what you will, Nurse Fields, but I happen to think you're much too emotional and far too sensitive. It's a wonder you've lasted in nursing this long. Why, I heard from the other nurses on duty today that you were crying with the Webster family over their boy!" She sniffed in what seemed like disgust. "A nurse must never let her emotions get in the way of her duty, Nurse Fields."

"Yes, ma'am." Renna endured the rebuke; she'd heard it many times before.

Nurse Ruthledge squared her wide shoulders. "Now, may I suggest that you leave your burden right here in this hospital bed and go home and get some rest. You're due back here at six a.m., and I'll expect you promptly!"

Renna nodded. Then, with a backward glance at Mr. Blackeyes, she left the sick ward.

Leaving the hospital minutes later, Renna rode the eight blocks in a hired hackney to the home in which she lived with her parents. She was the oldest child in the family, but at the age of thirty, Renna was what society termed "a spinster." Her two younger sisters were married and producing children galore, and her one younger brother and his wife were just now expecting their first baby.

Renna loved all her nieces and nephews. They filled her empty arms when she wasn't nursing, and Jesus filled her heart. Time and time again, however, Renna was asked by a young niece or nephew, "Why didn't you ever get married, Aunty Renna?" And her reply was always, "I never fell in love."

But the truth of the matter was no man would have her. . .even if she had fallen in love. At least that's what Renna thought, for she had a large purplish birthmark on the right side of her face. It came down her otherwise flawless cheek to the side of her nose and then down to her jaw. It was an ugly purple triangle.

However, what always unnerved her were the gawks, stares, and piteous glances sent her way at social functions. All dressed up and looking her prettiest, Renna still felt marred and ugly under the scrutiny of her peers—but especially when she was with the eligible men to whom she was supposed to be attractive and charming. Renna never felt she was either of those.

Nursing, however, was different. There in the hospital, Renna was confident of her abilities. Moreover, her patients were usually too sick or in too much pain to be concerned with her ugly birthmark. Rather, they just wanted her care and sensitivity, and that's what Renna thought she did best. . .in spite of what Nurse Ruthledge said about her being too emotional and too sensitive. God in all His grace had given Renna a wondrous work in nursing, and it pleased her to be used in that way. What more could she want? And yet lately—lately Renna had been desiring something more. *Is it a sin,* she wondered, *to be so discontented after so many happy years of nursing?*

The carriage stopped in front of Renna's house. She climbed out, paid the driver, and then turned to open the little white gate of the matching picket fence around the front yard. A slight breeze blew on this hot August evening, and Renna thought it felt marvelous after her day of sweltering on the second floor of the hospital.

"Well, there you are, dear," Johanna Fields said. She had been pruning the flowers that graced the edge of the wide front porch. "You're late tonight, Renna." She studied her daughter. "Mr. Blackeyes? Is he. . . all right?"

Renna nodded. "Dr. Hamilton thinks he may even live; however, he has an awful fever now. We're hoping it breaks by morning and that pneumonia doesn't set in."

"Oh. . ." Johanna shook her head sadly. "Well, we'll keep praying, won't we?"

Renna nodded, and then mother and daughter walked arm-in-arm into the house.

"I've made a light fare tonight, Renna. Help yourself."

"Thank you, Mother."

Renna fixed up a plate of cold beef, sliced tomatoes, and a crusty roll. While she ate, her sister Elizabeth walked in with her two babies, Mary and Helena. Renna delighted in her nieces and then visited with her sister before turning in for the night.

Upstairs in her small bedroom, Renna poured water from the large pitcher on her bureau into the chamber basin and then washed away the day's heat. She pulled her cool, cotton nightgown over her head, then took her Bible off the nightstand and continued her reading in John, chapter 9. As she read, Renna realized that physical ailments allowed God to show His glory, and she marveled as she read about the blind man who by simple faith and obedience regained his sight.

"Oh, Lord, that You might heal Mr. Blackeyes," Renna prayed fervently. "That You might show Your power to those who don't believe by healing him." Renna paused to remember her other patients then. "And please rain down Your peace that passeth all understanding on the Websters tonight."

Renna finished her Bible reading and then turned down the lamp. The breeze ruffled the curtains slightly, and somehow Renna knew that John Webster would not be in her sick ward tomorrow morning. Nor would his family be there. Somehow Renna knew that John was with the Savior already.

But Mr. Blackeyes. . .why, he might not even be a believer!

"Please heal him, Lord," she murmured.

And the darkly handsome stranger who lay fighting for his life was the last person on Renna's thoughts that night as she drifted off to sleep.

Chapter 2

It was nearly thirty-six hours later before Mr. Blackeyes' fever broke. His thrashing ceased, and he emerged from his delirium.

"Close the shades, Nurse Fields," Dr. Hamilton barked. "The sun is shining right in the poor fellow's eyes."

Renna went to do as she was told when Mr. Blackeyes weakly said, "The sun. . .what do you mean it's shining in my eyes?"

His voice sounded dry and hoarse, but his words alone stopped Renna in her tracks. With eyes wide, she looked to Dr. Hamilton.

"You can't see the sun shining in your eyes?" he asked the patient.

"No, and I would venture to say it's the middle of the night." The man turned his head toward the sound of Dr. Hamilton's voice. "Why are you questioning me in the dark, man? Are we in the bowels of a ship?"

"No, no, you're at Lakeview Hospital in Chicago." Dr. Hamilton waved his hand in front of the patient's eyes. Then he looked at Renna and mouthed the word "blind."

Her heart sank.

"What's your name, my dear fellow?" Dr. Hamilton asked. He pulled various gadgets from his medical bag, waving them in front of the patient. No reaction.

"My name?" The question seemed to stump him.

"Your name. . .what is it?"

"I—I don't know."

"Oh, come now," Dr. Hamilton said with a note of impatience. "Everyone has a name. What is yours?"

The patient seemed to grope for a reply. Finally all he said was, "I—I really don't know."

Renna's jaw momentarily went slack as she realized the implication. Looking to Dr. Hamilton, she mouthed, "Amnesia?"

He nodded. Clearing his throat then, he ordered her to fetch some salve and bandages from the supply cabinet. Renna hurried to get them; and when she returned to the sick ward, Dr. Hamilton was explaining the situation to Mr. Blackeyes.

"It's a result of your head injury, I'm afraid. Now the blindness may or may not be temporary; however, I'm inclined to believe that your memory will come back within a relatively short period of time."

Renna assisted Dr. Hamilton in applying the salve to his eyes. Next they bandaged them tightly.

"Since you can't see sunshine in your eyes, you won't be able to see other harmful things, either," Dr. Hamilton explained. "The bandages will protect your eyes until your sight comes back—if it does."

Mr. Blackeyes fell back against the bed, seemingly exhausted by this last endeavor.

"He'll sleep now, Nurse Fields," Dr. Hamilton said. "But when he awakens, feed him and clean him up. See if you can jog his memory loose, too."

"Yes, Doctor."

As Renna went about her business, she noted that Mr. Blackeyes slept all day. It wasn't until the end of Renna's shift when he finally felt strong enough to eat something. A coddled egg and milk toast were on the menu tonight, and Mr. Blackeyes grimaced at every spoonful Renna slipped into his mouth.

"Roast beef and potatoes would suit me just fine," he complained.

"Well, then you must be feeling much better." Renna spooned in another bite.

"What is your name?"

"I'm Nurse Fields," she replied, undaunted.

"Are you Miss or Mrs.?"

Renna smiled. "I'm Nurse Fields, and that's all you need to know."

A sardonic grin curved Mr. Blackeyes' mouth. "You've got some spirit, Nurse Fields. I like a spirited woman."

"You remember that much, do you?" Renna retorted.

Before he could reply, she spooned the last bit of his supper into his mouth.

He nearly gagged. "See here! That's not fair, Nurse Fields. I couldn't see that coming."

Renna smiled inwardly and moved off the side of the bed where she'd been sitting.

"Nurse Fields," he said, grabbing her white smock. "Would you stay and talk with me awhile?" His expression was serious, and there was a pleading sound to his voice. "Tell me what you know of me and my condition. Will you?"

Renna unloosed her apron and considered the request. "Oh, all right," she said at last. "But I have to finish writing up my charts and check on my other patients. Then I'm off duty, and I can sit with you."

Mr. Blackeyes grinned. "Your husband won't mind?"

Renna expelled a weary sigh. She was glad her patient was feeling better; however, she felt wilted from the heat and exhausted from twelve hours of working, and she was not up to playing cat and mouse.

"I am not married, sir," she said, sounding a little too harsh to her own ears. She forced herself to soften her tone. "Now let me go and finish up, and I'll sit with you awhile."

Strolling from bed to bed, Renna quickly wrote up her charts, checking on each patient as she did so. John Webster's cot was, as she suspected, empty this morning. He had died during the night. Mr. Taylor was much better and would go home tomorrow, and Mr. Anderson. . .

Renna felt his forehead and realized the man was burning with fever! Quickly, she ran from the room and fetched some cool water and a fever rag.

"What is it, Nurse Fields?" Nurse Ruthledge asked as Renna whizzed by.

"It's Mr. Anderson. He's fevering from his wounds."

"The man who lost his arm in a farming accident?"

"Yes, that's the one."

"You'll have to stay until that fever is down, Nurse Fields. I'm short of nurses tonight."

Renna nodded, for she feared that would be the case. With Mr. Blackeyes momentarily forgotten, she set out to sponge down Mr. Anderson.

He moaned and protested having the cool water on his body, but Renna fought to do her job. Then Dr. Hamilton was called in. Upon examining the wound, he shook his head, wearing a grave expression. "It's a blood infection."

"Oh, no!" Renna's heart sank. "I kept the wound clean, Doctor."

"Well, at times, Nurse Fields, that's not enough."

Renna tried to think of what more she could have done but thought of nothing.

"Don't blame yourself," Dr. Hamilton said as if divining her thoughts. "You did what you could. So did I."

With that, Dr. Hamilton packed his medical bag and left for home. All Renna could do was try to keep her patient comfortable—until death set in.

Sometime during the night, Mr. Anderson awoke.

"I'm dying, ain't I?"

Renna could only soothe his burning brow and try to smile. "It's God who controls life and death. Not me." She thought for a long while, then asked, "Is there anyone you want me to send for? A wife? Children?"

"No one," came the curt reply.

Renna had thought so since she hadn't ever seen anyone come to visit Mr. Anderson. He had said that he lived on his farm alone with just a few hired hands.

"My wife left me years ago."

"That's a shame, Mr. Anderson." Renna continued sponging his forehead.

"She said I was a no-account drunk, and I suspect she was right. I left her alone far too much of the time."

Renna though her patient was growing delirious. It wouldn't be long before he'd be uttering complete nonsense.

As she gave the fever rag another rinse, her heart became very burdened for this man. "Do you know the Lord, Mr. Anderson? Do you know Jesus Christ?"

He nodded. "He's the One who hung on a tree and died." Mr. Anderson turned his fever-bright eyes toward Renna. "I heard a preacher say that. . .once."

"Well, that's true. . .at least that's part of the truth. You see, God so loved the world that He gave His only begotten Son," Renna said, quoting John 3:16, "that whosoever believeth in Him should not perish, but have everlasting life. Would you like to have everlasting life, Mr. Anderson? Free from pain and suffering such as you're feeling right now?"

He closed his eyes and sighed, but a smile played on his lips. "If I die, I won't suffer no more."

"If you die and go to heaven, you won't suffer," Renna corrected. "You see, you have to make a decision, Mr. Anderson. Where will you spend eternity?"

He groaned. "You mean I gotta decide right now? While I'm lyin' here dyin'?"

"This is the best time to do it. I'm afraid indecision will send you to an eternity apart from God, Mr. Anderson. On the other hand, the Bible says that if you will confess with thy mouth the Lord Jesus," she said, quoting Romans 10:9, "and if you will believe in thine heart that God hath raised Him from the dead, thou shalt be saved. . . . For whosoever shall call upon the name of the Lord shall be saved."

"And God'll save an old drunk like me, huh?"

"We're all sinners. Just some of us are sinners saved by grace, and that's the difference."

Mr. Anderson was very quiet for a long while.

Renna, however, continued to soothe his burning brow and make him as comfortable as she knew how. She hummed a favorite hymn and tried not to think of how tired she was. She ignored her aching feet and the pain in the small of her back from bending over her patients all day.

Then finally in the wee hours of the morning, Mr. Anderson confessed his sin to God and cried out for Jesus to save him.

By daybreak, he went home to meet his Savior.

Renna was past the point of exhaustion, yet she rejoiced that Mr. Anderson had died a believer.

The day supervisor ordered Renna to go home and replaced her with Nurse Thatcher. Feeling so weary, she scarcely remembered the ride home in the hired hackney. She hardly felt the cool breeze against her hot skin as it blew in through the carriage window, and she was only vaguely aware of the towering masts of the vessels moored in the Chicago River. Normally, Renna liked to watch for them as they peaked and dipped above many of the city's buildings. But this morning, she didn't even think of them as she leaned her tired head back against the leather seat.

And it wasn't until later, after she arrived home, ate, washed, and had crawled into bed that she remembered Mr. Blackeyes.

"Oh, no!" She bolted upright in her bed. "He had wanted to talk awhile. . . ."

Settling back against her pillows once more, Renna realized that she'd done what she could: Mr. Anderson had needed her immediate attention, while Mr. Blackeyes was well enough to wait.

I'll make it up to him tomorrow, Renna thought with a yawn. "Maybe I'll even bring him some of Mother's apple pie. . . ."

On that thought, she fell into a deep sleep.

Chapter 3

Renna slept most of the following day and then all of that night. The next morning she awoke at dawn and felt refreshed. A cool breeze was blowing in through her bedroom window, and the sun was rising in the east. Birds were chirping, and suddenly Renna couldn't stay in bed a moment longer.

She washed and dressed and, as she did, she caught a glimpse of herself in the mirror. She paused to examine her attire and hairstyle, deciding that both were acceptable. Then she scrutinized her birthmark. How ugly she thought it was, that purplish mark, as though someone had taken a hot iron and branded the side of her face. Renna had tried everything from creams to powders, soaps, and herbal teas. Nothing, but nothing made the thing fade even slightly.

On a small sigh of despair, Renna turned away from the mirror. She took a few more minutes with her appearance and then took time for prayer. Leaving her bedroom, Renna made her way downstairs. She ate some breakfast and then took the remaining half of her mother's apple pie to the hospital with her. Renna wasn't about to forget Mr. Blackeyes today! She packed him a jar of milk, a napkin, and a fork along with the pie. It looked like a small picnic lunch.

She was early for duty and crept silently into the sick ward. Two new patients had been added sometime yesterday, but Renna hadn't met them yet. She checked on Mr. Blackeyes and suspected that he wasn't sleeping.

"Are you awake?" she whispered.

He turned his head. "Who's there?"

"It's Nurse Fields."

"Nurse Fields." Mr. Blackeyes smiled wryly. "I had thought you fell off the face of the earth. You haven't been around for days!"

Renna smiled, though her patient couldn't see it. "It's only been one day since I've been gone."

"Feels like years."

Renna's heart went out to the man.

"Nurse Hatchet has the coldest hands I've ever felt!"

"Nurse Thatcher," Renna corrected.

"Hatchet suits her perfectly!"

Renna pressed her lips together in an effort not to smile. However, his complaints told Renna that he was feeling better.

"And Nurse Ruthless."

"Ruthledge."

"I beg to differ! Why I'd go so far as to say that. . .person isn't even human!"

"Now, now, I'll have none of that," Renna chided him.

"And the food is awful!"

Renna had to agree with at least that much. "Well, I brought you some of my mother's apple pie for breakfast. How would that do? A special treat because I didn't get a chance to talk with you the other night." She paused in all seriousness now. "Mr. Anderson was, as you might know, deathly ill. In fact, he died that morning."

"I heard it all," Mr. Blackeyes said in a somber tone. He was momentarily silent and then asked, "Was that all true what you told him? About God and salvation?"

"Yes," Renna replied. "It was gospel straight from the Holy Bible."

Another pause. "Well, I prayed to God that night, right along with Mr. Anderson. When you led him in prayer, I prayed right along. I somehow knew it was the truth when I heard you talking, because Richard used to tell me about salvation and my need for it."

"That's wonderful!" Renna was heartened that her patient's memory was returning. And that he accepted Jesus Christ the other night was as much a thrill to hear as it was a miracle! "Richard?" she asked gently. "Who's Richard?"

She waited for Mr. Blackeyes to continue, but he didn't immediately. Finally he just said, "I don't know who Richard is. But I can see his face right now in my mind's eye. He's fair-headed and wears spectacles sometimes. . .when he does my books."

"He's your bookkeeper?" Renna sat down on the side of his bed, totally absorbed in this man's puzzle of a past. "You must have some kind of business if you have a bookkeeper. Do you remember your name and where you're from?"

"No. And it's most infuriating, too!"

"Be patient with yourself, Mr. Blackeyes."

He drew his chin back in surprise, and Renna laughed. "While you were unconscious," she explained, "I felt I had to call you something. So I made up the name Mr. Blackeyes. It's because of the color of your eyes. They're the deepest black I've ever seen."

Another hint of a smile shone through the man's dark beard. "I wish they worked."

Renna smiled sympathetically. "Perhaps in time they will. In fact, we'll ask God to heal them, all right?"

"Do you think He'd do that?"

"He might. God is all-powerful, and He can do anything. He created you, after all, so who would know better how to heal you than God?"

"He didn't let me drown."

"No, He didn't."

"I would have gone to hell if I had died in the water."

Renna chewed her lower lip in thought. "Do you think you were a believer before but just can't remember it now?"

Mr. Blackeyes rolled his head from side to side. "No. I laughed at Richard. And Sarah, too. . .she went to church with the children. . . ."

"You're remembering! How marvelous!" Renna paused. "And do you think Sarah is your wife?"

Mr. Blackeyes was momentarily pensive. "I. . .don't. . .know," he admitted at last.

"Hmm. . .well, it'll come."

Renna stood now and found a fork and a napkin. "I'm not on duty for another half an hour. Would you like your apple pie now? And I can stay and talk with you, if you're up to it."

"I've been longing for someone to talk to!" Mr. Blackeyes replied.

"Well, all right, then."

Renna propped him up in his bed and allowed him to feed himself. He did rather well, too. He used his fork and napkin in a mannerly way that suggested proper training. And the way he spoke, too—Mr. Blackeyes was obviously a learned man. There was an air of sophistication about him.

"How about a good strong cup of coffee to wash that down?" Mr. Blackeyes asked now.

Renna grinned. "How about a cup of milk instead? It's all I brought with me." She looked at the pie tin. He'd scarcely eaten even a quarter of the portion she'd brought.

"Milk will do nicely, thank you," Mr. Blackeyes said. He seemed tired.

Renna gave him the jar of milk, and he took a few long swallows; however, he didn't even finish half of it.

"I'll save the rest of this for you," she promised. "There's a good deal of pie and milk left."

Renna cleaned up and prepared to put the food in the ice box downstairs. She could keep it there for the day without a problem.

"Nurse Fields," Mr. Blackeyes said, "could I get a shave? I simply abhor wearing a beard!"

"Of course," Renna replied easily. "I'm quite good at shaving a man's face. I shaved so many faces during the Civil War that it would put the local barber to shame!" She laughed softly.

"I was on the Mississippi River during the war," Mr. Blackeyes stated. "I was on a gunner. . .I was wounded. . .discharged early. . ."

"You're remembering!" Renna cried with delight.

But Mr. Blackeyes only sighed. "That's all I remember. This is most frustrating!"

Renna smiled. "It'll come," she assured him. "Give yourself some time."

Renna cleaned up the remains of her patient's breakfast and then reported for work. She charted everything Mr. Blackeyes had told her, hoping that all the slices of remembrances would somehow come together as a whole.

Then she was introduced to her latest charges. One man, Mr. Abraham, was suffering from cholera. Another outbreak had recently struck the city.

"Make sure the man gets plenty to drink," Dr. Hamilton said. "He has severe cramps, but an unquenchable thirst. And look at his skin. . .it's gray and wrinkling. An indication, I'd say, of poor circulation."

Renna sobered. "Do you think he'll live?"

"I'm not sure," Dr. Hamilton replied heavily. "Time will tell." He sighed. "Thank goodness it's not contagious from contact; but mind yourself, just the same."

"Yes, doctor," Renna replied before she cleaned up the man. She managed to change his bed sheets, depositing them in the incinerator afterward. Then she scrubbed her own hands thoroughly. The water was cool and refreshing, and the air downstairs was mild; however, by the time Renna returned to the second-floor sick ward, she was perspiring again. The end of August was approaching, and the days were hot and humid. *How nice it will be*, Renna thought, *when September comes with the cool fall weather.*

Mr. Blackeyes hailed her then. "Nurse Fields? Is that you?"

"It is," she replied sweetly. "Oh, yes, about your shave. . ."

Renna fetched the necessary supplies and a good sharp razor before returning to Mr. Blackeyes' bedside.

"You've been very patient," she commended him.

"I've got no pressing engagements." A hint of a smile peeked through his thick beard. "Tell me as you shave. . .what do I look like?"

"Well," Renna began, "you have thick black hair." She frowned. "Do you remember what the color black looks like?" she wondered aloud.

"Yes, I know black. I'm in it constantly."

"Oh. . .of course. . ." She took off a good patch of beard and then continued. "You've got black eyes, as I've told you before. But they're not mean or menacing. They're like polished stones. . .like the kind you can find on the beach. . . ."

"You're a romantic, Nurse Fields," Mr. Blackeyes said with a grin.

Renna blushed, glad her patient couldn't see it. She continued shaving. "No more talking now," she warned facetiously, "or I'm likely to slit your throat, and then Dr. Hamilton will have to forgo his lunch to stitch you up."

She paused for several moments, but Mr. Blackeyes was soon urging her to continue with her description of him. "Well, all right. You seem to be a tall man," she told him. "And I would guess that you do some sort of lifting or pulling. . .you have well-developed shoulders and arms."

The corners of Mr. Blackeyes' mouth lifted sardonically. "And do you like tall men with well-developed shoulders and arms?"

At the question, Renna nearly lost the basin of water on her lap. She hadn't meant to get so personal. She was merely trying to do the man a favor and tell him what he looked like to jog his memory.

"Mr. Blackeyes, you are quite fresh. I believe I'll stop shaving your face right now, and you can just wear half a beard for the rest of the day!"

Renna moved to get up off the side of the bed and make good on her threat when her patient suddenly caught the edge of her apron.

"I apologize, Nurse Fields," he said quickly. "I shouldn't have embarrassed you that way. I couldn't seem to help it." He cleared his throat and then smirked. "You must admit that I am in somewhat of a compromising position here. . .and you. . .well, you smell. . .very good."

"I'm hot and sticky," she countered. "I doubt I smell very good at all."

"On the contrary, Nurse Fields. You smell far better than this sick room and one hundred times better than the food in this hospital!"

"Well. . .thank you, I guess."

Mr. Blackeyes chuckled.

Renna shifted uncomfortably then, thinking over all her patient had just said. She had taken care of hundreds of men throughout her nursing career, and had never thought of her role with any of them as compromising. She was a nurse. They needed medical care. That was all there was to it.

But this man was very, very different.

"Perhaps you're a pirate," she murmured, studying his face now. He had a very straight nose and a rugged-looking jawline. He was darkly handsome—more so without his beard.

Mr. Blackeyes laughed. "Like Edward Teach, perhaps? Are you familiar with him? He was an English pirate in the 1700s. . .also known as Blackbeard."

Renna grew wary, but his next remark disarmed her.

"I used to tell my two sons pirate stories all the time. . .before they went to bed."

"You have two sons? See, you are remembering!" She continued to shave his face. "Can you think of their names—your sons, I mean?"

Mr. Blackeyes was silent for quite some time, and it wasn't until Renna had finished with the razor that he replied, "I can't think of their names, but I see their faces in my mind's eye. I can see them. . .and two little girls. My daughters, I think. We're at a funeral. . . ."

Renna quietly cleaned up around her and then straightened the bed dutifully. *He has children*, she thought. *Four of them. So he must have a wife. He mentioned Sarah. . .that must be her. And he has a business, since he has a bookkeeper named Richard.*

"Your family must be terribly worried. Your children. . .and your wife, too—"

"No, I don't think so," Mr. Blackeyes replied in a low voice. "And I believe you may be right: I am more of a pirate than I ever was a husband and father. . . ."

Chapter 4

He could picture the whole scene in his mind. The beautiful woman laid to rest in the casket. The children hovering around his knees. He could hear the organ music as they stood in the small chapel. Somehow he knew that the beautiful woman was his wife, but he couldn't recall her name. He knew their relationship had been strained, if nonexistent, save for begetting the children, but he couldn't remember the reasons why. Was he sad that the beautiful woman was dead? No. He remembered feeling apathetic, even annoyed at having to leave his business for this much overdone funeral!

The service, replayed so vividly in his mind, ended then and he remembered calling for the children's governess. He recalled that she was one of many who had come and gone throughout the years. Yes, that's right; he and his wife had sported a very demanding lifestyle.

And then he remembered. . .the elegant dinners in lavishly furnished mansions, the parties and fine affairs. Was that what killed her? The beautiful woman? His wife? No. No. He remembered that she was frequently ill. . .sickly.

In his mind's eye, then, he watched as the governess prepared to take the children away, and he remembered promising, "I will see you at suppertime." However, he never made it home that night. He rarely did. Business took precedence in his life, and attending social functions was essential to his climb up the ladder of economic success.

Then he recalled how he had conversed with several prominent citizens who had come to pay their last respects. They were important people in the community, he remembered. . .except he couldn't think of their names or which community!

"Mr. Pirate Blackeyes?"

It was Nurse Fields. He recognized her voice at once, and it swung him back to the present. Her tone was laced with amusement, as it frequently was, and he imagined that she was smiling over her new nickname for him: *Mr. Pirate Blackeyes.*

He felt her hand on his arm, then. Her fingers were warm and gentle, and her touch was reassuring, somehow. This darkness could be so frightening at times, irritating at others. But Nurse Fields had become his fragile link to the world beyond this blackness and the images that taxed his memory.

"Are you awake?" she asked.

"Yes, of course I'm awake."

A pause. "Well, you've been sleeping for most of the day, you know."

"I have?" He felt puzzled. "But you were just giving me a shave—"

Her fingers gave his arm a comforting pat. "That was this morning, Mr. Blackeyes. It's suppertime now, and I brought you a tray. It's beef stew, I think."

"You mean you don't know for sure?"

He heard her laugh softly, a light and delicate sound. "Try it and let me know," she said on a challenging note.

He was then helped into a sitting position, and a tray was placed on his lap.

"On your right, at one o'clock, is your coffee—I managed to get you a cup."

"You're most kind, Nurse Fields," he said with a teasing grin. He felt her closeness and smelled the increasingly familiar scent of the soap she used, like roses and soft powder. And she was like a breath of fresh air compared to those women he knew who doused themselves with French perfume. How he wished he could know what she looked like. He imagined that Nurse Fields was very beautiful.

"And at about three o'clock are your utensils," she was saying, and he had to force himself to pay attention. "At nine o'clock is your napkin and at eleven o'clock is a slice of the apple pie from your breakfast."

"I'll eat that first. At least I know it's safe—and it tastes good. Compliment your mother for me, will you? My own cook, Isabelle, couldn't even match that, I'm sure."

Nurse Fields gasped in what sounded like delight. "You've remembered someone else! Very good! Isabelle, your cook."

He heard the rustle of her skirts now as she moved away. "Are you leaving?" he asked, hoping she'd stay. It was very lonely inside all this darkness.

"Yes, I am," she said, sounding sympathetic. "I am expected at home and I've already stayed here too long. But if you wouldn't mind, I'd like to ask my father to come back and visit you tonight. He works at the Chamber of Commerce—in the exchange room where they sample grains, and he is a very faithful man in our local church. Since you're a believer now, I think it would be very beneficial for you to learn God's Word. The Holy Bible." Nurse Fields paused, and somehow he sensed that she was smiling at him from where she stood at the side of his bed. "You may have come into this hospital a pirate," she said on a teasing note, "but you'll leave here a man of God!"

He sighed, unsure as to what that all entailed. That kind of change sounded drastic. From pirate to priest? Surely not! But something vague came to mind when Nurse Fields mentioned "grain exchange." Perhaps they would have more to talk about than the Bible after all. . . .

"All right. Ask your father to come," he finally replied. "I'm desperate for the company anyway."

Renna couldn't help smiling as she left the hospital and then all the way home, too. *Hearing the Word of God is exactly what Mr. Blackeyes needs*, she decided.

She had felt awkward all day after he'd commented on how she smelled. He had a virile way about him that frightened Renna, for it implied he knew women very well. And of course he would, since he was a married man; however, the very fact that he was married caused Renna a good measure of alarm. She wondered how he could speak to her in such a personal manner if he had a wife and children.

Then she reminded herself that pirates do those sorts of things. However, this pirate had been saved and, as Hebrews 4:12 said, ". . .the word of God is quick and powerful and sharper than any two-edged sword, piercing even to the dividing asunder of the soul and spirit and of the joints and marrow, and is a discerner of the thoughts and intents of the heart."

Yes, Renna thought now, *meditating on God's Word is just what Mr. Blackeyes needs to keep his mind off his situation—and off me!*

Renna continued with her walk home. Tonight she didn't hire a hackney since the evening was so pleasant and mild. Renna simply had to walk. The fresh breezes coming right off of Lake Michigan revived her senses after the hours she'd spent in the sick ward.

Renna worked and lived on Chicago's South Side. It was by far the most exciting part of the city. This side of town had the stores, hotels, and other public buildings, such as the Chamber of Commerce building—where her father worked—and the courthouse.

She nodded politely as she walked past those with whom she was acquainted. She had secured her bonnet just right so it concealed the birthmark on her cheek.

Then finally she reached her quiet neighborhood with its well-groomed lawns and picket fences. It was hardly like the neighborhood on Michigan Avenue with its lavish mansions. No, Renna's neighborhood was best described as slightly better than average.

"Well, it's about time you came home, daughter!" Wendall Fields declared as he climbed down from his buggy. His hazel eyes twinkled with merriment, and Renna knew he meant to tease her for arriving home as late as he had. "I suppose you're going to tell me that a man can work from sun to sun, but a woman's work is never done."

Renna laughed softly. "You're so poetic, Father," she teased right back.

Wendall tied his horse to the hitching post. Then he and Renna walked arm-in-arm through the gate and up the front porch stairs.

"You work too hard, my dear," he said at the front door. "It isn't right. You'll grow old before your time."

Renna swallowed a weary sigh. She and her father had had this conversation before; however, Renna wasn't sure what to do about it. She couldn't just quit nursing. What would she do? She was a spinster and had to bide her time somehow. At least she felt needed at the hospital.

"Father, are you busy tonight?"

Wendall looked a bit surprised, for she'd changed the subject on him right in the middle of his sentence. "Why do you ask, my dear?"

"Well, it's my patient. You know, the one you and Mother have been praying for. Mr. Blackeyes."

"Ah, yes. And what about him?"

They were standing in the front hallway now where Renna carefully removed her bonnet. "He needs some Christian fellowship, Father," she said. "He just became a Christian, and he's so lonely. I can tell. But what bothers me is that. . ." Renna tried not to blush as she confided in her father this way. "Well, from what Mr. Blackeyes has remembered, it's quite apparent that he's married. And, well, he's—he's all too familiar with me, Father. I believe he's probably been something of a lady's man and. . .well—well, it makes me terribly uncomfortable."

"I see." A heavy frown settled on Wendall's brow. "I take it that nursing Mr. Blackeyes was easier when he was unconscious, huh?"

"I'm afraid so."

"All right, daughter," Wendall said with a large smile, "let's see what your mother has planned for me tonight and, if there's nothing pending, I'll visit with Mr. Blackeyes for a while." He cocked a brow and added, "It would be my pleasure."

As it happened, Johanna Fields had nothing planned for her husband that night, so Wendall climbed into his carriage after supper and went over to the hospital. Renna paced, awaiting her father's return. She hoped that Mr. Blackeyes would somehow remember more of his past. However, she hoped most of all that he would get a taste of God's Word. . .and want more!

"Renna, what about tomorrow night?" her mother asked.

With her thoughts of Mr. Blackeyes interrupted, Renna turned her attention to the question at hand. Tomorrow night. The dinner party. . .

"Will you be able to join us?"

"I don't know."

"Did you tell the day nurse supervisor that you had to leave early tomorrow night?"

Renna shook her head, and her mother sighed.

"What will I ever do with you?" Johanna said, though she wore a slight smile as she said it.

"Mother, I don't want to meet Mr. Benchley. I know he's Father's newest associate, and I know he is an eligible bachelor. . .but—but. . ."

"And the right age for you, too, Renna," her mother said. "He's not too old." Johanna shook her head sadly. "Most eligible men are old widowers and not for you, my dear."

Renna cringed inwardly. She had met some of those "old widowers."

"However, Clyde Montgomery was rather nice. Nearly fifty, though. . ."

Renna smiled. Yes, Clyde was nice. His age hadn't bothered her, either. It was his lack of love for the Lord. He had claimed to know Him, but didn't want to speak of Him, and he only discussed business and politics—with the men. To Renna he spoke as though he were addressing a very slow child and not a woman with a brain in her head. Yes, Clyde was nice, but certainly not the one with whom the Lord would have her spend the rest of her life.

"I understand, though, why you didn't marry him," Johanna continued. She darned socks as she and Renna chatted in the small sitting room adjacent to the parlor. "But Mr. Benchley, your father told me, is quite different. He's not a widower. He has never been married, and Abigail Hoffmann told me that he's very charming."

Already warning bells were going off in Renna's head. Abigail Hoffmann was not a good judge of character, bless her heart anyway.

"So why don't you suppose Mr. Benchley ever got married?" Renna asked.

Johanna smiled. "Waiting till he met you, dear," she replied in a singsong voice.

Renna rolled her eyes heavenward. It didn't look like she could get out of tomorrow night's dinner arrangement in a dignified manner. She would just have to attend and do her best to have a good spirit about it.

"I hope you'll get out of work early, Renna," her mother said. "Or at least try to be on time. I'll hold dinner for as long as I can."

Renna grudgingly agreed.

It was nearly ten o'clock when Wendall returned. Johanna had gone to bed already, but as exhausted as she felt, Renna stayed on the front porch swing and waited for her father.

"How did it go?" she asked, meeting him at the front walk.

"Very well, my dear. Come inside, and I'll tell you all about it."

They walked into the house, and Renna had to chuckle at the way the nurses had allowed her father to stay so long in the sick ward. But he and Mr. Blackeyes were being quiet, Wendall said, and not disturbing the other patients.

"So what happened?"

"Well, I began in the book of Genesis. I figured that would be a good place to start. With God's creation. And, oh, Mr. Blackeyes had the questions! My, my. . ."

Renna smiled. "What else, Father?"

"I got as far as chapter 20. . .we made it through the destruction of Sodom and Gomorrah."

"That's good."

"But I didn't want to give Mr. Blackeyes too much too soon."

"Very wise."

"So, we talked awhile. . .about things in general."

"And?"

Wendall smiled. "And he's a widower, daughter."

Renna's jaw dropped. "A widower?"

"Yes. He remembers that his wife died—we figured about four months ago—but he can't recall her name. However, he knows he has children. Gabriel, Michael, Elizabeth, and Rachel."

"His memory is returning," Renna said with awe in her voice.

"Indeed." Wendall cleared his throat now. "And I have a vague sense that I've met this man somewhere, but I can't remember where or when." He shrugged. "Well, I'm sure it'll come back to me eventually."

"And what about his. . .well, you know. . .his. . ."

"About Mr. Blackeyes getting too familiar with you?"

Renna blushed.

"I talked to him, and he has promised to apologize in the morning. I believe him. He does nothing but sing your praises, Renna."

"Well, he should be singing praises to God, not me!"

Wendall chuckled again. "In due time, daughter. I'm going to visit him again tomorrow night—if your mother doesn't object, that is."

Renna's eyes grew wide. "The dinner party is tomorrow."

Wendall snapped his fingers. "Oh, I forgot!"

An idea formed. "We could cancel it."

"Yes, but—"

"Postpone it then?" Renna was fairly pleading now.

Wendall sighed. "You don't want to meet Matthew Benchley?"

Renna swayed to and fro, her skirts swishing around her ankles. "I'll meet him if you want me to, I guess."

Wendall shook his head. "Daughter, we've had this conversation before. . .about your birthmark. That's what this is all about, isn't it? The reason you don't want to meet Matthew?" Wendall sighed. "I would have thought you'd gotten over that. My dear, but I scarcely notice it at all. You see, you're beautiful on the inside, Renna, and that shows and makes you beautiful on the outside, too."

Renna felt like crying at her father's honesty; however, she held her tears in check.

"No one notices it, Renna. Just you." Wendall gave his daughter a loving hug. "Now, vanity is a sin, Renna," he said gently, "and it's vain to be so self-conscious."

"Oh, Father, you just don't understand!" She twisted out of his embrace. "And how can you say I'm vain? Have you ever experienced the look of horror on people's faces when they first meet you? No, of course you haven't. But I have!"

"Renna, it's not horror on their faces, it's just surprise. They're surprised to see the birthmark. . .at first. . .but then they get used to it. Now why can't you?" Wendall smiled. "I hope you're not harboring an unforgiving spirit, Renna."

She clenched her jaw and her fists, but turned around without another word. She was tired, and she didn't trust herself to reply. Of course she wasn't vain or unforgiving. Her father simply didn't understand a woman's delicate sensibilities, that's all!

"Good night, daughter," he called up the stairs after her.

At the top, Renna paused. Her spirit softened at the sound of his gentle voice.

Finally she turned. "Good night, Father," she said. Then she let herself into her bedroom, closing the door behind her.

Chapter 5

S o tell me. . .am I forgiven?"

Renna was gathering the razor, basin of water, and towels after she'd given Mr. Blackeyes his morning shave. She still had two other men waiting for her. Then those who were able would have a bath today and clean garments—shirts and drawers for the men, cotton gowns for the women. And there were two of them, women that is, in the next sick ward. They had been admitted with terrible cases of cholera; however, they were feeling much better, and Renna knew they'd love a bath. Today promised to be a busy one!

"Pirates aren't well versed in the way of propriety," Mr. Blackeyes was saying, and Renna forced herself to concentrate. After all, he was trying to apologize. "I realized some things last night after talking with your father and, well. . .I. . .well. . .I'm trying to be less of a pirate. All right?"

Renna felt heartened. "Yes, of course you're forgiven. And I believe you when you say you're trying. I think it's commendable."

"Commendable for a pirate. Is that what you mean?"

He smiled, displaying large, even white teeth, and Renna could well imagine him aboard a tall-masted ship, surrounded by his crew, counting the booty.

"Are you still there, Nurse Fields?"

"Yes, I'm still here."

"You don't appreciate my humor this morning, is that it?"

"No, that's not it at all. I guess I'm just tired."

And that was the honest truth, too. The hospital was near to capacity, what with the cholera epidemic. And today's heat was oppressive! Nearly one hundred degrees and no breeze. Already Renna's clothes were damp with perspiration—and she had nine more hours of nursing ahead of her.

And then the dinner party tonight. . .that obligation weighed heavily on Renna.

"I'll be back shortly to draw your bath," she promised Mr. Blackeyes as she crossed the room to where young Mr. Adams lay. He had been brought in after a fire. He'd been unconscious for days but seemed to be recovering nicely now. Complaints about the food always indicated better health.

"Yer an angel of mercy is what you are," Mr. Adams said.

Renna smiled. "I'm just doing my job."

"Well, I'm here to say ya do it a lot better than some of the other nurses on this floor." Mr. Adams smiled. "Them women are downright mean!"

"Oh, now, they're not really mean at all. They're just busy. In any case, don't let it spoil your day. And guess what? The orderlies are bringing up the bathtubs. You'll have a good soaking soon—and have some clean clothes." Renna wrinkled her nose. "You still smell a bit like smoke."

"Well, now, a good soaking will feel real good. . .'specially on my burned foot."

"Yes, it is time for us to soak your foot again, isn't it?"

Mr. Adams nodded, and Renna smiled as she finished with his shave. Most of the other nurses would never allow time for their patients to have such luxuries as a shave. But Renna thought keeping up one's appearance was conducive to the healing process.

Within the hour, two large tubs were brought into each of the sick rooms, and Renna filled them with tepid water. It was so hot, even an ice cold bath would be much appreciated. In fact, jumping into the Chicago River didn't sound like such a bad idea to Renna, and she joked about it with the orderlies when they helped her draw the patients' baths.

"All right, Mr. Blackeyes. You're first."

The orderlies helped him into the tub while Renna stripped his bed and then made it up with fresh linens. Afterward, she laid out clean garments for him.

"And I'm sure I don't have to tell you to use the soap," Renna called over the wooden screen.

"Are you sure it's safe?" he called back. "It smells strong enough to take my skin off!"

Renna laughed. Yes, Mr. Blackeyes was definitely on the mend.

It was midafternoon before things quieted in Renna's wards. All the other nurses said she was daft for taking on such a monumental project as bathing patients on a day as hot as today. But Renna had thought her patients would feel better if they were clean and cool and if their beds were changed. And it seemed she was right. There were no complaints being shouted from out of her sick wards as they were from out of the others.

"Nurse Fields!" Mr. Blackeyes hailed her from his bed.

"Yes, what is it?" she asked. She had been walking in the hallway between the wards when she heard him. "You're supposed to be napping."

"Would you talk to me for a few minutes?"

Renna thought it over, then acquiesced. She knew how disappointed he was since Dr. Hamilton had come in and changed the bandages on his eyes. There was no change; Mr. Blackeyes still couldn't see.

His head wound, on the other hand, had healed almost completely. Dr. Hamilton said his lungs sounded clear; however, because of his memory loss and weakened condition, Mr. Blackeyes would be staying for a while. After all, he had nowhere else to go.

"Your father told me your first name is Renna," he began. He was sitting up in his bed, although the exertion after bath time had exhausted him, and it showed on his expression. "Renna," he said. "That's a most unusual name."

She smiled but thought her name sounded differently, somehow, coming from his lips. As though he didn't speak her name—he caressed it.

Renna cleared her throat, wondering how she could think such things. Perhaps the heat was making her a bit daft after all. In any case, she forced herself to reply. "My given name is Lorrenna. Lorrenna Jane, after my father's grandmother."

"Lorrenna. It's beautiful," Mr. Blackeyes said. "Renna is a nickname, then?"

"Yes."

"Renna." He said the name again, sending a tiny shiver up her spine. What was it about this man, anyway?

"And if I roll the R with my tongue," Mr. Blackeyes continued, "it sounds Spanish, don't you think? Renna."

She smiled as she sat in a chair beside his bed. She had found a fan to cool herself, and she waved it back and forth as she conversed. It was a nice break.

"Do you think you're Spanish, Mr. Pirate Blackeyes?" Renna had to laugh at her own question. "I might think you are, because of your dark features; however you have more of a European look about you."

"Hmm. . ." The comment had Mr. Blackeyes thinking for a few moments. Then he shrugged. "I don't know."

"It'll come," she insisted on a more serious note.

"Your father said he'd return tonight."

Renna grimaced. "No, he can't come. He forgot about a dinner engagement. I'm sorry. I should have told you earlier."

"I'm disappointed. I was looking forward to hearing more about the Bible."

Renna was so glad—though she was just as disappointed, too. How much more important it was to share God's Word than attempt to marry off a spinster daughter. Renna hoped her father would realize it.

"What sort of dinner engagement is it?" Mr. Blackeyes wanted to know.

"Well, my father is entertaining an associate at our home."

"I can recall some very fine dinners that my wife and I hosted. She was very beautiful, but very cold. . .Louisa! That was her name!" Mr. Blackeyes snapped his fingers. "Louisa!"

Renna smiled. "You're remembering!"

He sighed and sat back against the metal headboard of his bed. "She's dead. My wife. . .Louisa. She was ill for a long, long time. But off and on."

"I'm so sorry. I'm sure you loved her very much."

A wry grin curved Mr. Blackeyes's handsome mouth. "Actually, I didn't love her at all."

Renna gasped.

"Does that disturb you? I suppose it would, and I apologize. You probably believe in falling in love and living happily ever after. Like in the fairy tales. But when you grow up a bit, you'll see that love is—"

Renna's laugh cut off the rest of his remark. "When I grow up a bit? And how old. . .or should I say, how young do you think I am?"

Mr. Blackeyes was frowning. "I assumed that you were. . .well. . . young. You're spirited. . .unmarried—"

"I'm thirty years old, Mr. Blackeyes," Renna said, as a kind of bitterness swelled in her breast; however, she immediately fought to tamp it down. God made her this way, and He had called her to nurse the sick. She enjoyed her work and had a family who loved her. Wasn't that enough? What more could she ask for? Quickly, she repented silently for what she perceived as ungratefulness.

Mr. Blackeyes, however, still hadn't said anything, so Renna decided to clear the air. It was as thick with sudden tension as it was with the day's humidity.

"I am a spinster," Renna told him. "But, I'm not a nun, as many nurses are. I'm just unmarried, and I like to take care of people. I went to a finishing school for two years, but I got my nursing training in a military hospital, and that's where I served during the war.

"You see, God never sent me a husband to take care of, but instead He sent me hundreds and hundreds of patients. And I have loved them all. Some just needed a kind word. Some have needed a tender heart and much understanding. Some needed a hand to hold and someone to cry with. Some, as they lay dying, needed me to write to their wives and mothers. And many have needed to hear about salvation through Jesus Christ."

"Hmm. . ."

Renna smiled. "Like you."

Mr. Blackeyes didn't say too much after that. He seemed to retreat inside himself somewhere.

Shortly thereafter, Renna was called away. She had much to do before she could leave for the day.

At six o'clock, Renna's father appeared and offered her a ride home. He looked very distinguished in his three-piece suit, his gold watch dangling from the pocket of his vest. But like everyone else, he looked very, very hot.

"The day is sweltering, Renna, and unfit for a dinner party," he blurted unceremoniously. "Matt has agreed. We've rescheduled for sometime in the fall. Your mother is extremely relieved. She's been wilting in the kitchen all day."

Renna sighed with relief while straightening her paperwork. All she could think about doing tonight was soaking in a large, cool bath!

"How's my friend, Mr. Blackeyes?"

"Fine for the most part," Renna replied. "But he's very disappointed. Dr. Hamilton changed his bandages today, and there's no change. He's still blind."

Wendall shook his head sadly. "That's a shame." He glanced at his watch. "How long till you're through here?"

"Another hour, I think."

"Good."

She lifted a brow. "Good?"

"I'll chat with Mr. Blackeyes while you finish up, and then I'll take you home."

"And Mother won't mind us both coming in late. . .again?"

"Not in the least. I've already forewarned her."

Renna gave her father the best smile she could manage after eleven hours in the sick ward. But she thanked God that she only had one more to go.

Chapter 6

Now he was curious. In fact, it was driving him crazy! So when Renna's father came to sit with him for a while, as his dinner engagement was canceled, he had to ask about her.

"Please tell me. . .how is it that your daughter is a—a spinster? She told me that herself. She said she's thirty years old and a spinster. I could hardly believe it."

There was no reply for many long moments, and he thought perhaps the question was offensive.

"Forgive me," he said at last. "I didn't mean to pry. It's just that—"

"Renna is a beautiful person," Wendall Fields answered at last. "That's what you mean, isn't it? And it's so true. She is a blessing to her mother and me. But the fact of the matter is, Renna is also intelligent. Smarter than most of the eligible men her mother and I have tried to pair her with over the years." Wendall chuckled. "You must admit, Mr. Blackeyes, that there isn't a man alive who wants his wife to be smarter than he is!"

He grinned. "Yes, I suppose you're right." But what he didn't say is that he thought an intelligent woman like Renna would be a far better companion than, say, his wife Louisa had been. Oh, Louisa had sense about decorating and fashion, but she had been sorely lacking on issues of real importance. Issues that mattered. And he wouldn't have even married her if not for his mother, Aurora Reil.

He sat up a little straighter and snapped his fingers. "I've just remembered my mother's name. Aurora Reil."

"That's wonderful!" Wendall exclaimed.

"I can see her in my mind's eye. She was a very beautiful but very eccentric woman. She insisted that I call her Aurora during all my growing up years. And my children called her by her first name also." He felt the rueful smile curve his lips. "She disliked being a mother and abhorred the idea of being a grandmother."

"Pardon my saying so, but that's rather strange. However, you did say that your mother is an eccentric."

"Was." He paused as the sudden rush of memories poured in. "She was on the boat. . .with me. . .the day of the storm. . . ."

"Oh, no."

"She drowned. I saw her waving her arms frantically in the waves. I couldn't help her."

"I'm so sorry. . . ."

"And Elise was there."

"Elise?"

He grinned sardonically. "I was romancing Elise."

"How tragic. You lost your love as well as your mother."

He laughed bitterly. "Elise wasn't my 'love.' I merely wanted her shipping company. I got it, too. I bought it from her."

Wendall Fields didn't reply for a very long time. Finally, he said, "I believe you must have been something of a pirate after all, Mr. Blackeyes." Then he patted his arm. "But God has delivered you out of that lifestyle. You are a new creation in Christ."

He didn't know what to say. The thought of Christ saving a wretch like him was an awesome one.

"Your last name is Reil, then?" Wendall asked.

He shook his head. "My mother had three. . .no, four husbands. And I don't remember my father. Aurora always told me he died of the smallpox when I was very young, and I have no reason not to believe her."

"I see." There was a pause. "Well, I'll do some investigating and see what I can find out about your mother. Perhaps it'll lead us to your real identity very soon."

He nodded but felt suddenly exhausted.

"Would you like it if I read some more of the Bible?"

"Yes, please," he replied.

"All right, then."

After the whispering sound of delicate pages being turned, Wendall began to read from where he had left off last night.

"So you see, daughter, the man has lived a life of lies and deception—and devoid of true love. His first marriage was more of a business arrangement that secured good social standing, and he was about to make the same mistake, until the boating accident occurred."

"How sad," Renna said as she sat beside her father on the front porch swing. The air was much cooler out here now that the sun had set. "But Mr. Blackeyes can begin anew—now that he's a Christian."

"Yes, and I told him the same thing."

Renna smiled. "Now if we could only find out who he belongs to."

"We will. I'm doing a bit of investigating, asking everyone I know who does business along Lake Michigan's shores. Surely there must be some news somewhere of a prominent man in a boating accident who is now presumed dead."

"Yes, of course. . .there must be news of him somewhere. The rescuing ship's captain said he and his crew found Mr. Blackeyes floating near the Wisconsin-Illinois border."

Renna's mind drifted far away as she imagined her patient's former lifestyle. A pirate, lady's man, and prominent social figure. . .everything Renna abhorred in a man. He probably danced with only the most beautiful women, drank only the finest wine, and dined with the rich and famous. He probably lived in the fanciest house in the best neighborhood and furnished it lavishly, from the paintings to the carpets. *A man to be wary of, for sure*, she thought.

"Renna, did you hear anything I just said?"

She pulled herself from her musings. "Sorry, Father, I must be tired. My mind wandered a bit."

"I said, after church tomorrow, since it is your day off, I thought we'd all go by the hospital and visit Mr. Blackeyes. Perhaps we'll even bring him back for a little supper—if he's up to it, that is."

"Bring him here? To our home?"

"Why not?"

"Well. . .I. . .Father, he's my patient! I can't bring home everyone I nurse back to health!"

Wendall chuckled heartily. "No, of course you can't. But Mr. Blackeyes is different, wouldn't you say? I mean, you were burdened for him right from the beginning. We all prayed for him, and God answered by sparing the man's life and saving his soul. That warrants a dinner invitation, I think."

"Yes. . .if you say so, Father."

However, Renna's heart began to pound, and she couldn't seem to shake the sudden feeling of impending doom.

Despite Renna's misgivings, the sun shone brightly the next morning. She chided herself as she dressed carefully, though she couldn't imagine why she fussed today more than any other Sunday. It wasn't as though Mr. Blackeyes could see, not that she was trying to impress him, of course.

Goose! she told her reflection in the looking glass. *You're acting as though you're sixteen years old and without an ugly birthmark on your face. Now, that will be quite enough!*

She nodded curtly at herself, as if she'd given a militant order and expected it to be followed to the letter. Then she walked down the stairs to meet her parents for church, wondering what on earth had happened to her and when it had happened.

Perhaps it was finding out that Mr. Blackeyes was, indeed, something of a pirate. Perhaps he frightened her. Or perhaps it was knowing that, if he could see, he wouldn't be quite so friendly toward her—the woman with the purple birthmark on her face. Certainly she'd never compare to the ladies of society with whom he was accustomed.

"Not that it even matters!" she muttered, pulling on her white gloves.

"Did you say something, Renna?" her mother asked, opening the screen door off the front porch.

Embarrassed, she shook her head and put on her bonnet.

"Oh, the cool breeze. . .oh, Renna, the wind has shifted. It's a glorious day." Johanna turned at the door. "Why, it's warmer inside this house than it is outside."

Her tumultuous thoughts momentarily forgotten, Renna strode toward the front door and stepped out onto the porch. "You're right. It is a glorious day, Mother." Turning back to her, she added, "Let's have a picnic today. By the lake."

"That's a splendid idea."

Smiling and arm-in-arm, they walked to the carriage where Wendall patiently waited. A couple of hours later, after church, they rode the carriage home, where the ladies prepared a delicious picnic basket. Next, it was on to the hospital, where Mr. Blackeyes was overjoyed at their invitation.

"A picnic, you say? I'd love to go. Anything to get me out of this hospital."

"But are you feeling up to it?" Renna asked, concerned.

"I should say I am!"

Renna had her doubts. Mr. Blackeyes still looked pale and weak, but he looked more desperate than anything, so she sent her father an approving nod. "Will you help him dress?"

"Yes, of course." Glancing at Mr. Blackeyes, he said, "I brought along a suit for you, since the clothing you wore when they brought you here was burned to disrepair. But these are well-tailored threads—my son-in-law's spares—and I think they'll fit you fairly well."

Renna and her mother stood outside the sick ward and waited while Mr. Blackeyes dressed. Finally, he appeared, his arm looped through Wendall's. He looked peaked, but he seemed steady on his feet. The borrowed clothes, however, didn't do the man justice. The pants were too big at the waist and too short at the hems and the crisp, white shirt stretched tightly over his broad shoulders. Even so, he was a handsome man, in spite of the fact that he was convalescing.

Oh, how could I even notice such a thing? Renna wondered as they all walked out to the carriage. But the day was so bright and fair that she put all her wonderings aside, choosing instead to enjoy this outing. There would be plenty of time to ponder tomorrow when she went back on duty at the hospital.

"The air smells so good," Mr. Blackeyes said after they reached the park. He inhaled deeply. "I feel like I can breathe again. I believe I was beginning to suffocate in that sick room."

"Nonsense," Renna replied with a little smile. "The window was open, so there was little chance of suffocation."

"An open window is not the same as the fresh air outside in the sunshine. It feels so good on my face. Thank you. . .thank you all for rescuing me today."

Wendall chuckled, looking thoroughly amused. "You're welcome, but I wouldn't say we exactly rescued you, Mr. Blackeyes."

He snorted in disgust. "And I say you are! Nurse Hatchet is on duty again today and—"

"Now, now, let's not speak badly of Nurse Hatchet—I mean, Thatcher." Renna stomped her foot. "Now you've got me calling her Hatchet. You're incorrigible, Mr. Blackeyes!"

Everyone laughed as Johanna spread out the picnic blanket beneath a leafy elm tree. They sat down on a grassy section of the park while just ten feet away lay a half-mile stretch of rocky shoreline upon which Lake Michigan's waves pounded continuously.

"I know this sound well," Mr. Blackeyes said, tilting his head from side to side and listening intently. "The sound of. . .water."

"Lake Michigan to be exact," Wendall replied.

"Ah, yes, Lake Michigan. The very smell of her. . ." He inhaled deeply. "Like the scent of a familiar woman."

Johanna cleared her throat. "I believe that smell belongs to the dead alewives," she quipped, "so don't blame the lake—or any of us women for that matter!"

Uproarious laughter emanated from the men, while Renna and her mother exchanged amused glances and served the picnic meal.

After about an hour of lunching and light banter, Wendall stood. He stretched and complained of stiffness.

"Should we go for a short stoll?" Johanna suggested to her husband. "Walk out the kinks, so to speak?" She gave a sweet but teasing smile.

"Are you suggesting that I'm growing too old for picnics, madam?" he asked tartly.

"Indeed," replied Johanna, taking his arm. "Shall we?"

Wendall grumbled slightly but acquiesced.

Watching her parents amble off, Renna smiled. "Even after thirty-two years of marriage," she told Mr. Blackeyes, "my mother and father are still very much in love."

"Yes, I've sensed that," he replied. "It's quite remarkable, too, since I have always imagined that kind of love happened only in storybooks."

Renna shifted uncomfortably, glad that Mr. Blackeyes couldn't see through his bandaged eyes. She didn't want to discuss the topic of love with him. Fortunately for her, Mr. Blackeyes had different ideas.

"At first I had hoped Louisa and I would have a strong love relationship; but, after our marriage, it was soon apparent that she wanted a socialite's existence. The wife and mother roles were quite boring and often a nuisance for Louisa. Even so, I had tried to give the children the nurturing I thought they needed by providing loving governesses; however, they never lasted very long."

"Why is that?"

"I wasn't ever sure. . .until recently. I've had time to think about things, and. . ." Mr. Blackeyes chuckled. "Well, after a few snakes in your bed, you'd move on, too, I think." He laughed again. "My boys are mischief makers."

"Aren't all boys?" Renna shook her head, recalling her brother's shenanigans in his younger days.

Mr. Blackeyes was still grinning. "Yes, I suppose they are." He turned silent for a few minutes. "Sarah was the only one who could put up with them. . .and they loved her for it."

"Sarah? You've mentioned her before." Renna arched a brow. "Another wife?"

"No, no," Mr. Blackeyes said with a smile. "Another governess."

"You remember!"

"Yes, I remember."

Mr. Blackeyes grew pensive, so Renna prompted him. "Sarah was a governess who stayed on?"

"Yes. I hired her for the summer, but I don't know which summer it was. This one, perhaps." He paused. "She fell in love with Richard. It was so obvious, too. Even Aurora commented on it."

"Richard was your bookkeeper?"

"Yes. Except Sarah couldn't make up her mind about marrying him, even though Richard loved her right back. You see, Sarah enjoyed living in my house and romanticized about the kind of lifestyle I led. She saw me rubbing elbows with the elite. She saw the parties, the dinners, the dancing—or at least she thought she did."

Renna nearly groaned. So what she had suspected was true; Mr. Blackeyes was a man among the high-society echelons. "And Richard?"

"Richard wanted to be a farmer."

Renna frowned. "But I thought he was a bookkeeper."

"He was. . .or is. . .I'm not sure; however, his ambition was to take over his father's farm. To work outdoors." Mr. Blackeyes chuckled. "He readily volunteered for any and every errand that involved leaving my store—"

"A store! You remember!" Renna was delighted.

Surprise shone on the man's face. "I own a store, yes, and my new shipping business."

"Ah," she said, smiling, "so you are the pirate I suspected all along." They shared a laugh.

Johanna and Wendall came strolling back to the picnic site, and Renna leapt up.

"Mother! Father! Mr. Blackeyes has just remembered that he owns a store and a shipping business! Isn't that wonderful?"

"I should say it is," Wendall remarked, eyeing the man a little closer now. "You've mentioned the shipping business, but a store? What kind of a store?"

Mr. Blackeyes shrugged. "I don't know. I wish I remembered more."

"It'll come," Johanna assured him. "It's coming already."

At that moment, a man approached them. Wendall looked up and grinned broadly. "Matthew! Matthew Benchley! What are you doing here?"

Renna groaned inwardly. So she would have to meet Mr. Benchley after all.

"I was taking an afternoon stroll," he said, "and I spotted you here, Wendall. This must be your beautiful wife," Benchley remarked, looking at Johanna.

"Yes, it is. Johanna, dear, this is my newest associate, Matthew Benchley."

Johanna smiled demurely. "Nice to meet you, Mr. Benchley."

Wendall cleared his throat and made the appropriate introductions. "And this is my daughter, Renna."

"Ah, yes, you've spoken of Renna to me before." He took her hand and pressed a kiss on her fingers, causing Renna to pull away at once. She hadn't expected such ardor—and from a stranger yet!

But then she looked up into Matthew Benchley's face and beheld his cold, calculating stare. Icy eyes, like the blue-gray color of Lake Michigan during the winter months, and a little chill passed through her.

"And this is the man I told you about. We know him only as Mr. Blackeyes," Wendall continued. "The poor fellow is recovering from a boating accident."

Benchley stuck out his hand. "Pleasure to meet you."

"Thank you." Mr. Blackeyes reached out in the direction of Benchley's voice, but it was Benchley who had to make the hand shake.

"Injury to your eyes I take it? They're bandaged securely."

"Yes."

An uncomfortable silence ensued, and Renna found herself wishing Matthew Benchley would continue his stroll. He had a presence that caused her to feel disquieted, and she couldn't figure out why. It was different from the unnerving affect Mr. Blackeyes had on her, even though Matthew Benchley was a handsome man in his own right. Little wonder Abigail Hoffmann found him so "charming."

"Would you care to join us, Matt?" Wendall asked, much to Renna's dismay.

"Yes, thank you."

Benchley sat down beside Renna on the picnic blanket, forcing her to move closer to Mr. Blackeyes. It was either that or rub elbows with Benchley, and Renna thought she much preferred a pirate to him!

"Our friend, here, was just remembering that he has a store and a shipping business," Wendall said.

"Is that so?" Benchley asked, looking interested. "And what is the name of your shipping business?"

"I—I don't know."

"Mr. Blackeyes has amnesia as well as being blind," Wendall informed him. "Both infirmities were incurred in that tragic boating accident I just mentioned."

"What a shame," Benchley drawled in the way that caused Renna to wonder over his sincerity.

"Yes, but his memory is returning, little by little," Johanna put in.

Wendall nodded. "Soon our Mr. Blackeyes here will remember everything, I'm sure."

"You're a very fortunate man, Mr.—Mr. Blackeyes," Benchley replied. Then he looked over at Renna, and suddenly she felt like a cold, bitter wind had just blown off the lake.

She shivered.

Chapter 7

The darkness, the stony darkness. It seemed to oppress him more in this hospital at night, when Renna wasn't around. She and her family were like a soothing sun shower—like the one he'd felt on his face this afternoon in the park. It had been something of a holiday for him. . .at least until Matthew Benchley appeared. After that, he sensed the atmosphere change.

Matthew Benchley. Renna didn't seem to like him one bit. After Benchley had joined their picnic, she had moved away from Benchley and closer to him. He had felt her tense on more than one occasion, and the sudden urge to protect her rose up within him. That urge surprised him. He'd never felt that way before.

Benchley. The name was familiar, but he couldn't place it.

Strange, he mused, as the darkness overcame him and he slept.

The calendar finally read "September," and Renna sighed happily as she walked to work. Fall was her favorite time of year. The leaves would soon turn shades of orange and yellow and a flaming red. Standing on a hill in front of the hospital now, Renna turned and looked out over the treetops toward Lake Michigan. She was reminded that when the Almighty Creator made something, He did it perfectly.

On that thought, she entered the hospital and set to work.

In her ward, she fed those patients who were able to eat, changed bedding, and shaved men's beards. Mr. Blackeyes was one of them.

"Are we alone, Renna?" he whispered.

Razor in hand, she paused to consider the question. "We're as alone as we can be in a room filled with sick people."

He grinned. "They're all unconscious, I hope."

Renna rolled her eyes. "Only three unconscious patients today. Two are asleep, and one is waiting for a bath."

"I just don't want to be overheard."

"Speak softly then. . .and please call me Nurse Fields here at the hospital."

"Aye, aye," he replied with a teasing smile.

Ignoring his sarcasm, she began to shave his whiskered cheeks. "Tell me about Matthew Benchley."

Again, Renna had to pause. "I don't know much."

"Then tell me what you know. I'm curious."

"Well, he's a new associate at the Chamber of Commerce and works with my father. He's been there for about a month now."

"What does he look like?"

"He's got light brown hair and. . ." Renna recalled his iceberg eyes and wondered if she should disclose her thoughts. *No,* she decided, *best to remain objective.* "He's got blue-gray eyes and a very straight nose. Fairly even teeth, though he doesn't smile much. When he does, it's rather lopsided." *Cynical,* is what she wanted to say, but she held her tongue. "And he reminds me of those men from the West—opportunity seekers. I met plenty of them during the war."

"Opportunity seekers, huh?" Mr. Blackeyes grinned, and Renna had to warn him to hold still. He kept talking anyway. "Do you mean to say that Matthew Benchley appears to be the sort who would take advantage of an unsuspecting young lady in order to seize an opportunity?"

"Oh, stop teasing me."

Mr. Blackeyes chuckled. "I sensed you didn't like him, Renna."

"Nurse Fields," she corrected him. She sighed and sat back. "All right. I admit it. You're correct. There's just something about him that gives me the creeps."

"Even more than I do—a pirate?"

Renna was glad her patient couldn't see the sudden smile on her face. "Believe it or not. . .yes!"

She finished shaving and put the razor and wash bin away. Then she allowed Mr. Blackeyes to get out of bed and stretch so she could straighten the linens. The night nurse had taken pity on him and rummaged through a box of donations, producing tan-colored trousers and a wrinkled white shirt. But even wearing those rumpled clothes, he was still a handsome man.

Then quite unexpectedly, Mr. Blackeyes asked, "What do you look like, Renna—I mean, Nurse Fields?"

"Me?" Instantly, her hand went to her cheek, the one marred by the birthmark. "I—I'm just regular-looking, I guess. Nothing special, and certainly not anything like the ladies with whom you're accustomed to socializing."

Mr. Blackeyes acted as though he hadn't heard her. "Could I. . .could I feel what you look like, Renna?"

Her mouth suddenly went dry at the thought of him touching her.

"Please," he persisted, "I—I just want to have an image of you in my mind—that is, I do already, but I'm wondering if it's accurate."

"Mr. Blackeyes, I don't think—"

Before she could say another word, he stepped forward and touched her hair. Most of it was covered by her stiff, white nurse's cap. "What color is it?" he asked, rubbing a few strands between his thumb and forefinger.

Renna could only stand statue still. She'd never had a man touch her hair like this before. "Reddish-brown."

"Curly?"

"Yes."

"I can tell by its texture." His hands moved to her face. "What color are your eyes?"

"Hazel," she squeaked.

His thumbs rubbed over her brows, then down her cheeks. "Your skin is so soft. . .are you fair-skinned? With a smattering of freckles, perhaps?"

"Yes."

"Most redheads are—and I speak of both males and females."

Renna lifted a brow and immediately found her voice again. "Thank you for clarifying that, Mr. Pirate Blackeyes."

He laughed and touched her nose. "Pert, just like your personality."

Renna couldn't help but smile now. Her father liked to lovingly tease her that way, too. A pert little nose on a pert little girl.

Mr. Blackeyes touched her mouth, then, and one finger lingered on her bottom lip for a long moment. Renna thought he seemed wistful and she wondered why, so inexperienced was she with affairs of the heart. However, it wasn't long until she realized that he might want to kiss her. A little frightened by the thought, Renna brought her head back, and

Mr. Blackeyes moved his hands down to her chin and neck.

"You're not very tall," he assessed accurately. His hands went to her shoulders. "And you're slight of build." He gripped her by her upper arms. "But strong for a woman."

"All right, that's quite enough," Renna said, stepping back out of his grasp. "There is nothing more for you to feel, so get back into bed."

He smiled and, much to her surprise, complied without a single complaint. He surprised her further by saying, "I knew you were beautiful."

Renna swallowed hard. She wasn't beautiful. Not at all. She had an ugly purple birthmark on her face that made men gawk and stare. Why, she'd even caught Matthew Benchley gazing at it with an expression of regret. He might as well have said, "I might have been attracted to you if it weren't for that thing on your face. Doesn't it come off?" Of course, Renna was actually glad that Mr. Benchley wasn't attracted to her. But that's what Mr. Blackeyes would say once he regained his sight. He would look at her face in horror, and his illusion of her would be shattered.

I should tell him, Renna thought. *I should tell him that I'm not what he has imagined.* However, she just couldn't. Somehow, somewhere, she'd formed her own illusions—that of an old maid becoming a new bride— marrying a pirate.

Oh, Lord, Renna whispered in silent prayer, *this has never happened to me before, and I've taken care of hundreds of men. Perhaps I am too emotionally involved in Mr. Blackeyes' case; however, I can't help but wish that—*

Renna halted her thoughts, remembering what Nurse Ruthledge once said. "If wishes were horses, we'd all take a ride. In other words, Nurse Fields, wishing is a waste of one's energy!"

Renna decided Nurse Ruthledge was probably right.

With renewed energy for her position, she finished up her day, pausing to say good night to all her patients before she left the hospital. Mr. Blackeyes was one of many who seemed disappointed.

"You're leaving already?"

"I've been here for twelve hours, and I'm tuckered out."

He smiled warmly. "Go home and get some sleep, then. You deserve it."

"Thank you. And don't forget, my father is coming to visit you tonight. He's been doing a bit of investigating and has gotten together a list of the names of persons presumed drowned in Lake Michigan from here all the way north to Green Bay, Wisconsin."

"Good. That may help jar my memory loose."

"And Dr. Hamilton may be by to see you, too," Renna added. "He had a surgery to perform today, so he didn't make his rounds."

Mr. Blackeyes chuckled. "I had better get an appointment book."

Renna grinned at the quip before wishing him a good night. Then she left for home.

The weeks passed swiftly, giving way to the cool fall air and autumn colors. Mr. Blackeyes grew continually stronger and less tolerant of his convalescing. He still could not see and remembered little else except for sketchy details, much to his frustration. Neither did Wendall's list of names help his memory to return. So, in an effort to cheer him up, Renna obtained Dr. Hamilton's permission to take Mr. Blackeyes for a walk outside every day for an hour, except when it rained. And, as long as she had his doctor's consent, Nurse Thatcher and Nurse Ruthledge couldn't say a word about their daily walks.

Renna secretly enjoyed being out of the hospital in the middle of the day. The fresh air revitalized her so that she finished out the day with more energy than she realized she possessed. And the company. . . well, Renna found her pirate to be quite charming, amusing, and, when their conversations turned more serious, he was a confidant. Like this afternoon. . .he listened patiently while Renna fretted aloud about this evening's mandatory dinner party.

"Mother has already put it off for a month, and my father always entertains his new associates. It just wouldn't be proper if we didn't invite Matthew Benchley over for dinner. It's just that I don't want to be there when he comes. My mother, bless her heart, is something of a matchmaker."

Mr. Blackeyes chuckled. "Ah, the real reason finally comes out. I had been wondering why this was such a big deal. Now I understand."

Renna blushed, glad that Mr. Blackeyes couldn't see. "Yes, well, when I fall in love, it'll be a man of my own choosing." Renna tried not to think that her heart might have already made its own decision.

"Oh, dear, you sound like those women suffragettes," Mr. Blackeyes stated on a dramatic note.

"Well, I don't mean to," she replied, uncomfortable with the association. "It's just that I don't want to be forced into a relationship."

Mr. Blackeyes seemed to ponder the statement. Finally, he said, "I believe that you're putting undue pressure on yourself. I was in several matchmaking situations last summer. Men, as you know, aren't required to mourn like women—especially if they have children, as I do. 'Get them remarried quickly' seems to be the general consensus, and soon after Louisa's death, my mother was plotting and planning romance after romance for me. . .that's how I met Elise. Yet, through it all, my attitude was lackadaisical at best. I never felt forced into any relationship in spite of my forced circumstances."

Renna listened intently, wondering if Mr. Blackeyes was right. Perhaps she was putting undue pressure on herself. After all, her father would hardly force her to marry—he was merely trying to encourage her along those lines.

Moments later, she smiled, realizing that Mr. Blackeyes had just recalled another little piece of his past.

"So you never fell in love with any of the beautiful women you were forced to escort?" Renna ventured, half teasing, half curious.

"Never," came his reply. "And many of those women weren't beautiful, either."

"Oh. . ." The remark caused Renna to be reminded of her birthmark. Sometimes when she was with Mr. Blackeyes, she actually forgot it was there. He treated her like a woman—like a beautiful woman. But what would he think of her if he ever saw it?

"Besides," he continued, "love is as real as the fairy tales all those governesses used to read to my children. At least romantic love anyway. I am, however, convinced of another love. . .the kind a father has for his children."

"You're speaking of yourself?"

Mr. Blackeyes nodded. "And of God's love."

Renna smiled broadly. She delighted every time Mr. Blackeyes made a spiritual reference. He was growing in Christ, learning more of God's ways as her father continued to read to him from the Bible.

"You know, Mr. Blackeyes, you're not half the pirate you used to be," Renna remarked with a little laugh.

A wry grin pulled at his mouth. "Thank you. . .I think."

That night, Renna dressed carefully for the "mandatory" dinner party. She had decided that Mr. Blackeyes was right and resolved that she would not be "forced" into a relationship with Mr. Benchley. She would, however, try to look her best and be polite to him for her parents' sake.

Examining herself in the mirror, Renna surveyed her birthmark. She tried to imagine what she'd look like without it and decided she'd be beautiful if not for that purplish triangle. Then she found herself dreaming of looking differently, feeling differently. Why, she'd be a whole 'nother person if it weren't for this ugly thing!

"Stop it, Renna," she chided her reflection. "This is the way God made you, and you're just going to have to learn to live with yourself."

Lifting a determined chin, Renna left her bedroom for the parlor downstairs, where Mr. Benchley was already comfortably seated.

"Well, well, Renna," her father welcomed her, "I'm glad you finally made it." Turning to Matthew Benchley, he added, "Renna is a nurse at the hospital and works much too hard. She finally managed an evening off."

Benchley nodded and stood politely. "Miss Fields, I am honored by your presence."

She gave him a tight smile. The man seemed pretentious to her, although her father was a good judge of character. Why didn't he see through Matthew Benchley—unless, of course, there was nothing there to see?

Just then Johanna Fields entered the room. She smiled approvingly at Renna. "Would you like an iced tea, dear?"

"No, Mother, but thank you." Renna sat down in the armchair across from her father. Johanna took the place beside him on the settee.

"How is Mr. Blackeyes today?" Johanna inquired.

Renna couldn't help a grin. "He's feeling better. The daily walks have improved his spirits greatly. Dr. Hamilton says he's well enough to leave the hospital. He says Mr. Blackeyes is taking up time and care that should be spent on those sicker than he. Unfortunately, Mr. Blackeyes has no money, nowhere to stay."

"What about family?" Benchley interjected, as though such a trifle thing had been overlooked.

"Mr. Blackeyes can't remember who he is and to which family he belongs," Wendall explained patiently.

"Dr. Hamilton is looking for a temporary home for Mr. Blackeyes," Renna added. "I requested a Christian home, but Dr. Hamilton said that he's too busy to consider religious beliefs. If he finds temporary housing for Mr. Blackeyes, he'll take it."

Wendall got a troubled look on his face, and it stayed there until Johanna announced that dinner was served. Renna took her place across from Matthew Benchley, and her parents were seated at each end of the tastefully decorated dining room table. When all were at their places, Wendall prayed over the food and they began to eat. Roast turkey and all its trimmings were the sumptuous fare tonight, and passing dish after dish, Renna was reminded of a Thanksgiving Day feast, only one of smaller proportions. The holiday was but a month away, and she smiled to herself, thinking of seeing the faces of her darling nieces and nephews. . . .

"Renna, did you hear what I said?" her father asked, bringing Renna to the present.

Smiling, she shook her head. "I'm sorry, Father. I must have been daydreaming. What did you say?"

"I said, I've figured out the situation with Mr. Blackeyes."

"Do tell, Wendall," Benchley said, looking interested.

"Why, Mr. Blackeyes can live with us!"

"What?" Renna shook her head. "No, that's not possible. Mr. Blackeyes is my patient. I can't take home every patient—"

"But Mr. Blackeyes is a—a *special* patient. We prayed for him as a family, and now we're deeply involved in his discipleship."

"I wouldn't mind it," said Johanna, "except what would I do with him while you and Renna are at work?"

Wendall smiled. "I'll take Mr. Blackeyes with me to the Chamber of Commerce."

"Hmm, the idea does have possibilities," Benchley concurred. "But what on earth can a blind man do at the Chamber of Commerce, Wendall?"

"I don't know," he replied with a slight frown, "but I'll think of something. And I believe that if Mr. Blackeyes were in such an en-vironment as the one we work in, he may get his memory back sooner. As I've said all along, I'm sure I've seen this man before."

"But you can't remember where?"

"No, and it's most frustrating, too."

"Renna, dear," Johanna said, changing the subject, "isn't the weather tonight perfect for a buggy ride? Perhaps Mr. Benchley would like to go. . . ." She looked at him. "Perhaps after dinner?"

Renna nearly choked on her mashed potatoes, while Benchley gave her mother a shrug. "Certainly. A buggy ride sounds pleasant enough."

"Renna?"

Suddenly remembering her promise to herself about not being "forced" into anything, she shook her head. "Thank you, but I'm not interested in a buggy ride tonight, Mother. And it was good of Mr. Benchley to agree to take me."

He merely smiled. "I'm still more of a stranger than an acquaintance, aren't I? Well, I don't mind taking a few minutes now to introduce myself."

"Oh, that would be nice," Johanna said, giving Renna a mild look of warning. "Where are you originally from?"

"Michigan, actually. I grew up in a small harbor town right on Lake Michigan. My parents died when my brother and I were but boys, so we were raised by a wealthy aunt and uncle." Benchley's ice-blue eyes bore into Renna's, causing her to look down at her dinner plate. "My uncle Ralph, now deceased, sent my brother and me to West Point, and we both held commanding positions during the war."

"Really? Did you see any action?" Wendall ventured.

Benchley nodded. "I was a blockade runner—" He suddenly stopped and sputtered. "That is to say, my brother was a blockade runner for the Confederacy. Our loyalties were divided at West Point. I sided with the Union while my brother supported the South."

"Brother against brother." Wendall shook his head sadly. "Very common. I'm glad the war is over."

"It's not over for everyone," Benchley replied in a strained voice.

"Yes, I suppose that's true enough," Johanna said. "My son served with an Illinois brigade but returned to us last Christmas unharmed. Many families aren't as blessed."

"Well, neither my brother nor I got wounded," Benchley said. "However, we'll never see eye-to-eye. We couldn't agree as children, as graduates of West Point, and now as businessmen." He suddenly seemed very far away. "But that shipping company will be mine regardless of my brother's lack of interest." He looked at Wendall, who was now wearing a curious frown. "My brother and I inherited a shipping company—from my late uncle."

"I see. . . ."

"Didn't you know that? It's worth a fortune!"

"Really?"

Benchley kept on talking about himself and his riches for a good hour. It was a subject he seemed to never tire of—even though his listeners did. And, finally, Renna excused herself and retired to her bedroom, glad that Matthew Benchley was so absorbed in himself that he forgot all about buggy rides. . .and her.

Chapter 8

"How was the dinner party last night, Renna?" Mr. Blackeyes asked as they left the hospital for their daily walk.

Renna smiled, her arm looped through his so she could guide him easily. "Actually, it wasn't bad at all, though Mr. Benchley is not someone with whom I enjoy conversing. He's much too narcissistic for my tastes, and he relishes his war memories, whereas I would rather forget mine."

Mr. Blackeyes chuckled. "Aurora—that was my mother—maintained that all men are narcissists and, as for the war, there is a kind of pride many of us men acquired while serving our country—a patriotic pride."

"Hmm, well, I dare say that last night Mr. Benchley's pride was in himself and nothing patriotic about it. But I won't complain since I was relieved that his pride caused him to forget he'd agreed to take me for a buggy ride after dinner as my mother had suggested."

"You were relieved, Renna?" Mr. Blackeyes asked softly.

"Yes, I was."

He paused momentarily. "I'm glad."

Renna looked up at him. "You are?" She held her breath, unsure if she wanted to know why, and yet she didn't think she could bear to not know.

But Mr. Blackeyes was a savvy pirate and obviously wasn't about to get sentimental here in the streets of Chicago. "The night air isn't good for ladies, Renna," he said with a handsome grin, "and whatever would I do if you caught a chill and couldn't take me for my daily walks?"

"I ought to leave you here in the middle of the street," she replied tartly.

He laughed heartily. "Yes, I suppose you should."

And that was all he said. He didn't even try to explain himself, although Renna found herself wishing he would. . .sort of. On one hand, she dreamed of hearing words of love from this man; however, there was still part of Renna that held her heart in check. It was that lifelong

209

insecurity that haunted her—and with good reason. As soon as Mr. Blackeyes regained his memory and sight, he'd go back to the life to which he was accustomed and forget all about the lowly nurse with the purple birthmark on her cheek.

And it's best he did, too, she decided. *I certainly wouldn't want to share his high-society lifestyle.*

Such a myriad of emotions. Renna marveled at them. Her feelings swung right and then left like the pendulum on the grandfather clock in her father's study.

"I have offended you, haven't I?" Mr. Blackeyes said after they'd returned to the sick room.

"Not at all," Renna replied.

"You've been so quiet."

"Just thinking."

"About what?"

Renna paused, unwilling to share her heart here at the hospital if she ever shared it at all. She tried to inflect a teasing note in her reply. "None of your business, Mr. Pirate Blackeyes. Now, rest, because Dr. Hamilton will be here shortly to recheck your eyesight."

"Aye, Captain." He grinned sardonically. "I feel like I'm back in the military." His expression suddenly changed to one of seriousness. "Captain," he repeated. "Captain. . .I believe that was my title. Captain."

Renna smiled. "Captain Pirate Blackeyes, huh?"

He didn't reply so lost was he in his sudden reverie.

The wind whipped off the dark Mississippi River with the onset of a storm. He remembered looking across the water for some of his men who had gone ahead in rafts to cut away the trees obstructing their ship's path. The gunner was headed toward Vicksburg to aid Grant in his mission to take the Confederate citadel on the Mississippi. He would see that they got there, too, right after this new canal was completed. The shortcut would open into a system of bayous that would take his ship to a secret landing just below the Vicksburg batteries.

"Captain, do you think they'll get back before the storm?"

He turned and regarded the young officer standing beside him. "I'm sure they will."

"I heard there's snakes hanging from the branches of them trees they're cutting down—poisonous snakes, sir."

He recalled smiling at the young man and thinking that snakes were the least of their worries. They were days away from facing Confederate gunfire. But if they could take Vicksburg, the Mississippi River would be completely open to Federal military. It was a battle they had to win.

"And we won," he murmured. "But I got wounded. . .my shoulder. . ."

"What was that, Mr. Blackeyes?"

The past blended into the present at the sound of Renna's sweet voice. "We won the battle at Vicksburg. I was remembering. . . ."

"How wonderful!" he heard her exclaim with genuine delight. "Little by little your past is coming back to you."

"I was a captain on a Federal gunboat."

"On the Mississippi. Isn't that what you had once told me?"

"Yes. But I wish I could remember my last name. It's right there, on the edge of my memory. . . ."

"It'll come, Mr. Blackeyes—or should I say Captain Blackeyes?"

He grinned at the smile in Renna's voice. Then her hand gently touched his shoulder, generating a warmth that spread through his whole body. He had always sensed her care for him but noticed lately that other male patients didn't get quite the same attention he got, and he was grateful for the special favor. Even more than grateful. If he believed in falling in love with a woman, he was sure he'd fallen in love with Renna—sight unseen. He didn't have to see her to know what a beautiful person she was. But, of course, he didn't believe in that sort of love—fairy tale love.

"Dr. Hamilton has arrived," Renna told him softly. He felt her breath on his cheek as she helped him sit up on the edge of the hospital bed. He was tempted to put his arm around Renna's waist and pull her close. She was right there, innocently pressing against his arm as she worked to remove the bandages from his eyes.

He sighed.

"I'm almost done," she said, misinterpreting a sigh of regret for one of impatience. "There. Now I'll clean the salve from your eyes."

He nodded, trying to ignore the desire in his heart, something new for him. He remembered that much. Before his accident and his conversion to Christ, he wouldn't have hesitated to take advantage of a woman who stirred him the way Renna did. On the other hand, he couldn't ever recall meeting a woman like Renna Fields.

"Thank you," he said simply, unable to express the feelings he had for her. . .whatever they were, whatever their names.

"You're entirely welcome, Captain Blackeyes," she replied tartly, causing him to smile again.

Moments later, Dr. Hamilton joined them. "All right, man, look around. Tell me if you can see anything."

He blinked. Once. Twice. There was light. Everything was a blur, but there was light. He turned his head and saw shapes and outlines, though not very clearly.

And then he saw the shape of the woman who had to be Renna. He could make out her white cap, her dress, but the details of her face wouldn't come into focus.

"I can see," he said, looking right at Renna, trying to force his eyes to focus. Then he sighed. "But I can't make out details, I'm afraid." He turned to Dr. Hamilton and smiled. "You've got bushy whiskers and gray hair. . .but I can't see your facial features clearly."

He heard Renna sigh. Was that disappointment? Or relief? Confused, he turned her way, studying her and trying again to blink her into focus.

Dr. Hamilton chuckled merrily. "I had my doubts, but now I'm certain your sight will be returning soon. Good job, Nurse Fields. I might be inclined to believe in miracles after all."

"I'm happy to hear that, Doctor." However, something in Renna's voice didn't sound happy at all.

"Well, carry on, Nurse Fields," the good doctor said. "As for you, Mr. Blackeyes, I'm told you'll be leaving the hospital soon."

"I will?"

"Yes. Another stroke of luck for you—or a miracle, whichever way you choose to look at it. The Fields family has offered to take you in until you've completely recovered—or until you've at least recovered your memory. And what better family than one belonging to such a devoted nurse? You'll be in excellent care. Wendall Fields assured me of that, and knowing Nurse Fields, I'm convinced of it."

"I am indeed a fortunate man," he said, looking in Renna's direction. But she was gone.

Several days later, Wendall drove his buggy for home with "Captain Blackeyes" in tow. Upon finding out about his commanding position in the war, Wendall had begun to refer to him as "Captain," as did Renna.

"Beautiful day," Wendall remarked.

Looking through the dark eyeglasses he'd been given, the captain nodded. "I can see how bright the sunshine is, and I feel its rays on my face, but everything else is still such a blur."

"Well, at least you can make out the shapes of things, people, horses, carriages, and such."

"I could make out the pointy nose on Nurse Hatchet this morning," he said dryly.

Wendall stifled a chuckle. "Now, now, Renna would have our hides if she caught us snickering over Nurse Hatchet's pointy nose. However, I will agree that the woman's manner this morning was unkind."

"She's always that way. More's the reason I preferred to be in Renna's care." He grew pensive, wondering over the change in Renna lately. Finally, he decided to ask. "Is Renna unhappy that I'm coming to stay with you?"

Wendall paused in thought. "Um, no, she's not *unhappy* about it."

"She's been very distant lately."

"Yes, I've noticed."

He waited for an explanation and, when none came, he pressed further. "I don't have to have my sight back to see there's something amiss between Renna and me. Did I offend her?"

"No, no, it's not you at all, Captain. It's Renna." Again he paused momentarily. "Listen, I'm going to be honest with you. You deserve that much and, since you're coming to live in our home for a while, I think it's best you should know. But please don't tell Renna I said anything."

"You've got my word, and from what I can recall, it's honorable."

Wendall nodded. "Very good. The problem is Renna is a very self-conscious and insecure young woman when it comes to the birthmark on her cheek."

"Birthmark?"

"You haven't seen it?"

"No. Facial features are still a blur."

"Hmm, well, Renna thought you hadn't seen it yet. But she's taking precautions for when you do. She's hardening that tough outer shell of hers because she's afraid to be hurt. You see, she is certain that you will decide she's an ugly toad of a woman once you see it."

"An ugly toad of a woman?" He hung his head back and laughed. "Wendall, your daughter would have to really be a toad before I thought she was ugly and, even at that, Renna would be beautiful in my eyes."

Wendall snorted out a chuckle. "I'm glad to hear that."

"But now I'm curious. What does her birthmark look like?"

"It looks like a violet triangle that goes from her jawline to her ear to her nose and back. But in all honesty, a person doesn't even notice it after a while—after the initial surprise wears off. In fact, Matthew Benchley, my associate, thinks highly enough of Renna to want to court her."

"Really?" For some reason, the idea troubled the captain greatly. The man's last name, Benchley, was still so familiar, yet he still couldn't place it. . . .

"Yes, Matt is looking for a wife," Wendall continued. "He feels being a bachelor holds something of a stigma in the business world. Matt says being unmarried makes him seem irresponsible, and he wants bankers to think his business ideas are worthwhile ventures."

"Hmm. . .and have you given your permission?"

"I would if Renna wanted me to. Matt would be a good provider, and I know Renna would like to have children someday. But, unfortunately, she doesn't like Matt well enough for a courtship. In fact, she doesn't like Matt at all." Wendall frowned. "But if she could only see him at work. He's so different. I can't figure it out!"

"Wendall, your daughter doesn't like Matthew Benchley period."

"Yes, well, I've told Renna that love might come later and she could build a good life with Matthew Benchley. He's got money—"

"Money isn't everything, Wendall. I'm learning that the hard way."

"How well I know that. But it's worth something—"

"But not enough to enter into a loveless marriage. My marriage was devoid of love, and I was miserable."

Wendall grew quiet as the horses clip-clopped down the streets.

"I'm an opinionated pirate, aren't I?" the captain said, chuckling lightly. "I hope I haven't offended you with my straightforwardness."

"No, you haven't offended me. In fact, I'll consider what you've said."

The captain couldn't help a smile. "Wendall, your daughter seems very capable of falling in love with the right man."

The remark was left hanging between them until they reached the Fieldses' home, and suddenly Captain Pirate Blackeyes was wishing Renna would fall in love with him. *Except I don't believe in falling in love,* he reminded himself sternly before Wendall helped him up to the porch.

Johanna Fields was there to greet him. "We're pleased to have you staying with us, Captain." She waved both men into the house. "Dinner will be in about two hours, and Renna has promised me that she'll make it home in time. So, if you'd like to rest, Wendall will show you to your room."

"Thank you."

"This way, my friend," Wendall said, leading the captain by his right elbow. "We had a large pantry off the kitchen that I converted into a bedroom for you. I thought it would be better if you were downstairs since your sight is impaired. Wouldn't want you falling down the staircase, you know."

"I appreciate your thoughtfulness."

Through the wide kitchen where wonderful smells lingered in the air, they made a right turn.

"Here we are. If you need anything, I'll be in my study, which is back through the kitchen and to the left before you reach the front door."

Nodding his thanks, the captain stretched out on the soft bed and thanked God he was no longer in that wretched hospital sick room! The only good thing about it had been Renna.

He thought about her, her sweet voice, her gentle touch, and the idea of another man courting her suddenly infuriated him. *If I don't believe in falling in love,* he mused, *then what are these emotions I'm feeling?*

He wanted to know—needed to know; however, one thing seemed sure. Without Renna, he would never find out. He would just have to do something—anything—to close the distance between them that she had created.

Renna arrived home a half hour late for dinner. "Where's our new houseguest?"

Her father stood, looking grave. "He wants to speak with you. Apparently leaving the hospital was something of a strain and. . .well, he's totally blind again."

"Oh, no!" Remorse flooded her being. "But he was doing so well."

"Why don't you go talk to him?"

Nodding, Renna walked through the kitchen and knocked on the door to the captain's bedroom.

"Come in."

She entered and found him sitting up in bed. He was fully dressed in the charity garb he'd received from the hospital, and over his eyes he wore his dark glasses.

"I understand you've had a setback," she said, coming to stand beside the bed, the door open behind her.

"Yes, and it's most discouraging."

"I'm so sorry."

He lifted his right hand in a helpless manner, and compassion ruled Renna's heart. She took his hand.

"Many times these things are only temporary," she told him, sitting on the bed next to him.

The captain had to force himself not to grin. Though he couldn't see her expression clearly, he sensed her genuine concern. She was holding his hand. He had been successful. The chasm between them was gone.

"Have you eaten your dinner?" she asked.

"No, I was waiting for you."

For the very first time, he saw her smile. The sight caused his heart to beat a little faster.

"Well, then, I would be happy to escort you to the dinner table, Captain Pirate Blackeyes."

He grinned. "I would be honored, madam."

Chapter 9

The captain sat in the cozy parlor, a fire blazing in the hearth. He waited patiently for the Fields family to ready themselves for dinner. A week had gone by since he first arrived, and he had regained much of his eyesight, though he kept it a secret from Renna and her family. He was certain that as long as he remained blind, Renna would remain attentive. However, it grew increasingly hard to continue his charade. Sometimes he had to close his eyes behind the dark spectacles he wore so he couldn't see the step in front of him, or know what was on the plate before him at the supper table.

But Renna was always there to help him, and he conceded to her coddling. He once needed it and looked forward to it; however, he now chafed beneath it, though he knew it was necessary if he was to continue the plan that seemed to be working better than he ever dreamed.

Renna was in love with him. He was sure of it. She looked up at him so adoringly, and it pulled at his heart in the most peculiar way. But he pretended he couldn't see. Except he did. Clearly. He had seen an ardent expression cross her lovely features on more than one occasion—and, yes, they were lovely features. He hardly noticed that birthmark at all, and the captain wondered over Renna's insecurities about it. She was such a beautiful person. Couldn't she see that? And, if he believed in falling in love, he would have to say he was in love with her, too. But, of course, that didn't happen in the real world. Something would change to prove his love-is-only-in-the-fairy-tales theory correct. He would just bide his time and guard his cynical heart.

"There you are," Renna said, entering the parlor. She wore a deep green corduroy dress with a fitted bodice and flaring skirt.

The captain rose from his chair politely, thinking the color of Renna's dress suited her features perfectly, her hazel eyes and wavy auburn hair. It was on the tip of his tongue to compliment her; however, he reminded himself that blind men can't see beautiful women.

"I see you didn't have any trouble dressing for dinner tonight," Renna remarked. "Even your tie is perfectly straight. And your hair. . ." She smiled. "You must be getting accustomed to the feel of things."

The captain cleared his throat. "Yes, I suppose I am." Next time, he would have to leave his tie a bit crooked. However, the cut of these clothes left something to be desired, and he longed for a visit to his tailor!

A knock sounded at the front door, and Renna bit her bottom lip as an expression of apprehension washed over her face. "Oh, dear, I suppose that's Mr. Benchley."

The captain smiled sympathetically, wondering why Wendall persisted in inviting Benchley over, insisting Renna be friendly to the man. Benchley behaved like a gloating buffoon! Men of real wealth and dignity didn't flaunt it, which meant Benchley was either new to having money or he was all talk. And Wendall was correct when he said Benchley behaved quite different at the Chamber of Commerce. Mild mannered and friendly. The captain had witnessed it himself. Perhaps the change in him was simply due to the fact that he was trying to impress Renna.

She excused herself and answered the door. "Come in, Mr. Benchley. May I take your coat?"

"Yes, thank you. And may I say that you look especially lovely this evening."

The captain rolled his eyes behind the dark glasses.

"Why, thank you," Renna replied, showing him into the parlor.

"Captain Whoever-you-are," Benchley said pompously. He then extended his hand. But since he was supposed to be blind, the captain didn't acknowledge the greeting thrust in his face. Eventually, Benchley dropped his arm.

"Please sit down," Renna invited, taking the chair closest to the captain. "I trust you had a good day today, Mr. Benchley."

"Quite good," he said with a slight frown in the captain's direction. But, at Renna, he smiled broadly. "Any day is a good one when money is earned and invested wisely. A new shipment came in today from China—"

"Japan," the captain corrected him.

"Oh, yes. . .Japan. Anyway, we were busy in our department. Working closely with the merchants made me long for the day when I'll be in charge of my own shipping company—mine and my brother's, that is."

The captain had heard Benchley mention this shipping company several times now, and his interest was piqued. However, until this moment, he hadn't had the chance to ask about it. "May I ask what the name of your shipping company is and where it's based?"

Benchley smiled menacingly. "It's Kingsley Shipping, based in Michigan. It belonged to my Uncle Ralph Kingsley," he said emphatically, "who willed it to my brother and me—and my aunt, Elise Kingsley, of course. It supported her while she was alive; however, she was killed this past August in a boating accident. And what a coincidence, huh, Captain? You were injured in a boating accident, too."

The captain's heart beat wildly as he realized Benchley was speaking of the same woman he knew—Elise Kingsley. . .yes, of course, that was her last name. He had just purchased her shipping company—the very one Benchley spoke of!

Sitting back in his chair, the captain asked as calmly as possible, "The names of your aunt's friends. . .do you know them?"

Renna gasped quietly, and he knew she suddenly understood why he asked. But he leaned over and placed a hand upon hers, praying she wouldn't reveal anything to Benchley. Not to him. Not now, though it was obvious that Benchley knew very well who he was.

"Well, let's see. . ." Benchley deliberately took his time searching his memory. "The only one I know who drowned was my aunt Elise's love interest, Kyle Sinclair—"

That's me! That's my name! I am Captain Kyle Sinclair! From out of the corner of his dark glasses he could see Renna's face paling slightly beneath the room's lamplight. He'd have to speak to her later.

"Ah, yes, Captain Sinclair. . . ," Benchley was saying. "I never met the man, but he was a blackheart. He wooed and cooed Aunt Elise until she lost her senses. Then he convinced her to sell our shipping company to him. She did. She was as smitten as a schoolgirl, and there was no reasoning with her. I tried on many occasions."

Renna felt queasy as the captain lifted his hand from hers and sat back in his chair once more. The captain most certainly had been a pirate, but for some odd reason he wasn't revealing his identity to Matthew Benchley. Renna didn't know why he'd keep it a secret, unless he didn't realize that he was this man—this Kyle Sinclair—and of course he was. There was no mistaking the circumstances and that woman named Elise. Hadn't he already admitted to all Benchley just said?

Wendall entered the room with Johanna, and still the captain didn't reveal himself. In fact, not another word was spoken on the subjects of shipping companies and boating accidents; however, Matthew Benchley's cold stare seldom left the captain. It was as if Benchley knew who he was, too—and he hated him.

Once they'd finished eating and everyone retired to the parlor, Renna excused herself as she always did when Matthew Benchley was visiting. However, she was unable to fall asleep, even after she heard Benchley leave and her parents turn in for the night. Climbing out of bed, Renna donned her robe and crept downstairs to the kitchen, where she lit a lamp and set a kettle of water on the cast-iron cookstove to boil for tea. She was unprepared, however, for the man who suddenly stepped out of the shadows. She gasped.

"I'm sorry. I didn't mean to startle you. I couldn't sleep."

"Me either."

Renna considered him beneath the smoky kerosene light from the lamp. His dark glasses were off, and he seemed to be staring right through her. Renna was only too glad that the captain was blind, or she'd be too ashamed to stand before him in her bedclothes. But he was a handsome pirate all the same. No wonder Elise Kingsley took leave of her senses.

"I've been doing a lot of thinking," he said, taking a step closer. The angles and planes of his swarthy features came into view, though a shadow of whiskers had darkened the lower half of his face. "I know who I am and where I've come from."

"You're Kyle Sinclair, aren't you?"

"Yes. I'm from Wisconsin, specifically Milwaukee. I remember everything. . . ."

"We should contact your family."

He nodded. "Would you help me write a letter to them?"

"Of course."

He took another step closer, and Renna admonished her foolish heart for hammering so loudly. Her pirate, just a foot away, was likely to hear it!

"Renna, please don't tell anyone who I am just yet. Not even your parents."

"Why?"

He paused. "I remember thinking that something was wrong with my schooner this summer—before the accident. You see, we were off course. I had never meant to get so far out into the lake and, when the storm approached, I couldn't maneuver the boat and get her safely into harbor."

"You think someone tampered with it?" Renna was horrified by the implication. "Who would do such a thing?"

"I don't know. And I don't want to falsely accuse anyone of. . .of murder. However, Elise told me about her nephews, Lars and Matthew Benchley. She had argued with Lars one week before the accident. I never met him—Lars, that is—but Elise said he threatened her with bodily harm if she sold the shipping company to me. Of course, she'd sold it already, but she wouldn't tell him. She was too frightened of what he'd do." A rueful expression crossed his dark features. "I shrugged off the threat as typical female hysterics, but I now know I should have taken it seriously.

"Elise told me that her nephew, Lars, was capable of anything. She said he was a blockade runner for the Rebs, not that he supported their cause, mind you. Lars Benchley was in it solely for the monetary gain. . . and he made a fortune. But, according to Elise, he gambled it all away and was seeking new money-making opportunities. She said he was the sort of man who'd let nothing and no one stand in his way. Elise was crying when she told me that Lars would murder for money."

"And you think Matthew, being his brother, is capable of the same thing?"

"I don't know. There's something odd about Matthew's character." Kyle paused before adding, "The man behaves quite differently while working with your father. It's as if he has a dual personality."

Renna gasped. "You think he's insane?"

The captain lifted a dark brow. "Perhaps, although I'm not convinced of it. And, until I can determine if there's any real danger surrounding my circumstances, I can only trust a few people with my identity."

"But Matthew obviously knows who you are."

"Yes, but he's playing along with me." Suddenly, his hands cupped her face, and Renna thought that surely he could see her as his black eyes bore into hers. But of course he couldn't. "Renna, is my secret safe with you?"

"Yes," she whispered hoarsely, her lips just inches from his.

He released her. "Good."

She sighed, feeling a tad disappointed. She had been certain that this pirate-captain was going to kiss her.

He just grinned, a pirate's smile if she ever saw one. "Renna, Renna," he said, "what shall I ever do with you?"

"W—what do you mean?"

He shook his head. "You were very close to getting yourself kissed just now—and quite thoroughly kissed, too."

Her heart leapt into her throat.

"But don't worry," he added assuredly. "You have my word that I'll never be anything less than a gentleman to you."

Renna thought it over and, pirate or not, she believed him.

The kettle's shrill whistle announced that the water was boiling. Renna turned and took it off the stove. "Will you have tea with me?"

"No tea, but I'll keep you company."

She nodded while he stumbled loudly to the kitchen table.

"Shh," she warned, "you'll wake my parents."

"Sorry, it's this. . .blindness."

"Of course, I understand."

With her tea steeping in a pretty china pot, Renna moved to the table. Next she took a cup from the shelf and sat down. Several minutes passed.

"Did you love Elise Kingsley?"

Kyle paused momentarily before answering, "No." Then he took one of Renna's hands in both of his. "Renna, please understand that I am not proud of the man I was before my accident. I've been thinking of all the wrongs I did, and I can't imagine how I'll ever make them right. My children may not want me back. I wasn't a good father." He sighed and dropped her hand. "They needed so much more than I was capable of giving."

"Do you think they were placed in an orphans' home?"

"I hope not. My guess is that the Navis family took them in."

"Friends of yours?"

"Sort of. They're Richard's family."

"The bookkeeper who turned farmer?"

"That's him. And the Navises are a strong Christian family, too. Both of his parents, along with Richard and Sarah, tried to tell me about Christ. In fact, the day of the accident, Sarah asked me to church.

I refused, of course. But later, as I bobbed in the dark, stormy waters of Lake Michigan, fighting for my life, I thought that if God gave me one more chance, I'd turn into a church-going man. I promised God."

Renna smiled. "I guess He heard you and took you up on your promise."

The captain nodded soberly as if realizing for the first time that a true miracle had occurred. "Yes, I guess He did."

Chapter 10

When Richard Navis got the letter informing him that the captain was still alive, he was both shocked and relieved— but mostly shocked. He looked down at the letter now, still in his hands. He'd read it three times already. It was written by a woman named Lorrenna Fields. She was apparently the captain's nurse and had seen him through the worst of a head injury. The captain was suffering from amnesia and could only recall "bits and pieces." However, he was still blind.

"Why the frown, Richard?" Sarah, his wife of just two weeks, asked.

"It's a letter about Captain Sinclair," he replied. "It just came today. I picked it up in town this morning."

"The captain?" The stunned expression on Sarah's face had matched his own earlier today. "You mean, he's alive?"

Richard nodded.

"I knew it!" she cried, smiling broadly. "I never gave up the idea that the captain survived the boating accident."

Richard grinned. "Yes, I know. And it seems you were right; however, I would like to investigate this for myself."

"Yes, definitely," Sarah replied, all humor aside. Then a worried expression crossed her features. "The children. . .what about them?"

"Let's not tell them just yet. I want to make sure."

"But he'll want them back—except they won't want to go! They love it here on the farm with us, Richard. Gabriel is just beginning to adjust—"

"Sarah, don't fret." Setting down the letter, he put his arms around her. "God loves these children even more than we do. As with everything, we'll just have to trust that His ways are best."

Somewhat reluctantly, Sarah nodded. "It's a good thing you didn't sell the captain's house and only closed up his store. It hasn't even gone into probate. How fortunate. But, you, Richard, are the one who has been marvelous at keeping up the books and running his shipping business. I hope the captain finally appreciates you."

"He always has. . .in his own way." Richard grinned sheepishly then. "However, I wonder what the captain will have to say about my marrying his governess."

Sarah smiled. "And don't forget you allowed his housekeeper to head off to the wild West with my brother Luke and our neighbor, Bethany Stafford."

"Looks like I'm in big trouble," Richard said teasingly. "But perhaps the captain won't remember that he had a governess and a housekeeper. The letter states that he was suffering from amnesia and that only some of his memory has now returned."

"Amnesia? Oh, dear. . .well, that does explain why it's taken months to hear from him." Sarah wore a concerned frown. "The poor man, he never did have a good memory."

"No, he never did." Richard sobered. "The letter also states that Captain Sinclair is blind, Sarah. Another consequence of the head injury he suffered. It's unknown if the damage is permanent at this point."

"Oh, no."

At her look of pity for the captain, Richard added, "But God can make the blind to see."

"Yes, He can."

"Now put that smile back on your face."

"Look who's talking," Sarah retorted playfully. "I was the one who caught you frowning so hard, remember?"

"You're right again, Mrs. Navis." With Sarah still in his arms, Richard twirled her in a full circle. She responded with a merry little laugh, and suddenly four children ran from the kitchen, eager to get in on the fun. Soon Richard was tickling the lot of them.

Kyle Sinclair sat in the small bedroom that the Fieldses had afforded him and secretly penned a second letter to Richard. He could trust him; Richard had always been a faithful steward. In his note, he divulged everything—that he knew who he was and that he could see. He explained about Renna, his feelings for her, whatever they might be, and went on to tell of his deception, something he wasn't proud of. "But you must not let on that I can see," he wrote. "For Renna's sake. . .and mine."

Kyle then wrote of his misgivings regarding Matthew Benchley and explained in detail what had happened out on the lake that fateful day. He instructed Richard to notify the authorities. With that information out of the way, Kyle proceeded to ask Richard to bring him some funds. He designated a generous amount for Dr. Hamilton and the hospital and, of course, the Fields family for their hospitality. Finally, he ended with, "And please bring me some clothes. Not to sound ungrateful, but I feel like some poor slob off the docks in these charity rags I've been given!"

Signing his name, Kyle sat back on the bed, his back against the cold wall. He wondered what he should do about the children. Move back to Milwaukee and insist upon becoming a family once more? Or should he take Renna's advice and stay here and allow the children "visits"—until they saw that their father was, indeed, a changed man?

Renna. The corners of Kyle's lips moved upward in a slow smile. Who did she think she was fooling, anyway? She didn't want him to leave, and truthfully, he didn't want to go. Yet, he had his children to think of. . .and he so desperately wanted to make things up to them. He had always loved them, always wanted the best for them. But he'd been very selfish, too, wanting to satisfy the desires of his own heart and hiring others to fulfill his responsibilities to his children.

A knock sounded at his door. "Captain, are you ready for work?" It was Wendall.

"Yes," Kyle replied. "Just give me one minute."

"Do you need some help?"

"Um, no, I believe I can manage." He slipped the letter into its envelope. The trick would be posting it today. "I'll be right out."

Moments later, he donned his dark glasses and left his room. In the kitchen, Johanna Fields had prepared breakfast. "Smells good," he remarked, taking a chair at the table. Oops. He wasn't supposed to see that there was a chair in front of him. He glanced at his host and hostess. They hadn't seemed to notice his blunder.

"Renna had to leave early this morning," Johanna said, setting a plate of steaming blueberry muffins on the table. Kyle had to force himself not to snatch one off the plate.

"Will she be working another twelve-hour day?" he asked as Johanna came over with her cast-iron frying pan and scooped two fried eggs onto his plate.

"Yes, she's working another of those long shifts," Wendall replied. "There ought to be a law against working a person to death like that."

Johanna served her husband and then sat down. Wendall prayed over the food, after which he explained to Kyle that there were muffins in front of him and eggs on his plate.

"There ought to be a law," Kyle remarked, "against the food they serve in that hospital. It isn't fit for animals, let alone humans." He turned toward Johanna. "My gratitude, madam, for your expertly prepared dishes."

Johanna blushed. "You're entirely welcome, Captain." With that, she poured him a cup of very strong-smelling coffee—just exactly the kind Kyle enjoyed in the morning. "Now don't burn yourself," she warned. "The coffee is to your left."

"Oh, mercy, don't go and burn yourself, Captain!" Wendall exclaimed, finishing his breakfast. "Renna would have a conniption if she found out we harmed her patient."

Kyle smiled; however, it bothered him to be referred to as Renna's "patient." Is that how her parents saw him? Only her patient and not possible suitor?

I'm crazy, Kyle thought. *I'm a pirate recently saved by grace. What father in his right mind would consider me a possible husband for his daughter? I'm a man with a past. . .and four children! Besides, I don't believe in fairy-tale love like Renna does. Wouldn't be fair to her. Wouldn't be right. . .*

But was it right to deceive Renna and her family? Kyle's conscience was suddenly pricked.

"Is everything all right, Captain?" Wendall asked as they rode in his buggy to the Chamber of Commerce building. "You've been awfully quiet."

"I don't mean to be. I've just been thinking."

"Hmm. . ."

Then, suddenly, Kyle could stand it no longer. His conscience bothered him too much. "Wendall, you were honest with me once—about Renna," he began, "and now I need to be honest with you."

Wendall turned. "You mean you've been dishonest?"

"Yes."

A frown settled on his brow. "All right. Go ahead."

"I remember who I am."

"Really? That's splendid!"

"My name is Kyle Sinclair, and I'm from Milwaukee, Wisconsin. It all came back to me in a rush. . .a few nights ago."

"Kyle Sinclair. Captain Kyle Sinclair!" Wendall had a look of awe on his face. "My, my, but I thought I had heard of you. Your name is well known at the Chamber of Commerce because of your business ventures. I believe I've even met you once or twice, but I've mostly dealt with your steward."

"Richard Navis."

"Navis. . .yes, that's him!" Wendall shook his head as if to alleviate his shock and surprise. "Well, knock me over with a feather!" he said at last. "Kyle Sinclair! *The* Kyle Sinclair!"

"There's no 'the' about it." Guilt and embarrassment formed a knot in his chest.

"Renna will be delighted that you remember."

"Renna already knows," Kyle stated on a serious note. "But I asked her to keep it a secret."

"A secret? From me?"

"Yes. You see, my life may be in danger," Kyle quickly explained. "I remember that the boating accident this past summer. . .well, it may not have been an accident at all."

"Not an accident. . . ?" Wendall looked shocked for a second time. "My, my. . .is that what you've been dishonest about?"

"That's part of it. The other part Renna doesn't know." Kyle paused to collect his thoughts. "Wendall, I'm not blind anymore. I can see clearly. I've been. . .pretending."

Wendall's jaw dropped. "Pretending? But why?"

Again Kyle paused, unsure of how to explain. Finally he just said, "Because of Renna."

"What? I don't understand." Wendall brought his chin back, giving him a curious look. But then an expression of understanding washed over his features. "It's her birthmark, isn't it?"

Kyle inclined his head, ashamed of his dishonesty. "She was so distant when she thought I could see and I. . .well, I wanted her. . . friendship." He turned to Wendall. "You were right. One hardly notices the birthmark at all. Renna is a lovely woman."

Wendall smiled broadly, but it slipped slowly away. "I've told her that a hundred times. But do you think she'll believe her own father? No!"

"And I didn't think she'd believe a pirate," Kyle said with a grin.

Wendall chuckled. "I understand now. And maybe it'll teach Renna a lesson." He sobered. "Have you prayed about this, son? Are you sure that this deception is what God wants?" He gave Kyle a keen glance.

Kyle shifted uncomfortably in his seat. He hadn't prayed about the little trick he was playing on Renna—and he realized now that he hadn't wanted to pray about it because he was quite certain that God would not approve of his deception. He met Wendall's eyes. "I know I have to be honest with Renna, sir. I just want to be sure I've won her. . .friendship."

"Hmm. . ."

They rode in amicable silence for several minutes and then Wendall turned to Kyle again, this time with a serious, very fatherly expression. "And just what, may I ask, are your intentions regarding my daughter?"

Now it was Kyle's turn at surprise. "Well, I—"

"You've got a reputation, Captain Sinclair, and I'm not blind," Wendall rushed on, "and I can see my daughter has feelings for you that go beyond the call of her nursing duties."

"Yes, but—"

"That's why I pushed Matthew Benchley on her. I thought that if Renna had an interested suitor, she'd turn her attentions from you to him."

"You did?" Kyle frowned. "I wondered what you were up to."

"Yes, well, Matt is interested, you know. He just behaves strangely around my daughter. Can't figure out why. Perhaps he's trying too hard to impress her."

"Perhaps. But he's hardly a match for Renna. He swings from mild-mannered and boring by day to overbearing and obnoxious by night. What's more, he's not a man with whom Renna could match wits. She'd grow tired of him. . .or be intimidated by him."

"Oh? And are you saying that you're the right match for my daughter?"

Kyle choked on a response. Was he?

"By the way, I don't believe a man and a woman can be friends, as you say. If you want my daughter's friendship, Captain, you're going to have to court her properly."

"Wendall, she thinks of me as her patient. She dotes on me like a mother hen."

"She thinks you're blind and in need of her nursing abilities."

"But if I tell her the truth, she won't want anything to do with me!"

Wendall frowned. "I see your point."

Kyle sighed. "Why is Renna so preoccupied with that birthmark anyway?"

"Oh, I don't know. Somewhere along the line she got the idea that she's not as pretty as other women. And while it's true that her birthmark is somewhat unsightly—at first glance—one gets used to it."

"It certainly doesn't bother me," Kyle stated candidly. He saw beyond the birthmark to real beauty, the kind that came from within.

"It doesn't bother Matt Benchley, either," Wendall said, as if to goad him.

Lifting a brow, Kyle turned to him. "Whose side are you on, anyway?"

Wendall, too, cocked a brow. "My daughter and a. . .*pirate?*"

"A *reformed* pirate," Kyle said in his own defense.

Wendall laughed. "True, true. You are a changed man."

"Besides, I'm a very rich reformed pirate."

"As well I know. But so is Matt Benchley. . .rich, that is."

"So he says."

Wendall wore a Cheshire cat grin. He was obviously enjoying himself.

Kyle, however, knew this matter was no joke. "Wendall, wealthy or not, the bottom line is your daughter isn't in love with Benchley!"

"Quite true." He turned to Kyle, a pleased look in his eyes. "All right, Captain, your secret is safe with me. Renna will never hear from my lips that you can see. You'll have to tell her yourself."

Chapter 11

Daughter, what's wrong? You've been moping around since last night and your disposition hasn't changed after a good night's sleep."

Spoon in hand, Renna made swirls in her porridge. "It's nothing. I–I'm just tired, I guess."

"You work too hard. I wish you'd quit that job at the hospital," her father said. "Either that, or demand shorter hours."

"I did ask. . .but my request was denied."

"Oh, Renna. . ." Her mother pressed her lips together in a worried frown.

"I'm think I'm beginning to—to hate my—my position. A couple of nurses at the hospital are constantly scolding me, and I'm feeling. . . well, discouraged."

"Sounds like it's time to move on," the captain said from where he sat across the table from her.

Her mother agreed. "Oh, Renna, there are dozens of things you could do instead."

Like what? Renna wanted to ask, but she dared not. She wasn't sure any employer would want a thirty-year-old spinster with a dreadful birthmark on her cheek.

Renna was suddenly sorry she'd said anything.

"Why are you being scolded at the hospital?" Kyle wanted to know. He appeared just as concerned as her parents.

Standing, Renna cleared her place. She now wished she wouldn't have even brought up the subject. But since she had, she'd might as well be honest. "Nurse Ruthledge called me into her office yesterday, and both she and Nurse Thatcher scolded me for getting too personally involved with my patients. They were referring to a young woman who's been very sick—dying, in fact—and she wanted me to write a letter for her. How could I refuse?"

"I'm sure I wouldn't have been able to," Johanna stated.

"And I couldn't either. So I wrote it for her." Renna shook her head. "I believe nursing goes beyond seeing to a patient's physical needs. It's seeing to their spiritual and emotional needs as well. However, as my superiors, Nurse Thatcher and Nurse Ruthledge don't agree, and they scold me for taking care of my patients the way I believe is honoring to God."

"Would you like me to talk to them?" her father offered.

"No. It's best to leave it alone, I think. If you talk to them, Father, they'll only get angrier and treat me worse than they already do."

"Oh, Renna, I'm so sorry," Johanna said sympathetically.

She looked at her mother and managed a smile.

"Are you going into work today, Renna?" the captain asked.

"No, I begged off. I've worked the last eight days straight, going in even on Sunday night and working through Monday. I need a rest."

"I have never known a woman to work as hard as you do."

Renna lifted a brow, determined to lighten the atmosphere. "Is that a compliment, Captain Blackeyes Kyle Sinclair?"

Everyone laughed. His secret was out—half of it, anyway. The Fields family knew that he remembered his identity; only Renna and her mother still believed he was blind. But Kyle hoped to rectify that as soon as the opportunity presented itself.

"Oh, poor Renna," Wendall said between chuckles, "she's got so many names for the captain here that she can't decide which one to use."

"Kyle would be fine," he replied, noting the pretty blush that suddenly colored her face. Her reaction, he thought, was so innocent, so precious.

Renna turned away, and Johanna cleared her throat. "Well, I guess Renna and I will see to these dishes."

Wendall glanced at Kyle. "Seems we've been dismissed."

"Undoubtedly."

The two men stood and ambled off to Wendall's study with Wendall, of course, guiding the poor, blind captain.

By Saturday afternoon, the wash had been hung out to dry, folded, and put away. With that and the tidying of the house accomplished, Renna and her mother paused for a short break in the kitchen and poured some tea. The men stayed occupied, and Renna was glad to see that her father and Captain Sinclair were getting along so well. Nevertheless, she still felt that the captain needed her, too. He seemed to need this family, for he was making great strides in his recovery. . .except for his blindness. Renna had thought the temporary setback would have corrected itself by now. Even Dr. Hamilton was stumped by it.

A hard knock sounded at the front door around mid-afternoon, and Renna answered it. A young man, blond and blue-eyed, stood before her.

"Is this the Fieldses' residence?" he asked.

"Yes." Renna's first thought was that the hospital had sent a messenger to fetch her for duty. She tried to suppress the rising dread of going into the hospital today.

"I'm Richard Navis, and I'm here to see Captain Sinclair."

Renna gasped in surprise. "Oh, yes. Of course. You must have received the letter."

He nodded, and she beckoned him inside.

"I'm Renna Fields, and I'm pleased to meet you."

"Likewise." He gave her a friendly smile.

"Let me get my father and the captain for you. Please, make yourself comfortable."

Renna ran out to the backyard and into the stables, where she found her father and Captain Blackeyes working on one of the horses' harnesses and having a lively political debate. However, they stopped when they saw her coming.

"What is it, daughter?"

"It's for the captain," she replied. She turned to him. "Mr. Richard Navis is here to see you."

"Richard? That's wonderful!" He started for the house but stopped in mid-stride as he reached the door. "I guess I need an escort. Blind men need escorts, don't they?"

Renna was quick to volunteer for the task. She looped her arm around his elbow and guided him back into the house.

Richard's face split into a broad grin when he saw him. "Captain Sinclair! It's so good to see you. We thought you were dead!" Richard shook his hand heartily but then embraced him in all his exuberance.

"It's good to see you, too—" The captain paused. "Well, you know what I mean. I'm blind. It's good to hear your voice."

Richard frowned slightly. "Yes. . .right." He glanced from the captain to Renna and back to the captain again.

"I hope you brought me some clothes."

Richard's smile returned. "I did, indeed. I brought you an outfit to wear home."

Renna's heart suddenly plummeted. Of course. Mr. Richard Navis had come to take her pirate home where he belonged. What had she expected? That he'd stay here forever?

Suddenly Renna felt as though her whole world was coming undone.

"They sure have been in there a long time," Renna remarked two and a half hours later as she pushed the buttered squash around on her plate. Normally she loved the vegetable; however, tonight she couldn't seem to even choke down a single bite—not with Captain Sinclair and his steward in her father's study discussing how he'd be walking out of her life forever.

"They'll come out when they're ready," Wendall said, buttering a warm, flaky biscuit. "Much to discuss. Many plans to make."

"I'm sure much of the talk surrounds his children," Johanna said. "The captain has mentioned all four of them to me on several occasions in the past few days."

"Yes," Wendall agreed, "he's concerned about their welfare—like any good father."

Renna had to smile. "The captain would be pleased, I think, to hear you call him a good father. He's admitted to me that he wasn't a good father at all, except now he wants to change all that."

"To God be the glory!" Wendall declared with a broad grin.

"Amen!" Johanna added heartily.

As if on cue, the captain and Richard walked into the kitchen. "We're not too late for supper, I hope."

"No, no, Kyle, sit down," Wendall invited. "Mr. Navis, too."

Renna stood and helped her mother serve up two more plates.

"Would you like me to cut your meat for you, Captain?" his steward asked with a sheepish grin. "Like the way I cut it for Rachel? In little squares?" He looked straight at Renna. "Rachel is the baby of the family."

"Oh. . .I see," Renna replied, not knowing what to make of the scene before her. Was the captain's steward teasing him? Because he was blind? How utterly cruel!

"Thank you, Richard," the captain replied on a sarcastic note, "but I can manage to cut my own meat."

"Are you sure, sir?"

"Positive!"

The steward seemed to swallow a laugh.

"The captain has adapted miraculously well to his condition," Johanna stated seriously. "But Renna told us that sometimes people without one of their senses make it up in the other five."

"Do you have your five senses, Captain?" Richard asked, regarding him askance. "Are you sure? Perhaps you've taken leave of them all."

Renna watched as the captain lowered his head and pinched the bridge of his nose between his left thumb and forefinger. He seemed annoyed. But then his shoulders began to shake and Renna realized that he—he was laughing!

She looked at her father, who was wearing a smirk, then at her mother who seemed as dumbfounded as Renna.

"Ladies, please excuse my steward, Richard," the captain said. "He has a peculiar wit that many find amusing—" he turned his face toward his steward—"but not everyone."

His last three words had a ring of warning to them, and Mr. Navis cleared his throat, donning a serious expression now.

Dinner was finished on a more somber note. Then, afterward, they moved to the parlor, where a fire burned in the hearth, lighting the room with glowing warmth.

"First of all," the captain began, "I'd like to thank you all for your hospitality."

Was this good-bye? Renna wondered. She steeled her heart for what was sure to come next.

"Words cannot express my gratitude, and neither can monetary means; however, I would like you to have this—"

As if on cue, Richard pulled out an envelope, thick with national bank notes. He handed it to Wendall.

"Oh, no, I can't accept this."

"You must," the captain said, "or I shall be deeply offended."

"But. . ." He counted the notes. "Kyle, I don't want your money!"

"Wendall, I always pay my debts, and I feel I owe this family a large one."

"Nonsense."

Johanna suddenly stood and walked over to her husband. Taking the envelope from him, she tucked it into the folds of her full skirt. "Thank you, Captain," she said graciously. "This money will be put to good use." She looked at Wendall. "There's a family at church, the Reids, with eight needy children. We'll consider it a privilege to help them out."

Wendall nodded; obviously he hadn't thought of the Reids. "Yes, and I guess we have a few needs here, too." He smiled, looking chagrined. "Forgive me, Johanna, for being so prideful."

Bending over, she kissed the little bald spot on top of his head. "All is forgiven, dear."

"Well, I'm glad that's settled," the captain said. "However, I do have a favor. Because of the circumstances regarding my boating accident this past summer, and because of the situation with my children, I would like to remain here at your home. . .for a while."

"Of course, Captain," Johanna said quickly. "You're most welcome here."

"Thank you."

Renna looked down at her hands folded in her lap and tried to hide her relief. He wasn't leaving. Not yet. She still had time. . . .

But time for what? Time to hope the captain fell in love with her? The very thought was ludicrous and virtually impossible. Kyle Sinclair was accustomed to having women around him who were ten times more beautiful and sophisticated than Renna could ever hope to be.

No. She must stop her fanciful ideas now while she could. Her pirate would leave sometime; she shouldn't attach herself to him. Perhaps Nurse Ruthledge and Nurse Thatcher were right—she got herself too personally involved with her patients. She'd only get hurt—they both said so. And they said they spoke from experience.

I should have listened to Nurse Ruthledge and Nurse Thatcher. Perhaps God in His wisdom put them in my path to warn and protect me. But too late. I didn't listen. . . .

Chapter 12

Renna was bone tired. She had worked the last eight days at the hospital, and three of those days had been eighteen-hour shifts. She could barely think, and that was good. Thinking lately made her heart ache, as she thought of little else but her pirate and her birthmark.

If you continue in My Word, that still small voice seemed to whisper in her ear now, *you shall know the truth and the truth shall make you free....*

"Well, good evening, Renna. . .or should I say good morning. It is two a.m."

Standing in the hallway between her father's study and the parlor, leaning against the wall with her coat still on, Renna started at the sound of the captain's voice. "Don't you ever sleep?" she asked on a defensive note.

"Don't you?" he countered.

Renna sighed. "We've been busy at the hospital. . .and short-handed."

"Well, your excuse is better than mine. I just have insomnia tonight."

Renna nodded for lack of a better reply.

"Would you like to share the rest of the firelight with me?"

"I don't think I'd be very good company. I was just trying to gather my strength to go upstairs to bed."

The captain stepped forward and helped her off with her woolen overcoat. He stumbled loudly before hanging it on the wooden rack near the front door. Then, turning back to her, he held out his hand. "Why not gather your strength by a warm fire?"

Renna considered him. Even through tired eyes, Captain Sinclair was a handsome sight. He wore his own clothes, which fit him much better than the old charity garb. A crisp, white shirt was tucked into suspendered, black pants.

"Renna?"

Mentally shaking herself, she accepted the offer she didn't have the energy to decline. In the parlor, an opened Bible sat on the coffee table in front of the settee. "Was my father reading to you tonight?"

"Um. . .well. . ."

"Saint John, chapter eight," she said, viewing the page at which the Bible was left open. "Was that the reading tonight?"

"Yes."

Renna studied the words, and the last part of verse thirty-two seemed to jump out at her: ". . .*the truth shall make you free.*" With a heavy sigh, she sat down on the settee beside the captain. Her conscience pricked her.

"You missed meeting my children," the captain said. "They arrived Friday evening on the four o'clock train and left yesterday afternoon."

"I'm sorry to have missed them. I adore children." Renna had been on duty all day Friday until three o'clock Saturday morning. Knowing her next shift began only a few hours later, she'd slept at the hospital.

"You've been so busy and gone so much," the captain said. "Why, you even missed going to church yesterday."

Renna nodded, and her conscience bothered her all the more. "How are your children faring?" she asked, changing the subject.

The captain shrugged. "My girls, Libby and Rachel, seemed glad to see me. No doubt Richard and Sarah had prepared them." He laughed. "Would you believe that my steward up and married my governess while I was convalescing?"

Renna grinned. "They got married?"

The captain nodded. "They're so in love, it's embarrassing."

Renna couldn't help a soft laugh. She wished she could have met the woman who married the smart-aleck steward.

"Anyway, my eleven-year-old son Michael was obedient but distant the whole weekend. And Gabriel. . ." The captain left his name hanging between them ominously.

"What about Gabriel?"

"He's my oldest son, and he hates me. He said he hates me."

"Oh, I'm so sorry, Captain. Those words must have wounded you terribly, but I'm sure your son doesn't really mean them."

He turned his face toward hers. "Please call me by my given name. Call me Kyle."

Renna felt a blush warming her cheeks. "But that's so. . .*familiar.*"

He laughed. "We are familiar." Then he picked up her hand, his expression turning more serious now. "Renna, I would like to be more than—"

"Don't say it." She stood abruptly, pulling out of his grasp.

"What's wrong? Have I misinterpreted your feelings somehow?"

Renna spun back around. "You noticed?"

He smiled warmly. "Renna, you're very transparent."

"Oh, dear. . ."

He laughed once more.

Renna just stood there, considering him.

"Come back here and sit down," he instructed her. "Let's talk about this once and for all. I've had to do some heavy soul-searching this weekend, what with my children here."

Renna sat down cautiously. She knew she should tell him about her appearance. And, again, she heard her conscience say, *The truth will make you free.* . . .

"Captain. . .I mean, Kyle," she began hesitantly, "I'm not the woman you think I am."

Sitting back against the settee, he frowned slightly but appeared unconcerned. "Oh? How's that?"

"Well, you said that I was. . .beautiful. But I'm not. I have a—a birthmark on my face. It's an awful sight, too. A purple thing—it even clashes with the color of my hair." She chanced a look at him, noting that he didn't seem appalled. . .yet. "People give me curious glances everywhere I go." Renna sighed. "I doubt a man of your caliber should be seen with a woman like me. It could ruin your social standing, affect your influence with prominent people."

"Hmm. . ." Kyle was momentarily pensive, wondering how he should reply. Renna was both right and wrong. Wrong, because his influence had never been based on appearance, though that was part of it, but on actions and wise decisions. However, the social standing part might be a legitimate concern. Kyle, on the other hand, couldn't care less what others thought of who he was with and why he was with them. Never did. In the past, he had always made his friends according to what they could profit him. Now, however, he was a changed man. But that he was romantically interested in a woman at all was sure to make the society page of the newspaper in Milwaukee, and the local gossips could be vicious. Oh well, he'd just have to make sure he protected Renna from all that. And he could.

Suddenly he wondered if he ought to be honest with her, too. Perhaps now was the perfect time to tell her that he wasn't blind and that he'd seen her every expression and that she was, most certainly, beautiful in his eyes. Then, thinking better of it, he decided to use the situation to his advantage.

"Renna," he asked, "are you ashamed to be seen with me?"

"What? Why would I be ashamed?"

"Because I'm blind. . . . What will your friends think?"

"No friend of mine would ever shame me for falling in love with a blind man." As she realized her admission, her cheeks flamed a deeper crimson than Kyle had ever seen.

He chuckled softly under his breath. "Renna, the same is true for my friends. No true friend of mine is going to look on you and judge you to be any less of a person because of your birthmark."

"And you don't. . .mind that it's there?"

"No."

"But you haven't seen it."

"I have a very good imagination."

"Oh."

Kyle smiled at her reaction. But then, he grew serious again. There was one thing he had to be boldly honest about with her.

"Renna," he began, "there is something I'm struggling with."

"Oh?" Expectancy shone from her gaze.

"After being around your family—your parents, your siblings and their spouses, and then after seeing Richard and Sarah together. . .well, I want to believe in romantic love. I guess I do believe it's possible now, whereas I didn't before. I've seen it. However, I've never experienced it." He paused momentarily to collect his thoughts. "I guess what I'm trying to say is, will you be patient with a pirate like me who's trying to figure out if he's in love with you?"

Renna's jaw dropped slightly. She was obviously taken aback by his candidness. But then her features softened and that sweet, gentle expression he was so fond of replaced her surprise.

Finally, she replied, "You're a worthy pirate, all right." She smiled. "I'll have no problem being patient."

"But you can't treat me like one."

She frowned, looking confused.

"I am not your patient, Renna, so don't treat me like one. I'm a man, and I don't want to be coddled."

"But you're blind."

"And I'll have to learn to deal with it. . .like a man."

Her gaze fell to her hands, folded in her lap. "I just wanted to help."

"You have. I doubt I'd be alive today if you hadn't taken pity on me from the beginning. But now I'm getting stronger and, if I need your help in the future, Renna, I shall ask for it."

She lifted her head, looking so hurt that Kyle was tempted to apologize. He wondered if she were going to cry. Oh, a woman's tears—Kyle had seen a million of them. A sea of them! Was Renna going to use tears as a form of manipulation to get her way? To make him feel guilty for his honesty?

Much to his relief, she was made of stiffer stuff. She turned back to him, appearing as tired as she said, but no worse for wear. "Your request is not unreasonable," she stated at last, "and I'll try to refrain from. . . coddling you."

He smiled. "My children could use the coddling, though."

"And wouldn't I love that job instead of my position at the hospital."

"Glad to hear it—but I could already tell you love children and people in general."

And I love you, too, she wanted to say, but she couldn't get herself to be that bold, especially as tired as she felt.

Then a swell of concern plumed inside of Renna. "Do you think you need to hire another governess instead of pursuing a romance with me? Perhaps that should come first."

"I thought about it. I thought about it a lot; however, hiring another governess won't change my feelings for you—whatever they are." He sighed. "And I need to find out what they are. My feelings for you, Renna, need a name so I can deal with them accordingly."

"Fair enough," she announced. "But you'll have to talk to my father."

Kyle grinned. "I will, but I don't think there will be a problem."

"Nor do I."

He smiled.

She tried to return the gesture but had to stifle a yawn. "Oh, please excuse me," she begged. "I'd love to sit here with you all night, but I'm nearly delirious with fatigue."

"Quite understandable." Kyle stood and helped Renna to her feet. "I hope you won't change your mind tomorrow," he teased, "after you come to your senses."

"I doubt it." Her smile broadened. "But now you sound like your amusing steward. Didn't he accuse you of losing your senses?"

Kyle laughed. "Yes, he did, and lately I've wondered if he's right. He's a card, that Richard. But he's a good man, a Christian, honest and loyal."

Renna sensed those qualities about Mr. Navis.

Kyle walked her to the stairs. "Good night, Renna," he said, taking her hand and pressing a kiss onto her fingers.

Her heart skipped a beat. "Good night," she replied. Then, turning slowly, she walked upstairs to her bedroom.

"He's courting her?"

Richard nodded. "That's what he stated in this letter."

Sarah smacked her palm to her forehead. "The captain and a courtship? Now I've heard everything."

Richard grinned. "I told you the captain was in love with her. I saw it that very first visit. And I told him he was in love, too—during our meeting that afternoon." Richard chuckled. "He had all the telltale symptoms—and so did Miss Fields. I even poked fun at him for his denial—told him he'd lost all his senses."

"Richard, you didn't!"

"I did." He grinned mischievously. "Needless to say, the captain didn't appreciate my humor."

"No, I don't suppose he did." Standing in the kitchen of the farmhouse, after tucking the children into bed, Sarah sighed deeply. "I wish I could have met her, this Lorrenna Fields, when we visited a couple of weeks ago. Too bad she was working all those hours at the hospital." Sarah paused momentarily. "What's she like, Richard?"

"She seems very nice. Rather quiet."

"Pretty?" Sarah ventured.

Richard shrugged. "I didn't notice. I'm newly married, remember?"

Sarah rolled her eyes but looked pleased with the reply anyway.

"Well, she must be beautiful if the captain is in love with her—of course, he is blind." Sarah frowned. "Should the captain be courting a woman if he can't even see her?"

"Love is blind, Sarah," Richard said. Then he laughed at his attempted humor.

Sarah just shook her head at him. "What else does the captain's letter say?"

Richard sobered. "He states he's coming home for the Thanksgiving holiday."

"Home?"

"Yes, home to stay. He's asked me to get his house in order. His former valet said he'd welcome his old job back, as did his cook, Isabelle. But I'll have to interview housekeepers."

"And the children?" Sarah wore a pained expression. "What about them?"

"The captain says they may stay with us for now." Richard narrowed his gaze. "He's going to want his children back, Sarah. You must accept the fact. Besides, they really do love their father, no matter what he's done or didn't do in the past. But you saw with your own eyes that he's a changed man now."

Sarah nodded. "Yes, the change in the captain is obvious."

"Gabriel, of course, is another story. He's at an awkward age in life and he's struggling in his relationship with his father. But he needs to work through it, because if he doesn't, it'll affect the rest of his life." Richard paused before adding, "It could even affect his relationship with God, his Heavenly Father."

Chapter 13

"Renna, I'm afraid I had to put my foot down this afternoon."

Taking off her coat, she hung it up. She'd put in another eighteen hours at the hospital, and she felt exhausted. "What are you talking about, Father?"

"You are working too much again, daughter. Things cannot go on as they are."

Renna walked into the parlor and stood by the fire. Seeing Kyle sitting in an adjacent chair, she frowned with concern. "Can't sleep again tonight?" she asked, as it was nearly two o'clock in the morning.

Kyle smiled from behind his dark glasses. "Your father kept me up."

Renna suddenly noticed the chess board. Obviously a game was in progress. "Chess? How can a blind man play chess?" She looked expectantly from one man to the other.

"Um. . .well. . .you see. . ."

"Chess is quite a challenge for a blind man," Kyle put in after Wendall fumbled for a reply.

"Yes, I'm sure it is," Renna said, puzzled by how they'd managed such a feat.

"We had to occupy ourselves until you came home," her father tried to explain. "Chess is a good occupation of time."

Renna nodded, too tired for challenges and debates.

"But I'll say this," Wendall told her with a stern countenance now, "I had made up my mind that if you weren't home by three a.m., I was going to fetch you myself!"

Renna frowned deeply. "But I've been working many long shifts this month."

"Precisely my point!" Wendall declared. "You're overworking yourself, Renna, and I'll not have it. I spoke to Dr. Hamilton about it this afternoon."

"You did? What did he say?"

Wendall smiled. "He said you can have off as long as you'd like, and Dr. Hamilton promised to speak to Nurse Ruthledge, who did the scheduling this month. It hasn't been fair, all the days she's assigned you to work. You'll burn out like an old candle, Renna."

"And besides," Kyle added, "I can't very well court you when you're always at the hospital."

Renna stood there, feeling a pinch of both indignation and pleasure. On the one hand, she was shocked that her father would step in this way and speak to Dr. Hamilton without consulting her first. On the other hand, she was relieved that he had. In truth, Renna had been wondering how long she was going to last, working as hard as she was, but she hadn't known what to do about it. However, she was mostly pleased by Kyle's statement about the courtship. Renna had been afraid he'd changed his mind, since their courtship hadn't a chance to get started yet. Then, again, Kyle was right—she hadn't been home much lately.

She smiled at her father. "Thank you for speaking to Dr. Hamilton for me. A few days off will do me a world of good."

Wendall suddenly looked chagrined and turned to Kyle, who smiled calmly. "Actually, Renna," he said, "I suggested an indefinite amount of time off. Your father proposed the idea, and Dr. Hamilton agreed to it."

"An indefinite amount of time off?"

"Yes, Renna, indefinite," her father said lightly. "You see, Kyle wants us to travel with him to Milwaukee for the Thanksgiving holiday. Won't that be a treat? We haven't been on a holiday in a long time. Besides, you need to meet Kyle's children, and your mother and I need to—to. . ." He waved his hand in the air, searching for the right word.

"Investigate my household," Kyle proffered with one of his darkly handsome grins.

"Well, yes, something like that."

Kyle laughed. "Investigate all you want, Wendall. Hopefully Richard will have hired all the needed household staff. I'm grateful that Richard, a farmer now, has the time to help me. I suppose he's in between harvesttime and spring planting, fortunately for me." Kyle sighed. "I guess I'm going to need a new steward, too."

"What kind of household staff do you have?" Renna wanted to know, although she suspected she already did.

"Well, in the past, I've employed only two live-in employees: a housekeeper and a governess. The others, like my valet Thomas and my cook Isabelle, both of whom Richard believes will return to their positions, go home to their own families at the end of the day. I never cared for an overabundance of live-in household staff. One tends to lose his privacy that way."

Renna nodded for lack of a better reply. She wondered if she'd get used to having household staff—that is, if Kyle ever proposed marriage.

Then, suddenly, she remembered. "What about your life being in danger?"

"I am in as much danger here as I will be in Milwaukee, and the authorities have been alerted. They're investigating last summer's boating accident."

"That's good. . .I guess." Renna frowned heavily. "But I still worry about you, Kyle."

He chuckled. "My dear Renna, I manned a gunboat on the Mississippi River during the war. My crew and I saw plenty of battles." He was grinning straight at her now. "I can handle Matthew Benchley."

"If it is Matthew," Wendall added, wearing a pained expression. "I don't want to believe that Matt is involved in anything illegal. He seems like such a fine man."

"I know, Wendall, and maybe I'm wrong. Time will tell. What does the Bible say. . .something about our sins finding us out?"

"That's in Numbers!" Wendall exclaimed, looking all the happy tutor. "Be sure your sin will find you out."

"Right," replied Kyle, looking pleased with himself. However, no one could have been more pleased than Renna. Her pirate was learning the Bible and putting it to practical use!

"So what do you say, Renna?" her father pressed, changing the subject now. "It's late, and I'm tired. We need your answer now. A holiday in Milwaukee, how about it?"

"Sounds wonderful." She pushed aside her sudden concerns. She knew what kind of man Kyle Sinclair was—a very rich, high society man—and Renna doubted she'd fit into his world.

Too bad he couldn't stay in hers forever.

Two days later, Renna looked around her bedroom, shaking her head in amazement. Dresses lay everywhere. Thirty of them, all store-bought. Then she looked at the list in her hand, the one Kyle had given her. "This is practically indecent," she muttered.

"The dress?" her sister Elizabeth asked. "Which one?"

"No, no. This list! Imagine having to own all these dresses!"

"You do own them. What's to imagine?"

Both Renna's sister and mother chuckled. They seemed more excited about the purchases than Renna. Of course, Renna's excitement was the nervous, anxious kind, not the happy kind her mother and sister were displaying.

"Oh, Renna," Elizabeth said, "this is a blessing not a curse. I mean, I wish I could afford store-bought dresses like these, not that I don't get one occasionally. It's just more economical for our family that I make all our clothes."

"Well, most everyone does these days," Johanna said. "Only wealthy people can afford wardrobes from a store."

Renna grimaced, hearing the word "wealthy." She wasn't, and she didn't think her parents were, either. So obviously Kyle had supplied the money for her new clothes, much to Renna's embarrassment. True, her wardrobe was lacking, since she mostly wore a nurse's uniform, but these dresses were much too extravagant for her tastes. They belonged on another woman in another world. That she couldn't afford them herself only served to drive the point home.

Renna reread the list in her hand. Kyle had said she'd need one or two velvet dresses, a few less extravagant evening gowns, breakfast dresses, dinner dresses, and several dresses suitable for various holiday receptions and parties.

She sank onto her bed, never minding all the dresses heaped upon it. "This isn't going to work."

"What isn't, dear?"

"Marriage to Kyle—that is, if he proposes." She sighed. "Oh, I want him to. . .I think I want him to. But I can't be one of these ladies."

"One of what ladies?" Elizabeth asked, pushing back a wisp of her brunette hair.

"Rich ones."

Elizabeth tipped her head, and her brown eyes darkened. "What's the difference if you're rich or poor? You're still Renna, aren't you? Will money change you that much?"

"No, of course it won't, you goose. It's just that. . .well. . ."

"Just be who you are," her mother advised gently. "That is, after all, the woman the captain was drawn to—the real Renna."

"And just remember," her sister added, "it's all up here." Elizabeth pointed to her forehead. "Who you are in your mind is who people will see."

"Sure, if they ever get past my birthmark," Renna replied sarcastically. Elizabeth and Johanna groaned in unison.

"Oh, go ahead," Elizabeth told her. "Go ahead and decide everyone you meet will judge you by your birthmark and not for who you really are. Sabotage yourself before you even get to Milwaukee. I guarantee you'll be miserable the whole entire time. It'll be like when we were girls, Renna, and invited to parties. You made up your mind to have a bad time before we ever arrived."

"That's not true!"

"Yes, it is."

"Now, girls, don't bicker," Johanna said. "The captain might overhear you. He's just downstairs."

Renna stood, feeling defensive. Elizabeth was her younger sister, charming and pretty with a flawless complexion. What did she know about Renna's thoughts and feelings?

Picking up a dress from the bed, Renna began to help her mother pack the trunk she would take on their holiday.

"Let go and be yourself," Elizabeth persisted, packing dresses alongside Renna. "Show the captain and his friends the Renna we, your family, know and love. And if they can't accept you, so be it. You'll always have us."

Suddenly touched by her sister's words, Renna fingered one of the lacy flounces they'd purchased. "Thank you, Elizabeth. I love all of you, too."

Johanna looked at Renna and smiled tenderly. "You see, dear?" she said. "What have you got to lose?"

My heart! Renna wanted to reply as she let the lace slip from her fingertips. *My very heart!*

The packing lasted for days, but finally Renna, her parents, and Mr. Pirate Blackeyes were on their way to Milwaukee. Renna couldn't help it sometimes, calling Kyle Mr. Pirate Blackeyes. He was a new creature in Christ, that was true; however, the name suited him well at those times when he looked so darkly handsome that it made her pulse race. Only a pirate could steal her heart that easily!

"So you still think I'm a pirate, eh?" Kyle asked as the train rocked them back and forth as it chugged north toward the Wisconsin border. A grin tugged at the corners of his mouth. "Then I'll be sure to show you a pirate's good time in Milwaukee."

Renna gasped, though she knew Kyle was teasing. "You'd better not."

He laughed rakishly, and the woman sitting across the aisle turned and gave them both a curious stare.

"Now you did it," Renna whispered, leaning closer to him. "There's a woman across the aisle with a large purple feather in her hat, and now she knows you're a pirate, too."

"I stand corrected," Kyle replied gallantly. "From now on, I shall keep my voice down—especially when we're speaking of my identity as a—a *pirate*."

"Good."

The easy banter continued for the rest of the trip. Finally, after four hours of travel time, the conductor made his way down the aisle. "Milwaukee!" he called. "All for Milwaukee!"

Renna's stomach fluttered with nervousness. "Kyle, do you think your children will like me?" Oddly, she hadn't concerned herself with his children until now. But Renna had always loved children. She appreciated their honesty, their innocence and, therefore, she had taken it for granted that she and Kyle's children would become fast friends. But now a small seed of doubt plagued her. "I do want your children to like me."

Kyle gave her a sad smile. "I have a feeling they'll like you a lot more than they like me—especially the boys."

"Well, I'll fix that." Her apprehension over Kyle's wealth and social status was suddenly replaced by a heartfelt mission. She could win his children—to herself, to Christ, and to their father. "By the grace of God, I'm going to help your children discover what a wonderful man their father really is."

Kyle's smile grew as he took one of her gloved hands in his. "By the grace of God, Renna, I hope you succeed."

Chapter 14

Adjusting her bonnet so it hid much of her cheek, Renna looked up in wonder. The captain's mansion stood three stories high against the backdrop of a cold, dark November sky. Renna thought it made an ominous sight if she'd ever seen one. It was red brick, its porch encased entirely in terra-cotta and the massive oak front doors had lead glass panels covered with wrought iron grillwork.

Renna breathed an awestruck sigh.

"Do you like it?" Kyle asked.

"I. . .well. . .it's very. . .um. . ."

"It's the most impressive house I've ever seen," Johanna said while Wendall nodded beside her.

"Thank you." Kyle held out his arm, inviting Renna to take it. When she did, he said, "Let's go in, shall we? Our luggage will be delivered shortly."

As they arrived on the front porch, the doors swung open and Richard greeted them. "Welcome home, sir!"

"Thank you." Kyle smiled, shaking the younger man's hand. "You've done over, above, and beyond the call of duty here, and I appreciate it immensely."

Richard grinned. "Just wait until you get my bill, Captain."

Kyle laughed but stopped short, as if realizing what this all might cost him.

Now Richard laughed. "Captain, I'm just teasing you. Come in, come in. All of you." He looked at the Fieldses and added, "Welcome to the captain's humble abode."

"Humble, indeed!" Wendall exclaimed, glancing around the magnificent vestibule with its terrazzo floor.

Johanna was speechless.

Renna said, "This is the kind of house I've only walked by and marveled at from a distance. Even some of the more elegant functions

I've attended because of Father's business endeavors were never held in a home of this magnitude."

Kyle patted her hand, still draped over his arm. "It's not so imposing, Renna, once you get used to it. I just call it home."

Richard stood there grinning at the two of them.

Then Sarah came down the front staircase, smiling a welcome. "Hello, Captain Sinclair."

Kyle shook his dark head at her. "Down the front stairs?"

She looked instantly chagrined. "Yes, sir."

"Hmm, I suppose I can't reprimand you for using the front staircase since you aren't my governess any longer."

"Oh, it was a stupid rule anyway, Captain," Sarah quipped. "Besides, you never reprimanded me. Gretchen did." Sarah turned and smiled at Renna.

Renna smiled back.

"Ah, yes, Gretchen," Kyle murmured. "I will miss her terribly, though I don't think she was happy here—hadn't been for years."

"Well, she's enjoying her journey west, Captain," Richard said. "We got a letter from Sarah's brother, Luke. He was able to post it in one of the bigger towns they were passing through. Anyway, Luke wrote that all was fine and Gretchen was. . .happy."

Kyle grunted out a pensive reply.

"But not to worry, sir. I managed to hire another housekeeper. Her name is—"

"What's goin' on in here?" A wiry little woman cried, entering the vestibule at a breakneck pace. "I may not know much about la-dee-da livin', but I know you don't leave company in the front hall with their coats on, grand front hall as it may be. Guests are to wait in the main reception hall—and shouldn't I be the one to answer the door?"

"What have you done, Richard?" Kyle asked, his voice just above a dark whisper.

The steward smiled, looking a tad less confident than Renna had ever seen him. "This is Hester, Captain. Your new housekeeper."

"Captain? Captain?" Hester moved toward him so quickly that she threatened the chignon, sitting precariously on top of her graying, light brown head. "Welcome home, sir," she said, shaking Kyle's hand vigorously.

Renna had to swallow a giggle, and she noticed that Sarah was hard-pressed to contain her smiles, too.

"I'm pleased as punch to meet you, sir," Hester prattled on. "Why, this job is the biggest blessing I've had this year. I lost my beloved husband seven months ago, and I was in sore need of a job and a place to live. Had to sell the farm, and my kids are all grown and gone." Hester wiped a tear off her cheek. "I just don't know what I would have done if young Richard, here, hadn't approached me after the morning service last Sunday." The woman suddenly smiled. "But he did, and here I am!"

"A pleasure to meet you, madam," Kyle said with a slight bow, and Renna was proud to see him act so gallantly toward the less than sophisticated housekeeper. She could tell he was disappointed. No doubt Kyle had wanted his housekeeper to be highbred, at least in the way of household staff.

"Now, come out of this front hallway at once," Hester insisted. "Lemme show ya to your rooms. Why, put 'em together, and they're bigger than my farmhouse was!" Her light laughter echoed through the foyer as she beckoned the Fieldses up the front stairs.

Renna moved to follow her parents, but Kyle held onto her hand. "What do you think?" he asked softly. "About Hester? Do I need to interview other candidates for this position?"

Renna momentarily fretted over her lower lip. Kyle was asking her opinion on the housekeeper? What should she tell him? She had no experience in these matters.

"Renna," Kyle insisted, "I want your heartfelt opinion, that's all."

"All right, Kyle. I think you ought to let her stay." Renna smiled. "There's something about her that's. . .unpretentious. I like her."

Kyle drew himself up, obviously thinking it over.

"She's very quick," Richard added. "She had this whole house clean in a matter of hours."

"And she loves the children," Sarah said. "She plays games with them and teaches them funny tricks. They like Hester, too. They call her 'Granny Hester.'"

"Oh, good grief," Kyle muttered.

"A governess and a housekeeper all in one," Richard stated with an enterprising grin.

Renna raised her brows. Sounded good to her—but what did she know?

"You really want her to stay, Renna?"

"Yes, I think she deserves a chance."

"All right, then. Hester may stay on as my. . .housekeeper."

Kyle stated that last word on a note of dread, and Renna could only imagine what all his elite friends would have to say. They'd take one look at her, with her birthmark, and then at Hester, with her flash-fire efficiency, and they'd think Kyle's head injury last summer did more to him than cause blindness. His friends would think he'd lost his very mind!

Sarah managed to pry Renna out of Kyle's possessive grip then. "Come with me, Miss Fields," she said. "I'll show you to your room. You must be tired from your traveling."

Renna gave the young woman a grateful nod and followed her up the front stairs. They traipsed down a long hallway and then turned to the left. Sarah opened the door to a bedroom with sunny yellow walls. The curtains on the windows were made of thick ivory lace, as was the wide canopy covering the bed. They complimented the thick Lost Ship quilt, which looked so soft and inviting it made Renna long to curl up on it and go to sleep.

"This house has seven bedrooms," Sarah explained. "One suitelike room is on the third floor, and that's where Hester stays, and the remaining six are here on the second floor. Those are the captain's chambers," she told Renna, pointing down another hallway. "The captain has a bedroom and a dressing room. Then there is a guest bedroom, across from yours, and that's where your parents are. The remaining bedrooms are reserved for a governess and the children." Sarah smiled, though her expression looked uncertain. "This was my bedroom while I was the governess here. I hope you won't be insulted that I've suggested you stay in it. It's the only other bedroom available—that is, unless you'd prefer one of the children's bedrooms. Or, perhaps, Hester will agree to a temporary trade—"

"This is fine," Renna replied. "I am not the least bit insulted." Turning, she began to take off her bonnet. "Where are the children?"

"They're with Richard's parents on our farm. We thought it best to let the captain and his guests get settled before bringing them home."

"Sounds like a wise decision."

Sarah paused. "Do you like children, Miss Fields?"

Renna turned back around to face her. "I love children." She watched, then, as Sarah took note of the purplish mark on her right cheek. "It's a birthmark," Renna informed her.

"Oh." Then, much to Renna's surprise, Sarah shrugged off the matter and continued talking about the children. "I'm so thankful to hear you love children." She looked relieved. "Poor Gabriel thinks you'll be the kind of stepmother who'll send him off to boarding school. Apparently Aurora threatened boarding school on numerous occasions."

"Aurora?"

Sarah nodded. "She was the captain's mother—the children's grandmother."

"Oh, yes." Renna was momentarily pensive. "She was killed in the boating accident, wasn't she?"

Again, Sarah nodded. "It was so sad." A moment later, she seemed to shake off her sudden melancholy. "Would you like a tour of the house before you nap?"

"Oh, yes, I'd like that very much. Thank you."

Sarah led the way up to the third floor and showed her Hester's suite. Next, she led Renna across the hallway, through a double set of doors and into a magnificent ballroom. Plaster sculpture work adorned the ceiling from which hung two crystal chandeliers. The walls were lined with matching crystal sconces.

"This is the most beautiful room I've ever seen," Renna breathed, stepping across the shiny, hardwood parquet floor.

"That was my reaction exactly!" Sarah exclaimed with a smile. "I was quite taken with this room—with the whole house, in fact." She shook her head as if remembering. "Why, I can still see Captain Sinclair and Elise Kingsley gliding across this floor. The children and I had to make an appearance at one of the captain's parties last summer, and the music and dancing. . .and the way the captain was holding Mrs. Kingsley—"

Sarah stopped in mid-sentence and blushed right up to her blond hairline. "Oh, Miss Fields, please forgive me! I—I didn't mean to run on like that."

Renna just smiled. "It's all right, Sarah," she replied gently. "I know all about Elise Kingsley."

"You do?"

Renna nodded. "And I know that Kyle was something of a—a pirate before his conversion to Christ."

"Pirate?" Sarah smiled, looking chagrined. "Yes, I suppose that might be an accurate description."

Renna chuckled softly. "Well, here's hoping Kyle's ballroom days are over. Perhaps this could be. . .a tea room."

"That would be lovely!" Sarah declared as they continued their tour.

Kyle stood in his study with Richard. He shuffled through his mail. "How many parties can people in this city attend?" he muttered aloud, looking at all the invitations.

"When news got around that you were still alive, sir," Richard informed him, "the invitations started pouring in."

"I don't remember attending this many holiday balls last year."

Richard seemed to mull over the remark. "Well, sir, I believe you attended more than I'd care to count."

"Hmm. . ."

"Will this year be different? With Miss Fields here?"

Kyle looked up from his stack of mail. "I should say it will be."

Richard sighed. "Glad to hear that. I'm sure Miss Fields and her family will be glad to hear that, too. They don't strike me as ballroom people."

"Hardly," Kyle replied. Then he sighed. "And I'm so glad for it, Richard. I've grown weary of these things." He slapped the mail down on his desk. Turning, Kyle considered the young man standing in front of him. Blond and blue-eyed, broad-shouldered and faithful. Richard Navis had always been a very, very faithful steward, a fact which, Kyle decided, would not go unrewarded.

He looked back at all the invitations on his desk. "I suppose I should have some kind of reception."

"A good idea, sir. Half of the city of Milwaukee will most likely pound your door down from curiosity if you don't." Richard laughed. "In fact, Lillian LaMonde has already been to your store, here, and at my house."

"What?" Sheer outrage caused Kyle to tense. "Your house, too? I'm sorry, Richard."

He waved off the apology and chuckled. "My mother was thrilled. Lillian LaMonde of the Milwaukee Sentinel, at our home, searching for tidbits for her society page—Mama will have stories to tell her friends for weeks now."

"Society page, my foot! That woman writes a vicious gossip column."

"I agree. Have you warned Miss Fields?"

"Sort of," Kyle said lamely. "But I will," he promised at Richard's look of warning. "I have no intention of subjecting Renna to the likes of Lillian LaMonde."

"Good luck, sir," Richard said sarcastically, grinning all the while. "And what about your sight? Does Miss Fields know you can see yet?"

"Um. . .no."

Kyle walked to the windows of his mahogany-paneled study and gazed out over the front terrace. "At first I withheld the truth because of . . .well, the personal matter I discussed with you in Chicago. But now the authorities have advised me to continue under this pretense They think it will be easier for an assailant to strike if I seem like more of a victim." He shook his head and glanced back at Richard. "But I hate lying to Renna. I have wanted to tell her I could see so many times, but I think the authorities are right: the more she knows could hurt her—perhaps even kill her."

"You really think someone may be trying to kill you, sir?" A grave expression settled over his features.

Kyle nodded. "I've thought it over, and I don't think I'm being overly anxious or paranoid. I know something was wrong with my schooner last summer. That's why we had the wreck. And then there are the Benchley brothers who are infuriated with me for buying Kingsley Shipping. Elise told me one of her nephews threatened her."

"Well, just to inform you, Captain, Mr. Norton, your banker, said one of the Benchley brothers had something of a temper tantrum when we wouldn't sell Kingsley Shipping to him."

"He wanted to buy it? Hmm, perhaps I should just sell it to the Benchleys and be done with it." Then Kyle shook his head, thinking better of the idea. "No, I can't do it. Three lives were lost on the lake last summer because of someone's greed, and one of those lives belonged to my mother. I owe it to her memory, Richard—and to the others' as well—to see that whoever is responsible for that accident is brought to justice."

"But how will you prove it? The schooner was completely destroyed."

Kyle grinned. "Yes, but the day before the accident, Toby Barton, the best dockhand a sailing man ever had, checked the schooner over and found it to be in excellent condition. Toby can testify to that."

Richard paled. "Sir, Toby Barton is dead—an accident down at the docks happened just last week. I'm sorry I didn't tell you. I didn't remember that you even knew him."

"I knew him," Kyle replied through a clenched jaw. His heart ached for Toby, while at the same time anger over the injustice filled his being. Toby Barton was just a boy! "I wonder," Kyle muttered, unable to keep the cynicism out of his voice, "just who might have been responsible for *that* accident."

Chapter 15

The children arrived the next morning. Richard and Sarah brought them in the rockaway, a multi-passenger carriage. Richard was in the covered driver's seat, while Sarah and the children sat all bundled up inside.

As Richard drove the carriage around the circular drive, Renna watched from the front windows of the enormous solarium. Her limbs tingled with nervousness as the children alighted and ran for the front porch. What would they think of her? Would they like her?

Renna was only too glad that Kyle had asked the Navises to stay for a few days. He thought it would make the transition easier on the children, and Richard and Sarah had agreed. Furthermore, Sarah had agreed to help Renna get to know the children.

Now if she could only help Renna find her way around this house!

She sighed, turning from the windows. She'd gotten so mixed up last night just trying to find her mother in the ladies' parlor. Downstairs, Renna had learned, there was a main reception parlor, a men's parlor, a ladies' parlor, a music room, a solarium, Kyle's study, a "great hall," and, of course, the dining room and kitchen area. Off the solarium, then, was a long, windowed hallway, which led into a pavilion that was closed off for the winter months. But, oh, how Renna could get herself turned around in this place!

Renna left the solarium and headed for the voices now coming from the foyer. She heard Kyle welcoming his children back home and then heard the sweetest little voice in response, "Welcome home, too, Papa."

Smiling, Renna entered the vestibule.

"And here's Miss Fields," Richard said, shrugging out of his wool coat. "She's the lady we told you about," he informed the children.

"Hello, Miss Fields," said that same sweet voice she'd heard before. "I'm Libby."

"Hello, Libby." Renna thought the little girl looked like a female replica of her father, with her blue-black hair and thick eyelashes. Why, she even had his ebony eyes. The only thing Libby possessed that Kyle didn't was a pretty little rosebud mouth.

"I'm seven," the girl announced.

"No, you're not," the tallest boy answered. "You're six."

Libby frowned. "But I will be seven in twelve weeks! Miss Sarah and I counted the weeks till my birthday."

Kyle laughed. "Libby, darling, that's three months away. A little soon to be counting down the days, don't you think?"

"But, Papa," she said, "I just love birthdays."

"Me, too! I wuv birfdays, too!" This declaration came from the smallest girl.

"You must be Rachel," Renna said, hunkering to the child's eye level. "How old are you?"

"I'm free."

"Oh, to be free again," Richard stated dramatically, earning himself an elbow in the ribs from his wife. "I meant three, Sarah," he quickly replied, a teasing gleam in his eyes. "Like Rachel. . .three."

Sarah lifted a brow. "Yes, well, sometimes I do wonder." She rolled her eyes and Renna chuckled, noticing that Libby had wandered over to her father and had slipped her hand into his. Then the little girl looked up at him with adoration shining in her dark eyes. Kyle bent and lifted her into his arms.

"See, you're still a baby, Libby," the tallest boy said on a cynical note. Standing once more, Renna wondered if the boy was jealous as he watched his sister get their father's attention.

"I am not a baby, you big galoot!" Libby shot back at her brother.

"Now, now, there'll be no name-calling in front of Miss Fields," Kyle told his daughter, pressing a kiss on her cheek. "Is that understood, Libby?"

"But Gabe started it, Papa," she said sweetly, and Renna wondered how Kyle could resist spoiling the little girl. Good thing he couldn't see the darling, little face that was now curiously examining the dark glasses he wore.

Renna turned her attention to the boys. "You must be Gabriel," she said to the one who had participated in the name-calling.

"Uh-huh." And that's all the response she got. Renna didn't think he seemed at all pleased to be home again.

"And you're Michael?" she asked the younger of the two boys.

He nodded. "I'm eleven years old and Gabe is twelve," he informed her, "and we don't need a governess. . .or a mother. And if we can't live with the Navises, we're going to be stowaways!"

Gabriel nudged him, as though Michael had given away their secret.

Renna looked at Kyle, who was quick to dispel any big ideas. "Stowaways? Why, that's a very serious offense. If you're caught, you could be beaten. . .or worse. And if you live, you'll be sentenced to a life of hard labor."

Gabriel was stone-faced, but Michael looked taken aback. His dark brown eyes were wide with horror.

"Now, get your bags," Kyle instructed both boys, "and go upstairs to your rooms and unpack."

Michael obeyed without incident, but Gabriel paused in front of his father and boldly stuck out his tongue in an act of rebellion. Then he followed his brother outside.

Kyle set Libby down at once, and Renna held her breath, certain that Gabriel was about to get disciplined, such was the stern expression on his father's face. But when he did nothing, Renna was reminded of the fact that Kyle couldn't see his son's defiance. It had to have been a mere coincidence that Kyle set Libby down on her own two feet just as Gabriel passed. Still, Renna didn't think the boy should be allowed to get away with such an act.

She looked at Richard, then Sarah, both of whom wore concerned expressions. Would they tell him? Should she?

Finally, it was Libby who tattled. "Papa," she said, tugging on his hand. "Gabriel did a bad thing. The worst thing I ever saw him do. He sticked his tongue out at you, Papa. Are you going to whip him now? He should get a belt-whipping, don't you think so?"

Renna bit the side of her cheek in an effort not to smile. She couldn't help it. She recalled numerous times in her childhood that she'd wished her brother would get a whipping. Saying nothing of the sort, however, she glanced at Sarah, who peered at her husband. But no help there; Richard stood staring up at the ceiling.

"Libby, darling," Kyle began, "thank you for your concern. Gabriel probably deserves a whipping, but I think I'll settle for a good talking-to."

"Yes, Papa," Libby said, wearing a disappointed little frown.

Just then the housekeeper appeared, and both little girls ran to hug her, crying, "Granny Hester! Granny Hester!"

"Well, now, look who's here." The older woman embraced the girls with a quick hug. "My two little darlings!" After placing kisses on the tops of their heads, she said, "Isabelle's making cake in the kitchen, and if you hurry, she'll let you lick the spoon. Mrs. Fields is in there, too. That's Miss Fields's mother, you know," Hester explained to the girls before setting them in the right direction. "Go see what's happening in the kitchen."

Libby turned to her father. "Can we, Papa?"

Kyle smiled. "Yes, you may."

Taking Rachel's hand, Libby dragged her off down the hallway.

"Isn't the kitchen that way?" Renna said, pointing down the other hallway.

Sarah nodded. "You can go that way, too."

Renna sighed. "Oh, dear." She looked at Kyle. "I think I need a map."

Kyle's laughter rumbled like thunder. "Renna, in a few days you'll know this place like the back of your hand. I promise. Now, then, turn me toward the front staircase. I need to deal with my oldest."

"Shall I guide you up the stairs?"

Kyle shook his head. "I know my way very well."

"All right." Renna took his hand and walked him to the first step.

"Thirty-six steps in a curving staircase." Kyle smiled. "Don't be surprised, Renna, if you see a couple of boys sliding down this banister from time to time."

She smiled. "I won't be surprised at all. In fact, the idea even appealed to me when I first saw this nice shiny railing."

Kyle paused, and a wry grin curved his lips. "Now that would be a sight, wouldn't it? Nurse Fields sliding down my banister."

"I did it once at the hospital," Renna confessed. "I slid side-saddle down the banister of the front staircase, though it wasn't half as grand as yours, Kyle. And besides," she added as he hooted, "I was in a hurry."

"I'll bet Nurse Hatchet gave you a piece of her mind, huh?"

"She didn't catch me," Renna replied tartly. "Now up you go, Kyle, your son awaits."

Kyle's expression sobered at once. "Pray for me, Renna," he said softly. "My relationship with the boy is already strained. I can't imagine what I might say to change his mind about me."

"I will pray," she promised, watching him ascend the staircase.

Kyle made his way to Gabriel's bedroom. He knocked once and then, without waiting for a reply, walked in. Gabriel was not unpacking, as he'd been told. He was lying on his bed, staring at the ceiling and wearing a dour expression.

"Gabriel, we need to talk."

No reply.

Kyle walked farther into the bedroom. He glanced around at all the unframed artwork tacked to the walls. Why hadn't he seen it before? The watercolors, ink sketches, and chalk drawings were all very well done.

"Are you the artist of all these pictures, Gabe?" Kyle asked before thinking about it. And then, too late, he realized his blunder. He was supposed to be blind. Turning toward his son, Kyle saw that Gabriel was scrutinizing him with a puzzled frown.

Kyle removed his dark glasses. "I'll be honest with you, son, although I pray I'm not endangering your life by doing so." He sighed. *Oh, well, too late now.* "I'm not blind, Gabriel, although I was for a long time after the boating accident. But I've agreed to pretend that I'm still blind so the authorities can discover if someone tampered with my schooner last summer. That same person—or persons—may still be trying to kill me."

Gabriel sat up and swung his legs off the bed. "You mean you can see?"

Kyle nodded and watched the boy pale slightly. "And, yes, I saw you stick out your tongue at me minutes ago."

Gabriel swallowed hard, obviously expecting impending doom.

"You deserve a good thrashing for that one," Kyle told him. "However, I think you're old enough now that we can. . .discuss the matter. Will you agree to that? A discussion?"

Gabriel nodded and followed his father over to the round table in the middle of the room. Four chairs surrounded it and pens, ink, paints, and brushes covered the top. Kyle sat down and gently moved the art supplies toward the middle of the table.

"You're a very talented young man, Gabriel."

"Thank you, sir," came the stiff reply. The boy still had a wary look in his eyes. No doubt he was thinking that after their discussion he might still get his thrashing.

Kyle tried in vain to stifle a grin. "You know, I remember when I was your age. Aurora didn't know what to do with me, so she did nothing. I was very bored one summer and spent my free time down at the docks. I met a man down there whom everyone referred to as Corky. Captain Corky." Kyle chuckled at the remembrance. "Corky was an old man with a sharp tongue, but he took pity on me that summer and taught me many things about ships. Once he even took me on a two-day journey across Lake Michigan. Aurora never even knew I was gone. But then the fall came, and I was talking of seafaring men and using bad language. Aurora was so aghast, she packed me off to boarding school. I never got to say good-bye to Corky and his crew. I hated my mother for that."

Kyle looked at his son. "But after a couple of years at boarding school, I realized that, even though Aurora had no mothering skills to speak of, she wanted the best for me and soon I wanted the best for me, too. I married your mother and we had four beautiful children, but I didn't know how to be a father because—well, except for Corky that summer I had no father figure in my life. Even so, I wanted the best for my children. . . just like Aurora had wanted the best for me. Do you understand what I'm trying to say, Gabriel?"

He shrugged. "I think so."

Kyle paused to collect his thoughts. "I know I haven't been a good father, but I want to be. And now I'm a Christian, so I know God will help me. But you're going to have to be patient with me, son."

Gabriel looked him squarely in the eyes. "Are you going to marry that lady and then send me off to boarding school like Aurora did to you?"

"No, not if you don't want to go."

"I don't."

"Then you won't go to boarding school."

Gabriel narrowed his gaze suspiciously. "How do I know that you'll keep your promise? You never did before."

Kyle expelled a heavy breath. He hated the fact his son spoke the truth. "I wasn't a Christian before my accident, Gabriel. I had no use for God. But now I know Him, and I'm studying His Word. I'm learning. I'm different. Everything is different now. I'm a changed man."

"All right," Gabriel replied grudgingly, "I'll give you one more chance."

"Only one more?" Kyle sent the boy a patient smile. "What if I need fifty more chances? If I remember correctly, Jesus said we're to forgive seventy times seven. That's four hundred and ninety chances, Gabe—for the same sin!" Kyle leaned toward his son. "Richard told me that you were born again, too—on the day of my boating accident. Is that true? Are you a Christian, too?"

Gabriel nodded.

Kyle smiled. "I'm glad."

"Michael got saved, too. And Libby. But Rachel's too little. She doesn't understand yet."

"We'll help her when she gets older, won't we?" Kyle's smile broadened. "And just think, we'll all be in heaven together one day."

Gabriel was studying him earnestly now. "You seem like you're really a Christian."

"I really am, but I'm still learning. As I said before, I'm going to need your patience." He chuckled. "Miss Fields even said that I'm not half the pirate I used to be."

"Pirate?"

Gabriel's young face split into a grin. "I remember all those pirate stories you used to tell Michael and me."

"I remember them, too."

Gabriel sat back in his chair, looking more at ease now. "How long do you have to pretend that you're blind?"

Kyle sobered. "I hope it's not much longer. But, please, Gabriel, keep this a secret from Miss Fields. She still thinks I'm blind. . .and I have to be the one to tell her the truth. I hate deceiving her this way; however, I don't want to put her life in danger, too." He gave his son a heartfelt glance. "I hope I haven't endangered your life, Gabe. Oh, God, may it not be so!" he added on a whispered prayer.

"Don't worry, Papa," Gabriel replied. "I'm brave and strong. Old Mr. Navis even said so. Besides, people don't pay much attention to children. We're just seen and not heard. . .but we listen a lot. I'll bet I can find out a whole ton of stuff."

"Now, Gabriel, I don't want you to involve yourself. Leave this to the authorities. They know what they're doing. One man has already lost his life because he knew too much."

"Really? Who?"

"Someone I had dealings with down at the docks. He repaired ships and had worked on my schooner just days before the accident." Kyle paused and gave his son an earnest look. "Gabe, you mustn't repeat any of what I've told you to anyone. Understood?"

Gabriel's eyes gleamed with a challenge. "Do you trust me?"

Kyle lifted a brow. "Can I? Are you a trustworthy man?"

"I am," Gabe replied, bringing his chin up.

"Well, then, I trust you, Gabe. I trust you with my life!"

Chapter 16

Thanksgiving Day was spent on the Navises' farm as Kyle wanted to give his staff the day off. But he realized too late that it meant more work for the women in his life, although they didn't seem to mind. They bustled around the kitchen, cooking and preparing all the food, and gabbing all the while. Kyle made sure he stayed out of their way.

The men, on the other hand, had an easier time of things. They sat in the parlor and talked of war days, since Richard's father had served in the Civil War, too. Marty Navis, called "Old Mr. Navis" by the children, was, in fact, confined to a wheelchair due to a back injury incurred during his time in the service. But he didn't harbor a bitter spirit and told lively battlefield stories. Kyle, too, had a few lively tales of his own. He spoke of his battles at sea and his shoulder wound which sent him home early. Gabriel and Michael listened with expressions of fascination, but Libby and Rachel preferred to be with the ladies in the kitchen.

"Smashed potatoes are my favorite!" Libby declared as she did her best with the metal masher in the boiled potatoes.

Finally, Richard's mother, Beatrice Navis, called, "Dinner is served!" and everyone flocked to the dining room.

"That's one bad thing about living on the farm," Gabriel mused aloud as he gazed at the turkey, roasted to a golden perfection. "You've seen the food when it's alive and running around the yard."

"Oh, now, don't turn your nose up at my dinner," Bea warned him. "I worked for hours. . .along with Sarah, Miss Renna, and Mrs. Fields." She smiled at the little girls. "And Libby and Rachel, too, of course. And we've got the pies to prove it."

"Well, I didn't mean I wouldn't eat dinner," Gabriel clarified with a hungry look in his eyes.

Kyle chuckled and tousled his son's hair.

Renna noticed that Kyle was getting very good at being blind. It was actually quite amazing. She'd also noticed Gabriel's attitude had done a turnaround for the better. In fact, Gabriel acted as though he and his father were the best of friends. He followed Kyle around like a puppy and did his father's bidding without a single complaint.

"What did you ever say to Gabriel to make him have a change of heart toward you?" Renna asked Kyle later that night, after they had arrived back at his home. They were sitting in the great hall with Wendall and Johanna. Hester had spent the day with her family and wouldn't be back until tomorrow morning, and the children were asleep upstairs.

Kyle smiled at Renna's question. "I'm not sure exactly. I guess I just talked to him like I'd talk to anybody else."

"Well, that's what did it," Wendall said. "Children like to be regarded as human beings, too. Very few people understand that these days."

"I suppose that's true enough," Kyle said. "But around here, things are different now. In fact, I want my children at the reception tomorrow night."

"What reception?" Renna asked, wide-eyed.

"Oh. . .did I forget to tell you? It's a very bad habit of mine. . . forgetfulness. I'm sorry, Renna," he said, looking sincere. "As for tomorrow night, I've circulated the news that I'm holding a reception here. It was either that or entertain curious, drop-in visitors from now until the New Year."

"I see." Renna tried to conceal her dread.

"It's just a reception," Kyle said, as if he could see her displeasure. "However, I will warn you, we're going to have to attend a ball or two. . . for propriety's sake."

"Yes, of course." She sent her mother a pleading look.

"Now, Renna, it won't be all that bad." Johanna glanced at Kyle. "Will it, Captain?"

He grinned. "No. And we won't stay long, I promise. We'll greet everyone and then make our excuses."

"I'm sure it will be fine," Wendall said with an air of confidence, while eyeing his daughter. "Renna, I wouldn't have allowed this man to court you if I didn't trust him."

"It's not a matter of trust," she began. "It's. . ." But then she thought better of bringing up the subject of her birthmark. "Never mind."

She steeled her resolve, willing herself to believe that the reception tomorrow night and the balls to follow wouldn't be as horrible and humiliating as she imagined.

The next morning, Renna and Johanna came downstairs and found poor Hester running hither and yon. "The captain is having a reception here tonight, and he didn't even forewarn me," she complained. "Told me just this morning. He invites the entire city of Milwaukee, and he forgets to mention it." Hester threw her hands in the air. "Hallelujah!"

Johanna smiled demurely. "What can Renna and I do to help you?"

Hester paused, looking surprised by the offer. But then she flung a list at them. "Here. The captain gave me these duties this morning. I've got to plan the hors d'oeuvres, hire some more staff—where will I get more people at this late hour? The captain is insisting on a butler and wants several maids, too. . ." Hester shook her head. "Impossible!"

Johanna frowned and glanced from the list back to the harried housekeeper. "Where's the captain now?"

"Oh, he and Mr. Fields went to his store on the riverfront. The captain wants it reopened soon. He said he's losing money every day that it stays closed."

"And the children?" Renna asked. "Where are they?"

"Oh, the captain and Mr. Fields took the children with them," Hester replied. "It was the captain's idea, actually. He told Gabriel and Michael that he'd like them to get involved in his business affairs little by little." Hester smiled for the first time since Renna had seen her this morning. "You should have seen those boys' faces, too. Beaming, they were! Why, the captain made his sons feel real important." But then her expression fell. "But the man's going to kill me with his lists and last minute receptions, that's for sure!"

"Oh, now, Hester, we'll help you," Renna promised. "Here—here, give me that list."

Johanna handed it over, and Renna sighed while reading it. But then she snapped her fingers as an idea struck. "I'll ask Kyle's valet. He should know who Kyle usually hires for these things."

Renna ran upstairs to find Tommy and, as it happened, he proved most helpful. By one o'clock, the staffing problems had been taken care of. By three o'clock the food was arriving with Isabelle, the cook, manning the kitchen. With a bit of monetary persuasion, Isabelle agreed to stay until after the reception and clean up. Then she even incorporated her thirteen-year-old daughter's help. Together they polished silver and prepared the hors d'oeuvres trays. After that, the children came home and the little girls took a short rest. Then there was a flurry of activity as everyone dressed for the evening.

"Hester, I am impressed," Kyle stated as he stood in the foyer with Renna at his side. "I gave you some tall orders, but you were able to follow them to the letter." He bowed graciously. "Thank you."

"You're welcome, Captain," Hester replied with a bit of a curtsey. She had donned a black dress and white apron that matched the serving maids'. "I must tell you, though, sir, I had help from—"

Hester paused and, from out of the side of his dark glasses, Kyle saw Renna shaking her auburn head vigorously. He tried not to grin. "Yes, Hester? You had help from whom?"

"Ah, well, I had to offer Isabelle a slight bonus for staying late tonight and helping me out."

"That's to be expected, and it's not a problem."

"Thank you, sir. Now I'll be running along and making sure those hired maids aren't slacking off."

"Yes, see that you do," Kyle replied, smiling in her wake. Then he leaned over to Renna and whispered, "You did a wonderful job with the preparations for tonight." He couldn't help placing a kiss on her temple then. "Thank you."

She blushed. "If you do that again, Kyle, my father will be upon us in a flash, standing in between us the rest of the night."

Kyle smiled at the threat, though he didn't doubt it. "I stand justly rebuked," he replied. "But you look so beautiful tonight, Renna, that I—"

She looked up at him with a puzzled frown.

Kyle smiled, chagrined. "Well, several people have told me how beautiful you look, and I can imagine it. . . ."

"Oh," Renna said, seeming to accept the explanation.

Kyle chided himself, first for the blunder and then the deception. He should just tell her. . . .

"Look, Renna, there's something that I—"

But, too late. Guests were upon them. The well-trained butler announced the invitees as they arrived.

"Mrs. Lillian LaMonde," he told them as the woman stepped right up.

Kyle forced a polite smile. "Lillian. How nice that you came tonight."

"How nice that you're not dead, Kyle," she quipped. "And who's this sweet-looking thing at your side?" She eyed Renna with a speculative gleam.

Kyle made the appropriate introductions, praying that his beloved would withstand the scrutiny tonight. "This is Renna Fields, from Chicago."

"Chicago? The Windy City. Are you a widow?"

Renna shook her head. "No, ma'am."

"You're married?"

"No!" Renna looked shocked by Lillian's implication. "I'm a nurse!"

Kyle grinned inwardly. Lillian, too, seemed rather amused. "A nurse? How interesting. You and I will have to talk soon." Looking back at Kyle, she added, "And you and I, Kyle, will have to talk soon as well."

"I look forward to it," he stated dryly.

Lillian LaMonde waltzed away, heading for the great hall.

Kyle leaned over to Renna. "Watch every word you say to that woman. She writes the society page in the *Milwaukee Sentinel*. Everything you say can and will appear in her gossip column."

Renna nodded, and Kyle wished he could erase the worried frown from her brow.

"Mr. and Mrs. Marcus Norton," the butler announced.

"Thank you for coming," Kyle said as he and Marcus shook hands. Then he introduced Renna. He knew she'd like the Nortons. They were decent, Christian people, though Kyle hadn't ever appreciated that fact until after his conversion to Christ. Now he saw it as a valuable asset in his trusted banker.

The Nortons walked off, and the butler announced the next set of guests. "Miss Fayre Waterford."

Kyle cringed. The woman was like his pirate's past hitting him right between the eyes.

Fayre walked up to him, standing barely an inch away. Then she greeted him with a pout. "You've been back nearly a week, and you haven't called on me once!"

Kyle felt Renna stiffen at his side. "Allow me to introduce Miss Renna

Fields," he said, patting her hand, looped around his elbow. "Renna is a nurse from Chicago, and we're likely to announce our engagement in the near future."

"Engagement?" After a scowl, Fayre lifted her gloved hand and struck the side of Kyle's face before he even saw it coming. But that was fortunately for him, since he was supposed to be blind.

Nevertheless, gasps echoed in the foyer, and Kyle feared Renna would faint from shock.

"Renna, I'm terribly sorry," he said leaning toward her. "Fayre is one of those females I escorted last summer. She took our relationship more seriously than I ever did."

"Obviously." The little frown marring Renna's brow deepened.

"I apologize for the embarrassment. Please don't be angry or hurt," Kyle pleaded. "I'm in love with you, not her."

A look of happiness transformed Renna features, and Kyle suddenly realized he'd labeled his feelings accurately. Love. That was it. Why else would he want to protect, cherish, and even show Renna off to all the world? She was, by far, the most beautiful person he'd ever met.

Kyle pulled her a little closer. "Fayre Waterford can't hold a candle to you."

"Why thank you, Captain."

The evening wore on. Renna met so many people that, after awhile, the names and faces all blurred together. She doubted she'd recognize any of them if she passed them on the street.

Just then a man pushed passed the butler. Guests in line gasped at his rudeness.

"Matthew Benchley," Renna murmured. "Kyle, it's Matthew. . .what on earth. . . ?"

"Stay calm, Renna," Kyle told her, narrowing his gaze at the other man.

"Captain Sinclair," Matthew said on an arrogant note, "I believe you and I have unfinished business."

"Oh?"

"Yes." Benchley stood just inches away, his chin raised in defiance. "Kingsley Shipping. I want it. My uncle willed it to my brother and me.

Aunt Elise had no right to sell it."

"Now's not the time or place—"

"Oh, no. . .you're not going to get rid of me that easily. I could care less about your ostentatious social affair." He cleared his throat, behaving as though he held the upper hand. "About Kingsley Shipping. . ."

"What about it?"

"I want it."

"It's not for sale. Now, get out!"

Renna gasped at Kyle's vehemence, while Benchley's face reddened with anger. Then Timothy and another man grabbed hold of Matthew's arms and hauled him from the foyer. Gasps and murmurs resonated through the house.

"Kyle. . .?"

"Never mind, Renna. I don't want you involved in this." A heartbeat later, he softened his tone and gave her a warm smile. "Nothing to worry your pretty head about."

Renna gazed up at him, thinking that if he could see, he might not be saying such things tonight—things like "beautiful," "pretty," and maybe even "love." On the other hand, she was grateful that he was blind to the blond, voluptuous Fayre Waterford in her shockingly low-cut silk gown. Renna hated to think that Kyle would be one of the half-dozen handsome men flocked around Fayre right now. But he had been once. . .that much was obvious.

And how could Miss Waterford remain at the reception, having slapped the host's face? How utterly rude—and even more confusing.

Lord, I don't know if I can fit into this world, Renna breathed in silent prayer.

Then she turned and looked right into the smirking face of Lillian LaMonde.

Chapter 17

G oodness!" Lillian LaMonde exclaimed. "Wasn't that. . . Benchley? Yes, that's his name! He certainly seemed agitated." She eyed Renna speculatively. "Perhaps he was jealous. . .a former love interest?"

"Hardly," Renna replied dryly, and beside her, Kyle chuckled.

"Well, there are certainly enough of those around here tonight—former love interests, that is." Lillian snorted, turning her scrutiny on Kyle.

He pursed his lips and shrugged as if he cared less.

Lillian tried a different approach. "Your children are up rather late, aren't they, Kyle?"

"My children are invited guests. They always make an appearance at my social functions."

"True, but they're usually accompanied by a governess. Why, those boys are eating up all the hors d'oeuvres. And your housekeeper, Kyle. . . why, she's conversing with the company!" Lillian brought herself up to her full height. "No doubt there are plenty of people who would gladly take advantage of your physical distress."

"Hester is new at housekeeping," Kyle replied, sounding a bit terse to Renna's ears. "I'll have to speak with her."

She looked at Kyle, taking in his stern expression. She hoped he wouldn't deal too harshly with poor Hester. The woman was trying so hard. . . .

"And, as for you, my dear," Lillian said, looking at Renna once more, "it was a pleasure to meet you—you and your parents." She chuckled merrily. "Kyle, things do seem topsy-turvy here, if you don't mind me saying so. I hardly expected your latest romantic interest to be of such. . .average stock. From what I gather, there aren't any fortunes to be won here."

"Things are most certainly topsy-turvy," Kyle retorted with a handsome smile, "because, for once, Lillian, you're right!"

"Hmm. . ." Lillian arched a well-sculpted brow. "Well, I must be off.

I have a column to write and a deadline to meet."

The captain bowed. "Thank you for coming."

She left, and Renna sighed with relief.

By now, the guests had stopped arriving, so Kyle pulled Renna toward the great hall, where everyone had congregated. "I know my way around this house like I know my way around a ship," he said in explanation. "Many a late night, I've had to find my way in the pitch dark, both in this house and aboard roiling vessels."

"You're doing very well," Renna replied, for Kyle hadn't stumbled once.

The great hall was filled to capacity. People stood in various small groups engaged in lively discussions which included the lastest gossip.

Then the children were suddenly upon them. Gabriel and Michael had mouths so full of food that their cheeks bulged and they were laughing obnoxiously, the way eleven- and twelve-year-old boys sometimes do. They earned a gentle admonishment from their father and composed themselves. Meanwhile Renna noticed that Rachel looked tired. As if to prove her theory, the little girl's jaw dropped in a wide yawn.

"Kyle, perhaps I should take the children upstairs and put them to bed," she suggested. "The boys are red-faced and over-excited, and little Rachel looks exhausted. Libby looks tired, too."

He smirked. "You're not getting out of this reception so easily, my dear."

"I'll come back," she promised. Renna looked across the room and spotted Sarah Navis. "I'll get Sarah to help me."

"All right," Kyle replied, albeit reluctantly. "I'll try not to get lost while you're gone." He wore a sheepish grin.

"I'm not worried," Renna retorted. "You do so well at being blind, and it's nothing short of a miracle."

Kyle's grin faded. "Just hurry back, Renna. . .you and I need to talk privately. Soon. Perhaps right after the party."

"Did I do something wrong?" she asked with growing concern. "Perhaps I'm in need of a talking-to like Hester. . . ?"

"No, no, nothing like that. And, as for Hester, I plan to merely point out a few rules of propriety so that—"

"Oh, don't speak to me of propriety, Kyle. This function smacks of politics and money, nothing proper about it—at least not in the Christian sense." Renna bit her lower lip, sensing she'd said too much. "Forgive me. I'm so opinionated—maybe too opinionated."

"We'll talk later, Renna," he said, giving her hand a gentle pat.

Nodding, she gathered up the children and then crossed the room and asked for Sarah's assistance.

"Of course. I'd love to help you!" she replied enthusiastically.

Children in tow, the women marched them around the kitchen and up the back staircase for "propriety's sake." Renna was completely disgusted.

"Do you think there are any God-fearing people here tonight?" she asked Sarah after they tucked the girls into bed. "Except for us?"

"Oh, yes," she replied. "The Nortons and the Talbots are believers, the Johnsons and the Smiths, just to name a few. Richard has had business dealings with them."

"Hmm. . ." Renna was momentarily pensive. "And how do they handle affairs like this? All the pomp and arrogance downstairs is suffocating me."

Sarah only smiled. "I know what you mean, and, if you'll notice, the couples I mentioned didn't stay too long." She sighed. "We should be on our way soon, too."

"But you have such a long ride home to the farm," Renna protested, not wanting to lose her one and only ally. "Why don't you spend the night here?"

"Actually, we are staying in town—with Richard's aunt and uncle. They live close by. So does his cousin Lina and her husband. They're here tonight, too."

Renna fought to hide her disappointment.

They walked down the hallway together and then checked on Gabriel and Michael. Each boy was in his own room, dressed for bed and reading quietly.

"I'm so glad you have a heart for the children," Sarah said as they made their way back to the reception. "It's easier for me to give them up, knowing you care for them. And they like you, too. That's obvious."

"A blessing all the way around, I'd say."

Sarah nodded. "I've grown particularly fond of the Sinclair children— so much so that I was ready and willing to adopt them had the captain really drowned."

"You're a special young lady," Renna told her, wishing she could promise Sarah more. However, Kyle hadn't proposed marriage, and Renna had no jurisdiction over the Sinclair children, though she suspected that Richard and Sarah Navis would always be special friends and welcomed into this household.

They ambled through the kitchen now, where things were much calmer than hours ago. The cleanup process had begun, and right in the middle of it was Johanna Fields.

"Mother, what are you doing in here?" Renna asked on a note of surprise. "I don't think Kyle will like it."

"I said the very same thing," Isabelle murmured. "The captain won't like it." She looked at Johanna. "Guests don't clean up with the hired help."

"Pshaw!" Johanna replied tartly. "I answer to my Master, Jesus Christ, not Captain Sinclair. Besides," she added with a wink at Renna, "that man will have to accept me just as I am if he wants to marry my daughter."

The sounds of amiable snickering went around the kitchen, and Renna shook her head at her mother.

"This house won't be the same if the captain does marry Miss Renna," Isabelle announced. "Will it, girls?" She chuckled. "Why, when Gretchen was here we all had our 'places' and she ran this house like Grant! But I think I could get used to Miss Renna and her mother running things. You two think of us workers as people, and that's refreshing."

"Of course we do," Johanna said, wiping clean a silver platter. "That's what the Civil War was all about—equal rights among people."

"I don't know," Isabelle replied skeptically. She was of German decent, though she didn't speak with an accent. Her hair was salt-and-pepper gray, worn pinned up at her nape, and little round spectacles rested on the wide bridge of her nose. "The captain told us the Civil War was a political issue and didn't have much to do with rights for slaves, though that was part of it. And last night Miss Ann Dickinson, you know, that female orator, spoke at Music Hall right here in Milwaukee. She said none of the issues of the war got solved and there's treason in the White House!"

"Oh, don't listen to her," Johanna said. "Miss Ann Dickinson, indeed! Ladies have no business talking politics. . . ." She lowered her voice. "That is, we ought not let the men hear us talking politics. We are entitled to our opinions, though."

"Yes, ma'am," Isabelle replied, laughing. Then she turned to the hired hands. "Don't be standing around now. We talk while we work. I want to be home before midnight."

The ladies in the kitchen returned to their tasks, Johanna included. She would not be persuaded to join the other guests.

Leaving the kitchen, Renna and Sarah returned to the great hall. They passed the vestibule where many of the guests were leaving as it had begun to snow outside. Several people called good-byes to Renna, and she replied with a smile and a wave. She suddenly thought that perhaps she could fit in here—at least among some of Kyle's friends and acquaintances.

However, the next scene that Renna encountered changed her mind. There, in the great hall, standing among a throng of people, was Kyle, acting all the pirate's part. He was laughing gaily with Fayre Waterford plastered to his side. More disturbing to Renna was that Kyle made no move to extricate the woman's arm, looped intimately around his.

Sarah cleared her throat and looked suddenly very uncomfortable. "Some punch, Miss Fields?"

Renna turned away from the heart-wrenching sight before her and forced a smile. "Yes. I believe I am quite thirsty. Thank you."

Renna followed Sarah to the other side of the room and gratefully accepted a glass of punch from one of the serving maids. Then they headed for the man and woman with whom Richard was conversing. Standing there beside Sarah, Renna was only too glad that she had her back to Kyle.

How can he say he's in love with me and then flirt with a woman who slapped his face?

"Miss Fields?" Renna brought her gaze up from her punch and regarded the woman addressing her. She was about the same age as Sarah and had huge blue eyes. Her hair was a light-brown color and curled into fat ringlets that fell all around her oval face. "I'm Nickolina Barnes," she said. "Please call me Lina. I'm Richard's cousin."

Renna smiled. "Thank you for reintroducing yourself. I'm afraid I don't remember many of the names I heard tonight."

"I wouldn't either," Lina replied, and Renna saw a look of under-standing in her eyes. "I'm a schoolteacher, and this fall I've had the privilege of instructing the three oldest Sinclair children. It was their first time at school and they had quite an adjustment. But they're doing wonderfully now."

Sarah explained, "In past years, the captain always hired a private tutor for the children. Either that or the governess taught them, although I've heard governesses didn't stay on very long."

"Yes, I've heard that, too," Renna replied, smiling in spite of herself.

"We're hoping Captain Sinclair will allow the children to stay in school," Lina continued. "They're just settling in and really beginning to learn. It's exciting. Perhaps you'd like to come to school on Monday morning and observe while I teach. . . ?"

"Thank you for the offer. I will consider it; however, I would suggest you speak to the captain. I don't have any say as to the children's education."

"You had a big say in Hester's position," Richard said. "The captain looked to you for advice and made his decision based upon your reply."

"But that was before—"

Renna stopped herself before saying *That was before this party, and now Kyle is obviously allowing himself to be drawn back into his old lifestyle.* She managed a tight smile. "I–I'm afraid you'll have to talk to Kyle about the children's education."

"What about the children's education?"

At the sound of his voice coming from just behind her, the tiny hairs on Renna's neck stood on edge. She wanted to turn and mimic Miss Waterford's greeting. How dare he allow that indecently dressed female to hang on him. But more than that, Renna hated feeling jealous and so insecure. With her marring birthmark, she couldn't compete with a woman as stunning as Fayre, and Renna wasn't about to try. Even blind, Renna was certain that Kyle's imagination would remind him of just how beautiful Fayre was. His memory would no doubt overshadow any image he had of her.

Then Renna was reminded of all the parties and social gatherings she'd been forced to attend from the time she was sixteen. She had never been able to compete with any of her female peers, so Renna never tried. She kept to herself at all the social affairs, but watched on with a secret longing—a longing to be beautiful!

"Please excuse me," Renna said in the gentlest voice she could muster between clenched teeth. She suddenly couldn't decide with whom she was more angry—herself or Kyle! "I'd better go see after my mother."

With that, she swung around and left the hall so quickly she had to remind herself not to run. She got as far as the vestibule when she heard someone call out her name. It was Richard Navis.

"Miss Fields, please wait up."

She paused.

"Please don't let Fayre Waterford upset you," he said, catching up to her. It seemed as if he could read Renna's thoughts. "I saw what happened but, honestly, it wasn't the captain's fault." He went on to explain. "Miss Waterford must have seen you coming with Sarah, and she attached herself to the captain like a barnacle. The captain, being polite, didn't overreact, but he did manage to shake her off—unfortunately, you hadn't seen that part. You had gotten your punch and had come to stand with my cousin and her husband."

Renna was tempted to be stubborn about this, but she knew Richard wouldn't lie.

"And this is exactly what Fayre wanted to happen," he added. "She'd like nothing better than to upset you and subsequently ruin your relationship with the captain."

It made sense, and Renna accepted the explanation. But in the next moment, she felt foolish for being duped so easily. On the other hand, she was inexperienced in these things—and in the ways of women such as Fayre Waterford.

At last, Renna nodded. "Thank you for taking the time and setting straight this, uh, misunderstanding."

Richard bent in a slight bow, but there was no mistaking his sheepish grin. "My pleasure, ma'am. Now won't you please rejoin the guests? The captain had a worried look on his face, and Lina wants so badly to discuss the topic of the children's education, or at least present it. However, my guess is Captain Sinclair hasn't heard a word Lina said so far."

A new resolve washed over her. "Yes, I'll go right now."

"And tell the captain that I'll return with his punch shortly. All the maids have gone to the kitchen."

"I'll tell him."

Renna walked back into the great hall and over to where Kyle was still standing with Lina, her husband, and Sarah. When she reached his side, Kyle interrupted the conversation to inquire over Renna's mother.

"She's in the kitchen," Renna explained. "She insisted upon helping clean up and seems to be enjoying herself, even though I told her you wouldn't like it."

Kyle smiled. "Well, if it's only that, Renna. I thought she was ill from the way you left in such a hurry."

"No, she's fine, Kyle. Everything's fine."

His relief was evident in the way his shoulders sagged. He seemed to relax. "Good."

He reached for her hand and looped it around his elbow, and Renna tried to still the persistent disquiet in her heart.

Chapter 18

The rest of the evening passed without incident, and by nine o'clock most of the guests had departed. Renna was more than glad to see them go; this evening proved the longest four hours of her life!

Once the last of their company had left, Kyle pulled Renna into his study. "Your father gave me permission to speak with you privately," he said, closing the oak-paneled double doors.

"Kyle, before you say another thing," Renna began, "please allow me a few words."

He inclined his head. "As you wish."

Renna groped for the right words, but then ended up just blurting it all out. "Oh, Kyle, you're not going terminate poor Hester's employment, are you? She tried so hard to please you today. She was such a help with all the preparations. She'll learn not to talk to your guests, and she needs a place to stay. . .and work."

Kyle expelled an annoyed-sounding breath. "Renna, I'm afraid Hester is not my idea of a housekeeper. I wouldn't have had to hire a butler tonight if Hester were well trained. I could have had her welcoming guests as well as overseeing the hired serving wenches."

Renna winced. "I abhor that word!"

"Which word?"

"Wenches."

Kyle laughed. "Renna, that's what they are."

"No, Kyle, they're women. Working women. Human beings. Like me."

"Tsk, tsk. . ." A wry smile played across Kyle's mouth. "The suffragette in you is coming out again, Renna."

His voice held an amused ring, though there was no mistaking the warning, and Renna bit her lower lip. Is that what Kyle wanted? A docile, beautiful little thing—an ornament to hang on his arm? Was he really like all the other men she'd met? Men who couldn't appreciate her for having a brain in her head?

Facing the windows that had been shuttered tightly for the night, Renna folded her arms across the bodice of her gown. She wondered what to do. On one hand, she was sure she loved this man, her pirate. On the other hand, she felt trapped. A square peg being forced into a round hole.

Suddenly Kyle's hands were on her shoulders. He stood directly in back of her. "If you want Hester to stay," he whispered, "then she may."

Renna sighed at her bittersweet victory. "Kyle, this is your household, not mine. I have no right to interfere."

Slowly, he turned her around to face him. He paused as if he could read her expression, and Renna was only too glad that he couldn't. Her face surely mirrored all the doubt and despair in her heart.

"I value your opinion," Kyle stated softly.

"But we're worlds apart." She felt the emotion accumulating in her throat.

"Only if you want us to be."

"As if I can change something like that?"

"Yes, of course, you can." Kyle dropped his hands to his side. "It's all in the way you think of yourself, Renna. You're as good—if not better—than anyone who attended the reception tonight."

"But I'm not rich."

"But I am."

"And therein lies the problem. Can't you understand? I don't come from money. I'm like Hester and the serving. . .*wenches*. I'm acquainted with simple folk."

"But your father is a successful businessman in Chicago, and he has a fine reputation. He mingled comfortably with all the guests tonight."

"He mingled comfortably with all the *businessmen*, you mean. And so would I, if it were a socially acceptable thing for a woman to do. I'd gladly talk business with men rather than gossip with bubbleheaded women—all except for Lina, Sarah, and Mrs. Norton, that is!"

At the tart reply, Kyle dropped his head back and laughed. In fact, he laughed harder than Renna had ever seen him laugh before. He laughed for a good minute, until Renna lifted an angry brow and threatened to leave the room.

"All right, all right, I'll stop," he said between chortles. "I will. I promise." He took another minute to collect himself. Then he sighed and took her hands in his. "Renna, your father warned me fair and square. It was while I was in the hospital. I was curious as to why such a beautiful angel of mercy was yet unmarried. Your father explained that it was difficult to find suitors for you since most of them were beneath your level of intelligence. Now I understand what he meant. . .and, Renna, I respect you for it. In fact, I love you more for it."

As if his own words surprised him, Kyle brought himself up short, shaking his head and suddenly looking very serious. "And that's what I needed to talk to you about. Twice, I professed to being in love with you, Renna, but it's like I want some guarantee that I've correctly tagged my emotions. I'm desperately trying to figure out what love is and just how real it is."

Renna pondered the idea for several long moments. Finally, she said, "I think that perhaps love is like faith. You know it's real, but you can't touch it or see it. . .except in action. Just like the Bible says that faith without works is dead, perhaps love without works is dead, too."

"And you think that since I've been working at them—both faith and love—that's what makes them real for me now?"

"Perhaps."

The frown on Kyle's face told Renna that he wasn't satisfied with her answer. With her hands still in his, he persisted. "Do you love me, Renna?"

She hesitated a moment, startled by his blatant question. "Yes," she whispered at last.

"How do you know?"

Her eyes widened. "I just do."

"You just do?" He sighed, sounding exasperated. "That's not helping me, Renna."

She laughed and squeezed his hands. "Do you believe in something called the wind, Kyle?"

"The wind? Of course I do. What kind of question is that?"

"Well, how do you know there's a wind?" Renna queried. "You can't see it or hold it in your hands."

Kyle looked chagrined at her challenge. "I can feel it."

"You can feel love, too. And faith. When I sing hymns to praise my

Savior, I feel my faith stirring in my heart. What joy!" Renna smiled at her own enthusiasm. "And when I'm with you, Kyle, and you accept me for who I am and the knowledge I have—because of our friendship first—I feel love for you in my heart."

"I am. . .overwhelmed by your honesty," Kyle said, though he looked pleased all the same.

Renna's smile grew. "Honesty is what a relationship is all about. I learned that the night I told you about the birthmark on my cheek. I kept hearing the words of our Lord: *The truth shall set you free*. . .and it did that night."

Kyle dropped her hands and gave her an uncomfortable grin. "Renna, I need to tell you something."

"All right. But first let me just say that you're the first man—besides my father, of course—whom I could trust. And trust is essential to every relationship. Don't you agree?"

"Ah, yes. . .absolutely. Trust. That's why I need to tell you—"

"Like Matthew Benchley, for instance," Renna continued, "that cad. I wouldn't be able to trust a man like him."

"Renna—"

Suddenly a large crash rocked the house.

"What in the world. . . ?" Kyle ran to the doors, swinging them open. Renna was right behind him, and they met Hester and Johanna in the foyer.

"Must have been a tree that fell on the house, Captain!" Hester exclaimed.

Wendall came running from the men's parlor, wearing a concerned expression. "I think it came from the pavilion."

Kyle nodded. "Let's investigate." He turned to Renna. "Will you and your mother please go upstairs and check on the children?"

"Of course."

"Then stay up there until your father and I come to fetch you. You, too, Hester."

"Yes, Captain."

All three ladies took the wide front staircase at once. Reaching the top, they found the two little girls asleep and Michael quietly occupying himself in his bedroom.

"What was that crash?" he asked. "Was it Granny Hester in the kitchen?" Michael chuckled, so typically boyish and unconcerned.

However, Gabriel was nowhere to be found, much to Renna's dismay.

Then, about a half-hour later, Wendall came up with the news. "Gabriel is downstairs with his father. Apparently, he crept down for more food and was eating in the hallway between the solarium and pavilion when the crash occurred. Gabriel was shaken but unharmed."

"Oh, I'm so glad," Renna breathed in relief. "When we couldn't find him, I imagined the worst."

"I'll go up to Hester's quarters and let her know Gabriel is all right," Johanna said, leaving the room.

"So, what was that awful crash?" Renna wanted to know.

"It was an odd-looking metal object, weighing nearly four pounds," he said, looking grave. "Upon closer inspection, Kyle identified it as a piece of propeller from a ship. Someone heaved it through one of the glass walls of the pavilion." He shook his head sadly. "Such damage. Kyle has summoned the police. Meanwhile, Gabriel claims to have seen a man running from the scene. He's sketching a likeness of him for the authorities."

Renna shook her head incredulously. "Vandals?"

"More than vandals, I'm afraid. There was a note tied around the piece of metal. A threat."

Fear prickled inside Renna's limbs. "What sort of a threat, Father?"

"Renna, you should know that this is the third threat made against Kyle's life since we arrived in Milwaukee."

"The third. . . ? But Kyle hasn't mentioned any threats to me."

"He didn't want you to worry, daughter."

Renna threw her hands up in exasperation. "I would have prayed, not worried!"

"Oh, don't be too hard on the man, Renna, he's trying to protect you. The less you know, the better—that's what Kyle told me."

"Father, I'm not some swooning little morsel of a woman. I was a nurse during the war, and I don't need protecting."

"Maybe not in that sense, Renna. But a man needs to feel that he can protect the woman he loves. So, let him. Let Kyle protect you."

Her father's words made their mark, and Renna softened. Poor, dear Kyle. Since he was blind, the only way he felt he could protect her was to withhold information from her. Well, she'd "let him," all right.

Smiling, she gave her father a kiss on the cheek. "Thank you for the advice. I shall take it to heart."

"Good night, daughter," Wendall said.

"Good night."

With that, Renna left the room her parents occupied and walking across the hall, entered her own room. Her mother came in moments later with an offer to help her undress. It was then that Renna noticed the two pairs of eyes, gazing back at her from under the quilt on her bed.

"I believe I have company, Mother." With a little smile, Renna pulled back the quilt, revealing pink, lacy nighties and two little girls.

Wide-eyed, Libby looked up at her. "We were scared. We heard lots of loud talking. . .it woke me and Rachel up."

"Woke me up," Rachel mimicked.

"I see," Renna said, sitting on the edge of the bed.

"And we wished we had a mama to sleep with when we're scared."

"A mama when we're scared!" Rachel said, bolting upright and smiling impishly at Renna.

She was touched, and yet she sensed a little manipulation here. Nevertheless, these little girls were in obvious need of some motherly affection.

"Libby, Rachel," she began, "there is nothing to be afraid of. Your father has everything under control."

"He does?"

"Yes. He's a very brave man, you know. We don't have to be afraid with your father taking care of us."

Libby smiled. She seemed glad to hear that.

"However," Renna continued, "if you'd like to sleep with me, you may. Mercy, this bed is big enough for all of us."

"Yippee!" Rachel cried, throwing her arms around Renna's neck.

She hugged the little girl tightly.

"Will you read us a story, too, Miss Fields?" Libby asked, her black eyes shining with hopefulness.

"Of course, I will."

"But first, Miss Fields needs to undress," Johanna said. "You girls can help her. Then I'll go to bed, and all three of you can enjoy your story and fall asleep."

"Hooray!" Libby cried, getting up and jumping on the bed. She was immediately followed by a bouncing, giggling Rachel.

Renna laughed as she watched them. She noticed how happy they looked—happier than she'd ever seen them—and hope was restored in Renna. It was a hope that she could fit in here after all, a hope that she could fulfill the need for nurturing that lay deeply in these little girls' hearts, perhaps the boys' hearts, too.

Thank You, Lord, she prayed silently. *Thank You for another answered prayer.*

The next day, the sun shone brightly, but the ground remained brown and as bare as the branches on the trees. The wind was cold, but Renna and her parents traveled with Kyle to his mother's home in spite of wintry air. There was still the matter of her estate to settle. By carriage, the trip took nearly forty-five minutes, and when they finally arrived, Renna felt frozen solid. But inside the house, with its gray stone exterior, a fire burned in the hearth, warming the parlor.

Aurora Reil's butler greeted them enthusiastically. "I'm the only staff member left, sir," he told Kyle. He was an older man, perhaps the same age as Renna's father. He had white hair and well-groomed white whiskers that came down along his jowls. "But I never gave up hope," the butler added, his English accent suddenly apparent. "Since your body was never recovered, sir, I just knew you were still alive."

"Thank you, Ramsey," Kyle replied gratefully. Turning, he then introduced Renna and her parents.

"I started packing Madam's things," Ramsey said, speaking once more of his former employer. "Her clothes and belongings. . .they're packed in wooden crates, sir. I left them upstairs until further notice."

"Thank you."

Watching the exchange, Renna sensed the butler's remorse. Kyle had said that Ramsey had been working for Aurora for the past twenty-five years. No doubt he missed his employer.

"May I take your coats?" he offered. Turning to Kyle, he asked, "Sir?"

Kyle nodded and helped Renna off with her woolen cloak before removing his own. Likewise, Johanna and Wendall handed their winter wear into Ramsey's waiting arms.

The butler grinned broadly. "It's good to be of service again."

"Would you consider coming to work for me, Ramsey?" Kyle inquired. "I have a new housekeeper, but I will be in need of a butler as well." With that, he gave Renna's elbow a knowing little squeeze, and she smiled inwardly. Hester could stay!

"Sir," Ramsey began, taking a small bow, "I would be honored to work for you."

"Very good. We'll talk business later."

"Yes, sir," he replied, taking the coats away.

Turning, Kyle asked, "Would you all like a tour of my mother's home?"

"A splendid idea, Kyle," Wendall replied.

"And how shall we tour it," Johanna asked, "since you're. . .blind?"

"Wendall can lead the way, and I'll narrate from what I can recall." Kyle wore a sentimental-looking grin. "I grew up in this home, and I'd wager it hasn't changed in years." He went on to explain. "Aurora was married several times during my upbringing. Each time we moved into a different house; however, Aurora never sold this place. She loved it. She called it home and, after her last husband died, she moved back here to stay."

The tour began outside in the back. The wide yard gave way to a gently sloping hillside, which led to the sandy shores of Lake Michigan. To the right was an elaborate stable.

"Aurora loved to ride," Kyle said. "Every day at dawn she'd saddle her favorite horse, and with her hair loose and billowing behind her, she'd gallop along the beach." Kyle shook his head. "She didn't sit sidesaddle, either. I used to think that if her socialite friends saw her, they'd be aghast! But Aurora didn't care, and she was an excellent horsewoman. I believe she had my children on a pony by the time they were two years old."

Listening, Renna looked out along the shores and tried to imagine such a woman. So eccentric, she rode like the wind and insisted that her son and grandchildren call her by her first name.

Renna turned, surveying the yard. Except for the small, gray stone cottage, which Kyle pointed out were Ramsey's quarters, there wasn't a neighbor for miles. The bustling city seemed so far away with its crowds and clamor. *Refreshing*, Renna thought. She turned, still content to observe her surroundings.

The property was bordered by evergreen trees, and the terrace looked like a marvelous place for children to play. In the summer, Renna could well imagine moonlit walks along the beach—and, of course, she imagined Kyle by her side. At that moment, she experienced a sense of peace unlike she'd known since arriving in Milwaukee. She thought she could be happy in this place. Such a pity Kyle was talking about selling it.

"This home originally belonged to my grandmother, and I hate to part with it," Kyle said. "My grandmother lived with Aurora and me until I was about ten years old. When she died, I missed her terribly. My grandmother was more of a mother to me than Aurora." He paused in momentary reflection. "I believe she was a Christian," he finally said. "I can recall my grandmother reading the Bible and doing all kinds of charity work. She belonged to a local church, though I can't remember the name of it. I do, however, remember attending services with her from time to time. I have very pleasant childhood memories, and they're a result of my grandmother's nurturing.

"But then, about two years after she died," Kyle continued, "Aurora packed me off to boarding school and remarried. I never lived in this house again."

Renna turned toward Kyle, wondering over his melancholy. In a flash, his sentimental expression was gone. "Well, let's move on, shall we?"

Back inside the house, Renna and her parents toured the first floor kitchen, dining room, solarium, parlor, and sitting room. The latter, Kyle said, had once served as his grandfather's study.

As they walked about, Renna observed that each room opened to the next, save for the sitting room, which opened only to the foyer. This made the sitting room more private but allowed for easy access to and from the other rooms. The floor plan seemed more homey to Renna and, though it was a much larger home, it wasn't too different from the one she'd known all her life.

In Kyle's house, on the other hand, each room seemed like a separate entity, opening only to the grand foyer. This made the house seem impersonal, and Renna didn't think she'd ever be able to call the place her home.

Another dilemma, she thought glumly, following Kyle up the stairs to the second floor. Wooden crates lay neatly stacked in each of the four bedrooms.

"Aurora had clothes in every closet," Kyle murmured. "I'm grateful that Ramsey felt like packing them." He sighed. "I haven't a clue as to what to do with them, either."

"Charity?" Johanna suggested.

"I don't imagine any charitable organization would want them." A wry smile curved Kyle's lips. "My mother had extravagant tastes. She took great pains to see that no other woman in the city had dresses even similar to hers."

Wendall walked over to one of the crates, opened it, and pulled out a green concoction. "Yes, Kyle, I see what you mean," he said with a curious frown. It seemed as if he were trying to discern what manner of outfit he held in his hands. "It looks like the carcass of a great, green bird."

Upon closer inspection, Renna identified it as a silk taffeta having green feathers and beads sewn all over the entire bodice.

"Oh, my!" Johanna exclaimed, fingering the gown's low neckline. Then she frowned disapprovingly.

"You know, Kyle," Renna began, "a good seamstress would know what to do with these gowns. I'm sure there are yards and yards of material that could be salvaged and made into all kinds of things. Children's clothing, for example."

"Why, Renna, what a good idea!" Johanna exclaimed. "I hadn't thought of that, but you're right. There are so many needy families. . . ."

Kyle chuckled. "In that case, congratulations, Mrs. Fields, you've just inherited my mother's clothing."

She gasped. "But there must be at least fifty crates full of clothes."

"They're yours."

Johanna looked momentarily stunned, but then smiled. "Thank you, Captain. You're very generous."

As they walked back downstairs, Renna could practically hear her mother's mind working on a plan for Aurora Reil's clothing. No doubt it would be put to good use.

While they had toured the estate, Ramsey was busy preparing hot coffee, which he now served in the parlor by the fire. Only then did Kyle excuse himself to talk business with his newly acquired butler.

Johanna sipped her coffee. "Do you think the captain is getting ready to propose to you, Renna?"

"I'm not sure. He's trying to discern the true meaning of love."

"Oh, dear," Johanna said with a frown, "that sounds complicated."

"He wants to be sure," Renna stated on Kyle's behalf.

"Well, it's obvious that he cares very deeply for you," Wendall said.

"The question is, do you care for him?"

"Yes."

"Enough to marry him, daughter?"

"Yes. . .but—"

"But?" Johanna's frown deepened. "No 'buts,' Renna. You must be sure."

Renna had stood and strolled to the front windows, her back now to her parents. Only too late, for her mother had caught her troubled expression.

"You're never going to find the perfect man," Johanna stated as if she had divined the problem. She hadn't, of course.

"On the contrary," Renna replied, "Kyle is the perfect man for me. It's just that there is such a difference in our upbringings." She turned, facing her parents. "Kyle grew up wealthy, living among aristocrats and socialites. I've had a very average upbringing—not that I'm complaining, mind you."

"Of course, you're not complaining, Renna," Wendall piped in, "and your point is well taken. However, if Kyle doesn't mind the background difference—which he has told me he doesn't—then neither should you. It's that simple.

"And, really, daughter," Wendall added, "if you were to compare social standings and wealth, Kyle and I aren't worlds apart from one another. We've just made different decisions along the way. Kyle chose money, glamorous parties, and the social spotlight, whereas I chose my God, my wife, and my children, putting my business only second to them." Wendall added emphatically, "Kyle now wishes he would have done the same. But he has been granted a second chance. Will you stand by him, Renna? Will you be his help meet if he asks?"

The question was left hanging in the air, however, as Kyle suddenly appeared at the doorway.

"Ramsey has prepared a light lunch for us," he said. "He'll serve it in the dining room."

"Wonderful!" Wendall declared.

As they left for the dining room then, Kyle held out his hand for Renna. She took it, and he gave her such an endearing smile that she wondered what she was ever fretting about.

Chapter 19

A nother party. . .this time a holiday ball. Kyle said holiday balls ran now until the end of January; however, he promised Renna they'd only attend a few. A few, in Renna's estimation, was "a few" too many. But she had resolved to have a cheerful spirit about attending so as not to embarrass or disappoint the man she loved.

Helping Renna dress for the evening, Johanna styled her hair. Then she helped Renna into a black velvet gown. It's popular design included a fitted bodice with a V-neck filled with lace. Lace trim also circled the wrists and the full, velvet skirt flared gracefully.

"You look beautiful," Johanna said, taking a step back and examining her handiwork.

"Thank you," she murmured, glancing at herself in the looking glass. Her hair concealed her birthmark, while curly, wispy tendrils framed the rest of her face. The black velvet gown was as elegant as Renna had ever worn and its dark color seemed to accentuate her hazel-green eyes. Tonight, for the first time, Renna felt beautiful.

"The captain had better propose quickly," Johanna teased, "or some handsome swain will beat him to it."

Renna laughed softly. "If Kyle does propose tonight, Mother, I'm inclined to accept."

Johanna replied with a pleased smile.

"Everything has been going so well the last couple of days," Renna said happily. She did a little pirouette and her full, velvet skirt swirled around her ankles. "And did you hear what Michael said to me this afternoon? He said, 'You're different from the other ladies I thought Papa would marry. You're like a. . .mother.'"

"Oh, how sweet," Johanna purred.

"And Gabriel asked me to come into his bedroom, which is something of an art gallery, and look at his artwork. He's quite good, Mother, and we had a very friendly conversation. Then, he said, 'I like you, Miss Fields,' and he told me that he was going to paint a special picture for me."

"It sounds as though you've won the children's hearts as well as the captain's."

"Yes. . ." However, in spite of her victory, Renna suddenly grew troubled.

"But?" Johanna prompted.

Renna sighed. "But I simply abhor these social functions."

Her mother chuckled softly. "Oh, is that all?"

"That's a lot! Kyle is expected to show up at all these things."

"But I don't think the parties hold the same appeal for him as they did before his accident."

"I don't know, Mother. Kyle hasn't proved that much to me yet. He seems to enjoy himself." She turned from the looking glass. "And it still bothers me that Kyle bought my new wardrobe. I feel like some peasant upon whom he has bestowed his pity."

Johanna's expression looked somewhat rueful. "I think if the captain heard you say that, Renna, he would be hurt. He wanted to give you something special. He loves you so much. . .it's obvious. I just pray he'll act on his feelings soon. Besides, dear," Johanna added gently, "every good and perfect gift comes from above. It is God who is the ultimate provider."

"I hadn't ever thought of it that way. . . ." Renna chewed her lower lip pensively. "How rude of me; I never thanked Kyle for the clothes. I never even tried. I was never thankful."

"Then you know what you must do."

Renna nodded. "I will thank Kyle—and God—immediately," she replied, feeling humbled.

Once downstairs, Renna and her mother entered the music room where the children were entertaining Kyle and Wendall with their newly acquired piano skills. Taking in the homey scene, Renna had to smile. Then all at once she felt lighthearted. . .why, even this house didn't seem so imposing anymore!

Kyle heard the rustling of skirts and made a subtle glance toward the door. Even through his dark glasses, the sight of Renna standing there in an elegant black velvet dress rendered him momentarily senseless. She was captivating, and Kyle decided it was a good thing that Renna never knew how really beautiful she was. If she had, she might have become another Fayre Waterford!

"Captain Sinclair, did you hear me?"

He lifted Rachel, who had been sitting on his lap, and stood politely. "Mrs. Fields, I apologize. My thoughts were elsewhere. What did you say?"

"I said, Renna is here and ready for the ball tonight. I'll take the baby from you, though Rachel is hardly a baby anymore. . .are you, darling?" she purred, taking the little girl from him.

Kyle smiled and murmured a "thank-you" to Mrs. Fields, though he was still enthralled by Renna. *Tonight*, he promised himself. *Tonight I will tell her the truth at any cost. Tonight she'll know I can see and that I—I think she's beautiful.*

"Well, I suppose you two should be off," Wendall said, giving Kyle a friendly slap on the back.

His thoughts immediately returned to the present, and Wendall gave him a knowing grin. For the first time in years, Kyle felt embarrassed. Why, he'd been gawking like a schoolboy, and no doubt Wendall had noticed. However, even the "schoolboys," Gabriel and Michael, weren't gawking. What in the world was wrong with him?

Kyle cleared his throat, hoping to conceal his discomfort. "Thank you both for agreeing to watch the children for me tonight."

"Oh, we're seasoned grandparents, aren't we, Johanna?"

"Indeed."

Kyle smiled. "Very well. Renna and I shall take our leave, then." He held his elbow out for her. "Shall we?"

"We shall," she replied impishly, putting her gloved hand around Kyle's elbow.

"You're feeling more at ease," Kyle remarked after their driver saw them comfortably settled into the carriage. A slap of the reins, and they were off.

"Oh, Kyle, I've been stubborn, vain, and. . .proud. How have you managed to put up with me for the past month?"

He laughed. "My dear Renna, what on earth are you talking about?"

"I never thanked you for the new gowns, Kyle. Please forgive me for that oversight. They're beautiful and. . .well, I can't help but feel beautiful when I'm wearing them."

"You are beautiful, Renna."

"Thank you." She felt the heat of her embarrassment creep up her neck to her cheeks.

Then she turned thoughtful for several long seconds. "It occurred to me earlier," she said at last, "that when I performed my nursing skills, my birthmark didn't affect me personally. If a patient happened to see it and was put off by it, I still knew that I was a good nurse. But outside of my profession, I never allowed myself the same confidence in who I am as a person. Would you believe that I used to purposely take very little time with my appearance because I figured no young man in his right mind would want to court me anyway."

"Well, I can't say I'm sorry to hear it," Kyle told her with a sardonic grin. "That logic, ill as it may be, worked to my advantage."

"Oh, hush," Renna chided him. "It's just a good thing you're blind."

She was being flippant, Kyle knew. However, now seemed the perfect time to reveal the truth.

He took her hand. "Renna about my being blind—"

The carriage lurched to a stop, and Kyle heaved a frustrated sigh. "The Carpenters don't live very far away," he explained. "We'll have to resume this conversation on the way home."

"All right," she said, looking somewhat concerned.

The driver swung open the carriage door and Kyle climbed out with the aid of his servant. "Thank you, Wallace," he said. "I'll send word when we're ready to leave."

"Yes, Captain." The man bowed respectfully as Kyle helped Renna alight from the carriage.

They walked to the house, which was lit up brightly. There was a candle in all of the eight front windows, signaling a welcome.

At the front door, the butler welcomed them stiffly but politely. Then he took Renna's woolen cape and then ushered them into a large hall. A small quartet played an upbeat tune, and couples waltzed to the music.

They were immediately offered a glass of punch, and both the captain and Renna accepted. The room was nearly filled to capacity, but the object of Renna's attention was, oddly enough, the chandelier. It was the most hideous thing she'd ever laid eyes on.

"Kyle," she whispered, "there's a chandelier hanging from the ceiling and it looks to be made of wrought iron and. . .antlers! Have you ever seen it?"

"No, but I imagine it's an original TC." Kyle laughed. "Ted Carpenter, whose home we're visiting, is a sought-after artist. He first made a name for himself in the theater, but lately his forte is unusual artwork. My guess is that before this evening is over, someone will offer him millions for that piece."

"The chandelier? A piece of art?" Renna shook her head in disbelief. "Why, Gabriel's drawings are finer than that horned thing."

"Are you telling me that I had better not purchase it?" Kyle asked with a darkly handsome grin, indicating that he was teasing her.

"I would never tell you what to do," Renna retorted. "I'm merely voicing my opinion."

"Of course, you are," he replied, his grin broadening. "And I suppose I had better get used to it."

Before Renna could inquire over the remark, Ted Carpenter appeared and shook Kyle's hand. Then he looked at Renna. "I never forget a name," he said. "Miss. . .Fields, isn't it?"

"Yes."

"Thank you so much for coming tonight," he said, gallantly bowing over her hand.

"A pleasure to see you again, sir."

"Sir?" With a frown, Ted looked at Kyle then back at Renna. "I'm not a 'sir.' I'm a 'Ted.' Please call me by my given name. All my friends do."

"Thank you. Then you must call me Renna."

"Renna. Interesting name." He pointed behind him. "See that blond? The most beautiful woman in the room? That's my wife, Cyndie," he said. "You two will have to get acquainted."

Renna spotted the woman she thought Ted meant. She was in a daring white gown with tiny red bows sewn to its full skirt and draped across her shoulders was a fluffy, red boa. Her blond hair was styled in a chic but carefree manner, and she was laughing gaily with another couple.

Ted turned to Kyle. "The authorities were here this afternoon," he said, seriously now. "They asked about Lars Benchley, and he is invited tonight. However, I told them, as I'll tell you, we're not likely to see him. He owes me money for a sculpture I sold him. I made it from a ship's propeller." Ted beamed. "It was a magnificent thing, Kyle. You would have appreciated it."

"I believe I saw a piece of it," he replied tersely.

Renna gasped, catching the implication. "The other night, Kyle? The pavilion?"

"Yes."

"A tragic thing," Ted said. "I heard about the damage to your home. But as for Lars. . ."

"Lars?" Renna didn't understand. She thought the authorities were concerned with Matthew Benchley, not his brother.

"One moment, Ted. Let's talk about this in private." Kyle disengaged Renna's arm. "I won't leave you for long," he promised.

Hiding her concern and discomfort, Renna nodded. Then she watched Kyle and Ted cross the room. *He's trying to protect me again,* she thought.

Renna watched the couples dance by.

"Well, well, we meet again."

Renna turned and came face-to-smiling-face with Lillian LaMonde.

"Good evening, Mrs. LaMonde," she said politely.

An inquiring frown caused her left eyebrow to dip slightly. "What on earth are you doing with a man like Kyle Sinclair?"

"I beg your pardon?"

"He's a rogue and a rake and this entire town knows it! Didn't your parents do any kind of a background check on him?"

"Yes, of course, they did. But—"

"Then there must be something else. . ."

"Mrs. LaMonde, Kyle is—"

"A marriage of convenience, perhaps. . .because of the children. Kyle is too cheap to hire another governess—they never stayed anyway—and you'd make a fine example for his brood. Is that the scenario?"

"No," Renna replied in all honesty.

"Well, that's what everyone's saying."

Renna tried to ignore the sudden stab of hurt, and she quickly swallowed down the impulse to defend herself. She and Kyle had had this very conversation, and she believed him when he said he wasn't pursuing her for the sake of the children. Besides, Kyle wasn't cheap!

"Mrs. LaMonde," Renna stated at last, "you and everyone else are free to think what you like."

"Yes?" She stood there expectantly.

But Renna merely shrugged. "What more can I say?"

"So it's true?"

"No, but are you really concerned with the truth?" Renna gave her a patient smile. "It probably won't make as good a story as all the gossip."

Lillian LaMonde's face cracked into a genuine grin. "You know, I think I like you. Spunky, that's what you are." She paused, narrowing her gaze and scrutinizing Renna. "So you think you can tame a man like Captain Kyle Sinclair, do you?"

"Tame him?" Renna chuckled lightly. "Hardly, Mrs. LaMonde. I don't have that kind of power and influence. Only God can change a man's heart, and that's exactly what He did, too. God changed Kyle."

"God?" The probing journalist seemed suddenly at a loss for words.

"But Kyle will have to give you his testimony," Renna added. "It wouldn't be right for me to share it."

"Testimony?" Lillian LaMonde looked positively stunned—

"Kyle will have to tell you, Mrs. LaMonde."

"I'd like to tell Lillian many things," he said, coming up behind her. "But, what specifically did you have in mind?"

At the retort, Lillian lifted her chin. "You are so droll, Kyle."

He just chuckled.

"I mentioned that you're a believer now," Renna explained to him. "But I didn't think it would be right if I said any more. I told Mrs. LaMonde that your testimony would have to come from you."

"Yes, do tell, Kyle," Lillian said. A mischievous gleam entered her eye then. "In fact, why don't you tell everyone here what happened to you." She turned around. "Everyone, listen here!" She clapped her hands, getting all the guests' attention. The musicians stopped playing.

The din in the ballroom slowly ceased while Renna's heart plummeted. "Kyle, make her stop," she whispered. "I had no idea she'd go this far so as to embarrass you."

"Renna, I am not embarrassed. If these people want to hear, let them hear. I'll gladly tell them what happened to me."

Every eye was upon Kyle now, and Renna hesitantly stepped back to allow him room to speak.

"Kyle had a religious experience," Lillian announced. "Can you imagine?" She laughed as did several others. Then she turned toward him. "We must hear the story, Kyle. Please, tell us."

"My pleasure," he replied, and Renna thought Kyle looked as confident as ever.

The room was packed with affluence—men with whom Kyle had business dealings—men with whom he had friendships. Didn't he understand that publicly professing Christ could endanger his reputation with this crowd? Obviously, he didn't care, and suddenly Renna's heart swelled with joy. If she ever thought she loved Kyle Sinclair before, she was certain of it now.

"As you all know, I was in a boating accident this past summer. I watched as my mother, her escort, and Elise Kingsley all drowned. It was a heart-wrenching scene, even for me, a man who has lived something like a. . ." He cleared his throat. ". . .pirate."

Renna smiled.

"I'm not a stranger to death," Kyle continued. "During the war, I saw men die bravely and honorably. On the gunner, my crew and I viewed death as a tragedy, of course, but we determined our cause was worth dying for. However, last summer, death was not brave nor honorable. It was swift and mighty, and I helplessly watched as, one by one, each life was consumed. I could do nothing to save anyone, nor could I save myself."

Sympathetic gasps emanated from many of the women. Some touched their lips with their gloved fingertips.

"I would have drowned also," Kyle continued, "except a ship in passing saw me and its crew pulled me aboard. But I don't remember anything except the dark stormy waters and then waking up in a Chicago hospital. That's where I met and—" He paused momentarily. "And that's where I fell in love with Renna."

A heated blush warmed her cheeks and all around her Renna heard curious murmurs. Yet she looked at Kyle and smiled happily. She could tell he meant it, too. He loved her!

"Then while I was in the hospital," Kyle continued, "I was saved once more. Just like the crew of that passing ship pulled me from the dark waters of Lake Michigan, Jesus Christ pulled me from the darkness of my sins." He grinned sardonically. "No one had to point out the fact that I was a sinner. Even suffering from amnesia I remembered I was—and still am, for I'll never be perfect in this lifetime. But upon my belief in Christ, who willingly shed His blood for a sinner like me, I was promised eternal life in heaven, where I will be made perfect in the likeness of Him."

"Who promised you that, Kyle?" Fayre Waterford asked, making her way toward him.

"God makes that promise Himself. The Bible says it, and I believe it."

Standing beside Renna, Lillian LaMonde laughed cynically. "Kyle, if God will let you into heaven, He'll let anyone in."

"You're right. . .well, almost." Kyle moved toward her. "Help me out," he said to Renna. "That verse. . .how anyone can be saved. What is it?"

" 'Whosoever shall call upon the name of the Lord shall be saved.' Is that the one you mean?"

"Yes. Whosoever. . .that includes anyone here in this room. But you have to want it and believe in it, just as it's laid out in the Bible. Then God will give His salvation to whosoever shall ask. It's a gift, you see. God's given it, and whosoever shall take it will be saved."

The room grew so still that Renna could hear Lillian LaMonde breathing. She glanced over at the woman who seemed dazed by what she'd just heard.

Then suddenly a gunshot exploded from somewhere behind Kyle. The result of a bad aim, or just a warning shot, the ball hit just above the ugly, horned chandelier, sending it crashing onto unsuspecting guests. Women screamed, men yelled, the injured moaned.

Amidst the commotion, Renna frantically looked for Kyle. He had been standing right in front of her. Now he was nowhere to be found.

Chapter 20

Renna temporarily gave up her search for Kyle as there were people needing immediate medical attention. Someone announced that Dr. Welch had been summoned but, in the meantime, Renna was on her own. Several small fires had started as a result of the fallen chandelier, but they were quickly extinguished. Unfortunately, an older gentleman incurred an awful burn to his left hand. Renna ordered one of the Carpenters' maids to fetch a bowl of ice cold water. Then she told the man to soak his already blistering hand in the water until the doctor arrived. He readily complied.

On to the next victim. It was Fayre Waterford. She had a nasty gash on her shoulder. Her expensive gown had been torn irreparably. Taking a strip of it, Renna instructed Lillian to hold it firmly to Fayre's wound.

"Pressure will stop the bleeding," she told Lillian, who nodded obediently.

Renna moved on to help a man with a large lump on his forehead. He was conscious, however, and seemed alert. Grabbing a chunk of ice out of the punch bowl, Renna instructed the man's wife to hold it on his head.

"The ice will prevent excessive swelling."

"Oh, yes, of course. Thank you, dear."

The next victim was a man with a wrist injury. Having seen the chandelier falling, he'd held up his arm in an attempt at defense.

"I'm afraid your wrist is broken," Renna told him. "The doctor will have to set it when he arrives. Meanwhile, hold ice on it." Again, Renna went to the punch bowl and returned with a palm-sized block of ice.

The guests became her patients, and suddenly Renna was in her element. She went from one to the next, triaging them in the same manner she used to triage wounded soldiers. But unlike the enlisted men, most of the Carpenters' guests had minor cuts and contusions.

Dr. Welch finally arrived, and Renna helped him stitch Fayre's shoulder. She wailed and cried and begged Dr. Welch not to leave a scar.

"I'm afraid that can't be helped," he told her. "But I'll do my best stitching, Miss Waterford."

After the sutures were in place, Renna assisted Dr. Welch with bandaging the burned hand and setting Mr. Brisbane's wrist.

"It's a miracle more people weren't hurt," Dr. Welch said when they were all done. He combed his chestnut-brown hair back with the fingers of his right hand. "Thank you for your help. . .Miss. . .ah—"

"Fields. Miss Renna Fields." Almost everyone had gone now. The gala had come to an abrupt halt.

"Well, thank you, Miss Fields," the young doctor said. His brown eyes shone with gratitude. "You're a most competent nurse. You wouldn't, by any chance, be seeking a position? I could use an assistant."

Renna was flattered. Even more so since the young Dr. Welch was quite handsome. "I appreciate the offer, Doctor, but, no, I'm not seeking a nursing position at this time."

"I rather thought so but figured I'd ask anyway." He smiled. "Well, thanks again for your help. I'll be taking my leave now. Um. . .perhaps we'll see each other again soon."

"Yes, perhaps." Renna gave him a parting smile, wishing she could say she was betrothed—and then she remembered. . .how could she forget? Kyle!

She glanced around the ballroom. What a shambles! Leaving the room, then, she immediately spotted Kyle. He was standing in the foyer with several policemen, Lillian LaMonde, and Ted Carpenter. Matthew Benchley was there, too, dressed all in black, his hands tied behind him.

Kyle turned around and smiled at her. "Renna! Are you all through?" he asked, his black eyes gazing directly into hers.

"You can. . .see?!"

Kyle nodded. "I can see."

"That's wonderful!" Renna exclaimed, coming forward and taking both of his outstretched hands. "Did it just happen? The excitement, perhaps. The trauma?"

"No, no. . ."

"Then when? How did Matthew Benchley come to be apprehended?"

"That isn't Matthew, Renna. It's his brother, Lars."

She felt her brows furrow as she tried to understand.

"They're identical twins," Kyle explained. "Lars has been impersonating his brother in Chicago. The man who dined at your home was Lars. The man who works with your father is Matthew. They may look identical; however, Matthew is quite different."

Renna was stunned. "Identical twins. . . ?"

"Yes."

"Then both brothers were threatening you?"

Kyle shook his head. "Only Lars. However, Matthew went along with his brother's schemes to take back Kingsley Shipping at first. Matthew told the authorities that, in the beginning, Lars's plans seemed harmless enough, even though he knew they were above the law. But after the boating accident, Matthew got worried. Lars seemed out of control, governed only by his obsession to take Kingsley Shipping away from me. Lars even offered to buy it, but after it was discovered that I was alive, Norton, my banker, wouldn't continue with the sale. Had I died, Lars would have obtained the shipping company, but since I'm alive, he couldn't get it. So Lars thought he'd help me get to heaven sooner than God planned."

Kyle gave Renna a warm smile. "Knowing Lars and what he's capable of, Matthew agreed to cooperate with the authorities in exchange for a pardon for his involvement. Matthew warned us that something might happen tonight. We just weren't sure what. . .or when it was going to happen."

"And what exactly did happen tonight?" Renna asked.

Kyle drew in a deep breath. "As I was giving my testimony, here by the entryway of the parlor, I could see from out of the corner of my eye that someone was sneaking up behind me. I wasn't sure there was any danger, after all, it could have been one of the servants. But then I saw clearly that it was Lars Benchley, and I watched as he pulled out a revolver. He aimed, and just before he fired, I quickly turned around, knocking the gun out of his hand. Lars ran toward the back of the house and I went after him, leaving the chaos in the ballroom. I'm just grateful that more people weren't hurt."

"Wait a minute," Renna said, narrowing her gaze and trying to understand. "You *saw* Lars Benchley sneaking up behind you? How can that be?"

Kyle took her elbow and led her a few steps away from the police and Benchley. "Renna, I've been able to see since my discharge from the hospital."

"Yes, but then you lost your sight again."

Kyle shook his head, looking rueful. "I'm sorry I deceived you, but I did. I sensed your distance, and I thought that if I were blind again—"

"You deceived me? On purpose?"

"Renna—"

She pulled her hands from his. "Why would you do such a thing?"

"To close the distance between us." Kyle shook his dark head. "Let's not discuss this here, Renna. We'll talk on the way home."

The butler brought her cape, and they walked out to the awaiting carriage. Kyle helped Renna inside and then climbed in after her. Wallace closed the door. Staring straight ahead, Renna was so angry she barely heard Kyle's explanation. Oh, it made perfect sense; he deceived her to get close to her because he was in love with her. Then he wanted to tell her the truth, but the authorities advised him not to. And look how he was able to apprehend Lars Benchley—he couldn't have done that without feigning his blindness.

"Your father agreed that I should listen to the authorities."

"My father. . . ? He knows you're not blind?"

"Yes."

"Then why did you have to keep the secret from me?" Renna asked. "I wouldn't have said a word to anyone." She lifted a derisive brow. "Or don't you trust me?"

"Of course I trust you. Trust isn't the issue here."

"It's the very issue here, Kyle. Can't you understand? Relationships are based on trust, not secrecy. For all I know, you're not telling me something else and I'll have another shock to contend with."

"Do you really believe that? Never mind. Of course you do, or you wouldn't have said it."

Renna clenched her jaw and willed herself not to say another thing. She was hurt—hurt that Kyle hadn't trusted her enough to tell her the truth.

"I was trying to protect you," Kyle said tightly.

"Hogwash!"

He swung around, looking at her with an expression of surprise at her exclamation.

"I don't need protecting," Renna said stubbornly. "I'm a nurse who made it through the Civil War and—" She paused, her heart softening, breaking. "I need the man I love to be honest with me, not deceive me."

"Renna, it's not as though I plan to make a habit of it."

She closed her eyes, too hurt and angry to discuss this further. Fortunately for her, the carriage lurched to a stop before any more could be said.

Renna placed her hand in Kyle's long enough to climb down from the carriage. Then she pulled out of his grasp and ran to the house without his escort. She opened the heavy front door by herself and, without even acknowledging her parents, who had just stepped into the foyer, and without taking off her cape, she ran upstairs to her room.

Wendall frowned as Kyle entered the house. "Trouble?"

"Your daughter is one stubborn woman!" Kyle said, fuming.

"Oh, my!" Johanna exclaimed. "What happened?"

"You're not wearing your dark glasses, Kyle," Wendall observed. "Does that mean Renna knows about—"

"She knows, all right. And she's as angry as a little wasp."

"Knows? Knows what?" Johanna asked, looking from her husband to Kyle, then back at Wendall again.

"Kyle isn't blind, dear," Wendall explained. "He's kept it a secret. . . mostly because his life was in danger."

Johanna's lips made an O, though no sound passed through them.

"I'll explain everything later," he promised his wife. Then to Kyle, he said, "As for Renna, well, we knew she'd react like this. She's just in a bit of shock, that's all. Tomorrow she'll be back to her same sweet self. That's one thing about Renna—she's reasonable."

"I never want to speak to that man again as long as I live!" Renna declared the next morning.

"Now, daughter," Wendall said, "stop that packing and listen to me. Kyle did what he thought he had to do. You ought to be grateful he had your best interests at heart."

"Oh, pooh!"

"Now, Renna, I'll have none of that talk. I raised you to be a lady and, I might add, Kyle Sinclair is a fine gentleman, a suitable match for you if I ever knew one." Wendall took his daughter by the shoulders and gave her a mild shake. "Don't ruin this chance to marry for love, Renna. Don't let your stubborn pride get in the way."

"Easy for you to say. You weren't the one deceived." She frowned, standing with arms akimbo. "And you deceived me, too, Father. How could you?"

"I didn't do it to hurt you. I thought it was for your own good."

"The truth sets us free, the Bible says, and Satan is the father of lies. How then could deceiving me be for my own good?"

Wendall looked momentarily pensive. "I'm sorry, Renna," he said at last. "Perhaps I shouldn't have gone along with it. But if you weren't so insecure over your birthmark, none of this would have even happened. Think about that for a while!"

She did, too, after her father left her bedroom and all the while she packed her gowns. She felt duped. . .and so stupid! Why hadn't she detected that Kyle could see?

No wonder he could play chess with my father, Renna fumed. *I should have seen through his charade. I'm a skilled nurse. . . .*

Then the words "stubborn pride" crept into her thoughts. She didn't want them there. They made her feel uncomfortable. She had a good reason to be angry!

And, perhaps, Kyle had a good reason to act blind. . . .

"Oh, I suppose I was insecure," she mumbled, dropping the dress she held in her hands. She didn't want Kyle to see her birthmark. She feared that if he saw it he wouldn't fall in love with her. It was true.

But he did, she realized. *He said he loves me and all along he could see this ugly mar on my cheek.* In spite of herself, Renna reveled in that fact. Kyle loved her for who she was, intelligent, with an uncomely birthmark. Yes, and it was true, she was a tad opinionated—Kyle loved her despite that characteristic, too.

"Lord," she whispered in prayer, "perhaps I am being stubborn. On the other hand, Kyle's deception might be a sign from You that I ought not marry him." Renna sighed. "What should I do. . . ?"

A knock sounded at the door.

"Yes?"

Slowly it opened, and a pair of hazel eyes peeked around the corner.

"Gabriel." Renna smiled. "What can I do for you?"

"Can I come in?"

"Yes."

The door opened wider and Gabriel slipped in, shutting it behind him. He held something behind his back and then slowly brought it around and into Renna's view.

"What's in the newspaper that you're hiding it?"

"It's the society page," Gabriel whispered.

"Oh," Renna whispered back.

"I'm not supposed to be reading it, but I do anyhow." Gabriel was still whispering. "I've been reading it since I was nine. That's how I kept up on what my parents were doing."

"Gabriel!"

He shrugged. "Never did read anything good about them, though."

Renna shook her head at the boy's disobedience.

"It isn't right, is it? My reading the society page when my mother told me not to a long, long time ago?"

"No, it isn't right."

He nodded. "I won't do it again. I promise. But, here, take a look at what it says today."

"Gabriel, I don't think—"

"It says Papa's a hero!"

"It does?" Renna took the newspaper from him. Sure enough. Lillian LaMonde had described last night's events and made Captain Kyle Sinclair look like a hero, to be sure!

"Read what it says about you!" Gabriel insisted.

"About me?"

"Here, look!" Gabriel sounded so excited, and his expression shone with boyish pride. "Miss Renna Fields is an angel of mercy," he read from the newspaper. "She willingly tended to all the wounded at the Carpenters' ill-fated ball. In addition, Miss Fields has so obviously won the heart of Captain Sinclair and, by her love and devotion, has rendered him a new man!"

Renna rolled her eyes. "It's God who rendered your father a new man, not me, Gabriel."

"I know, but don't you see, Miss Fields? This is the best thing I've ever read. . .or even heard about my father! Lillian LaMonde usually writes about what Miss Sarah calls 'sandals.' You know, the stuff children shouldn't hear about."

Renna was hard pressed to conceal her grin. "I think the word is 'scandals,' Gabriel."

"Yes, that's it. My father's name usually appears in one of those articles, along with whatever lady he escorted." Gabriel shook his head, looking disgusted. "Most times I knew what the newspaper said wasn't true, but it hurt me anyway, and I hated my father for it." Gabriel suddenly smiled broadly, looking up at Renna. "But that was before his accident. . . and before he knew Jesus. . .and before you!" Throwing his arms around Renna in a way that seemed very uncharacteristic of Gabriel—or so she had thought—he hugged her so tightly she thought her ribs might crack. "You could be a real mother to us, Miss Fields," he said, his head on her shoulder. "We could be a real family now."

Tears stung Renna's eyes. The artist-child who could both hate and love so passionately merely wanted what every child wants: a mother and father who love him.

Pulling back, Gabriel spotted Renna's trunk. A flash of horror crossed his features. "You're not leaving. . . ?"

She stuttered a reply. "N–no. I. . ." Renna pulled a gown from out of the trunk. "I was merely unpacking some more clothes." It was a half-truth, but she couldn't hurt Gabriel. He'd been hurt enough. As for unpacking, Renna realized God had given her all the signs she'd ever asked for. And she would most certainly unpack—right after she had a heart-to-heart talk with Kyle!

Meanwhile, Gabriel looked relieved. "Well, I'd better go now." He walked toward the door but stopped before reaching it. Turning and walking back to Renna then, he handed her the newspaper. Looking chagrined, he said, "I promise I'll never read the society page again. . . unless you say I can."

Renna nodded, donning her best mother's expression. "Very good, Gabriel. I'll hold you to your word."

He smiled and, with that, left the bedroom.

Renna looked down at the newspaper in her hand. *Dear Lord,* she prayed, *please forgive me for my stubborn pride and please prepare Kyle's heart. . . .*

Renna prayed for nearly an hour. She needed wisdom and patience, both of which came from the power of the Holy Spirit. Finally feeling ready to face Kyle, Renna left her bedroom and walked down the back stairs. The house was stone silent.

"Where are the children?" she asked Isabelle, who was baking bread in the kitchen.

"Oh, your folks took 'em downtown. Some of the Christmas decorations got put up today."

"I see." Renna momentarily fretted over her lower lip. "Is Kyle around?"

"The captain? Yes, ma'am. He's in his study, but the door is closed and he didn't look too approachable today."

"Hmm. . .well, I guess I feel brave enough to approach him anyway. No closed door is going to keep me from saying what needs to be said."

Isabelle raised her brows and then a little smile curved her lips. "Yes, ma'am."

Renna left the kitchen and walked through the foyer that echoed eerily in her ears. At the study door, she knocked firmly.

"Whatever it is, Isabelle, it can wait," came the growled reply.

But Renna was not to be put off that easily. "It's not Isabelle, and it cannot wait. Let me in!"

The door opened almost immediately. Kyle met her with a surprised expression on his face. His chin sported nearly a day's worth of beard, his dark, wavy hair was rumpled, and the black circles beneath his black eyes indicated very little sleep last night.

"You look awful," Renna said.

Kyle narrowed his gaze. Then he grabbed her elbow and pulled her into the study, closing the door behind them. "I don't want any of the servants to overhear us," he explained. He considered her, head to toe, before turning to the windows. "I suppose you've come to tell me you're leaving. You can't marry a pirate like me." When Renna didn't reply, Kyle turned back around. "Well? Is that it? Just say it, woman!"

Renna gasped.

He came toward her. "Well?"

Renna refused to be intimidated. With hands on hips, she lifted her chin. "I'll thank you to mind your manners, Kyle Sinclair, and, no! I did not come here to say anything of the sort."

Kyle lifted a brow.

Renna swallowed hard. "I came to apologize," she said softly. "I behaved badly last night, and I'm sorry."

All Kyle's defenses seemed to crumble before her very eyes.

"I should have allowed you to explain. I should have listened—"

Renna didn't get a chance to say another word before Kyle crushed her to him. He held her so tightly she could barely breathe.

"Oh, Renna," he murmured, his lips next to her ear, "I thought I'd lost you forever."

"No, Kyle. . .I was just being. . .stubborn. I'm so sorry."

He pulled back. "Renna, I'm the one who's sorry. More sorry than you'll ever know. And I'll never deceive you again. Ever."

"I believe you."

Kyle smiled and the dark, worried circles beneath his eyes seemed to fade. "I love you, Renna," he said earnestly. "I want to marry you. Will you marry me? Say yes."

"Yes."

He looked startled by her compliance, and Renna laughed.

"Are you teasing me?"

"No."

"You'll marry me, then?"

"Yes!"

"Tomorrow. Let's get married tomorrow. I can't wait another day."

"I'm sure my mother will be delighted."

"A reception will follow after our honeymoon and. . ." Kyle shook his head disbelievingly. "Renna, I've had all night to think about this, dream about this. I prayed, I begged God. . .I just didn't dare believe it would come true!"

"Oh, Kyle. . ." At least now she knew where Gabriel inherited his passionate nature.

"You've made me the happiest man alive." He cupped her face with his hands. "I'm going to sell this house, Renna, and we'll move to my grandparents' home on the lake. I could tell you liked it there. . . ."

Happiness assailed her. "Oh, I did, and I'd love to live there with you." She paused to tease him a bit. "But only if we can take romantic, moonlit strolls on the beach."

"Every night," he promised. Then he smiled into her eyes, and Renna thought her heart would melt. "And we'll live happily ever after, Renna."

"Just like in the fairy tales?" she quipped.

"No," Kyle replied, his black eyes darkening with ardor. "Just like a never-ending love story, just the way Christ intended it to be."

Tend
the Light

Susannah Hayden

Chapter 1

Lacey Wells pretended she did not hear them and, closing her eyes, she lifted her face to the spring sun and held still. She had not felt the sun on her skin for months. The northwestern Wisconsin winter had been long and harsh, and twice her family had been snowed in and could not leave the lighthouse for days.

The bark of the tree that she was leaning against scratched through her calico dress, but she paid it no attention. She felt only the crisp air cooling her cheeks and rustling the fine hair around her shoulders. Lacey sighed. Strands of her golden brown, wheat-colored hair had come loose, and she moved her hand to brush her hair clear of her face.

In this place, this private clearing of the peninsula's forest, Lacey Wells could dream and imagine. Here no chores had to be done, no music lessons had to be endured, and every reminder of responsibility was out of sight. If she kept her blue-gray eyes low, she could not even see the lighthouse from this spot.

If only she could stay here all afternoon. But she heard them calling, even though she pretended not to. Still, she refused to answer. She knew that someday she would have to get off the peninsula.

Seven people in those small, awkward rooms of the lighthouse afforded little opportunity for thinking or dreaming. Because Lacey was the only daughter in the family, she had a tiny cubbyhole downstairs that she could call her own. Her parents were in the cramped room across the hallway from Lacey, and her four brothers shared the large upstairs bedroom. Her mother never missed an opportunity to remind Lacey of her privileged privacy.

The shouts from her three little brothers were louder now, and they would find her in a few minutes. They were as eager as she was to be roaming the peninsula, escaping their mother's strict regimen of schooling. Three little boys could not be cooped up for weeks at a time without

313

bursting the seams of rebellion, and the coming of spring was the last push they needed to put them out on the land. Jeremiah and Joel were eleven-year-old twins always competing to lead the forays into the forest. Seven-year-old Micah trailed behind, knowing that he was allowed to come along only because their mother insisted that the twins include him; he mimicked everything they did.

Lacey could hear Jeremiah and Joel robustly shouting her name, demanding that she reveal herself. Micah's cry was thinner and less certain. In more sentimental moments, Lacey wanted to respond to Micah's voice, and she almost did today. But she stopped herself. If they wanted her, they would have to find her, even Micah.

"Why didn't you answer us?" Jeremiah demanded, bursting into the clearing.

Lacey reluctantly opened her eyes and confronted her brother. "I was busy."

"Doing what?" Joel wanted to know. "There's nothing to do here."

Lacey sighed. No answer she could give would satisfy Joel.

"Hi, Lacey," Micah said timidly.

"Hello, Micah," she answered, her voice softening slightly for the little blond boy. "What are you up to today?"

"Mama sent us for you," Micah explained.

Jeremiah twirled theatrically on one foot. "Mama says you've probably been daydreaming again." His arms swept over his head in a gesture of mock elegance.

"Stop it, Jeremiah!" Lacey said.

Jeremiah twirled again, and this time Joel joined him. "Mama says you're too fanciful for your own good."

"That's nonsense," she said.

"No, it's not. You can even ask Micah. Mama said so at lunch today. She had to fix lunch all by herself, you know. You weren't there."

Lacey glared at her brother. "I imagined that one of you would offer to help."

"It's not my job to make lunch. That's your job. Mama says so."

"I wasn't hungry," Lacey said.

Joel snickered. "Mama said you would say that."

"Looks like she's got you figured out," Jeremiah added.

Lacey shook her head and rolled her eyes. "Why do you insist on bothering me so?"

"Mama sent us," Micah repeated.

"Time for you to come home," Joel said. "The supply boat's coming in. Papa saw it from the lighthouse."

"Of course, the lighthouse," Lacey muttered.

"Lacey?"

"Yes, Micah?"

"Why don't you like the lighthouse?"

"What makes you think I don't like the lighthouse?" Lacey asked, taking Micah's hand.

Jeremiah snorted. "It's plain as the nose on your face you hate that lighthouse."

Micah, confused, looked from Lacey to Jeremiah.

Lacey sighed. "I do not hate the lighthouse. It's just. . .It's only a lighthouse. Why does everyone get so excited about it?"

"Our family has tended the lighthouse for fifty-four years," Micah said, proudly relaying the facts. "It's an important job, and we're honored to do it."

Lacey gave a half smile at the perfect display of family pride. She had repeated those words herself hundreds of times when she was small, but as she grew, her voice held less conviction. Now, at nineteen, she was nearly persuaded that keeping the lighthouse was no honor at all. Rather, it meant sacrifice and isolation.

She had grown up the same way that her father had before her, cut off from regular schooling, from friends and parties, even from church services. Their lighthouse sat solidly atop a cliff at the peak of the peninsula, and to get to it by land took courage and determination. Perhaps that would change someday as the lumber industry and growing towns edged northward, but for now crude roads threatened the axles of wagons and carriages, and unseen breaks in the rugged ground could snap a horse's leg in an instant.

By water, the lighthouse was accessible for most of the year. A supply boat came every two months to bring the family flour, sugar, various dry goods, and, of course, oil for the lighthouse. During the winter the waters never quite froze but were, nevertheless, treacherous and rarely did anyone venture up to visit the Wells family during those months of short days and long nights. By November, supplies were laid in for the winter against the possibility that they would not be replenished until spring.

It was true that Lacey's father and her grandfather had been the lighthouse keepers for more than fifty years. Her sixteen-year-old brother, Joshua, would be next in line.

"Where's Joshua?" Lacey asked abruptly, remembering that the boys had come to tell her that the supply boat was arriving and that Joshua should be there to help unload.

"At the lumber camp."

"Again?" Lacey moaned. Joshua was spending every spare moment working at the lumber camp on the other side of the peninsula. He would quickly satisfy his mother's educational requirements and then be gone for days at a stretch. But whenever he was gone, Lacey seemed to inherit his share of the chores on top of her own.

"He will be back tomorrow," Micah said, seeming to sense her irritation.

"Yes, but the boat is here today. We'd better go," she said.

Jeremiah and Joel immediately raced ahead of her, clearly glad to be rid of Micah. Lacey gave Micah's hand a squeeze, and he smiled up at her. "I like it when the boat comes," Micah said, "don't you, Lacey?"

She tried to respond as sincerely as he had asked the question. "Yes, it is a little exciting. We're never quite sure what Gordon will bring us."

"Mama says we really need flour, and if he doesn't bring it, she's going to make him go back and get some!"

Lacey laughed. "I bet she will, too."

"Maybe if we hurry home, we can go up in the lighthouse and see the boat come around the bend."

Lacey nodded. "Sure, Micah. I'm sure Papa would let you go up today."

"I love the lighthouse," Micah said simply.

"That's nice." The last thing Lacey wanted to do was disillusion a seven-year-old child. "Maybe someday you'll be the keeper."

"Do you really think so? I hope so!"

When they were out of the clearing and on the path, Lacey raised her eyes to the lighthouse. The gleaming white tower with its bright red cap rose proudly above the craggy cliff just like it had for eight decades, since just before the dawn of the nineteenth century. The original circular wick that burned whale oil had been updated to four wicks burning vegetable oil and then kerosene. Daniel Wells had taken great pride in installing prisms that magnified the light as far as twenty miles. A railing, also painted red, circled the tower. Lacey's father had built a bench so he could sit and look over the railing, sometimes scanning for ships, sometimes. . . She was not sure what he did some of the time.

Lake Superior bent just at that point, and under the water the mountain of rock was less visible. Without the lighthouse, especially at night, it was next to impossible for a craft of any size to estimate distances and navigate around the curve. Aged and rotted wooden memorials dotted the far shore to mark the failures of the past.

Daniel Wells was as serious about maintaining the outside of the lighthouse as he was tending the light at the top, and never did he postpone the upkeep or allow any blemish to obscure the visibility of the lighthouse. Tending the light was not simply the way he earned his living; it was a calling, which he answered enthusiastically.

Daniel Wells had grown up on the peninsula, learning from his own father how to keep the light burning and how to sound the foghorn in the darkness. His two sisters and one brother had left long ago, but he had stayed, never grumbling about the isolation or the difficulty of life on the peninsula. He had met his wife, Mary, on a blind date arranged by one of his sisters, and she had accepted the lot of a lighthouse keeper's wife. She raised her children in the house attached to the tower, insisting that they learn to read and appreciate literature and to play several musical instruments.

Several times Lacey had visited her grandmother's home in Milwaukee, where her mother had grown up. On her first visit she felt as though she were on a different planet with the spacious rooms, the wide streets, and the shops at the center of town. She could still hear her mother chastising, "Lacey, don't stare!"

Since her eighth birthday Lacey had known that someday after she finished high school she would go to a place like Milwaukee to stay. Now, three years after having finished high school, Lacey was even more determined to leave but, somehow, she had not made any serious plans to go. Her mother refused to let her go without some proper purpose for leaving; she also insisted that Lacey was still needed at home and certainly did not need to be wandering around the state unattended.

Micah was tugging her hand. "Let's hurry, Lacey. The twins will get there first, and then Papa will say it's too crowded for me at the top." Lacey stepped up her pace, playfully pulling Micah along.

Chapter 2

"I see the boys found you," Mary Wells said to her daughter as Lacey and Micah reached the edge of the yard behind the house. "I could have used your help with lunch."

Lacey touched Micah's shoulder. "I'll see you down there," she said, sending him off scampering gladly toward the boat. Lacey made no response to her mother who was tossing another handful of feed to the chickens. Lacey wondered why Jeremiah had not done so earlier.

"Did Joel do the milking?" Lacey asked, glancing around for the cow.

"I had to remind him three times," her mother said. "There's butter to be churned this afternoon."

"I'll do it as soon as we finish unloading the boat," Lacey offered.

"Your father will be down in a few minutes with the cart," her mother said. "Go ahead and start unloading without him."

"If you give me the list," Lacey said, "I'll see if everything is there."

Her mother reached into the pocket of her apron and fished out a crumpled scrap of paper. "Make sure he leaves flour. We don't have enough to last until the next trip. And don't let the boys play with the ropes."

Without comment, Lacey turned away. Her mother gave the same warnings every time the supply boat came. Lacey scanned the list and she saw the usual items, dominated by the need for oil to keep the lamp burning at the top of the lighthouse.

The rugged cliff rose steeply from the supply boat. The nearest place to actually dock a boat and and unload it was three miles away, around the bend. For years Daniel Wells had talked about carving out a road that would let them unload supplies on more level ground and carry them over the land. But the road was never made, so he and his sons used a network of pulleys and ropes to haul supplies up the cliff from the boat. Once, the twins had gotten their fingers caught in the ropes. Micah was forbidden to touch them, but he could not keep himself away from the unloading process.

Lacey did not share her brothers' passion for the supply boat, and she thought she was much too old to be forced to take part in the ritual unloading. But long ago she had accepted the task, for it was not a point worth arguing with her mother. Mary Wells had a system for everything, and her systems had worked well over the years to keep the family going in such an isolated place. But Lacey was ready to break out of the system.

The lighthouse, with their family home attached, sat right up at the edge of the cliff, so it took only a few steps for Lacey to reach the spot where the supplies would appear. A three-foot-high fence, painted luminescent white, marked the edge of the yard and the beginning of danger. Mary Wells had insisted that her husband build the fence before Lacey learned to walk; it had been freshly painted every summer since.

Joel and Jeremiah were already leaning on the pulley crank at the gate, moving a load. Micah chinned himself on the fence to survey the activity below. Lacey paused to stand behind him for a moment, and she saw that the deck of the small boat was laden with barrels and crates. Lacey hoped for some new calicos.

"There she is, the love of my life," boomed a voice from the craft below.

Lacey rolled her eyes, for Gordon Wright was the last person she wanted to see right then. Looking down over the edge of the cliff, she forced herself to say, "Hello, Gordon."

He grinned up at her from the ship's deck forty feet below, his sweaty face glinting in the sun and his mouth cockeyed. "What do you say I take you for a nice boat ride today? The water's calm as can be." He had asked her the same question on every visit for the last three years, whether the water was calm or not.

"Thank you, Gordon, but not today. Have you got flour this time?" she asked.

Gordon snorted. "Flour. All your mama thinks about is flour. Does she think she's the only one in the world who needs it?"

"She has a family to feed," Lacey said. "We're not farmers; we can't grind our own."

"You never tried." He spat tobacco over the side of the boat. "Put in some wheat with those vegetables you always plant."

"Have you got the flour or not?"

"Why don't you come down and see for yourself?" His grin was turning into a leer.

"Gordon, please." She glanced at Micah's hopeful, innocent face. The boy was mesmerized with the pulleys and seemed not to notice the conversation. She moved away from the edge to where the twins were working the pulley.

"I'll come up and get you," Gordon persisted. "You can hang on to me all the way down. That rope ladder is sturdy enough for the two of us."

Lacey was glad he was out of her sight, even if just for a moment. "Just send up the flour, or I'll go get my mother." Lacey yanked on a pulley, jerking Gordon's arm at the other end.

"Woman, what are you doing?" Gordon burst out. He scowled up at her. "Don't know why I waste my time chasing after you when any woman in town would be glad to be my bride. A man like me makes a good living around here."

"Don't be too sure about that," Lacey snapped.

The twins giggled at the exchange, but Lacey paid no attention for it was all part of the ritual that they loved and she abhorred. Even when she was sixteen she had not been fooled by Gordon's attentions, though she had been the tiniest bit flattered. Now she was strictly annoyed. She glanced back over her shoulder, hoping her father would appear with the cart soon.

Lacey leaned into the pulley alongside Joel and Jeremiah, and a barrel of kerosene crept up the side of the cliff. Cautiously, she looked over the edge to make sure Gordon was cooperating by tying on the next item. Fortunately, his back was to her as he sorted the crates.

As she watched his movements, another figure emerged from the hold of the ship. Usually, Gordon came alone for his was a small boat and he always made a point of letting people know he did not carry passengers. Had he hired some help? Lacey could not hear what the man said to Gordon, but she kept her eyes fastened on him. He was tall with broad shoulders and brown, thick curly hair, exuding a gentle quality that Gordon's friends did not usually have. He moved smoothly across the deck of the ship and laid a fifty-pound sack of flour at Gordon's feet. Somehow he did not strike Lacey as the type of man Gordon would bring along to help with the heavy load.

Lacey was determined to meet him. For a moment, she even thought of descending the rope ladder to the rickety dock, something she had not done since she was a little girl. Instead, she called down, "Hello!"

The man looked up. "Hello!" His dark eyes met her gaze.

"Are you a friend of Gordon's?" she asked.

The man smiled. "A passenger. How about you?"

She looked up, questioning.

"Are you a friend of Gordon's?" the man asked.

"We've known each other a long time," Lacey said awkwardly, perhaps not loud enough for him to hear.

The man turned back to his work, methodically moving supplies closer to the pulley so Gordon could unload them. Lacey and the boys continued winding. But it was hard to wind the pulley and look over the edge at the boat at the same time, so Lacey had to surrender her curiosity to the immediate task.

"Look, he's coming up!" Micah squealed from his outpost.

Lacey's head shot up, and she looked at the ladder. If Gordon came up, it would take all afternoon to get rid of him. She would rather risk her mother's wrath and abandon her task than have to stand face-to-face with Gordon Wright and endure his pawing and leering. But it was not Gordon. It was his passenger who had placed his foot securely in the bottom rung of the rope ladder and who, with a small pack tied to his back, gripped the ropes and skillfully maneuvered himself up the ladder.

"Push harder, Lacey," demanded Joel, pulling her back to the task at hand.

She cranked the pulley frantically, wanting to be free to greet the visitor. Out of the side of her eye, she caught his movements as he pulled himself up over the top, brushed himself off, and extended to his full height.

"Hello. I'm Travis Gates," he said.

"Lacey Wells," she responded, immediately wishing she had said something more creative.

"I've heard all about you. Gordon is quite smitten."

Lacey blushed, sweat trickling down one temple.

"Harder!" Joel insisted. "He's putting on another barrel of kerosene."

"Maybe I can help," Travis said as he moved in between Lacey and Joel.

Lacey hastily introduced her brothers. Travis's hand gripped the crank handle along with hers, and together they turned it. Immediately the task eased, and in a few moments, the barrel tumbled over the top and the twins steadied it.

Lacey tried to steady herself. She did not know what to say to Travis Gates, but she wanted to say something. "Did you see any more flour on the boat?"

"Several sacks," he said.

Then Lacey glanced down to see Gordon loading another fifty-pound sack on the pulley. "Thank you for helping," she said.

"It's my pleasure."

"What have we here?" a voice asked.

Lacey spun on one heel to see her father behind her. "Papa, I didn't hear you." She faltered only a moment before regaining her poise. "This is Mr. Travis Gates. He's a passenger on Mr. Wright's boat."

Travis extended his hand to Daniel Wells. "Actually, I've reached my destination," he said.

"Well, then, welcome to the peninsula," Lacey said graciously, all the while wondering why anyone would choose to come to a place that felt like the end of the earth.

"What is your business here?" her father asked.

"I've come to work in the lumber camp for a few months." Travis offered no further explanation. "I'm told that I can find the road to the camp not far from the lighthouse."

"That's true," said Daniel Wells, "but the hike is several miles, and the road is more like a trail. Why don't you come up to the house for some refreshment before starting out?"

"I would not want to inconvenience you," Travis said.

"It's not an inconvenience. We don't often have guests on this side of the peninsula. My wife will enjoy talking with someone from the city." He turned to his sons. "Joel, Jeremiah, Micah, run up and tell your mother we have a guest."

The twins groaned, but Micah jumped to his feet. "I will!" he said and then he was off.

Travis glanced at the wooden cart that Daniel Wells had dragged to the cliff. "Can I help you load your goods?"

"We'll get it later," he said, looking at the barrels and crates his sons had dutifully lined up. "Looks like everything is there."

Lacey fumbled for the list wadded up in her hand. "Yes, it's all there. Enough oil for at least two months."

Her father leaned over and waved at Gordon. "Do you want to come up for some refreshment?"

Lacey's heart nearly stopped. Did her father always have to be so hospitable? He knew how she felt about Gordon Wright.

"Daniel Wells, you don't know what real refreshment is," Gordon called up, laughing. "I'll just go back to where I can get a real drink. Tell your friend Saget that next time I'll have supplies for the lumber camp and I'll expect to be paid." Then he pushed his boat away from the edge and jumped on it.

Travis hoisted a sack of flour. "Perhaps I'll work my way into your wife's good graces if I deliver some flour."

Daniel Wells laughed. "Her reputation has preceded her, I see. But the need is genuine. With five children in the house, we go through it pretty fast."

"Five? I counted only four, including Lacey, that is."

Lacey was at the same time grateful and embarrassed by Travis's acknowledgement that she was not a child.

"My son, Joshua, is the fifth," Daniel Wells explained. "I imagine you'll meet him when you get over to the camp. He spends as much time there as he does at home." He raised his eyes to the side door of the little house. Mary Wells had opened it and stepped outside, and Micah was at her side. "I see Mary is ready for us."

Lacey fell into step between Travis and her father.

Chapter 3

M ary Wells, holding a pitcher, stood poised over Travis Gates. "Thank you, yes." He held up his glass for a refill.

"So you've come to the peninsula for only a few months?" Daniel Wells resumed their conversation. Lacey waited eagerly for the answer.

"My schedule is rather indefinite," Travis replied, "but I expect I will be here less than a year, perhaps only until winter sets in again."

"Are you a lumberjack?" The question came from Micah, perched on his father's knee.

"Not exactly," Travis replied, tilting his head. "But I want to learn about it."

"My brother is a lumberjack," Micah boasted.

"Then maybe he can teach me," Travis said.

Lacey was bursting with questions. Most of the men who came to work at the lumber camp stayed there for years; she had not known anyone who came for only a few months. Also, Travis did not look like a lumberjack. Joshua did not look like a lumberjack, either, but he was still a boy. Travis was a man, in his midtwenties, Lacey estimated, with smooth hands and trimmed nails. Wherever he had come from, he had not made his living felling trees and hauling lumber.

"How do you know Gordon Wright?" Daniel Wells asked. "He's never been one to carry passengers."

Travis chuckled. "Well, it was a bit of a challenge to get him to take me, but he was paid well for it. He's an acquaintance of someone my father does business with."

"What kind of business is your father in?" Daniel Wells asked.

"Industry," Travis answered.

What kind of industry? Lacey wanted to know, but she did not ask. Travis seemed relaxed in her family's home, yet at the same time he gave guarded answers that did not fully satisfy her curiosity.

Mary Wells took her seat. "Are you sure you can find the camp on your own? The light may fade before you get there."

Daniel Wells pushed back his chair and nudged Micah to his feet. "Mary is right. You should be on your way before it is too late to go today."

"Perhaps you could just point me toward the road," Travis said.

"I'll walk with you," Lacey said impulsively. She had not spoken much during the previous conversation, and her mother now looked at her with raised eyebrows. Lacey continued, "Showing you will be easier than telling you how to find it."

"Yes, that's sensible," her father said.

Lacey glanced at her mother, who set her jaw but did not speak.

"Can I come, too?" Micah's hopeful blue eyes looked up at his father, and Lacey's heart sank for she knew that expression was hard to resist.

Daniel Wells stroked the boy's head. "How about if you stay here and help me and the twins with the supplies?"

"Okay." Micah was easily diverted from one pleasure to another.

"I would be happy to help, too," Travis said.

Daniel Wells shook his head. "You'd better get going. I don't want you lost in the woods after dark."

"Well, all right, then." Travis stood up and smiled at Lacey. "Is my guide ready?"

Lacey felt the color rise in her cheeks, but she held her composure. Once outside, she gestured across the yard toward the edge of the forest. "This is the quickest way," she advised and then did not know what to say after that.

Travis came to the rescue. "Micah seems like a delightful child," he said as they fell into step together.

Lacey smiled, grateful to talk about something familiar. "He is. He's not like Joshua or the twins."

"They are not so delightful?" Travis teased.

"They're, you know, boys!" Lacey said emphatically. "Actually, Joshua is nearly grown and has turned into a likeable person, despite my doubts of a few years ago. I think you'll enjoy him. The twins, though, they're in their own world most of the time. Since they have each other, they don't seem to need anyone else."

"Least of all, Micah," Travis offered.

"Exactly. Mama tries to make them include Micah, but they avoid it whenever they can."

"I've never seen twins look so much alike!"

"If you spend any time with them, you'll be able to tell them apart," Lacey said.

"I hope to have the opportunity."

Involuntarily, Lacey glanced sideways at Travis. Was he simply being polite?

Leaving the yard, their path began to wind around the trees, and Travis said, "I can see how easy it would be to get lost."

"You'll get used to it," Lacey assured him. "The trail is used just enough to keep it beaten down. Joshua goes back and forth a couple of times a week." She looked at his profile. "Do you know anything about tracking?"

"Tracking?" He looked dubious.

Lacey laughed. "You really are a city boy, aren't you?"

"Guilty as charged," Travis said, also laughing. He gestured to his wide surroundings. "But this is beautiful. I'm going to love it here, I'm sure. It must have been wonderful growing up here."

"Funny, I was just about to say that about growing up in the city."

Travis shook his head. "Where I come from is not much of a city, really, just a town. People work too hard and drink too much. They forget to look at what's around them."

Lacey surveyed the familiar territory that had become her prison without walls. "I guess it's all a matter of perspective," she said quietly.

Travis glanced at her sideways. "Don't you like living here?"

"It's beautiful, no question about that. But it's. . ."

"Lonely?" Travis asked quietly.

She nodded.

"Have you no friends up here?"

"One," Lacey answered. "Abby Saget. Her father has been cutting wood for years. She grew up as the only child at the lumber camp. But the boys have never had any friends."

"At least they have each other, especially the twins."

"They don't see it that way. Having brothers is not the same as having friends."

"It is far away from a lot of things that I take for granted," Travis admitted. "School, church, friends. It must be hard for you sometimes."

Lacey wanted to shout that it was hard all the time, that she wanted nothing more than to leave the peninsula, that he was lucky he was only here for a few months. Instead, she simply said, "Yes, it can be hard."

"Have you lived here all your life?" Travis asked.

Lacey launched into her family's history of fifty-four years of tending the lighthouse, schooling at home, living miles away from playmates and hundreds of miles from relatives.

"Will Joshua take over the lighthouse, then?" Travis asked at the end of her explanation.

"That's what my father hopes."

"But what about the lumber camp?"

"I think Joshua is just trying to save up some money, something that he can call his own. My mother hates it that he goes to that camp. She would never stand for having him there all the time."

"Why does she hate it?"

Lacey shrugged. "She thinks it's an uncivilized way of life and not a suitable environment for her children."

"But Joshua is not a child."

"To Mama he always will be."

"I suppose mothers are that way. But perhaps it will not always be so uncivilized."

Lacey wondered what he meant. She had not seen much progress toward civility in her lifetime, certainly not any standard that would please her mother. The men slept in crude cabins without feminine influence, chewing and spitting what they pleased, and consuming a dubious diet. Moonshine flowed freely. Lacey wondered how someone like Travis Gates would fit in.

"Does your mother read the Bible a lot?" Travis asked.

Lacey was startled by the shift in conversation and furrowed her brow.

Travis explained. "Your brothers' names, three prophets and a courageous leader."

"Let's just say she made sure we learned our Bible stories, even without a church to go to."

"And your name? It's unique."

"Letitia, my grandmother's name." The truth was out before Lacey could stop herself. "But Joshua couldn't say it when he was little. The nickname stuck, especially after the twins were born."

"I like it."

Lacey laughed.

"What's so funny?" Travis asked.

"Some people have known me nearly all my life and they don't know my real name is Letitia. Even I hardly ever think about that. Yet I'm giving away my secrets to someone I hardly know."

"I assure you, your secret is safe with me."

Smiling, Lacey let the comment roll off and the conversation moved on to the habits of the squirrels darting across their path. Inwardly, though, Lacey replayed her interchange with this strange man. Why was she talking so freely to Travis Gates? After the conversation with her father back at the house and the discussion on the path, Travis knew a fair amount about the Wells family in general, and Lacey in particular. But, beyond his name, she knew practically nothing about him, not even the name of the town he had grown up in or the real reason why he had come to the peninsula. Was he hiding something or simply being casual? Intuitively, she did not believe that he had come to earn his fortune by cutting lumber.

"Gordon Wright is right, you know." Travis interrupted her reflective mood. "You have spunk."

Lacey slowed her steps and looked at Travis. "Gordon said that?"

"The exact quote is, 'That girl has more spunk than ten city girls rolled into one.' "

"I'm sure he was exaggerating. He drinks too much, you know."

"That much was easy to see. And when he drinks, he talks. . . about you."

"Why would Gordon do that?"

"He's stuck on you."

"Nonsense!"

"No, it's not nonsense."

"But he's a blathering, blubbering boob who has no idea what to say to a woman. Most of what he does say is offensive. I've never given him the least bit of encouragement."

"Doesn't matter."

"Oh, let's talk about something else," Lacey said, exasperated. Any other topic would be more interesting than an analysis of Gordon Wright's emotional state. "You know all about my family. Now, tell me about yours."

"Not much to tell. I'm an only child, and my mother died when I was twelve. My father spent most of his time working while I was growing up."

Apparently, Travis intended to say no more. With a summary like that, Lacey was sure there was more to the story—much more. But she could not be pushy with a stranger.

"I'm sorry about your mother," she said softly.

Travis shrugged. "It was a long time ago."

They had come to her clearing, and she stopped to lean against her favorite tree. "You can pick up the path right over there," she said, pointing to the other side. "After a mile or so, it curves a little to the north. Otherwise, it's pretty direct."

"I appreciate your bringing me this far," Travis said.

"I'm surprised someone didn't meet you," Lacey said.

Travis smiled slyly. "They didn't know I was coming today. And I'm told most of the men come over the land route from the southern part of the state."

"Yes, that's true," Lacey conceded, at the same time wondering why Travis had chosen the water route. "Well, I'm sure they'll be glad to have another pair of hands."

"I'll look for Joshua."

"Please do. My mother would like that. And I'm sure you'll meet Abby."

"Perhaps I'll see you again, Lacey Wells." His dark eyes held hers for just a moment.

Lacey blushed. "Perhaps so." She looked away awkwardly.

With a final wave, Travis turned and headed for the path. Lacey watched him recede into the woods and, in only a couple of minutes, he was beyond her sight. Yet his presence lingered in the clearing, and Lacey took a deep breath of his scent, manly, but not sweaty. She wondered what he would smell like after a stint in the camp.

She was tempted to settle in the grass for another private session in her clearing, but it was not worth annoying Mama two times in one day. Mama would have calculated how long it would take for Lacey to walk Travis to the clearing and when she should be back. Besides, she had promised to churn the butter. Soon it would be time to get supper going, and if she was not there to help, Mama would send the boys after her again. Reluctantly, Lacey turned her feet back toward the lighthouse.

Travis's comments about Gordon hung in her mind. If she had so much spunk, more than ten city girls, why did she feel so trapped? A woman with spunk would have found a way off the peninsula by now, instead of going home for supper to avoid a scolding. But Lacey did not see that she had any options. Mama was not going to let her go without a good reason to leave, and so far Lacey had not been able to offer any that qualified. Even if her mother changed her mind tomorrow, what would Lacey do? Where would she go?

She kicked the dirt, wishing she at least had an answer that would satisfy herself.

Chapter 4

The lilac would peel off the wall with the slightest touch, Lacey knew. No doubt her grandmother, for whom she was named, had lovingly papered this tiny room, hardly more than an alcove, with enthusiasm and expectation that it would bring pleasure to the occupants. And perhaps it had, at one point. Surely the wallpaper had been clean and vibrant in those days, the flowers brightening the walls as the breeze stirred the curtains. Lacey knew that her aunts, her father's sisters, had shared this small space while they grew up.

Now, however, the wallpaper was yellowed and cracked and the lilacs on one wall were so faded from the sunlight that they were barely visible. Lacey lay on her bed, with her arms thrown up over her head, and picked at the seam in the corner. She scraped at the paper's edge with her thumbnail as miniscule flakes scattered on her pillow. Years ago, she had gotten excited about redecorating her room, and she had it all planned out. When they went to visit her mother's family in Milwaukee, they would buy new wallpaper, paint, and fabric. The room was tiny, and it would not take much. She would do the work herself, from stripping the old wallpaper to pasting the new and carefully stroking paint onto the trim around the window and door. She had drawn a picture for her mother to show the color scheme she wanted.

Even now Lacey could see her mother's raised eyebrows, for she thought the room was serviceable the way it was. Lacey needed to concentrate on her schoolwork and chores, not on changing something that did not need to be changed. But Mary Wells had finally relented and allowed Lacey to freshen the trim. The new paint, however, simply made the wallpaper look more dull, and Lacey was sorry she had done it.

That was when she first became convinced that she needed to leave the peninsula, years before it would become possible. Daniel and Mary Wells had made a life for themselves here, and they would never leave.

But when Lacey pictured her future, she was always somewhere else in a place with people, activity, and maybe even a family of her own. When she was fourteen, she had determined that she would suffocate if she stayed here. But, at nineteen, she was still here.

Lacey swung her feet over the side of the bed, sat up, and sighed. The house was quiet. Her mother had sent the boys to their room hours ago, and Micah had lain in bed singing until the twins made him stop with threats of physical harm. It was a nightly ritual, an argument that Lacey had grown weary of overhearing. After having sat in the living room with the mending pile for an hour or so, Mary had gone to bed herself.

The house was still, but Lacey's mind was far from quiet as the events of the day tumbled through her mind, from her quiet hours in the clearing to the mysterious Travis Gates. At the supper table, everyone had had a comment to make about the newcomer. Jeremiah was impressed by his physical strength. Joel was suspicious that he was too good to be true, and that distressed Micah. Daniel was impressed with his pleasant demeanor. Their mother took a let's-wait-and-see attitude. Lacey had not known what to think, and she shared with her family very little of her conversation with Travis, thinking that probably she would not see him again, anyway. To Travis, she had simply been a young girl who could point him in the direction he needed to go, and he had been polite enough to make pleasant conversation along the way. Lacey had not even undressed for bed yet, somehow knowing that she would need to get up and go out. Now, she slipped her feet into her shoes and pulled a shawl around her shoulders, for although the spring days were warm, the nights could be brisk.

In the kitchen, a lamp glowed softly on the table, and that meant that her father had not yet gone to bed, either. No doubt he was up in the lighthouse now. In this way, Lacey and her father were more alike than anyone else in the family. Neither of them was able to leave the cares of the day and go to bed and fall instantly into a sound sleep. Lacey had been Micah's age when she began creeping out of her room after her mother was asleep to go see her father. Over the years, he had come to expect Lacey's visits, and Lacey took refuge in knowing that she could make them.

Lacey stepped outside the back door and looked up. The light in the tower burned fiercely bright against the black sky. Truly it was a beacon in the darkness to anyone on the water at night. In its yellow hue, Lacey could see her father leaning over the red railing encircling the peak of the tower. Had the night been much colder, he would have been inside the light room, but in fair weather he could not resist the railing. Daniel Wells was exactly where Lacey had expected to see him. From this distance, he looked oddly small; perhaps it was the overpowering presence of the light distorting his proportions.

Moving swiftly with the confidence of a long habit, she moved along the side of the stone house and let herself in through the small wooden doorway at the base of the lighthouse. Though the stairwell was pitch dark, she did not bother to light a candle, for she knew the path well with each of its turns and upward curves. As she wound her way up, she let one hand drag along the cold stones.

When she emerged at the top, her father turned toward her. "Thought you might have been up here an hour ago."

Lacey smiled gently. "I should have come sooner. I knew I would not sleep tonight."

He turned his gaze back toward the water; a sliver of moonlight reflected on the water below. Intermittent clouds hid most of the stars, but the tower's light would have obscured them anyway. Lacey moved in next to her father and laid her head on his shoulder.

"How can you think this is not beautiful?" he asked softly.

"It is beautiful," she replied simply.

"But not beautiful enough? Not enough to hold you?"

Lacey sighed. "I do love the view from up here. But, no, it's not the same for me as it was for you. . .or for Grandfather."

"Ah, I had hoped it was in the blood of all my children. Nothing would give me greater pleasure than to have another generation of the Wells family tend this light."

Lacey did not respond. As much as she longed to leave the peninsula, she hated to disappoint her father. But she was not his only child. Perhaps Micah's passion for the family heritage would survive his adolescence.

"Your mother tells me you will not be with us much longer," he said quietly.

Lacey snapped her head around to look at him in disbelief. "She said that?"

He nodded.

"But. . .I don't understand. When I wanted to go last year, she wouldn't let me."

"She didn't think you were ready."

"Because I had no husband?"

"Because you had no purpose, except to leave. She just didn't think you were ready."

"But how will I know what purpose might be out there until I go?" Lacey protested. "Why can't she understand that?"

"Your mother has developed some harsh ways over the years. It's my fault, I guess, for bringing her here and expecting she would love it as much as I do."

"Doesn't she?"

He shook his head. "No, but she has made a life for us all anyway, and I'm grateful for that. But she knows that she cannot hold any of you here. The time will come."

"Does she really talk to you about these things?"

He looked at his daughter and chuckled. "Do you really think we're so old and feeble that we cannot sustain a conversation about our children?"

Now Lacey laughed. "I'm sorry. I sound ridiculous. But Mama. . .she is so strict and hard to please."

"She is that way because she wants you to be prepared when the time comes."

Lacey was silent. She had never thought of her mother's viewpoint, instead focusing only on her own inner struggle for a place to belong. "Why does she think I'm ready to leave now?"

"Not now," he corrected, "but soon. I'm afraid that's a question you'll have to ask her."

"Did you ever think about leaving, Papa?"

He shook his head slowly. "Briefly, when I was twelve and your grandmother, Letitia, tore up my favorite shirt for a rag. But I could never leave, not really. I was fortunate enough to have found someone willing to come here, instead of making me choose between the peninsula and a home and family."

They fell into silence, Lacey pondering her father's last comment. For her, such a choice would be simple: leave the peninsula. But she knew that her father's heart would have been wrenched out of him if he had had to face such a choice. His calling and his dedication were a mystery she admired but never hoped to understand.

"Gordon Wright would take you away, you know," he said.

"Papa! That's nonsense."

"I don't think so."

"But I could never. . .ugh! I'd be just as happy if he never spoke to me again."

"I'm not saying he's perfect, but he does have some redeeming qualities."

"Such as?"

"He works hard, and he makes a good living. He also adores children. He's a little rough around the edges, but I think that's because he genuinely cares about you and doesn't know how to express himself. If you were to—"

Lacey cut him off. "Papa, you're not suggesting—"

"I'm not suggesting anything, Lacey. How you respond to Gordon Wright is your decision. But whatever you do, be sure to look beneath the surface."

Lacey got his point. More than once she had been accused of impetuousness and hasty decisions. No doubt this was one of the reasons her mother was so firm with her, even though she was nineteen years old.

"Papa, don't you ever wonder what else is out there?" she asked.

"Sure, sometimes," he answered. "But there is so much here, and I feel no urgency about what else there is out there."

Lacey stared into the night. Below them the water slapped the rocks and reminded them of hazards that had demanded a lighthouse in that place. Together they soaked up the nighttime beauty and their closeness. Unlike her father, though, Lacey felt the urgency.

Chapter 5

Having gratefully escaped from her mother's watchful eye, Lacey had spent most of the day with Abby Saget, her best friend, really her only friend. But, right now, if Lacey could have picked up a tree and thrown it across the forest, she would have. Had Abby lost her mind?

Abby's father, Tom Saget, managed the lumber camp and Abby had grown up on the other side of the peninsula and much closer to the camp than the Wells family. Tom Saget had been consistently discouraged from bringing his wife and daughter to the camp and for years, the three had lived in a rugged lean-to while Tom built a house and furnished it with creations of his hands.

Soon after the Saget family had arrived, the two girls, who were eight years old, had discovered each other. After that, Lacey and Abby had nagged their parents incessantly to be allowed to be together and, under the joy of friendship, the rugged miles between their homes disappeared. Lacey thrilled at every chance to be with Abby and away from the tower. Abby loved to visit the lighthouse, even stay overnight, and, eager to learn alongside her friend, she dutifully copied Lacey's lessons. Her own mother was not as conscientious about schooling her only daughter as Mary Wells was.

But all that was going to change soon for, because of what Abby had said and done, nothing would ever be the same between them again.

As Lacey passed through her clearing, she wanted to collapse against a tree trunk and let all the frustration bleed out of her. But she had been away all day, and there was always a price to pay for temporary freedom. In the mood she was in, the last thing she wanted to do was endure her mother's scowls if she missed supper. She would have to go home and start peeling potatoes. Quickly and without stopping, she forced herself to cross the clearing. She stormed through the yard, scattering the chickens and rousing the cow from its midafternoon snooze. Her mother had been digging in the garden, and Lacey stirred up the loose dirt as she tore through the garden. But she noticed none of the disturbance her return caused and, taking a deep breath, she prepared to enter the realm of decorum required inside the house.

Despite her effort, she let the back door bang behind her as she entered the kitchen. The noise made her mother jump, and she turned to examine her daughter's disarrayed countenance. "What has gotten into you?" she asked directly.

"Just having a bad day," Lacey muttered.

"But you've been with Abby, haven't you?"

Lacey nodded.

"You two haven't quarreled in years. I thought you'd outgrown that sort of thing."

"We didn't quarrel." It was true; they had not quarreled. Lacey had held her disappointment until she was out of Abby's sight.

Mary Wells gestured that Lacey should sit down, and she complied. Then she picked up a knife from the table and attacked a potato viciously, knocking a chunk to the floor.

"Lacey!" her mother said. "Just take off the peel, please."

"Sorry."

"Tell me what happened," her mother insisted.

Lacey considered her response. Did her mother really want to know? Would she understand? "Abby's getting married," Lacey blurted out.

Mary Wells raised an eyebrow. "This is cause for such anger? She's eighteen years old, and I've always thought she was a sensible girl."

Not like me, though, Lacey thought. *You never thought I was sensible.* Aloud she said, "I think she's making a mistake."

"Is the man a lout or a drunkard?" her mother asked.

"No."

"Is he a believer?"

"Yes, I think so."

"Does he genuinely care for Abby?"

"Yes."

"And she cares for him?"

"Mama, he's a lumberjack!" Lacey knew she would get her mother's sympathy with that fact.

Mary Wells pressed her lips together. "Well, after all, Abby's father is a lumberjack, and he has managed to provide a home for his family. Perhaps this is not a bad thing."

"It's not what she wants. She never wanted to marry a lumberjack. We made a pact that we would never do that."

Mary Wells now seemed amused, which irritated Lacey. "Girlish promises mean nothing in the face of a man's love."

"It wasn't a girlish promise," Lacey muttered. She stabbed an eye out of a potato and held herself from saying more. Her mother had made great sacrifices to come to the peninsula with her father and had endured decades of isolation and harsh living. How could her daughter sit before her and say that she and her best friend had promised each other that they would never settle for what their mothers had done? She kept her mouth shut.

"When is the wedding?" her mother asked.

"In August. She wants me to be her bridesmaid."

"You should be honored."

"She doesn't have any other girlfriends. It's me or nobody."

"Lacey, don't be so harsh. I'm sure she asked you out of genuine affection." Then she changed the subject. "We'll have to talk about this later. Now that you're here to work on supper, I want to give the twins their music lessons." She left the room to find the boys.

Lacey groaned inwardly. Now she would be trapped in the kitchen, listening to Joel and Jeremiah hit every wrong note they could find on the piano. The twins hated their piano lessons, but Mary Wells persisted, as she had with Lacey and Joshua and no doubt would with Micah.

Lacey decided she had peeled enough potatoes and, reaching to the shelf above the old black stove, she grabbed a big pot and then went out to the water pump in the yard where she could escape a few minutes of torture. Outside, she set the pot under the spout and started to work the handle. The physical effort felt good, and she started to calm down as the water began to flow. She pumped harder. When the pot was full, she leaned down to splash her face with the cool water and take in a deep, quieting breath.

"That looks like just what I need," a voice said.

Lacey looked up through the wetness to see sixteen-year-old Joshua approaching. As he strode across the yard toward her, she marveled at how much he looked like a man, not like a little brother. "So the rumor is true," Lacey said, drying her face on her skirt. "You came back."

"I have to come home every few days for a decent meal," Joshua said.

"Mama will never let you come to supper looking like that," Lacey warned.

"I know. Keep pumping." Joshua leaned down and vigorously rubbed water into his face, while his sister pumped.

"Don't lumberjacks believe in bathing?" she asked.

"Too much trouble," Joshua said, chuckling. "I'm hoping Mama will take pity on me and heat enough water to fill the tub."

"She might if you take in a load of wood for the stove."

Joshua rubbed his hands under the last spoutful of water. "I understand you had a visitor here yesterday."

Lacey startled. "Do you mean Travis Gates?"

"He's the one."

"You've met him?"

Joshua shrugged. "Sure. Everybody did. He went around and introduced himself to everyone in the bunkhouse."

"Don't you like him?" Lacey sensed her brother's reserve.

"He's all right. But he doesn't really say much."

"I thought he was quite pleasant." Lacey surprised herself, since she actually shared Joshua's observation.

"Sure, he's pleasant enough," Joshua said, "but something doesn't quite fit. Nobody is sure why he showed up at the camp. It's obvious he's never done this kind of work before."

"He can learn."

"But why would he want to?"

"I thought they were expecting him," Lacey said cautiously.

"Did he tell you that?"

"Well. . .no, not exactly."

"Precisely my point. He doesn't exactly say anything."

"Joshua, don't be ridiculous. You've known him less than twenty-four hours."

Joshua shook his head. "I just don't see how he's going to fit in at the camp."

"Don't jump to conclusions. Give him a chance," Lacey argued, continuing to rise to Travis's defense for reasons she did not understand.

"You can't expect to know someone's life history in one day."

"He seemed to know a lot about yours," Joshua said, one corner of his lip turning up, "Letitia."

"Let's change the subject," Lacey said pointedly.

"Okay. Let's talk about Abby. I heard the news. Peter is telling everyone he sees that Abby has agreed to marry him."

Lacey rolled her eyes. Another favorite topic.

"What's the matter?" Joshua asked. "Aren't you happy for Abby? She's your best friend."

"If you want to know the truth, I think she's making a big mistake."

"Now who's jumping to conclusions?" Joshua retorted.

"This is different. I've known Abby more than ten years. Now she'll spend the rest of her life in a log cabin on this peninsula. She never wanted that."

"Peter is going to build her a house, probably as nice a house as her parents have."

"That's what he says. We'll have to see." Lacey was muttering, her irritation renewed.

"Well, I for one think that this is great news. Except for Abby's father, no one else has tried to build a home and raise a family near the camp. Abby and Peter will be pioneers."

"What are you talking about? It's just a lumber camp, and it's as isolated as we are over here."

"Yes, but it doesn't have to be that way forever. We could have a real town on the peninsula. All we need are people willing to build a life and raise their children here. If Peter and Abby do it, some of the other young men will follow."

"Just where are they going to get these wives? I don't see women flocking to the peninsula."

"You're here. That's a start." Joshua grinned.

"You're as crazy as Abby is."

"We're not crazy," Joshua insisted. "Just because you don't want to live here the rest of your life does not mean that it is a bad place to be."

Lacey swallowed and did not respond.

"This peninsula has a future, Lacey. Just wait and see."

Lacey was not convinced. "You'd better go get some clean clothes on. Don't let Mama see you looking like that."

Obediently, and with a parting smile, Joshua turned and went into the house. Lacey slowly picked up the pot, now heavy with water, and followed him.

Mary Wells was in the kitchen now, with the stove growing hot. "There you are," she said. "As soon as the potatoes are done, we'll be ready to eat."

"How did the music lesson go?" Lacey asked, for lack of anything else to say.

"They don't practice nearly enough," her mother responded.

"At least Joshua made it home."

"And he'll stay home for a good while," her mother said insistently. "He's got schoolwork to catch up on."

A thud and a yelp captured their attention. "Joel! Jeremiah!" Mary Wells called out, heading toward the sitting room. "How many times have I told you not to get rough inside the house?"

"Sorry, Mama," came the usual response in unison.

"Go get cleaned up for supper."

The boys shuffled off, snickering about something.

"Will Abby go to the city to get married?" her mother asked while dropping potatoes into the water.

"She wants to get married here," Lacey mumbled.

"But there's no church."

"The minister will come here, and the wedding will be outside."

"The weather should be nice by August." Mary Wells set the lid on the pot.

"I suppose so," Lacey muttered distinterestedly.

"She's only getting married, Lacey. She's not dying, or even moving away."

"I know." Lacey sighed. She should be glad that Abby had found someone who made her happy. But things would never be the same, she was sure of that. All that day Abby had talked of little but Peter, and how much they wanted to have a baby right away. Soon there would be no room in Abby's life for a girlhood friend. Lacey would really be alone then, trapped in the wide open spaces of the peninsula. What pierced her heart most was that at that moment there was not a single person in whom she could confide.

The back door opened and Micah and his father entered. "Just in time," Mary Wells said. "Supper will be ready in ten minutes."

Daniel Wells breathed in the aroma. "Smells delicious."

"Micah, why don't you set the table?" his mother directed.

As he always did, Micah compliantly took the dishes off the shelf and arranged them around the wooden table. Lacey watched his habitual and familiar movements. The family would soon gather for the evening meal, as they always had. Another day had passed, no different from the one before, but nothing would ever be the same for Lacey.

Chapter 6

Don't forget that basket on the bench behind you," Mary Wells reminded Lacey as she removed her patched apron and hung it on a nail in the wall.

Lacey, her arms already full, leaned down and looped two fingers through the basket's handle. "This is a lot of food, Mama," she said. For four days her mother had been cooking: three different kinds of bread, spinach puffs, hundreds of meatballs, rice pudding casseroles, and cakes and cookies.

"Today is a celebration," her mother said. "It's Abby's engagement party. She's your friend, and her mother is my friend. So, of course, I want to help."

"Will there really be so many people there?" Lacey asked.

"The whole camp, I would imagine. That's more than a hundred people." She glanced at her daughter. "Just wait for your turn. I'll do this and more for your engagement party."

Lacey held her tongue. She hoped that by the time of her engagement she would be far away from the peninsula. "I'm surprised all the men would be interested in an engagement party," she said.

"Stress the party concept, Lacey," her mother said. "They get to eat something that their cook didn't prepare."

Lacey chuckled. "If Joshua is to be believed, all the men are desperate for real food."

"Papa has the cart ready." Micah burst through the back door with his announcement. "This is going to be so much fun. I can't wait to see the lumber camp."

His mother scowled. "Just remember, we're going there for Abby's party. Don't wander off."

The twins thumped their way down the stairs and into the kitchen, and their mother immediately put them to work. "Here, boys, take these crates out to your father."

"I want to ride the horse," Joel said.

"I'm going to do that!" Jeremiah responded emphatically.

"You can take turns," their mother said. "Now go on, load the cart." She handed Joel a crate.

"What about me?" Micah trailed plaintively behind his brothers. "I want a turn."

"The trail's too bumpy. You'll fall off." Jeremiah was leaving no room for argument.

"That's not fair!" Tears sprang to Micah's eyes but, with a basket full of bread in his arms, he followed his brothers out the door.

"I wish there were someplace else to have this party," Mary Wells said, smoothing down her hair. "I hate taking the little boys to the camp."

"The boys are not so little anymore, Mama," Lacey said.

"I just don't want them getting any ideas, that's all."

"You always let me go see Abby."

"That was different. I didn't have to worry that you would decide to be a lumberjack."

Lacey held her tongue. She knew her mother disapproved of Joshua's choice to work in the camp.

"We'd better get going." Mary Wells nudged her daughter, and both of them, loaded down with baskets and platters, joined the rest of the family in the yard.

The weeks since Abby had announced her engagement had brought vibrant, warm weather, and Mary Wells's vegetables sprouted through the black earth in perfect straight rows. Daniel took over loading the small wooden cart that their one horse would pull, wedging each item securely enough to survive the ride intact.

"Are you going to ride in the cart, Micah?" he asked.

The boy's bottom lip was hanging out. "I want to ride the horse," he muttered.

Daniel Wells glanced at the twins, already grabbing at the reins; the old mare seemed disinterested in the process. "Maybe we can work something out on the way home. If you change your mind about the cart, let me know."

They started out, heading across the property to the edge of the woods. Joel was on the mare while Jeremiah trotted alongside, complaining. Daniel

Wells made a good-natured attempt to distract Micah, and Mary Wells and Lacey walked side by side at the rear of the caravan, each absorbed in her own thoughts.

Finally, the miles were behind them and they emerged from the forest into the small dirt street that ran the length of the camp. Buildings erected two decades ago in a makeshift effort still stood, giving shelter for cooking and sleeping. A rickety stable housed a dozen horses used to haul logs. The only substantive structures were the common hall where the lumberjacks ate their morning and evening meals and the house where Abby's family lived. The house was at the end of the street, set well back from the flow of traffic around it and isolated by a large lawn that Abby's father tended faithfully over the years.

Abby and Peter stood holding hands in the yard in front of the house, and Lacey stood down the street and watched them as they greeted their guests. Reluctantly, she had to admit that they looked happy. Gone was the wistful expression that her friend had carried for years. In its place was a relaxed smile that Lacey envied. Abby may have compromised her youthful ambitions, but at least now she knew what her future was.

Lacey started toward them to offer her congratulations, but her eyes fastened on the couple as she saw Travis Gates approach them. He slapped Peter on the back and shook his hand heartily. Resting his hands on his hips, he seemed content to stand and chat for a few minutes. Lacey hesitated, but Abby had spotted Lacey and was waving for her to join them. Lacey put a smile on her face and moved more quickly.

"Travis tells me he's already met your family," Abby said. She smiled at Travis as she squeezed Peter's hand. "He and Peter have become great friends."

"Oh? That's nice," Lacey said. "Hello, Travis. I'm glad to see you again."

"And I'm delighted to see you, too."

"Maybe the four of us could spend some time together," Abby gushed.

Lacey caught herself before gasping out loud.

Travis came to the rescue. "Are your brothers here, too?"

Lacey nodded. "The three youngest are beside themselves. They love to come here."

"Having been here for a few weeks, I can see why boys would find it exciting." Travis glanced around. "Something tells me the twins are all right on their own. But would your mother mind if I gave Micah a tour?"

Lacey tilted her head in the direction she had come from. "He's back over there. . .and I'm sure he'd rather be with you than with Mama."

"I'll go with you," Peter said. "I'd like to say hello to Lacey's mother."

The men left, and Abby turned to Lacey. "I'm so glad you came, Lacey."

"Why wouldn't I come?"

"Something tells me you're not keen on my marrying Peter."

"Don't be ridiculous. I want you to be happy," Lacey said sincerely. "If marrying Peter will make you happy, then of course I'm happy for you."

"Thanks. You're the only real friend I had growing up. I know we always said we were going to get away from here, so you must think I'm crazy for staying. But Peter and I are going to make a life here, and we'll have lots of children. I'm going to teach them all the way your mother taught all of you." Abby glanced up toward Peter and Travis as they walked away. "Peter likes Travis a lot. He's going to ask him to help build our house."

Lacey raised an eyebrow. "I thought Travis was here temporarily."

"He's not sure when he's leaving," Abby said. "I hope he'll stay a long time. And I hope you'll get a chance to get to know him."

Lacey did not respond. Abby had verbalized what she secretly hoped but dared not say.

"Oh, look! The string band is starting to play." Abby pointed across the street.

"Where did you get a band?" Lacey asked in astonishment.

"Anything is possible when my mother puts her mind to it," Abby answered.

"The food tables look incredible," Lacey added. "When our two mothers put their minds together, there is sure to be enough to feed the multitudes. Let's go get something to eat."

Abby put her hand on her waist. "I'm so excited that I don't think I could eat anything."

Lacey pulled on her friend's elbow. "Oh, come on. It's your engagement party. You have to at least try. My mother made those spinach puffs you like."

Abby followed reluctantly as Lacey retraced her steps to where she had left her mother setting up food.

"Mrs. Wells, everything looks wonderful!" Abby exclaimed. Her fingers traced the edge of a meat platter.

Mary Wells gave a satisfied smile. "As soon as your father gives the signal, everyone can start eating."

Abby rolled her eyes. "I hope he's not going to make one of his speeches."

Lacey laughed. "Of course, he will. That's what fathers do at moments like this."

"Come with me, Abby," Mary Wells said. "Let's find your father."

"Lacey!" Micah's shrill cry took her by surprise.

"Micah! What is it?" He flew into his sister's arms.

"Travis is showing me everything. I got to see the big saws! And where they put the logs in the water to float them to the mill!"

"Even Joshua didn't get to do that until he was ten!" Lacey joined her brother's delight. She raised her eyes to see Travis, coming up behind Micah. "You've made my brother really happy."

Travis grinned. "It was my pleasure, I assure you. There is no one else around to show off my newly found knowledge to."

Lacey laughed. "From what I hear, you're getting to be an old hand around here."

Travis set his hands on his hips, a gesture Lacey had noticed several times. He exuded contentment.

"Abby says you and Peter have become friends," Lacey said.

Travis nodded. "He's a thinker, that Peter. He has big plans."

Lacey was not sure what to say. She had known Peter slightly for several years and had never seen him in this light.

Micah was tugging on Travis's arm. "Come on, show me more."

"Be patient," Lacey chastised gently.

Travis smoothed the boy's hair. "I have a lot more to show you. Why don't you meet me in front of the band in a few minutes."

"I'll be there! But don't take too long." Micah shot off directly for the string band.

Travis turned to Lacey. "This is a party, with a hundred things going on, but I'm glad I got to see you."

"Likewise," Lacey blushed.

"How do you spend your Sundays?"

"Oh, I. . .Well, there's no church, you know, so we just. . .Well, it's pretty much a regular day."

"Well, everyone in the camp has Sundays off," Travis said. "I'd like to come and see you. Would that be all right?"

Lacey swallowed, hardly believing her ears. "I'd like that," she said. "How about a picnic? We could eat in the clearing where the path comes out."

"Perfect. I'll look for you there about two o'clock."

"Travis!" Micah's soprano voice somehow carried over the growing noise of the crowd.

"Gotta go," Travis said with a quick smile.

Lacey turned around and nervously rearranged the food trays. Once she glanced over her shoulder to see Travis drape his hand around Micah's shoulders.

From his vantage point across the street, Travis could not tell that her efforts were needless. He simply admired her slim form and the thoughtful tilt of her head as the sun burnished golden highlights in the hair falling around her shoulders.

"My sister is really nice," Micah said. "Do you like her?"

Travis looked down at the boy, wondering how much those blue eyes understood. "Yes, Micah, I like your sister."

Chapter 7

Meeting Travis in the clearing on Sunday afternoons quickly became a habit, and one that Lacey welcomed. Knowing that she could look forward to his companionship on the weekends made the drudgery of the week more bearable. She found herself plunging into laundry and cooking and gardening without the usual exhortations from her mother. She even nagged at the twins to be more helpful, pleading the cause of their mother's enormous workload. As she tended the vegetables that year, pressing the seeds into the dark soil and pulling weeds, she looked forward to their sprouting and sprawling all over the plot, rather than dreading the fact that she would still be there to see the late-summer harvest that would carry the family through another winter.

Lacey hardly noticed when spring blended into summer and, before she knew it, the grass in the meadow was knee high and Micah was spending his afternoons there while the mare and the cow grazed. He had started a butterfly collection, and Lacey laughed riotously as she watched him chase the colorful flutters with his homemade net. Miraculously, he caught several.

By the time the hot days of July were upon them, Lacey and Travis were used to each other and content to indulge in extended speculation about life on the peninsula and life in a real town. Lacey liked best the times that Travis wandered through his memories and described the town he had grown up in with its school, a church, neighbors, and shops—all the things Lacey had hungered for as a child, and still did.

The first few times they agreed to meet, Lacey was not sure Travis would come. She imagined dozens of reasons that would keep him away, not the least of which was her own personality. She longed to pour out her feelings to someone who had lived somewhere else and might understand her drive to find a life away from the peninsula. But Travis had chosen to come to the peninsula, though Lacey never quite understood why, and she did not want to drive him away with chronic complaining.

Her brothers, of course, taunted her mercilessly. Joel called her picnic basket the "love basket." Not to be outdone, Jeremiah kept a running log of "the love food" that she put in it each week. Micah won coveted approval from the twins for his part in the onslaught. Naturally, they did all this behind their mother's back, and Lacey was much too old to go sniveling to her mother to make them stop. At first she had been infuriated and demanded that they mind their own business, but this sent them howling into mimicry and only made the situation worse. Eventually, Lacey steeled herself to ignore them, and she managed to hold her tongue.

Even her mother took a different attitude toward her. Wordlessly, she made sure Sunday afternoons were free of activities that would tie Lacey down. And when Micah chattered on about his fascination with Travis, she looked over her son's blond head at her daughter's brown-haired one, her faced covered with a knowing look and a vague smile.

In between Sundays, Lacey made her habitual visits to the clearing alone, for it was still her escape—the place where she could let her thoughts run free and close her eyes and dream of another place. Also, Travis's presence lingered in that place, drawing Lacey to it even more than ever.

Every week, when Travis arrived at the clearing, she relived their first meeting there. She had snuck out of the house with the prettiest quilt handed down to her from her grandmother, and she had reached the clearing early. Cold chicken, chocolate cake, and a jug of sweetened lemonade comprised the picnic lunch that she spread out on the quilt and then waited. Without a clock nearby, she was not sure how much time had passed, but it seemed like far too much. Travis had realized his folly and changed his mind, she had told herself. So she might as well pack up and go home.

But, just as she was convinced that Travis was not going to come, he had emerged from the woods, paused at the edge of the path, and smiled at her. The sun was in front of him, throwing a magical golden glow across his tanned face. Lacey lurched to her feet to greet him, nearly kicking over the basket of chicken.

"Hello," he said simply.

"Hello," she answered, and their friendship had begun.

The day came when Mary Wells suggested that it was time that Lacey should bring Travis home for dinner one Sunday afternoon. Inwardly, she resisted. When she was with Travis, she was in a world of fresh perspectives, dreams, and a vision of the future. To take Travis home for dinner would taint her new world.

But she knew it had to be done, and so she had done it. The twins snickered, and Micah climbed all over Travis. Mary Wells kept the food coming while managing not to miss a word of the conversation between her husband and the handsome young man. Lacey said little that day and breathed a sigh of relief when she and Travis finally broke away for a walk.

In the weeks that followed, Abby pleaded that she needed Lacey's help to prepare for her wedding, and Lacey gladly took advantage of this as an excuse for frequent trips across the peninsula. They stitched beads on a gown made of white silk that Abby's mother had been saving for years for just this occasion.

In the past, Lacey had not paid much attention to news about the camp or the lumber business, but now her ears perked up when Abby mentioned these things. According to Abby, Peter raved about Travis Gates.

"What does he say?" Lacey asked.

"Travis is a fast learner, and strong. He can handle the saws as well as men who have been there for years."

Lacey thought about how she had noticed his soft hands becoming calloused and rough. How his hands must have hurt in the first few weeks, yet he never complained.

"Peter says everybody likes him," Abby continued. "Usually the new men have to prove themselves, and they get the worst jobs, the heaviest loads, the most danger. It's a test, to see if they can make it as lumberjacks. Travis has never let anyone down." Abby looked slyly at her friend. "But of course you know that, don't you?"

Lacey blushed. Abby knew that she was seeing Travis every week, but Lacey guarded against divulging too many details of their conversations.

During one session at work on the dress, Abby stood on a stool wearing the gown while Lacey, on her knees, pinned the hem in place. "There he is," Abby said suddenly.

"Who?" Lacey mumbled through the pins in her mouth.

"Travis. He just passed by the window. I think he's coming to the door," Abby said.

A few seconds later, they heard his solid rap.

"It's open! Come on in," Abby called.

The door swung in, and Travis poked his head around it. Lacey spat pins into one hand.

"Hello," she said.

He smiled. "I didn't know you would be here. I would have cleaned up."

"You look great." To her own surprise, Lacey meant what she said. His face gleamed with sweat, and his shirt was smudged with layers of sap and mud. She could see he was being careful not to touch anything with his dirty hands. Never before had a grimy lumberjack looked so appealing to her. He was looking for Tom Saget and, after having gathered Abby's opinions about where he might be, Travis was on his way.

"See, it can happen," Abby said.

"What do you mean?"

"It is possible to fall in love with a lumberjack."

Lacey stuck a pin through the hem, hitting Abby's ankle.

"Ouch!" Abby cried.

"Sorry," Lacey said.

"You don't have to stick me with a pin just because I can see what's happening between you and Travis."

"Regardless of what may or may not be happening between us, Travis is not a lumberjack."

"He works in a lumber camp."

"It's temporary. He said from the start that he would only be here a few months."

Abby shrugged. "It doesn't look to me like he's in any hurry to leave."

Lacey bit back her response, for Abby had touched on the one thing that troubled her about Travis. It did seem like he was settling into life on the peninsula rather well. When he first arrived, she had thought he was a breath of fresh air, but if he stayed too long. . .she hated to think what might happen. She had grown attached to Travis, yes, but not enough to be content with the peninsula.

There was a day not too long ago when Lacey realized that her relationship with Travis had taken a new turn. They had been walking in the woods after eating, and she had pointed out the complexity of the wildlife existing along the edge of the trail: small rodents burrowing into the ground; birds nesting in the high branches; ants marching out in force in search of food; tiny bugs clinging to the wildflower petals. They had bent over a blue wildflower, daring not to breathe on it lest the object of their fascination flitter away. With their heads bent low, close together, Lacey could feel his breath on her neck. When they stood up, he had taken her face in his hands to kiss it, and she did not resist. In fact, she had hoped for weeks that this moment would come.

She had indeed fallen in love with Travis Gates. But could she love a lumberjack?

She shuddered at the thought of it. Travis had not said anything to her about staying on the peninsula, and she refused to believe he would. And, when he did leave, she sincerely hoped he would take her with him.

Chapter 8

S ullen gray clouds clumped in the western sky, readying for a summer thunderstorm. Wind blew through Lacey's hair as she studied the formation, and she pressed her hand to the back of her neck to keep her hair under control. The clouds were the sort that could produce a quick shower and pass by or barrage the peninsula for hours. Her father, she knew, would know the difference. His weather-watching habits had spanned the five decades of his life. Each day he carefully logged signs of change and later noted what had resulted.

Lacey stood on the lighthouse balcony, looking out over the passageway. This was the best time of year for boats to navigate the passage, and even as a child, Lacey had loved to come to the balcony and watch for boats. She would make up stories about the people on them, stories of adventure, daring, and romance in faraway places.

Sometimes, standing on the balcony high above the water and scanning the horizon, she felt as if she were at the edge of the world. She knew she ought to step back from the edge, step back to safety, yet she wanted to lean farther over the railing. What was over the edge? Was there a whole new world she could not see from where she was?

Lacey took her eyes off the clouds and glanced at the water. A boat was coming; it was Gordon Wright's supply boat, right on schedule. Gordon knew the rocks of the passageway better than anyone else who sailed through. Lacey watched now as he swung the wooden vessel around a curve and straightened its path toward the Wells family's dock below. Joshua and the twins were taking their places, and her mother had come out of the house with a crumpled list in her hand. Her father tousled Micah's hair and smiled at his enthusiasm. It was all so predictable, Lacey thought. It was just a rickety boat with its rude owner bringing them the bare necessities for their survival in this place. Why was that worthy of celebration every few weeks?

Daniel Wells cupped his hands around his mouth and called up to his daughter. Although his words were carried away on the wind and she heard only drifting tenor tones, Lacey knew he was summoning her to come down and take her place in the drama. This time Joshua was there to help with the heavy work, so Lacey would help her mother put the food and household supplies in their proper places.

Reluctantly she pulled herself away from the railing and turned to find the small door to the spiral iron staircase when a patch of red flashed to one side, and she automatically raised her eyes. The red was a shirt, a lumberjack's shirt, but not Joshua's and, to her delight, she saw that Travis and Peter were in the meadow. Peter patted the rump of a horse and left it to graze. Lacey scrunched up her face in a puzzle. What were they doing here in the middle of a workday at a busy time of the lumber year? Instinctively she raked her fingers through her windblown hair, wishing she had taken the time to tie it back properly that morning. But windblown or not, she was glad to see Travis and now felt no reluctance to descend from the edge of the world.

She reached the bottom of the stairs and pushed open the door. She squinted for a moment, for even the dull afternoon was brighter than the dank stairwell inside the tower. She saw that Peter and Travis had reached the edge of the garden. Ignoring the twins who were calling her, she walked toward the visitors instead and, when they were near each other, she pivoted and fell into step with them.

"Hello, Lacey," Peter said. He reached into his pocket for an envelope. "Abby sent this."

"Oh. Thank you." She stuck the note in the pocket of her skirt to read later and smiled at Travis, awaiting his greeting.

"Is Gordon here yet?" Travis asked, glancing toward the dock.

"Gordon? He's just about to dock."

"Good. Excuse me. Peter, I'll catch up with you later." With a wordless glance at Lacey, Travis quickened his step and trotted ahead of them.

Lacey's steps slowed as she scowled. "What was that all about?"

"He's expecting some important mail. He's hoping Gordon will have it."

"Does that mean he can't even say hello?" Lacey heard the sharpness in her own voice. "Joshua would have taken the mail when he goes back to the camp tomorrow."

Peter shrugged. "I'm not sure what's going on."

"And what brings you here?"

Peter grinned. "Abby's father sent me. They're expecting some fancy things for the wedding. City stuff."

"Oh."

They continued walking toward the edge of the cliff. By the time they reached it, Travis was winding the pulley with the first load; the twins were glad to be relieved of the effort. As the barrel tipped over the top of the pulley, Joshua pushed it off onto the ground. Under their mother's supervision, Joel and Jeremiah started rolling it toward the house. Micah squirmed in under Travis's chest to help with the crank.

"Where's my Lacey?" Gordon called out.

Lacey rolled her eyes and then glanced at Travis for his reaction. He had none; he just cranked.

"Lacey Wells, come and say hello!" Gordon insisted.

She craned her neck to see him. "Hello, Gordon. How are you?"

"Not as well as I would be if you could take a boat ride with me."

"Not today, Gordon," she said flatly, as usual.

"I'll be asking again. You know I will."

Peter chuckled beside her. "He never gives up, does he? I wonder if he knows about you and Travis."

Lacey thought to herself, *And I wonder what there is to know.*

The next load up had a small canvas pouch tucked between the ropes. It was the mailbag, and Travis plucked it off the crate before anyone else could reach it. Glancing over his shoulder, he said, "Hey, Pete, put yourself to work over here." Then he turned and walked away from the crank, unfastening the buckle on the mailbag as he went.

Mystified, Lacey watched as Travis sat on a boulder across the yard and started flipping through the letters in the bag. Finally, he pulled one out and held it in his hand. He glanced at her for a fraction of a second, then pulled his eyes away.

What will she think? Travis wondered. *Have I gone too far?*

Mary Wells called for Lacey, and she turned to help her mother. Travis watched her movements: competent, smooth, efficient. But he knew she cared little about what she was doing. She always urged him to talk about where he had come from, as if she could sit for hours and listen to stories about life in a real town. Would she ever know contentment, here or anywhere else?

He tore off the end of the envelope and slid out the papers. They were exactly what he was hoping for.

"Hey, Travis!" Micah called, running toward him. "Did you know Peter is even stronger than you are? He's turning the pulley fast!"

Travis smiled and held out his hand to the boy, who perched next to him on the rock. "Peter has been working outside for a long time. He's used to the hard work."

Looking up from her work, Lacey saw Travis chatting with Micah. That was one of the things she liked most about Travis: his willingness to take his time with Micah. She watched as he folded up his letter and tucked it in his shirt pocket. *What was that all about? What could possibly be that urgent?* He once mentioned that he had almost been engaged to a girl in his hometown and that they were still friends. *What did that mean? Are they sending letters back and forth? That might explain why he practically ignored me earlier.*

"I'll be right back, Mama," she said, having decided to approach Travis again, this time with Micah as a buffer. Resisting the temptation to gather her skirt in one hand and run toward the rock, she walked casually with her hands in her pockets. She felt Abby's note waiting for her attention.

"Hello," she said lightly. "I hope Micah is not disturbing you."

"No, of course not," Travis replied. Lacey thought his voice sounded strained. "But I suppose I'd better get back to work soon or Peter will tell tales on me."

"I'll help!" Micah's enthusiasm never waned.

"Great. I'll tell you what. You go over and see what's going on, and I'll meet you in a few minutes." Travis glanced up at Lacey.

"Oh. You want to talk to my sister," Micah guessed.

Travis laughed, and Lacey felt awkward. "I can't fool you, can I?" Travis said.

"Don't take too long." Micah scurried over to help Joel and Jeremiah roll kerosene barrels.

"Hello." The long-awaited greeting came.

"Hello," she responded.

"Micah's right. I did want to talk to you about something." Travis gestured that she should sit down.

Lacey swallowed involuntarily, for she was hearing a tone in his voice she had not heard before.

He slid the envelope out of his pocket. "I've been waiting for this to come," he said. "It's addressed to me, but actually it's for you."

Puzzled, she took the envelope from his hand, extracted the paper, and read the letter.

Dear Mr. Gates,

Thank you for inquiring about the teaching position on behalf of your friend, Miss Wells. We would be happy to consider her application. From what you have said, I am sure she would have no difficulty passing the qualifying examination.

Lacey absorbed very little after that. "Teaching position?" she said, incredulous.

Travis nodded. "I haven't said anything to you, because I wasn't sure it was my place. But. . .well, we have become friends, and I care about your feelings. I thought. . .perhaps you would be happy to have an opportunity to leave the peninsula, at least for a time."

"But, Travis, teaching? I don't know." She swallowed her true thoughts. *Yes, I want to leave, but not alone.*

"I think you would be good at it. From what I've seen, your mother has done a better job than most organized schools in educating you and your brothers. The twins get on your nerves, they're at an awkward age, but I see the way you are with Micah. Imagine the effect you could have on a whole class of children like him."

"But I've never even considered being a teacher! I wouldn't know where to begin."

Travis paused and lowered his eyes. "I know you're not happy here, Lacey, but when I try to picture what would make you happy, I can't quite fill in all the colors. After a while, I realized that no one can do that for you and that you have to do it yourself. I do know that God has given you some wonderful gifts, and you should find a way to use them."

Lacey swallowed hard. "But, Travis—"

"The teaching position is only for nine months," Travis continued, "because the regular teacher has to be away. But she's coming back. They're just looking for someone to fill in."

"How did you know about this job?"

"A friend of my father mentioned it in a letter, and I wrote for more information." Travis reached for Lacey's hand. "I kept wanting to say something, but I wasn't sure how you would react."

"I am not sure what to say. You've gone to all this trouble. I suppose I should be grateful." Confusion overwhelmed her.

"It's for only nine months. If you hate it, then you'll know teaching is not for you. But you might love it!"

"Where is the school?" Lacey asked. Her mother, she knew, would ask sensible questions.

"South. It's not a big place," Travis explained, "not the city that you would prefer. But after you get some teaching experience, you could apply for a better job somewhere else."

"It doesn't matter how small the town might be. It's sure to be bigger than here."

Travis smiled. "You're seeing the advantages already."

Lacey focused her eyes on a mushroom at her feet. "Are you leaving the peninsula, Travis?"

"I don't know. I came here because I felt led to come here."

"Led? By God?"

He nodded. "And I'll stay until it's time to leave. In the meantime, I'm content. I just want you to be content, too. You have to make your own decision, find your sense of call."

"I don't know what to say, Travis." Her voice was low, but her heart was screaming, *I thought you would take me away from here, not send me away!*

"Just think about it, Lacey. But they need an answer soon because the job starts in two months."

"Gates! Go get the horse and help me with this stuff!" Peter held a large canvas bag in his arms, and another lay at his feet.

Questioning, Travis looked at Lacey and drew her eyes up to meet his.

Silently, she nodded.

Chapter 9

The train slowed. Being careful to keep her hat on straight, Lacey pressed her face as close to the window as she dared. The blur of golden trees gradually gave form to trunks and limbs embellished with burnished leaves. Carefully painted wooden homes stopped spinning and announced that the train had arrived in a town. Abruptly, the train lurched to a stop and the whistle blew. Lacey's stomach flipped with uncertainty about the commitment she had made.

Travis had not proposed. Instead, he had found Lacey a job. He was giving her what she had said she wanted: a reason to leave the peninsula with which even her mother could not argue. Lacey was going to be a teacher for the next nine months, and it was her mother who had prepared her so well for this role.

But was she truly prepared? Lacey wondered. Yes, she had always been a good student, and now she even helped her mother with lessons for the twins and Micah. But that was very different from a whole classroom of children she did not know. She had passed the qualifying test with one of the highest scores ever seen, but did that make her a teacher?

Around her, the other passengers were gathering their things and leaving the train. Now Lacey did the same. She had not brought much, for she did not have much to bring. Her hand-me-down trunk was in the baggage car, and she had only a small bag of essentials, which she now grasped tightly. Smoothing her skirt and wrapping her coat tightly as she walked, Lacey made her way down the aisle to the door at the back of the train car. Now she could get her first real look at this new town.

Outside the train, Lacey scanned the station. Most of the people on the train had gotten off at this stop, and the platform bustled with confusion and greetings. A few feet from Lacey, a young wife with three children in tow greeted her husband with a kiss. Down the platform, a businessman dressed in a shiny black suit barked orders at his junior companion. Lacey got bumped from the back by a thin, teenage boy lumbering along the platform with his mother's trunk.

Where was Maria Johnson? Lacey wondered about her teaching partner who was supposed to meet her. But Lacey did not even know what Maria looked like.

"You look lost," said a voice behind Lacey.

Lacey spun around, grasping for words, as she faced a stout woman, perhaps ten years older than herself. "I—I'm to be met here, I think."

"I know. I'm meeting you," said the woman.

"Miss Johnson?" Lacey asked, hope rising within her.

"Maria," came the reply. "You match the description perfectly."

"Description?"

"Yes, the chairman of the school board gave me a written description. When did you meet him?" Maria turned and started to walk down the platform.

"I haven't," Lacey said. *Travis*, she thought. *Travis must have written the description.*

"He seems to know all about you," Maria said. "I have a wagon hitched up to the horse. Let's find your trunk." She walked toward the baggage car that was already unloaded, the trunks and bags heaped on the platform.

"There it is," Lacey said as she pointed at the the faded green metal trunk that her mother had brought to the peninsula as a bride more than twenty years ago.

"Wouldn't you know, it's at the bottom of the pile," Maria grumbled. "I'll just have a word with a porter." Briskly Maria marched down the platform in pursuit of a porter.

It was not long before the trunk was extricated from the heap and loaded onto the waiting wagon. Maria gestured that Lacey should climb onto the bench at the front of the wagon, behind the horse. From the other side, Maria heaved herself up and picked up the reins.

"Ready?" Maria asked.

"Ready," Lacey answered softly, even though she was not sure she was.

The horse trotted down the street, the wagon rattling behind. By usual standards, the town was not large but to Lacey it seemed enormous. A row of shops nearly made her burst out like a child, and the steeple of a church convinced her she was going to like this town. A few houses were clustered in neat rows, just like a real neighborhood! Gradually, the houses were spaced farther and farther apart. Now they were headed out on an open dirt road. Confused, Lacey could not contain her questions.

"Aren't we headed out of town now?" she asked.

Maria nodded. "We're leaving Paxton. That's just where the train comes in."

"Oh," Lacey said.

Maria turned to look at Lacey. "Did you think that was Tyler Creek?"

Now Lacey was more confused. "What's Tyler Creek?"

"The town where you will be teaching. Didn't they tell you anything?"

"They told me to take the train to Paxton, and that you would meet me there."

Maria threw her head back and laughed. "No doubt they were afraid you would change your mind if you knew the truth about Tyler Creek."

Lacey's stomach was in a knot now. "Please tell me what you are talking about."

"Tyler Creek is a small, small community about five miles from here. That's where the school is."

"Small?"

"We have about six hundred people," Maria explained. "A few have small shops, more are farmers or millworkers."

"Six hundred people?" Lacey echoed.

"I know that doesn't sound like many people to folks who live in the city."

"To me, six hundred is a city!" In her mind, Lacey added up the lumberjacks who made up the population of the peninsula; perhaps a hundred, she thought. "What is the school like?"

"Not all of the children come to school," Maria explained. "We have an enrollment of about fifty, split into two classes."

"And I'll have the lower grades?"

Maria nodded. "That's what Victoria was teaching before she had to go on leave."

Lacey's curiosity got the best of her. "Why did she have to leave?"

Maria's jaw stiffened and her face clouded over. "She became ill, and her family thought it best that she go home for a time of rest."

"Ill?"

But Maria said no more.

"Is there a mercantile in Tyler Creek?" Lacey asked, changing the subject.

Maria's smile returned. "No, no mercantile. But there is Mister Edgars who comes around every few weeks with his wagon loaded down with everything a body could want."

"What about food?"

Maria gestured widely. "Look around. This is farm country. Folks grow what they need."

"But you don't farm," Lacey pointed out.

"No, just a few vegetables. But I never lack for food. And neither will you. I'd wager that we'll send you home a good twenty pounds heavier."

Lacey put her hand on her slender waist. "I hope not!" She shivered and crossed her arms to hug herself. "I hadn't expected it to be so cool in September. My home is so far north. I thought it would be better down here."

"This is still Wisconsin," Maria reminded Lacey. "And winter is not far off. We don't have too much farther to go."

At last the horse lumbered into a small gathering of houses, and the animal seemed to know where he was going without further prodding. He turned left off the main road and trotted lazily down a dirt path.

"Here we are," Maria said finally, pulling on the reins gently. "Home, sweet home."

Maria jumped down and unhitched the horse. Lacey moved more slowly, inspecting her surroundings at the same time that she found the ground under her feet again. Before her was a small house, just a cottage. No doubt, its clapboard had once been a shiny white, but now it was dull gray and chipped. The three steps leading up to the front door sagged precariously.

Lacey turned slightly to see what Maria was doing. It was then she noticed the small building separated from the cottage by a small yard. A well-beaten path led directly from the cottage steps to the other building. *The school*, Lacey surmised.

"Do you want to take the trunk in now or get cleaned up first?" Lacey had already figured out that Maria was a practical soul.

"Let's do it now," Lacey mumbled. Without the help of a porter, managing the trunk would be much more difficult than earlier.

Maria heaved the trunk down off the back of the wagon, and dirt sprayed as it hit the ground. Lacey winced, glad she had not brought anything breakable.

"You've got more than clothes in here," Maria announced.

"Books," Lacey confessed. "I wasn't sure what there would be here."

Maria nodded knowingly. "You did the wise thing."

"Let me help you with that."

Together they carried the trunk into the house. Lacey glanced around the sitting room as they passed through. An overstuffed chair and a well-worn table were the predominant features, arranged on a faded braided rug that had once been a rich green.

"This is your room." With one hand, Maria pushed open a door. They set the trunk down with care on the bare wooden floor. "I'm going to put the kettle on while you settle in."

Lacey's room was not much bigger than her room at home. The bed swung low to the floor, and the iron headboard needed a fresh coat of paint. Sheets and a patchwork quilt were neatly folded at the foot of the bare mattress. A small dresser was wedged under the window. Four pegs in the wall would serve as a closet. Lacey slowly opened her trunk and considered how to arrange her things. The options were few, and the task was soon complete.

Lacey went out to the sitting room that she would share with Maria. Her new roommate stirred up the fire in the old black stove, and then she wiped her hands on a dingy apron.

"This is for heat and for cooking," Maria explained. "It's not fancy, but nothing in Tyler Creek is fancy."

No, it's not fancy, Lacey thought silently, *but it's not the peninsula. I said I wanted to leave, and I have.*

"Are you hungry?" Maria moved toward the nook of a kitchen. "I'll fix you some bread and tea."

Lacey nodded gratefully. *Father, keep me thankful,* she prayed silently as her heart raced slightly, *and show me what it is I am here to do.*

Chapter 10

Lacey struck a solid chord on the decrepit spinet with a cracked top that was at the back of her classroom. The tinny clang made her wince, for the instrument was badly out of tune and at least a dozen strings were missing. Sometimes she wondered why she bothered to try to teach music with that piano, but it was all she had. According to Maria, no one had taught music to the children in more than seven years. Lacey was determined to change that, but the idea of an a cappella choir appealed more every day. But she was committed to the piano for now.

Winterfest would begin the next day and Tyler Creek, as tiny as it was, would gather all its citizens to celebrate that winter was nearly over. Soon, they would have some relief from pelting sleet and howling wind, but slick, icy roads would turn to mud, which would no doubt mean broken buggy axles and chronically sloppy floors.

The fall weeks had blurred together as Lacey had sorted out the task before her. Lacey's first day in the classroom had been a mixture of terror and delight. Helping her mother give lessons to Micah and the twins was one thing; facing a roomful of children ranging in age from four to ten years old was something else entirely. She had stood before them, immobilized. The little ones in the front turned their faces up expectantly. In the back of the room, two older boys leaned toward each other and muttered, looking at her suspiciously all the while. In Lacey's mind the words were flowing, but somehow they did not seem to come out of her mouth. At last a little girl named Sally had asked, "Are you all right, Miss Wells?" and Lacey had snapped herself together and gone into action.

Lacey had learned from her mother to stay in control at lesson time, and the shenanigans of her twin brothers had prepared her for what she faced now. The muttering boys in the back were gently but firmly reprimanded, and class had begun.

It took nearly two weeks for Lacey to assess every student's abilities and discern their temperaments. She knew that the students in her class would be as different from each other as Micah was from Joel and Jeremiah. Yet, they all had to learn to read and do basic figuring. And Lacey wanted to add music, geography, and art to the curriculum. She was not teaching one class; she was teaching several classes. Dalton and Denys, the two biggest boys, were old enough to be in Maria's class. But they had missed too many days of school in the last two years, and they did not read well enough to move on to the next class. Lacey's dilemma was that she was not sure they wanted to learn to read and that they might very well spend yet another year in the same classroom.

At the other end of the spectrum was a child who was not even five years old but who insisted on going to school with his older siblings, and his mother had allowed it. Little Jonathan was well-behaved and was really no trouble, but Lacey did not feel she could extend the curriculum to such a young age, and so she was not sure what he was learning.

At the end of each day, Lacey gathered papers and books and scurried across the clearing between the school and the cottage. It was too cold to be outside, and everywhere she went, she went quickly. With Maria, she huddled around the blackened stove they used for both heat and cooking. The evenings were crammed with lesson planning. The previous teacher had left some notes and outlines, but most of her scribblings were not meaningful to Lacey, so she had to start over from the beginning. Maria was some help, although most of her experience was with the older children. Night after night, Lacey sat up late with a candle, a wool shawl wrapped around her shoulders, planning lessons that would teach Roger how to add double figures and Bessie to sound out the words on the page. She had to find a way to make Wiley pay attention and stop looking out the window. And TJ simply needed encouragement that he could succeed at school.

Books were in shockingly short supply, and three children shared one copy of a basic textbook. Victoria had left behind a few storybooks, and Lacey added some of her own to the meager collection. Maria had scowled when Lacey announced she was going to let the children borrow the books and take them home to read. It was a risk that some of the books would never make it back, but Lacey was compelled to act on her conviction that children must be stimulated with new ideas and experiences. She found it difficult to believe that even tucked away on a distant peninsula, she had grown up with more books than many of these children would ever hold. She had begun to see her own mother in a new light.

Christmastime had come, and Lacey had remained in Tyler Creek. A couple of times she took the wagon into Paxton where the festive spirit was more evident. An array of sugary cakes and candles made Lacey pine to be with her family. But that was not possible. There would be other years, she told herself, to savor her mother's roast duck on Christmas Eve and to tie bows to the window panes.

On Christmas Eve she went to the midnight service at the small church in Tyler Creek. While singing the carols, for the first time with more people than her immediate family, her heart surged to receive anew the gift God freely offered.

After Christmas, the weather took a severe turn. School was shut down several times and families huddled at their hearths, but Winterfest would bring them out and Lacey wanted the children to be ready.

Children bustled around her, jostling each other for a space in the front row. They had worked hard already that afternoon, and Lacey knew she would not have their attention for much longer.

She struck the chord again, raising and lowering her hands to the keys four times. "Children, children," she said, "we're almost through."

Maria had raised her eyebrows at Lacey's idea that a children's choir should sing at Winterfest but Lacey was determined, and for the most part, the children were enthusiastic, if not attentive.

"How can we practice without TJ?" a thin voice asked. Rebekah looked at her teacher, wondering.

Lacey sighed. It was a legitimate question. TJ had the solo part in the last song. This was the final rehearsal before the performance, and TJ was nowhere to be found. He had not been in school for two days.

"I suppose we can't wait for him any longer," Lacey conceded. "He learned the part so well, and he has such a beautiful voice. Are you sure none of you know where he is?" She scanned fifteen faces hopefully.

"He's probably sick again," Joey said. "He gets sick a lot."

Lacey's mind raced. If TJ were sick, he might not appear at the performance, either. "Joey, do you think you can sing TJ's part?" Lacey asked.

The little boy's eyes glowed. "We practiced it together lots of times. I know it just as good as he does."

"Just as *well* as he does," Lacey corrected. "Let's try it." And she struck the chord for the third time. This time the children began to sing.

Letters from home came irregularly. Lacey knew it was difficult to mail a letter from the peninsula, and she had not expected that there would be much mail for her. Her family either would have to wait for Gordon Wright to appear and carry a letter, and hope that he would remember to mail it from some town along his route, or they would have to entrust a letter to a lumberjack who might be traveling off the peninsula. Still, she hoped. One note came from Micah, sweetly written in his awkward handwriting. The form was perfect, with a salutation, two paragraphs in the body recounting recent deer sightings in the meadow, and a closing that read, "Sincerely yours, Micah D. Wells." Lacey pictured her mother making a lesson out of writing a letter. No experience was ever wasted if Mary Wells had anything to say about it.

The other letter Lacey received was from Travis. He seemed quite satisfied with work in the lumber camp—too satisfied in Lacey's opinion. In what little spare time he had, he was helping to build Peter and Abby's new home and was clearly pleased with his new carpentry skills. He asked politely about how her work was going but gave no further indication of his feelings.

Joey's voice glittered in the air as Lacey played the notes on the piano from memory. Joey did, indeed, know the part. His voice was not as unfaltering as TJ's, but he sang earnestly.

The song ended. "Joey, I'm so glad you practiced with TJ," Lacey said enthusiastically. The little boy beamed. "Whatever would we have done if you hadn't learned the part?"

"Are we done now?" Roger wanted to know.

Lacey nodded. "Yes, we're done. I'll see you all at the meeting hall at three o'clock tomorrow afternoon. Don't be late!"

Her students clamored into their coats and bolted through the doorway. Lacey moved to the window to watch them disperse across the clearing and head toward their homes. She could not help wondering where TJ was. He had been a steadfast student throughout the fall semester. He was dedicated and craved learning. But in recent weeks, he had been missing school more and more often. Lacey was not convinced that he was just sick.

Chapter 11

"M iss Wells! Miss Wells!"

Lacey pivoted just in time to find Patsy and Maggie tumbling into her skirts. She stooped to give the six-year-old girls a proper embrace before they knocked her over completely. Patsy slobbered on Lacey's face, and that reminded her of Micah.

"Do you like my dress?" Patsy asked, twirling her new calico garb proudly.

"You look very elegant," Lacey replied, and Patsy beamed at her teacher with satisfaction.

"When do we sing?" Maggie demanded. "I want to sing!"

Lacey chuckled at her enthusiasm. "Soon, Maggie. It will be our turn soon."

"You said we would sing after lunch. I'm all done eating," Maggie said.

"We have to be patient, Maggie. It won't be much longer."

"When you give the signal, right, Miss Wells?" Patsy asked.

"Right. When I put up our special flag on top of the piano, it will be our turn to sing. Don't forget to watch!"

"We won't," the little girls promised and then scampered off.

Lacey surveyed the crowd. It was a good turnout. Winterfest extended through one entire Saturday. A tradition that had begun in Tyler Creek ten years earlier now beckoned residents from the other small towns in the region. The meeting hall, which served as a church on Sundays, was not built for nearly as many people as were crammed into it that day. But it was the biggest building in Tyler Creek, and there was nowhere else to go; the town council refused to take Tyler Creek's Winterfest to Paxton just for the sake of a bigger space.

The temperature was well below freezing that day, and only the most hardened snow fans insisted on outdoor activity. Toboggans sliced their way down the hill, only to be hauled to the top by the next waiting team. An army of snowmen stood guard around the meeting hall, but no one lasted more than a few minutes in the biting wind. With icicles dangling from their clothes, one by one the outdoors enthusiasts sought the refuge and warmth of the meeting hall.

Inside, the temperature climbed steadily throughout the day as more and more people filtered in. The festivities had begun at eight in the morning. Quilts, the products of long winter evenings, adorned the walls of the meeting hall. In one corner men huddled to discuss their optimism for a good spring planting, surely only a few weeks away. Mothers kept one eye on their roaming children and the other on the sketches of new fashions that were making their way around the room. Games for the children lined the far end of the room. At noon, the long tables down one side of the hall were laden with everyone's best potluck dish, providing twice as much food as the hundreds of people there would require. Lacey had eaten heartily, something she had come to regret as her own nerves became unsettled while she considered the fact that the chidren had never before participated in the Winterfest program. Lacey had put herself out on a limb when she had suggested that they should. If the children's performance was not perfect, she would be ridiculed and no one would ever be convinced of the place of music in the educational program at Tyler Creek.

Lacey did not dare leave her music on the piano. Clutching it close so it would not be mangled in an inevitable collision, she scanned the crowd. She looked for one small head that could easily be lost in the throng of milling adults.

Maria came to stand beside her. "Have you spotted him yet?" Maria asked.

Lacey shook her head.

"Perhaps TJ is still ill," Maria offered.

Lacey nodded. "Perhaps. Sally was in school yesterday. When I asked her about her brother, she didn't answer. She acted like she didn't hear me, but I'm certain she did."

"I'm sure it's nothing." Maria abruptly stepped back to let a teenager hurtle past her.

"I'm not so sure," Lacey answered. "I'm worried about TJ. He really wanted to sing that solo. I can't understand why he wouldn't send word to me if he couldn't do it."

Maria shrugged. "Children often change their minds for reasons adults don't understand."

"I had to give his solo away," Lacey said. "I can't take it back from Joey now. But I'm still worried about TJ."

"I'll keep looking," Maria said. "If I find him, I'll tell him you are looking for him." Then Maria faded away as the crowd jostled them.

Lacey was polite to anyone who spoke to her, but her mind was on one thing, and at last she glimpsed a swatch of light brown hair that looked familiar. The child stood and watched as other children tossed darts at a target. Smiling at the people she squeezed past, Lacey moved steadily toward the bobbing head. Periodically she lost sight of him, but each time she glimpsed the child, she was more convinced it was TJ. Determined, she made her way past Mrs. Childer's apple pie and the group huddling around Mrs. Graves and her new afghan. She continued past the new calico samples from the mercantile in Paxton and the farmers bartering for horses and cows. Finally, she reached the other end of the hall.

"Hello, TJ!" she called.

The boy barely lifted his eyes. "Hello, Miss Wells."

"I understand you haven't been feeling well." Lacey kept her tone cheerful, while her heart swelled in sympathy.

TJ did not answer. His right foot slid forward and then back again several times. His hands stuffed in his pockets, TJ had not met Lacey's eyes.

"We missed you in school," Lacey said, "especially during the spelling bee yesterday. I know how much you like the spelling bees."

The foot slid forward again. "Who won?" he asked quietly.

"Roger. He spelled 'educate.'"

TJ nodded. "That's a hard one. But I can spell it."

"I'm sure you can."

TJ turned his head and looked over his shoulder. The black-and-blue patch on the bottom of his chin was unmistakable. When he turned his head again, Lacey saw the mark on his forehead, just under the lock of hair that hung down over his left eye. Fury stirred within her.

"TJ—," she started to say.

His eyes pleaded with her to say no more.

"Are you sure you're all right?" she asked quietly, her tone no longer chipper.

He nodded and looked over his shoulder again.

This time Lacey saw what he had been looking at. Bert Richards approached, and he clapped a hand on his son's back. TJ immediately tensed.

"I hope the schoolmarm is not making you do your lessons here," Bert said jovially.

"No, sir," TJ muttered.

"I was just inquiring about TJ's health," Lacey said. "I was concerned that he might not be feeling well yet."

Bert squeezed his son's shoulder in an unconvincing way. "The boy has been sickly lately. But he was just dying to come to Winterfest, and I didn't want to deny him that."

Lacey fumed. *You deny him school,* she thought, *and there's no telling what you do to him at home. But at Winterfest you want us all to believe you have a happy household.*

Aloud, Lacey said, "TJ, when you didn't come to the last practice, I had to give your solo to Joey. But I hope you'll sing with us anyway."

TJ shrugged one shoulder.

"I'm not sure the boy feels well enough for that," Bert said, more loudly than was necessary. "We'll be sure to listen to every note of your little choir, though."

Lacey saw the sneer behind Bert's broad grin. With a flash of horror, she realized that TJ had been beaten because of his interest in the choir. She changed the subject.

"Your son is quite a speller, Mr. Richards."

"He's a book learner, that's for sure. Sometimes he forgets to get his nose out of a book to do his chores, ain't that right, son?" Bert clapped TJ's back again.

"Yes, sir."

"Book learning is fine, but a man's got to have his head in the real world."

Lacey could hardly contain herself. "A good education will prepare TJ for a very productive life, no matter what he chooses to do."

"I just don't want him getting airs about himself, that's all." Bert stared deep into Lacey's eyes. "Come on, TJ. I'm sure your teacher has things to take care of."

Bert Richards led his son away. TJ never looked back—because he did not dare, Lacey was sure.

Maria appeared. "I see you found TJ."

Lacey nodded. "Something horrible is going on in that house."

"Lacey, you can't be sure of anything."

Lacey turned and stared at her fellow teacher, whose eyes flickered away. "You know, don't you? And you haven't said a word!"

"It's time for your choir to sing," Maria said. "You'd better get the children together."

Maria turned away. Lacey glanced at the clock. Maria was right. It was time to slither through the crowd back to the piano and give the signal that the children should gather. As soon as the bright orange and blue triangle flag was set on the piano, Patsy and Maggie appeared; Roger, Rebekah, Joey, and the others were not far behind. Many of them had anxiously been waiting nearby for the secret signal.

Lacey's hands shook as she placed her music on the piano and scooted the bench a few inches closer. The children bumped and jostled until they had finally formed two reasonably straight lines.

"Joey," Lacey said, her voice quavering, "you'd better stand in the front row so everyone can hear you."

"I can't see you, Miss Wells," Patsy complained.

"You may come and stand on this side," Lacey said, "right next to Joey."

More jostling ensued.

Dear Lord, Lacey thought, *still my soul and hands.*

Gradually the notes on the page in front of her fell into a pattern, and Lacey played a lively introduction to get the crowd's attention. Out of the corner of one eye, she saw the thatch of light brown hair. She turned, and at last TJ met her eyes.

Chapter 12

S atisfied that the fire had caught, Lacey leaned against the stove's heavy black door to make sure it shut securely. Then she wrapped her arms around her chest and huddled over the stove, waiting for warmth. Though the morning light had not yet come, she could tell that the early spring day would be a brisk one, and she was determined that her schoolroom would be warm when the children arrived. Four weeks had passed since Winterfest. Spring was stubborn in coming.

When she accepted the teaching contract, it had not occurred to Lacey to ask about things like heating the school. On her second day in Tyler Creek, Maria had meticulously demonstrated how to get the stove started. Then they alternated the chore. In addition to the unpleasantness of leaving her warm bed and going outside while it was still dark, the stubbornness of the stove aggravated Lacey. The door was hinged badly, and she was not convinced that the stove was vented properly.

Gradually she warmed up just in time to dash across the yard to the small house she shared with Maria. She knew Maria would have the fire going and breakfast waiting. A mug of steaming coffee greeted her.

Two hours later, they were both in their classrooms, waiting for the children. Lacey greeted the children at the door, mentally taking attendance as they hung their coats and stored their lunch buckets. The morning bustle was typical; the children chattered with each other and crowded around the stove for warmth. Some of them had walked several miles to come to school. Lacey had learned from experience to allow them a few minutes to recover from the cold outside before insisting that they take their seats.

TJ was missing again. But Sally was there. Lacey glanced over at the girl's tattered coat on its hook and saw no lunch bucket beneath it. She had not really expected to see one, but she kept hoping.

Then she walked up behind the huddle of children and made herself cheerful. "Good morning, everyone. Are you feeling warmer?"

She glanced at Sally as the children responded, but the girl did not even turn her head to acknowledge the question. Her hair badly needed combing, and her dress was much too thin for the weather.

Lacey laid her hand lightly on Sally's shoulder. "Where's TJ? I hope everything's all right."

"He's sick," Sally said sullenly.

"I hope he'll be better soon."

Sally shook her head. "No. He's real sick this time."

Lacey sighed. TJ had been "sick" too often. Sally always gave the same explanation. But Lacey was not fooled, for sometimes the bruising and swelling were not quite healed when he returned to school. A lump hardened in her stomach at the thought of what was happening to that eight-year-old boy at the hand of his own father.

"Are we going to do math today?" someone asked, and Lacey was pulled back to the task at hand.

"Yes, we're going to work on subtraction. But first, let's finish reading the story we started yesterday."

The children reluctantly left the warmth of the stove and took their seats. The day was underway.

At the lunch break, Lacey was relieved to see some of the other girls offering bits of their lunch to Sally. More than once, she herself claimed to have more food than she could eat and insisted that Sally or TJ help her by eating some bread. But it seemed easier for Sally when the other girls wordlessly set something in front of her. Today she gobbled up a slab of bread with butter and two apples. Obviously she had had no breakfast, and she may not have had anything last night, either. Lacey watched from her desk, trying not to let Sally notice.

After school, Lacey fell in step beside Sally outside the building. "Hi, Sally. I thought I'd walk home with you today. I'd like to check on TJ."

Alarm flashed across the girl's face. "He's sick."

"I know. I'd like to see if there is something I can do to help."

"He'll be sleeping."

Lacey hesitated. "Well, I wouldn't want to disturb him, of course. Perhaps there is something I can do for your mother. I could sit with TJ while she does some of her chores outside."

"I'll do the chores today. No need for you to come."

Lacey could not push the six-year-old girl any further. The look of fright on her blanched face told the whole story. Something was going on in that house, and Sally did not want her teacher to see it.

"I'll see you tomorrow, Miss Wells." Sally dashed off, running faster than any of the other children and disappearing around the bend in the road.

"What was that all about?" Maria asked.

"I wanted to walk Sally home," Lacey said.

"Why?"

"To see TJ. He was absent again today. Lately, he misses more days than he attends."

"His mother says he's always been a sickly child," Maria observed.

"I don't believe that for a moment, and neither should you!"

"Lacey! What's gotten into you?"

"Open your eyes, Maria. TJ is not sick. Not this time, not any time. His father. . ." She could hardly bring herself to say the words aloud. "His father beats him."

"You don't know that for sure."

"Yes, I do."

"Have you ever seen it happen?"

"No, but—"

"Does he come to school with bruises?"

"He's not allowed to come after it happens, not till the bruises are nearly gone."

Maria shook her head. "Look, Lacey, I'll admit the family is a bit odd. Mrs. Richards will hardly look anyone in the eye, and Sally acts like she's scared to death of something."

"Then you agree!"

Maria held up her hand. "Hold on. I didn't agree to anything. I said the family is unusual. Maybe they have some problems, but you have no proof of what you suspect."

"I don't suspect it, I know it!"

"You can't prove it. And you don't want to tangle with Bert Richards."

"Why not?" Lacey asked, defiantly shaking her head.

"Because if you do, you'll stir up this whole community and get a lot of people angry at you. Then what good will you be to anyone?"

"There must be a way!" Lacey insisted.

Maria shook her head. "Do what you can for TJ when he's in school, but stay away from his father—for your own good."

"What about TJ's good?" Lacey snapped.

Maria did not answer. Instead, she pushed a basket she had been holding into Lacey's hands. "Mrs. Larsen came by with a basket of fresh muffins. Would you mind taking them back to the house? I have a meeting with another parent." Lacey was silent, but Maria met her eyes before turning around and going back inside the school. She had said all she had to say.

Lacey sighed and looked down at the basket in her arms. She pulled back the napkin for a peek at the muffins. They were still warm, and thin steam rose and dissipated in the cool air. Lacey shivered, suddenly feeling the cold, for in her haste to catch Sally, she had not stopped for a coat. The wind whipped her skirt around her ankles and sliced through her. Reluctantly, Lacey retrieved her coat from her classroom, adjusted the stove door, and trudged across the yard to the house, carrying the muffins. Once inside, she sat down on a kitchen chair, cradling the basket in her lap.

She refused to accept that there was nothing more she could do for TJ. Maria was wrong. When she thought of TJ, she could not also help thinking of Micah, with his slender frame and tender disposition. She would never stand for anyone hurting Micah, so why should she stand for anyone hurting TJ?

Sally's frightened eyes haunted Lacey. Sally rarely missed school, but she was constantly tired and so thin!

Lacey looked at the basket of muffins. Many of the children's mothers were generous with gifts for the two teachers, and they always had more than they needed. More than likely, these muffins would go stale before she and Maria could eat them.

Abruptly, Lacey stood up, reached for a box on the bookshelf, and began transferring muffins from the basket to the box. Maria, she knew, would say that Mrs. Larsen would be insulted if she knew they gave away her muffins. But, at the moment, Lacey did not care about that. Sally and TJ needed those muffins more than she did. She tucked one of her own red napkins around the top of the box, turned up the collar on her coat, and headed out the door.

The Richards family lived nearly two miles from the school, on the outskirts of the little town. Lacey marched down the road, politely nodding her greetings to passersby but intent on her mission. The Richards house was in need of repair. One window was broken and boards were nailed across it, but the wind howled through the cracks. The third step up to the sagging porch had a hole through it, and Lacey saw it just in time to step over it.

She knocked on the door and waited. She heard unmistakable scuffling from inside the house, but no one came to the door. She knocked again. "Mrs. Richards? It's Miss Wells. Please open the door."

Lacey saw a tattered curtain move ever so slightly and caught a glimpse of Sally's profile. She held her breath. After a moment, the door opened about two inches.

"Hello, Mrs. Richards," Lacey said.

"Ain't Sally behavin' herself at school?" Mrs. Richards asked.

"Oh, she's fine. She's doing very good work. I—I brought you some muffins," Lacey said, holding the box out. "I know TJ is sick, and I thought the muffins might save you some work for supper."

"Thank you, but I already made biscuits."

"Oh. Well, then, perhaps for the morning." Subtly she set them on a half-rotted barrel next to the door. "How is TJ doing?"

"He's mendin'," came the reply, and Lacey noticed the mother's choice of words.

"Might I see him?" Lacey asked.

"He's sleeping now. He needs his rest."

"Of course he does." Lacey looked into the tired eyes of Alvira Richards. She could not have been more than thirty years old, barely ten years older than Lacey herself. But she was worn out, and Lacey wondered how much longer she would last.

Despite the knot in her throat, she persisted in her attempt to make conversation. "I hope he'll be able to come back to school tomorrow. We miss him."

"Probably not tomorrow. Maybe the next day."

After the swelling goes down, Lacey thought. Aloud she said, "Please tell him I stopped by."

"No need to leave those muffins," Mrs. Richards said.

"Well, perhaps—"

"You heard what she said!" a voice boomed from behind Lacey.

She wheeled and was face-to-face with Bert Richards. Lacey swallowed hard. "I meant no harm. Just trying to be neighborly."

"You ain't our neighbor. You're the teacher."

"I—I—I heard TJ was sick. I just wondered how one of my students was doing."

"At school, he's your student. Here he's my boy, and he ain't no concern of yours." His voice boomed into her face, and the smell of alcohol sprayed out of his mouth while fire burned in his eyes.

Involuntarily, Lacey took a step backward. "I meant no harm," Lacey repeated. She glanced at the window and saw Sally, her face scrunched up in horror at what might happen next; Lacey's resolve to confront Bert Richards disintegrated. Obviously, he was raging drunk. There was no telling what might happen to Sally and Alvira if she persisted.

Quickly she turned and went down the steps, intentionally leaving the muffins. She walked as calmly as she could, determined not to run and let Bert think she was afraid of him. From a safe distance, she stepped off the road and slid behind a tree to look back at the house. The porch was deserted, except for the box of muffins topped by the bright red napkin. Her heart pounded.

What am I getting into? she thought. *Lord, You know I mean to help those children. Show me how.*

Chapter 13

Lacey sniffed her dripping nose, wiped a tear with the back of her hand, and reached for a fresh sheet of paper. A half-dozen crumpled sheets were scattered across the small table next to the stove in the cottage. She had been trying for an hour to find the right words for the letter. Dipping her pen into the inkwell once again, she made another attempt.

> *Dear Members of the Board,*
> *It is with great regret that I tender my resignation as teacher of the lower elementary grades at the Tyler Creek School, effective immediately. I am not unmindful of the inconvenience this will cause. Nevertheless, I believe my action to be in the best interest of the children.*

That she must resign, Lacey was sure. After her encounter with Bert Richards, she had stumbled back to the cottage, shaken and befuddled about what to do next. Somewhere, about halfway home, her confusion got the best of her. If she could not reach out to a child like TJ, and actually help him, then she had no business calling herself a teacher and all the children would be better off with someone more competent, both in the classroom and with the families of the students.

Sighing, Lacey laid down her pen. If she left Tyler Creek, she would have to go home to the peninsula. Where else could she go? After her grandmother in Milwaukee had died, the rest of her mother's family had moved west. Papa's siblings were scattered around the country, too, and none of them would welcome a wayward niece who had failed at the first job she ever had. What other skills did she have except teaching? No, she had nowhere to go except home. From Paxton she could take the train as far as she could and then follow the land route in the back of a jarring wagon. She would go home a failure, and her mother would be proven right that Lacey was not ready to leave the peninsula.

Lacey snatched up her paper and crumpled it into the seventh wad. How could she even think of going home? No explanation in the world would be good enough to offer to Travis. He had gone to a great deal of trouble to get her this job. She did not want to face the disappointment she would see in his eyes if she left Tyler Creek now.

On the other hand, how long would she be home before Travis noticed? She had barely heard from him in seven months, and even then he kept his feelings carefully hidden. His few letters summarized life in the lumber camp with interesting language but far more detail than Lacey wished for and closed with a bit of news about her family. He said little about himself or his own plans. He had already stayed at the camp a full year, far longer than he originally intended.

What did I expect? Lacey asked herself. *Did I think that if I did what he wanted me to do and took this job, he would give me undying admiration? Why did he think I could do this? He's thrown me to the wolves.*

Lacey wiped her nose and chided herself for thinking such harsh thoughts about Travis. He had not forced her to come to Tyler Creek. When she signed the contract with the school board, she was truly excited about the challenge that lay before her. But she had not counted on Bert Richards. She was almost at the end of her contract with only two months remaining. Lacey put the lid on her box of paper. She had made a promise, and she would fulfill it.

The door creaked open, and Maria entered. "What is all this?" she asked, pointing at the seven wads of paper.

"I tried to write my letter of resignation," Lacey confessed.

"Why would you do that?" Maria hung her coat on the peg beside the door.

"Because I'm no good here, that's why."

"From what I have observed, you have the makings of a fine teacher. You just need some experience in the classroom."

Lacey rose to her feet and grabbed at the wads of paper. "Is experience in the classroom going to tell me what to do with Bert Richards?"

"Don't tell me you went out to the Richardses' place."

"All right, I won't tell you."

"But you did."

Lacey nodded.

Maria sighed heavily. "I know you mean well, Lacey. You would move heaven and earth for that boy. But what you did today did not help him."

"I know that," Lacey mumbled as she opened the stove door and dropped her wads into the coals. She watched them catch and burst brilliantly before sizzing into cinders. "But I couldn't just do nothing."

Maria took a pot off a hook and filled it with water. "I'll fix you something to eat. Where are the muffins I sent home with you?"

"I took them to the Richards."

"Then we'll have no bread for supper."

"We could never have eaten all those muffins before they went stale."

"We could have eaten two with our supper while they were fresh." Maria whacked at a carrot and tossed the pieces into the pot.

"Sorry," Lacey mumbled.

"It's no matter. We have a bit of dried beef from the Muellers and plenty of potatoes. I'll have a pot of soup ready before you know it."

"I'm really not hungry."

"Apparently not, or you would not have given away our muffins."

Lacey sank into the easy chair. "Maria, how do you do it?"

"I've been making soup since I was ten." Maria thwacked a potato.

"You know what I mean," Lacey prodded. "You've been teaching here for years. Bert Richards can't be the first difficult parent you've ever known."

"Some children don't get to come to school at all," Maria said, "especially girls. I take the ones I can get and try to open their minds to learning, so that no matter where they end up they will want to learn."

"And the ones you can't get?"

"I can't save the world, Lacey Wells, and neither can you." Maria set the pot on the stove and stirred the contents.

"Is that what you think I'm doing?"

"I imagine that's what Bert Richards thinks you're trying to do. And that's not going to help TJ."

"I've made a mess of everything. Maybe I should work on that resignation letter again."

"And what good will that do?" Maria had a point.

"Maria," Lacey said, "I know you are not very religious, but do you believe in having a calling? Are you here because you have a calling for teaching?"

"I'm here because there's a job to be done," Maria said simply as she took two bowls down from a shelf.

"But how do you know if this is the job you should be doing?"

"I'm here, aren't I?"

"You could be teaching in Milwaukee or Detroit or anywhere else," Lacey challenged. "Why are you in Tyler Creek?"

"I'm far too practical for these philosophical questions," Maria responded. "There is a great deal of work to be done right here in Tyler Creek, and I've invested seven years already. I don't need to look any further."

Maria Johnson and Daniel Wells had a lot in common, Lacey decided. There was a job to be done, and they were in the right place to do it.

Sinking back in the easy chair, Lacey watched Maria work. As the soup simmered, Maria stacked the dishes from earlier in the day and wiped off the butcher block where she had chopped the vegetables. Lacey made a mental note to offer to do the dishes after supper. She tried to do her share of the housework, but in many ways the cottage was Maria's home in a way that it would never be Lacey's. The dishes were stacked the way Maria liked them and the furniture placed the way with which Maria was comfortable. Maria moved around the small kitchen competently and efficiently. She was home here; she belonged.

But do I belong? Lacey asked herself. *Will I ever belong anywhere?*

"Come and eat," Maria said, ladling the soup into the bowls.

"I'm sorry about the muffins," Lacey said, as she pulled herself out of the overstuffed chair and moved to the table.

"Pay no mind. It's just as well we have no muffins. I'm getting far too plump."

"You have a practical perspective on everything."

"That's how the work gets done."

Lacey sat and put a napkin in her lap. She paused to give silent thanks for the meal, knowing that Maria was watching her out of politeness. Lifting a spoon, Lacey said, "You remind me of both of my parents at the same time, if that's possible."

"Anything is possible," Maria responded.

Lacey chuckled. "And that sounds like a friend of mine."

"The friend who suggested you for this position?"

Lacey nodded. "But maybe being practical is not always the right thing to do."

"It has always worked for me."

"Maybe so, but I'm not sure it will work for TJ Richards."

Maria looked at her, puzzled. "We've come a far piece from talking about your resignation, haven't we?"

Lacey tasted the soup. "Yes, I suppose we have."

"Well, you can just put any thought of resigning out of your head once and for all. It's the most impractical thing I've heard in weeks."

"Why?"

"You signed a contract. You can't just walk away from that. Where will the board find a teacher to fill in? And what about the children who have grown fond of you already? Will TJ be better off if you leave now? You only have a few weeks left. There's a job to be done. Stay and do it."

Lacey sighed. "I suppose you're right. Staying is the sensible thing to do."

"Stay, and enjoy it!" Maria admonished.

That Lacey could not promise. If she had to spend the next two months watching TJ suffer, how could she enjoy Tyler Creek?

Chapter 14

As Lacey walked, she fingered the letters in the pocket of her skirt. Micah's letter, flawlessly spelled and punctuated with the lettering in perfect, straight lines, reported that he had at last been allowed to help polish the brass railing around the top of the lighthouse. "Papa is persuaded I shall not be careless and tumble from the balcony," Micah had written. "I got brass polish under all my fingernails." In her mind, Lacey could see the pride beaming from her little brother's face.

The letter from Travis was the fourth he had sent since Lacey had arrived in Tyler Creek. The first three were enthusiastic reports of the booming lumber business on the peninsula. Travis had begun to speak of the lumber camp as if it were a small town. But it was the fourth letter that Lacey now carried in her pocket and her heart. At long last, Travis had written how much he missed her and how much he was looking forward to her homecoming in another six weeks.

Six weeks! Since her disastrous—in her eyes—encounter with Bert Richards, Lacey had thought of little else but how to finish out her contract with dignity. Long after Maria finished marking papers and went to bed, Lacey sat up with her books spread around the small table. All her carefully constructed lessons were stacked neatly in a box. *Even if I never use these again,* she told herself, *I will do the very best job I can as long as I am in Tyler Creek.* Then she could go home holding her head high, having done her job well.

Still, six weeks seemed an interminable time to wait for release and, despite her long hours with the candle, Lacey was not convinced that things were getting better in the classroom. The two older boys still sat in the back and whispered, although not as often. The younger children seemed genuinely fond of their teacher, and she of them, but she was not sure what would happen when examination time came. Lately, TJ had been in school more than usual, and for this Lacey was grateful. Perhaps her appearance at the Richards house had done some good after all. Drunk as he was, Bert Richards might have realized that he would eventually face the consequences of his actions. Lacey liked to think her trip had not been wasted, but still she heeded Maria's advice and stayed away from the Richards home.

At every opportunity, though, she paid special attention to TJ. But he was painfully thin and seemed distracted most of the time. Lacey shared her lunches and encouraged his every effort, but she could not make him stop staring out the window, sullen and silent.

One Sunday afternoon, after having attended church in the meeting hall, Lacey had pushed her papers aside, put on her sturdiest shoes, and had headed for the fields beyond Tyler Creek. The day was brisk and bright, with billowing clouds riding the breeze, and Lacey imagined that Micah would be lying on his back in the meadow behind the house, calling out the animals he saw riding the clouds. She wondered if TJ ever did that.

Despite the logic of her mind, her feet carried her down the dirt road toward the Richardses' farm. She had promised Maria she would not go there again; her presence at the Richardses' place would pose too much of a danger to TJ, and maybe even to Sally. Even so, her feet seemed to follow that path for there was a pleasant clearing that reminded her of the clearing on the peninsula, the place where she had met Travis on Sunday afternoons last spring and summer. With Travis's letter in her pocket, she wanted to be in that clearing.

She reached her destination and stopped for a drink from her water jug. With her back to a tree, she faced northwest, in the direction of home. Lacey took the letter from her skirt pocket and unfolded it once again. She settled into a comfortable position on the ground to read it.

Dear Lacey,

Ed is heading down to Milwaukee for a few weeks with his family. I did not want to miss the opportunity to mail a letter. As wonderful as the peninsula is, I do miss regular mail service!

In a few weeks, you will be home and we will have the whole summer together. I hope you will want to meet me in the clearing on Sunday afternoons. I've missed you quite profoundly in the months you've been gone, and I am eager to be together once again, at least until the fall. I imagine you will seek another

teaching position, so I must take full advantage of every moment
we have together during the summer.

Fondly,
Travis

The breeze stirred and the clouds morphed into new configurations. "Lord, You make such beautiful things," Lacey prayed aloud. "Why is Travis's heart not as clear to me as this day? And what do You really want me to do for TJ? I'm listening. Help me to hear Your voice above the others."

A sneeze made Lacey start, and she scrambled to her knees and looked around. Another sneeze came and she asked, "Who's there?"

"It's me," a voice answered.

But, as timid as the voice was, Lacey recognized it. "TJ, where are you?"

The bushes behind her parted, and TJ crawled out. Instinctively, Lacey scanned his face and arms for new marks. His forearms were bright red. "Are you all right?" she asked.

He nodded. "Who were you talking to?"

Lacey responded with a puzzled look. "No one. I'm alone, just out for a walk on a fine day."

"But I heard you say something."

"Oh, I was praying. I didn't realize I had spoken aloud."

"Praying?"

"Talking to God about some of the things I'm concerned about."

"Who's Travis?"

"A friend," Lacey said firmly. She could not ignore the fresh marks any longer. "Are you sure you're all right?"

He nodded again and stuffed his hands into the pockets of his overalls. "It's not as bad as usual. My mama told me to get out and stay away for a few hours. By the time I get back, he'll be sleeping it off."

"Oh, TJ, I'm so sorry."

"It's okay. I should be able to come to school tomorrow."

"Of course I'm glad you're not hurt more seriously, but he shouldn't be doing this to you."

"He don't mean no harm. He just gets mad about stupid things when he drinks."

"But he seems to be drinking all the time now."

TJ sat down next to Lacey. "You were praying about me, weren't you?"

"Yes, I was. I believe God wants me to help you, but I'm just not sure how."

"Ain't nothin' you can do. Excuse me, there *isn't* nothin' you can do."

"You mean 'There isn't anything you can do,'" Lacey said, finishing the correction that TJ had begun. "But I can't accept that."

TJ shrugged. "Other folks do. They say you have trouble mindin' your own business."

"Yes, I know they say that."

"Seems true, don't it?"

"*Doesn't* it. No, I don't think so. I just have a different idea of what's my business than other people do."

"Am I your business?" TJ asked, looking up at Lacey.

"I think you are," Lacey said softly.

"Did God send you to me?"

"I think maybe He did."

"Am I God's business, too?"

Lacey's heart filled her chest. "Of course, you are."

"Then why did He wait so long to send you?"

The question cut through Lacey. How could she possibly think about abandoning TJ?

"TJ," she said, "how would you like it if you didn't go home?"

"You mean today?"

"Yes, for today, maybe a few days."

"Maybe not ever?" he asked.

Lacey nodded. "Maybe until your father gets better."

"Where would I go?"

"Well, to begin with, you could come home with me."

"Miss Johnson won't like that."

"No, I don't suppose she will. But you let me worry about Miss Johnson. You concentrate on keeping yourself safe."

"Would I have a bed?"

"Of course."

"And lunch? Would I get to eat lunch?"

"I promise you will eat lunch every day."

TJ turned his head in the direction of his home. "You make it sound right nice."

"It would be nice. And your father wouldn't hurt you."

"Yes, he would. Somebody would make me go back to my own folks, and he would be steaming mad that I left."

Lacey picked up one of TJ's bony hands. "TJ, I can't make any promises about what will happen next. But if you want to come home with me, I will do my best to protect you and make sure no one hurts you."

TJ slowly shook his head from side to side as a tear rolled down one cheek. "I can't go with you."

"Yes, you can," Lacey urged.

"No, I can't. If I leave, he'll start in on Sally. As long as I'm there, he leaves her alone."

Lacey squeezed his hand.

"No, I can't go. Sally is too little. She can't run as fast as I can. I have to protect her."

"What if we found a safe place for Sally, too?"

Still, TJ shook his head. "That would break Mama's heart. Sally is her special baby. She would die if Sally went away, she would just die."

Lacey held back her own tears. She tried to imagine Micah, at the tender age of eight, taking on the responsibility for the safety and welfare of two other people. Rage swelled within her at the thought of Alvira Richards allowing her small son to be in such a position. But Alvira would never leave her husband, of that Lacey was sure.

"I'd better be goin'." TJ stood up abruptly and wiped the tear from his cheek.

"But you can't go home!" Lacey insisted.

"Not yet. I'll wait awhile."

"I'll stay with you."

TJ shook his head emphatically. "No, you'd best be on your way, too."

Lacey stood also. "If you change your mind, TJ—"

"I won't. But if you really think I'm God's business, you might ask if He has another idea."

Lacey could not help but smile. "I will, TJ. I will."

TJ turned, plunged his hands into his pockets once again, and shuffled away from her. He did not look back.

He was small and thin. Lacey had learned a lot from having four younger brothers. She wanted to run after him. She knew she could swoop him up and carry him off, and he would not be strong enough to stop her. Instead, she leaned against the tree and prayed, *Lord, be with him. Let him know that he is Your business.*

Chapter 15

Lacey cast a sharp look at Denys and Dalton, the older boys in the back of the classroom. Those two were more exasperating than Joel and Jeremiah on their worst days. Three times during the semester Lacey had separated them and then relented and let them sit together. It did not seem fair to seat them with younger children, whom they would only torment endlessly. If they were together, at least they kept their scuffling among themselves. But why was it so difficult for them to understand that silent reading time meant no talking?

Pretending that they had not seen Lacey's look, the boys shuffled apart and turned to their books. Lacey's eyes wandered around the classroom. Even with her own books, brought from the peninsula, there were not enough to go around at reading time. Some of the younger children shared simple storybooks. Patsy, Maggie, and Rebekah, always eager to please the teacher, had read everything in their grade level at least four times. Soon, Lacey would let them attempt some of the longer books.

TJ clutched his book with both hands and buried his face in it. If he heard the whispering behind him or the chairs scraping in front of him, he did not let on. Only the words on the page mattered; his lips moved as he struggled to make out the sounds.

Lacey watched him. He had missed far too much school this semester, and probably every semester since he first started school. He was a bright boy, but too many missed lessons and too little food and sleep made it difficult for him to keep up. Lacey hated to think that in a couple of years TJ would be one of the bigger boys at the back of the classroom, that is if he stayed in school at all.

Lacey turned back to her own book. When the children read, she read also. It was the pattern she had learned from her own mother more than fifteen years ago. Reading was important, and if it was important for children to do, it was important enough that children should see adults doing it. So she read.

She straightened her chair and turned a page at the same time, and the two sounds covered the noise of the classroom door opening. Lacey's brown-haired head remained bent over her novel. It was only a few minutes before the whispers swelled into murmurs, and she had to lift her head to see the reason. She stifled a gasp and rose to her feet. What was Travis Gates doing, standing in the back of her classroom?

Grabbing for composure, she smiled at the children and walked down the aisle between the desks to meet him in the back. As she passed each row, curious heads turned to follow her path.

"What a surprise!" she whispered. She wanted to embrace him, but she dared not in front of the children. "What are you doing here?"

"Visiting you, of course."

"But it's so far from the peninsula. Are you on your way home to the city? Have you left the lumber camp?"

He smiled and shook his head. "No, I love it there. But I got wind that a friend of mine was coming this way, and I couldn't pass up the chance to see you."

"And Tom Saget let you go?"

"I didn't give him a choice."

Lacey's heart warmed in a way it had not for weeks. "How long can you stay?"

"Just for the evening. I leave on the early morning train out of Paxton."

"Oh."

"Sorry it couldn't be longer."

"You've come a long way for an evening."

"I'm sure I won't regret it."

Travis's eyes held Lacey motionless. What did it mean that he had gone to such lengths to see her?

"Miss Wells," Patsy said as she tugged on her teacher's sleeve, "who is that man?"

Lacey jumped back to reality. The entire class had twisted in their chairs to watch her conversation. The older boys snickered; the little girls glowed with curiosity. She pushed out a quick breath and said, "We'd better get this over with."

"Class," Lacey said in a loud, steady voice, "this is Mr. Gates, a friend of mine. I hope you will give him a warm welcome to Tyler Creek." Then, leaving Travis behind, Lacey marched with a straight back to the front of the room. "We are just about out of time today. In the morning, we will begin with arithmetic."

The groans were louder than the cheers as the children pushed back their wooden benches, gathered their lunch buckets, and prepared to leave.

"I like arithmetic," said Patsy.

Lacey smiled and stroked the child's head. "I know you do. And you're wonderful at doing sums."

"Are we going to have spelling tomorrow?" asked Maggie.

"In the afternoon," Lacey assured her.

Travis leaned against the back wall and watched with contentment as Lacey moved around the classroom helping her students collect their things. It seemed to him that she was quite comfortable and confident in the role. Her letters had described the room well, including the two boys in the back who were likely to drop out soon. But she had underestimated her ability to handle herself in the classroom. She had described nervousness and anxiety, but he saw only warmth and competence. She showed the same tenderness toward her students that he had seen her give to Micah.

What her letters had not said, however, was how she felt about being off the peninsula, and whether she would ever want to return to live there. He hoped so, because he wanted her to return. But it would have to be her choice.

TJ was taking longer than the others to gather his things, so Lacey crossed to his desk and asked, "Are you all right?"

TJ smiled slyly. "This is the friend you were praying about, isn't it?"

Lacey felt the blush rise in her cheeks. "Yes, this is my friend."

"Did God answer your questions yet?"

"Not entirely. I'm still listening."

"When He tells you about His business, let me know, okay?"

"Of course. Now why don't you catch up with Sally and walk home together?" TJ scuffled out of the building, and Lacey was left alone with Travis.

"What was that all about?" Travis asked, smiling, and Lacey wondered just how much Travis had heard.

"Just following up a conversation we had on the side of the road one day," she said. Then, restraining herself no further, she opened her arms to Travis, who took her in tightly. She buried her face in his chest and breathed in his scent. "It's so good to see you," she said.

"I was hoping you would say something like that," came his gentle reply.

"I've been so homesick," Lacey admitted.

"You? Homesick?" Travis stroked the back of Lacey's head. "I didn't think you would admit to missing the peninsula."

Lacey laughed. "Don't tattle on me to my mother." She picked up her shawl and led the way out of the classroom and down the path that led out of Tyler Creek.

"Micah misses you terribly," Travis said. "He wants to write you a letter every day, but of course your mother is too sensible for that."

"Of course."

"She makes him stick to his lessons and reminds him that he can mail a letter only when Gordon Wright comes anyway."

"And the twins? They haven't written a single word."

"Rambunctious as ever, but your mother does her best to keep them reined in. I was there for their twelfth birthday party."

"I've never missed a birthday before. Now I've missed all my brothers' birthdays."

"Micah is quite proud of being eight, instead of a mere seven."

"I'm sure he is."

"Joshua tries to go home every Sunday now."

"I'm sure that makes Mama happy. How is my father?"

Travis shrugged. "You know your father. He doesn't say much, but I know he wonders how you're doing."

"He hasn't written. But putting words on paper would be hard for him."

Travis looked back over his shoulder. The row of buildings had disappeared behind them. "Are we out of town already?"

Lacey laughed. "It's not much of an effort to get out of Tyler Creek. There's almost as much wide open space around here as there is on the peninsula."

"Are you disappointed that it's not a bigger place?" he asked.

Lacey grinned. "I still think I could do well living in a real city, but Tyler Creek has its own charms, as well as its own troubles." She gestured widely ahead of them. "Off in this direction are several farms. Some of the children come in to go to school, but many of them don't stay past the fourth grade."

"How is school going?"

Lacey rolled her eyes. "I'm doing the very best job I can. I'm just not sure it's enough."

"What do you mean?" Travis responded. "I saw you with the little girl who tugged on your arm and with the boy who left last. They both seemed quite fond of you."

"Yes, I suppose they are."

"Then what's the problem?"

"The people here live difficult lives. Some of them are trapped in vicious circles that go on for generations." Somehow she could not bring herself to speak of TJ in detail.

"Then what you are doing is important. Education can be the way out for some of these children—better jobs, stronger families."

"I want to believe that," Lacey said softly, "but I don't know if book learning can touch the problems they have. I have to keep reminding myself that God can."

"I had no idea Tyler Creek was such a dismal place. I should have never suggested you come here."

Lacey put her hand on Travis's arm. "Oh, no! You did the right thing. And it's not dismal all the time. Some of the families here are doing quite well. We had a wonderful community festival a few weeks ago. The children sang, and they did beautifully."

"So you're not sorry you came?" he asked.

Lacey shook her head. "Every day I want to go home. And every day I'm glad I came."

Travis tilted his head back and laughed. "I suppose in an odd way, that makes sense."

"Tell me about Abby," Lacey pleaded.

"Hasn't she written?"

"Not one word."

"I suppose she hasn't felt well enough to write."

"Abby's ill?" Lacey asked, alarmed.

Travis smiled. "Not ill, exactly. Expecting."

"Expecting?"

"Yes. A little one. A baby."

Lacey's eyes grew wide. "Abby and Peter are having a baby?"

"Yes, it's to be born in the late summer."

"I suppose it was only logical that they would want to have a family. I just didn't think it would happen so fast."

"Their house will be finished soon," Travis said excitedly. "It's not large, but it is quite grand. Peter has been meticulous about every detail. I've learned a lot of carpentry skills working with him."

"So they are really going to settle in and raise a family in the lumber camp."

"It won't be just a camp for long," Travis said. "You'll see. It's becoming more like a town every day."

Lacey shook her head in shock. Inwardly she wondered, *Could I be happy doing what Abby's doing? As inadequate as I feel in Tyler Creek, would I be happier married and living in a lumber camp?*

"We'd better turn back," Lacey said aloud. "Maria will want to meet you."

Chapter 16

I have to warn you," Lacey said to Travis as they approached the cottage, "Maria is rather direct."

"That can be an admirable quality," Travis responded. "Does she know who I am?"

"She only knows that a friend helped me find this job." Lacey pushed open the door, and they stepped into the cozy kitchen. Maria was bent over a steaming pot. She looked up.

"So this is your friend, Mr. Gates?" Maria asked.

Lacey and Travis exchanged a look. Smiling, Travis extended his hand to Maria. "Travis Gates, at your service. It is a pleasure to meet you."

"Travis, this is Maria Johnson," Lacey said to complete the introduction. She glanced at the table, set for three. "How did you know—"

"That your friend would stay for supper? Where else would he eat? Tyler Creek doesn't have a restaurant, unless you count Selma Parker's annual summer picnic buffet."

"But how did you know he was here?"

Maria chuckled. "Everyone in Tyler Creek knows. Mr. Gates here hitched a ride in with Tom Saunders, who wastes no time remarking on strangers. And of course the children in your classroom were quite fascinated that someone would appear so unexpectedly."

"There was no time to write," Travis explained. "It was a spur of the moment trip."

"Of course," Maria said as she stirred her pot.

"I would have cooked. After all, Travis is my guest," Lacey said.

"No need for fussing. Everything's under control. You two enjoy yourselves."

Lacey felt the blush rise in her cheeks. "Then, what can I do to help you?"

"Not a thing," Maria said. "The two of you should make yourselves comfortable in the sitting room. With a little notice, I might have prepared a meal worthy of our guest, but I'm afraid we'll have to settle for boiled chicken. We don't want to waste any time. Tom Saunders will be looking for Mr. Gates before long."

"Tom is taking you back into Paxton?" Lacey asked.

"He kindly offered," Travis said, "and I was afraid you wouldn't have a carriage."

"We've got a wagon and an old mare," Maria said, "but Lacey would have no business driving into Paxton by herself late at night. Shoo. Go sit down. I'll call you when the food is ready."

Obediently, Lacey and Travis moved to the other room, hardly out of earshot of the kitchen.

"Is she always like this?" Travis asked, his voice hardly above a whisper.

Lacey covered her mouth to conceal her laugh. "Not this bad, usually. But we don't get many guests."

"We'd better keep talking," Travis said softly.

Lacey took his cue. "How was the train ride?" she asked in a louder voice.

"A bit bumpy."

"I suppose the tracks need some repairs."

"Yes, I suppose so."

Maria poked her head around the corner. "You two will have to do better than that. I would think you would have more to discuss than the quality of Wisconsin's railroad ties. Come to the table for some real conversation."

Holding back their laughter, Lacey and Travis obediently moved to the table. Maria gestured that they should sit next to each other, and she settled into a chair across from them. Lacey gave thanks for the food then raised the platter for Travis to serve himself.

"I hope Lacey has been telling you all the delightful things she has been doing," Maria said.

Travis's eyes lit up. "I'd like to hear about that."

"Then she hasn't told you?"

"I was anxious to hear news from home," Lacey said in her own defense.

"Of course, but your family will also want news of you when Travis returns."

"Tell me all the wonderful things she has been doing," Travis urged.

"The first thing that comes to mind is the choir for Winterfest," Maria started. "We've got that wretched piano in the back of the schoolhouse, but until now no one bothered to see what it could do. Lacey worked wonders with the children, despite the fact that the piano hasn't been tuned in twenty years."

"Why didn't you write me about that?" Travis chided.

"It was just a couple of songs," Lacey said. "Simple ones I learned from my mother. All my brothers would be able to sing them."

"But the children here don't get music like that," Maria said. "You brought that to them. I'm sure they'll want to do it again next year."

Travis's head snapped toward Lacey. "Next year? Will you still be here?"

She shook her head. "No, my contract runs out in June. I'm sure of that."

"Someone else will have to take it up, then," Maria said. "Everyone enjoyed the performance. Some of the students who have a difficult time in the classroom sang quite nicely. It was good to see them succeed at something."

Lacey scooped some rice onto her plate. "But I'm not sure I'm reaching those children with their lessons."

"Of course, you are. From everything I've seen, Dalton and Denys are at last ready to move up into my classroom. They'll have a much better attitude about school once they are in with the older children. You haven't let them dawdle for a single day."

Travis smiled. "That sounds exactly like the teacher you had, Lacey."

Mary Wells did not believe in dawdling, that much was certain. Lacey had learned well from watching her mother handle Joel and Jeremiah together.

"Ask her about the reading chart," Maria urged.

Travis complied. "What about the reading chart?"

"It's nothing, really," Lacey said, "just a chart that shows all the books the children have read this semester."

"And is it a lot?"

"There aren't many books."

"Nonsense," Maria interjected. "Nobody has been able to get those children to read as much as you have. I can't wait until they're all old enough for my class."

"Lacey didn't say a word about any of this," Travis said. He looked at Lacey with a pride she had not seen in his eyes before. Hastily, she looked away and concentrated on her green beans.

"And I suppose she didn't say anything about the class play, either?" Maria said.

"No, not a word."

"The children have written their own play, to be performed on the last day of the school year," Lacey supplied.

"That's quite an undertaking."

"The credit belongs to my mother," Lacey explained. "She used to make Joshua and me write plays when she was schooling us."

"When I go back to the peninsula, I'll be sure to let her know that her legacy has extended to Tyler Creek."

"All the parents are quite pleased with Lacey," Maria said. "Many of them have told me so. Of course, there are always one or two who simply cannot be pleased, and their children do not get everything from school that they might. But Lacey is a fiesty one," Maria continued. "I suppose growing up on that remote peninsula has made her quite independent."

"Yes, I suppose so," Travis said thoughtfully.

"Perhaps she's too fiesty and independent," Maria continued. "When she gets an idea in her head, she means to do it, even if it means tangling with a man like Bert Richards."

"Who is Bert Richards? And why shouldn't Lacey tangle with him?" Travis's questions bore an edge of concern.

Lacey quickly explained. "I promised I wouldn't go back, not beause I was worried about myself, but because I was concerned for the rest of the family."

"I'm just glad you came to your senses," Maria said sternly.

"TJ hasn't been 'sick' since I went," Lacey observed.

"I do hope you'll be careful," Travis said.

Lacey grabbed a plate of biscuits and thrust them at Travis. "This is a delicious supper, Maria," she said. "You must let me cook for the next few nights."

"Selma Parker is sending Sam over with a ham tomorrow," Maria said. "That should keep us going for a while."

Travis ate a biscuit eagerly. "For some reason we don't get food like this in the mess hall at the lumber camp. I wish I could send the cook over for a few lessons."

"I'll send some biscuits back with you," Maria offered.

"Thank you. I would like that. Has Lacey mentioned her friend Abby to you? She married one of the lumberjacks. She takes pity on me and invites me for supper nearly every Thursday night."

"Abby was never any good at cooking!" Lacey said.

"She is now. You'd be surprised what you can learn to do when you have to."

"Oh, I don't know," Lacey said lightly. "I've learned to keep that decrepit stove in the classroom going. If I had a pitchfork, I'm sure I could tune the piano."

"I don't doubt that you could do anything you set your mind to do," Travis said.

"She's proven that already," Maria added.

Travis pushed his chair back. "I hope you'll let me help you clean up."

"Certainly not." Maria snatched his plate from him and stacked it on top of her own. "Tom will be here soon. Lacey can walk you out to the road."

Lacey shrugged. They both knew there was no point in arguing with Maria. Lacy wrapped her wool shawl around her shoulders and led the way.

"Maria recited quite a litany of your accomplishments," Travis said.

"When I came, I was full of ideas, most of them from my mother, actually. I have a whole new perspective on what she did for us."

"She would be proud to know what you are doing for these children."

"I'm doing what I can. But I'll be gone in a few weeks. Victoria will be back in the fall. All I've really done is keep things going in her absence."

"I think you've done far more than that."

"Will it matter in the end?" Lacey asked. "After I leave Tyler Creek, I'll never see these children again. How will I know if anything I did helped TJ Richards have a better life?"

"Do you remember how we used to climb the stairs to the tower?" Travis asked.

Lacey nodded, confused.

"I didn't know the way in the darkness. But you did. I had to trust you for every step we took. You know what I'm saying, don't you?"

Lacey nodded again. "Yes, I think so."

"We have to go a step at a time. Someone else is carrying the light and knows where He's leading you."

They reached the edge of the road and turned toward each other. "I'm proud of you, Lacey. You should be proud of yourself," Travis said.

She turned her face up and searched his eyes. Was pride all that he felt? "I'm glad you came," she said, "even for a few hours."

"So am I."

A few yards away, a carriage rattled toward them.

"There's Tom," Lacey said.

Quickly, smoothly, Travis bent his head and kissed her mouth. Lacey smiled in the darkness.

The carriage rumbled to a stop. "Evenin', ma'am," Tom Saunders said.

"Good evening, Tom. How are you?"

"I'm right fine. I'll make sure your friend here gets to town safely." And Travis was gone into the darkness.

Leaning against the fence, Lacey turned and faced the cottage. The old kerosene lamp glowed in the kitchen where Maria worked.

I should go in and help her, Lacey told herself.

But Lacey wanted to savor the evening for just a moment more. Travis had come to her.

Chapter 17

The weeks since Travis's visit whirled around Lacey so fast she could barely keep up. Maria had hinted that Lacey should plant the year's vegetable garden, since she had been consuming last year's harvest of green beans, turnips, and carrots for the last few months. It seemed only fair, so Lacey did not protest. She had helped her mother plant a vegetable garden since the time she was two, and even the thought of putting in a garden made Lacey hear the hymns her mother used to hum while she worked.

Every afternoon, in the oldest muslin dress she had brought with her, Lacey crouched in the dirt and plunged her fingers into the silky black soil. The birds were far too interested in what she was doing, and before long she had taken on the task of rigging a crude scarecrow.

"That's not a very menacing face," Maria commented one day.

"But he's good and big," Lacey responded. "That's what frightens the birds."

"Victoria has never been much help with the garden; she is too much of a city girl. But you seem to know what you're doing."

Lacey smiled as she surveyed her tidy rows, marked off with string and miniature signs to tell Maria what she had planted and where. Lacey had planted more variety than practical Maria would have bothered with: tomatoes, green beans, radishes, corn, sugar snap peas, and lettuce. Mary Wells would have been proud of the sight.

"You and Victoria will be well fed next year," she said to Maria.

Maria scowled. "I don't think Victoria will come back."

Lacey snapped her head around. "Not be back? Why not?"

"It's just a feeling I have."

As the garden sprouted, rehearsals for the end-of-the-year class play intensified, and every afternoon was taken up with working on the play. What had begun as a short skit billowed into a full-scale theatrical production. The older children in the class had written a script that Lacey thought was quite clever, although she had had to expand it to create enough parts for everyone in the class. For weeks, the students had been pilfering hats and odd clothing from their parents' closets and arriving at school with pieces of small furniture in tow. The youngest girls had cut and pasted elaborate invitations for all the children to take home.

Only two days remained now, and Lacey was unsure of what to expect. She hoped that enough of the parents would come to the performance so that the class would not be entirely disappointed.

But, even without the pending performance, the children would have been agitated, Lacey was certain. An ambivalent spring had burst into robust summer, and Lacey found herself frequently reorganizing and enlivening her lessons to keep the children focused on their assignments. If she left them to do silent reading or sums for very long, their heads would turn and stare out the open window. At the lunch break they tumbled out of the building to frolic in the grass, and they resisted as long as they dared the bell that beckoned them back.

In two days, the performance would be over, and so would the school year. In three days, Lacey would be on a train heading north to the peninsula. There she would spend the summer and sort out her feelings about teaching. Maria insisted that Lacey was doing a spectacular job and had no hesitations to say so to anyone who would listen. But Lacey had such a difficult time separating classroom instruction from the rest of her students' lives. What would it matter if she taught a six-year-old to do sums if no one else cared that the child could do them?

TJ's attendance during the spring had been better than the winter months. Sometimes his father kept him home to do chores, but Sally no longer reported that he was "sick." A knot tightened in Lacey's stomach every time she thought about TJ and Sally. Had she really done them any good by coming to Tyler Creek? Should she just be satisfied that they could do their figures and read a few books?

The children, including TJ, had just cleared out of the classroom. They would have a few minutes to enjoy the afternoon before a dress rehearsal for the play. Lacey was using the time to gather some of her personal items from the classroom and put them in a crate to take to the cottage. Some of the books she would leave; she had already decided that. Even on the peninsula, she could get new books more easily than most of these children could.

She gathered her lesson plans and a few pictures she had tacked to the walls. When the door creaked open, she was surprised that the children would be coming back in so soon. She struggled to take down a picture without tearing the corner.

"You may play a few more minutes if you like," she said, without turning around.

"I'm quite sure I've played enough," said a deep male voice.

Lacey spun around, flushed; the picture floated to the floor.

"Mr. Duncan," she said to the chairman of the school board. "What a pleasant surprise."

"I trust you've had a productive day," he said. "The children certainly look vivacious."

"They are quite excited about our end-of-the-year play. I'm sure they would be very pleased if you could attend."

"That's the day after tomorrow, isn't it?"

"Yes, that's correct."

"I'm afraid I'm due for a meeting in Paxton that afternoon. But I wish you well in your endeavor."

"Thank you. That's very kind to say."

Lacey had spoken to the chairman of the school board sporadically since she had arrived in Tyler Creek, and usually it was in his office in Paxton. Why had he come to Tyler Creek today?

Mr. Duncan cleared his throat. "We've received quite complimentary reports on your performance from your co-teacher," he said.

"Maria is very kind."

"We have always found Miss Johnson's assessments to be reliable." He shuffled his feet and reached into his coat pocket for an envelope. "It is largely on her recommendation that I am pleased to offer you this contract."

Her hands shaking, Lacey reached for the document. "A contract?"

"For next year, with an option for the two years following that. We have received word that Victoria Stempel will be unable to return. Her health demands that she remain in the city near her doctor. The board discussed the situation at length. We see no need to begin a full-scale search for a new teacher when you have done such an admirable job. It's clear the children are smitten with you. A new teacher would have to begin again, whereas you would be able to build on the progress you've already made."

"I am very flattered, but I had not expected this," Lacey said. "My things are packed to go home."

"And go home you may. There is no need for you to stay here in the summer, if you do not wish to. We would welcome you back at the start of the new school year. I think you'll be pleased with the increase in salary."

Lacey could not focus on the words on the page in front of her. "I'm sure it's very generous."

"May I report to the school board that you are ready to take up the position on a permanent basis?"

Lacey swallowed. "Please do not think me ungrateful, Mr. Duncan," she said. "Your expression of confidence in my ability means a great deal to me. But I would like some time to think about the offer."

Mr. Duncan nodded. "Of course. You will want some time to read over the details of the contract and make your needs known to the board."

"I'm sure the contract is fine."

"Perhaps we are mistaken in assuming you have not received another offer."

Lacey shook her head. "No, I don't have another offer. But when I accepted this position, it was temporary. I need some time to consider if it is the right position for me in the long term."

"Naturally. We will await word from you, then," Mr. Duncan said. "However, you will understand that we will need adequate time to recruit another teacher if you decide not to return."

"I will do my best to make a speedy decision," Lacey assured him. "I will send word before the end of June."

Mr. Duncan excused himself then, and Lacey looked at the document in her hand. It was a contract that would allow her to teach the lower grades at the Tyler Creek school for another three years. Travis had challenged her to leave the peninsula for a few months and consider her calling. Had he expected this might happen?

As Mr. Duncan left, TJ slipped in through the open door. Lacey did not notice him at first. "Miss Wells?" he asked.

Lacey stared at the paper in her hand.

"Miss Wells?" he repeated as he walked quietly toward her.

Slowly, she looked up. "Yes, TJ? What do you need?"

"I know you're going away," he said, his voice quavering. "I wanted to tell you something first."

"Of course. What is it?"

"Before you came here, nobody every told me that I was God's business. I know God must be really busy, but it's still nice to think that I'm His business. I think He sent you here to tell me that."

"Oh, TJ, that's good of you to say." She reached out to stroke his face. He blushed. "It's true."

Lacey nodded as tears pooled in her eyes. "Thank you, TJ."

"Miss Wells?"

"Yes?"

"I was wondering about the questions you had for God. Did He answer them?"

She swallowed hard and fingered the edge of the contract in her hand. "Some of them. And I'm sure He'll answer the others when it's time."

"Do you think it will be all right if I asked Him some questions?" TJ asked.

"Absolutely! Ask Him anything you want."

TJ shook his head. "No, I'm going to think of the most important questions, so I don't take up too much of His time."

"God has all the time in the world for you, TJ."

"I guess that's what it means to be somebody's business."

Once again the door opened. Patsy planted her feet and said firmly, "It's time to practice, Miss Wells. Are you ready?"

Lacey reached for a book and tucked the contract inside the front cover. "I'm ready!" she said enthusiastically. "Please tell the others it's time to begin."

Chapter 18

Coming through the clearing, Lacey drew in a deep breath of the sweet summer air, then she paused and leaned against her favorite tree. She was glad for a moment in her own clearing. Her weeks home on the peninsula had passed pleasantly. She had immediately resumed the late-night chats with her father on the tower's balcony, and confusion had tumbled out of her as she told her stories of Tyler Creek. Her questions remained, but she felt calmer for having talked about them.

Joel and Jeremiah treated her with new respect now that she was a "real" teacher. Micah, small for an eight-year-old, crawled into her lap at every opportunity and pleaded with her to teach him. Even her mother had changed, and she no longer told Lacey what she ought to be doing all day long. But having lived on her own, Lacey no longer needed promptings to do what needed to be done.

Lacey had spent the morning with Abby, nearly eight months pregnant. Peter and Abby's house was sparsely furnished, but Abby appeared thoroughly satisfied with the progress they were making toward establishing a real home outside the lumber camp. Lacey had to admit the house was beautiful. Wood was easy to come by, obviously, and Peter had chosen well. As she walked through the house and let her fingers trail along the railings and bannisters, Lacey was momentarily envious of Abby for having a home of her own. Nevertheless, she had a difficult time picturing Travis doing the detailed carpentry work she saw all over the house.

Abby carried the baby well. Only twenty years old, she hardly slowed down with the growing weight. Her robust cheeks glowed in the golden summer sun, and her eyes shone with a happiness that Lacey envied. Peter insisted, sensibly, that Lacey should come to Abby rather than Abby walking to see Lacey. And Peter would not allow Abby anywhere near a horse.

During their visit, Abby had jabbered on about the new family. The owner of one of the mills who bought wood from the camp had decided to station a representative to make sure they got the best quality wood possible. The man, George Stanton, had a wife and small son. Peter and Travis, along with several others in the camp, were hastily putting up a house for the new family. Abby was thrilled to be getting neighbors so soon.

Lacey had been home for two weeks. The contract offered by Mr. Duncan lay on the top of her dresser, where she looked at it every day. She had promised him an answer by the end of June.

When she had arrived back on the peninsula, Lacey had showed the contract to Travis immediately. If he was going to give her a reason not to accept the offer, she wanted to know soon. Travis was pleased that she had received the contract and in front of her family retold the accounts he had heard of her work from Maria. Lacey listened carefully for any hint that he wanted her to stay on the peninsula. But none came. She had seen Travis several times, including that very morning, and she had raised the subject of the contract. He said nothing. She pointed out it could be a three-year commitment, and still, he had said nothing. Instead, Lacey's compulsion to return to Tyler Creek grew steadily each day.

Yesterday, Lacey had sat up on the balcony of the lighthouse with her father. "You're not the same as you were," he had said, the breeze lifting his graying hair, which needed to be trimmed.

"How am I different?" she had asked.

"You have your calling now."

"Yes, I suppose I have."

"Your mother and I prayed every day that you would find your calling. . .and your peace."

"Mama prayed for me?"

"Why do you find that so surprising?"

Lacey shrugged. "I guess I shouldn't. I know her faith is real."

"Your mother has a tender heart," Daniel Wells said. "But she has had to adapt to life on the peninsula, and she has done so with a good spirit."

"When I went to Tyler Creek, I started to understand that. I had wanted to leave for so long. But Tyler Creek was not at all what I expected."

"Just as the peninsula was full of surprises for your mother." He turned to look at her. "You're going back, aren't you?" It was more a statement than a question.

"Yes, I believe I am."

"Even though it was not what you hoped for?"

"I don't know much about the voice of God, Papa. I don't hear words in quiet places; I don't have prophetic dreams; verses don't leap off the page when I read the Bible. But I think this is the right thing to do."

"Then you should do it."

They had sat in contented silence after that.

Lacey left her tree and headed out of the clearing. She would go home and sign the contract that afternoon. The acceptance letter could go with Gordon Wright next week, and Lacey would return to Tyler Creek at the end of August.

She could see her mother in the garden now. Mary Wells was hunched over the turnip patch, no doubt weeding and thinning as she went down the row. What had started as a small patch twenty-five years ago had grown to a plot that would provide vegetables for seven people all winter. Tending the garden was time-consuming work and not always comfortable in the summer heat. Lacey determined to help tend her mother's garden through the summer and go back to Tyler Creek and harvest the vegetables she had planted there.

The twins would be off hunting rabbits this afternoon, Lacey knew, and Micah would have insisted on going with them. Joshua was out at the camp. Lacey and her mother could have a peaceful afternoon in the garden, and Lacey would find a way to tell her mother how she felt.

Mary Wells rose to her feet awkwardly and, with the back of one hand, she wiped her forehead wearily. For her, this was an unusual gesture and, even from a distance, she did not look right to her daughter. Lacey quickened her steps.

Suddenly, her mother lurched, lost her balance, and, with no attempt to right herself, slumped to the ground.

Lacey broke into a trot, screaming, "Mama! Mama!"

Sluggishly, Mary Wells rolled over and she struggled to her knees before collapsing again, face forward in the dirt in the middle of her garden, and then she lay very still.

Keeping her eyes on her mother, Lacey stumbled over a root, took two steps to regain her balance, and then raced ahead. Finally, Lacey reached her mother and fell to the ground beside her.

"Mama? Mama, can you hear me?" Lacey pleaded.

Looking around, Lacey could see no reason for the collapse. Her mother had not tripped over anything. Lacey checked her mother for broken bones, and then she grasped her mother's shoulders and carefully rolled her over. In her mother's eyes was gratitude. . .and desperation.

"Mama, can you hear me?" Lacey repeated.

"Hear," Mary Wells said so softly that Lacey almost missed it. "Ca–ca–ta–" She seemed to choke on her own words.

"Mama, do you know where Papa is?" Lacey asked, scanning the yard. Then, at the top of her lungs, she screamed for her father as she pulled her mother to an upright sitting position. She felt the limpness in her mother's limbs as her body fell back against Lacy's chest.

"Ca–mmm–" Mary Wells said.

"It's okay, Mama, I'm here. Don't try to talk." Once again Lacey screamed for her father, who she realized must be up in the lighthouse and could not hear her above the wind. Still, she screamed.

"Mama, we're going to try to go to the house," Lacey said as she staggered to her feet, raising her mother's uncooperative body as she did so. She took a few tentative steps, stopped to regain her own balance, and then she stepped again.

"Lll–no–mmm."

"Just lean on me, Mama," Lacey said, knowing full well that her mother could do nothing else at that moment.

Lacey looked across the yard. They were more than fifty feet from the back door but, undaunted, she resumed the trek toward the house. Periodically, she stopped to readjust her mother's weight against her body and to call for her father. She looked toward the meadow; if only the boys would come home just now. Her mother grew heavier and heavier; her head sagged to one side. Lacey had never known her mother to admit to being sick even for a day. Even on the day Micah was born, Mary Wells was checking on her garden eight hours later.

At last Lacey reached the back porch and she sat on the step, cradling her mother's head and shoulders. "Papa!" she screamed. "Come! Now!"

Daniel Wells now thundered down the stairs and burst out of the bottom of the tower. His face paled at the tangled forms of his wife and daughter on the sagging wooden step.

"I found her in the garden," Lacey explained as he reached them. "I saw her collapse as I came out of the meadow."

"So it just happened?" he asked.

"Yes, just now."

He took his wife's face in his hands. "Mary? Mary?"

For a moment her eyes seemed to focus. "Da–Da–hhh. . ."

"I'm going for the doctor," he said resolutely. "It's a stroke, I'm sure of it."

"You'll be gone for hours!" Lacey said.

"I'll help you get her inside first," he said. "The boys should be back soon. You can send Jeremiah for Joshua before it gets dark."

With her father's help, her mother was soon laid out on her own bed, just off the kitchen. After a few more futile attempts to talk, she fell asleep. She had not moved a muscle by her own volition since she had collapsed in the garden.

"I've got to go," her father insisted. "I'll be back as soon as I can."

And he did go, leaving Lacey standing in the doorway and staring at the stranger on her mother's bed.

Chapter 19

Lacey shoved the window up as high as it would go, but her effort made no difference. The air in the bedroom weighed thick and still, laden with humidity and lacking any breeze. On the bed, Mary Wells groaned under the thin sheet Lacey had tucked around her. The toes on her right foot twitched restlessly.

"Are you thirsty, Mama?" Lacey asked. Without waiting for a response, she poured water from the pitcher into a small cup and sat on the edge of the bed to offer it to her mother. Putting one hand firmly behind her mother's neck, Lacey helped her sit up enough to sip the water.

"Hhh–tt," her mother whispered. Then she swallowed awkwardly.

"Yes, it's hot," Lacey agreed. "It's the middle of July. The worst of the hot weather should be over soon."

Mary Wells's right leg kicked at the sheet.

"You have to stay covered," Lacey insisted as she tucked the sheet back in place. "The mosquitoes are terrible because of the wet spring. You'll get bitten up if we take the sheet off."

"Hhh–tt."

"Yes, it's hot. Let me sponge you off." Lacey dipped a cloth in a bowl of cool water and began wiping her mother's face. "Abby's baby will come soon. Peter wants a boy. Abby says she doesn't care, but I think she really wants a girl."

Mary Wells's eyes followed the motion of Lacey's hand as she moved the cloth to the basin and wrung it out.

Three weeks had passed since Mary Wells's stroke in the garden, and she was not better. Her right arm and leg moved freely, while her left side grew thinner every day with the lack of movement. The determined look in her eyes told Lacey that she understood every word that was spoken around her. More than once, Lacey had chastised the boys for speaking in the room as if their mother could not hear what they said. But the best

413

Mary Wells could say for herself were hoarse sounds, no real words. Lacey could only imagine the frustration welling up inside her mother.

Mary Wells might not ever be any better, the doctor had said when he finally reached the peninsula seven hours after her collapse. Daily exercises on the right side of her body might help her regain control of her muscles, and she could perhaps be helped to sit up in a chair for a few hours a day, but he did not think she would ever speak again.

"Will Mama die?" Micah had asked, his chin quivering.

The doctor had shrugged and looked over Micah's head at Daniel. "With good care, she should be comfortable and might be with you a long time. But we can't be sure of anything."

"So Mama won't ever be all right?" Micah persisted.

The doctor shook his head. "I'll try to come up and check on her from time to time," he said. "Be careful not to let bedsores develop, and do what you can to get her to eat."

"I'm going to pray that she will get better!" Micah declared.

The doctor laid his hand on Micah's head. "Only God can help your mother now."

Micah had slunk away to hide his tears. Lacey had seen his slender shoulders shaking.

Lacey's contract still lay on her dresser top, unsigned. She had prevailed upon the school board to give her a few more weeks to reach a decision because of the change in her personal circumstances. But she had not given up hope of returning to Tyler Creek. The boys could learn to manage Mama, and Daniel would have to take over lessons for Micah and the twins. Lacey had been sorting through her mother's boxes of lessons and books. She did not remember a time her father took part in her formal education, or Joshua's either. But he could guide Micah through a spelling lesson as well as anyone, Lacey was sure of that.

She squeezed out the rag and hung it on the side of the bowl. Her mother's eyes had closed. The air in the room was finally beginning to move. Then Lacey stole out to the kitchen, where Micah sat with a spelling list on the table in front of him. She leaned over his shoulder and looked at his work.

"I'm going to use my best penmanship," he announced, "so Mama will be proud. I'm going to write each word ten times, until I'm absolutely sure I can spell them perfectly."

"Mama will be proud, I'm sure. And when you've finished your spelling, you can do some arithmetic. I'll check it when I come back."

"Where are you going?"

"Travis is waiting for me. I won't be long."

"I'm going to finish before you get back."

"If Mama needs anything, you go tend to her, okay?" Lacey smiled and went out the back door.

Travis lounged on a bench along the side of the house. "This is the hottest day yet," he said, wiping sweat from his forehead. "I'm not sure I want to move."

Lacey reached for his hand. "There's a tree with some good shade on the other side of the chicken coop, but we may have to chase away the cow."

They strolled across the yard and settled onto the grass beneath the tree; shade had kept the ground cool. Before them, the tower looked over the cliff and, even from this distance, they could heard the water slopping over the rocks and lapping at the craggy cliff. On a windless day in the bright sunlight, it hardly seemed necessary to have a lighthouse at this location, but Lacey knew the terror that darkness and bad weather could bring. She pushed that thought out of her head and raised her face to the sun. At least the air up here was clean, not musty or sick smelling.

"You're doing a wonderful job," Travis said.

Lacey looked at him, a question in her eyes.

"I'm talking about the way you're holding the family together. I see what good care you are taking of your mother, and Micah is doing lessons, even in the summer."

Lacey sighed. "The twins haven't opened a book all summer. Mama would not be happy with that. When fall comes, Papa will have to insist that they get back to work."

"Are the boys all right?" Travis asked quietly. "I see Joshua quite often. He's concerned about your mother, of course, but he keeps to himself quite a bit. At least he's working and keeping busy. But the twins and Micah. . .are they all right?"

"It's hard to say. Jeremiah acts like nothing has changed. He spends all day tromping through the woods, doing who knows what. He has always had a mind of his own, and these days he gets to use it as much as he wants."

"And Joel?"

"He tags along with Jeremiah for lack of anything else to do. He doesn't seem to concentrate on anything. I don't think he cares if they ever catch a rabbit or not. And Micah, poor little Micah spends all his time doing things to make Mama proud. I'm sure she is proud, but he needs so badly to hear her say it, and she can't." Her voice was shaking. She stifled the torrent of words.

"Lacey, no one would blame you if you felt overwhelmed," Travis said quietly.

She shook her head. "There's no point in that."

Travis chuckled. "Now you sound like your mother. No time for feeling overwhelmed and discouraged, too much to be done."

"I'm beginning to think she was right all these years."

"What will happen in September?"

"Papa has talked to Joshua about cutting back on the time he spends at the lumber camp. If Joshua can come home a couple of times a week and help with chores, they'll manage. The twins are bright; they just have to be nagged into concentrating. The music lessons will have to stop, of course. Even Papa's patience won't extend that far."

"It sounds like you've thought everything through."

Lacey shrugged. "If Mama stays stable, it's only a question of setting up a routine that all the boys can help with."

"So you will be going back to Tyler Creek without fail?"

Lacey turned and looked at Travis. His dark eyes met her gaze but betrayed nothing of what he was thinking. "I have not signed the contract yet," she said slowly. "If you think I should reconsider—"

Travis shook his head. "This is your decision, Lacey. I'll not stand in your way."

Lacey turned back to the water. "Travis, would it be so difficult to really tell me what you think, what you feel?"

He did not respond.

"I know my family needs me," Lacey continued, "but there is important work for me to do in Tyler Creek, as well. I have a calling to be there."

"I understand."

"Do you?" she said. "Do you really understand?"

"Of course. And I care about your happiness, Lacey Wells."

"Then why have you no opinion about what I ought to do?"

"Because this is your calling, not mine."

"And have you found yours. . .an educated city boy working in a lumber camp like a country bumpkin?"

Travis turned away, obviously stung by her words, and she wished she had not spoken them. "I'm sorry, Travis. That was unkind."

Travis stared across the yard. "Sometimes obedience takes you to strange places." He leaned toward her and nudged her with his shoulder. "You have ears to hear, Lacey. And you will hear God's voice when it is time."

Just then a shriek pierced the air. Travis jumped and looked around, but Lacey merely sighed. "That's Micah," she explained.

"It sounds like he's hurt," Travis said, alarmed.

Lacey shook her head. "Persecuted perhaps, but not seriously hurt. The twins must be back."

As she headed across the yard to sort out the disturbance, she wondered if she would recognize the voice of God so easily.

Chapter 20

A few days later, Lacey sank into wooden chair in the kitchen, a towel in one hand and her apron half off. She could not believe what she had just heard Joshua say.

"You're leaving?" she echoed weakly.

"Leaving is the only way. If I stay I'll never reach my dream." Her brother sipped his thick hot coffee, calmly holding his ground. When had he started drinking coffee? He had become a man while she was away.

"Joshua, I don't know what you're talking about. I always thought you loved the peninsula. For the last two years, you've spent every moment you could working in the lumber camp."

"I do love it here, and I hope that I can come back someday. But it will be a long time."

"I don't understand."

"I want to study, Lacey. I want to go to college."

Lacey's jaw dropped. "If Mama were not so sick already, this would put her into shock. She always had to nag you about keeping up with your lessons. College?"

"Yes. I want to become a doctor."

"A doctor? Joshua, I had no idea."

"No one knows."

"What made you decide to do this?"

"Lumbering is dangerous work. I've seen a lot of accidents. Men have died because there was no doctor on the peninsula. And look what happened to Mama. Maybe if a doctor had been here sooner. . ."

Not a day went by that Lacey did not have the same thought. "Is that what you want to do. . .come back to the peninsula as a doctor?" she asked.

Joshua shrugged. "I think so. The peninsula is getting more and more people every year, and we need a doctor here."

"What about the lighthouse?"

Joshua shook his head. "No, I'm not going to work the lighthouse. I outgrew that notion years ago."

"Have you told Papa that you're not interested in the lighthouse?"

"I think he knows. He makes comments about how much time I spend at the camp. Besides, he's not an old man. He doesn't need someone to take over yet. Also, he has three more sons."

"Ordinarily, I would agree with you, but taking care of Mama is going to wear him out. He's going to need help just to keep the household running smoothly."

Joshua looked down at his mug. "He keeps telling me how grateful he is for my help, now that Mama is sick. I didn't want to tell him I was leaving until I was sure."

"And you are sure now?"

"Absolutely."

Lacey could hear from his voice that Joshua meant what he said. "But Papa has a point, Joshua. The twins are only twelve. They can't do the heavy work that you can do. And what about Micah? Somebody has to pay some attention to him."

"Believe me, I've thought about all that." Joshua pushed his chair back. "But I have to go."

"Do you have to go now? Why not wait a couple of years? Joel and Jeremiah will be older." Frenzy rose within her.

"No, Lacey, I have to go now. The college has accepted me, and they may not take me later. Or things will get worse around here, and I'll never be able to leave. I can't put this off."

Lacey's throat tightened. She knew only too well how Joshua felt. "But Joshua, I'm due to go back to my teaching job in a few weeks. I can't ask the school board to indulge me any further. They must know if I am coming back."

"I know that," Joshua said quietly.

"Mama is so sick. The doctor doesn't think she's going to get better. She could be like this for years."

"I know that, too."

"We can't both go, Joshua." Lacey's fingers gripped the table.

Joshua was silent for a long time. He studied the coffee mug he held in both hands. Finally, he said, "I'm going, Lacey. I have to go, and I have to go now."

"Where does that leave me?" she cried out, nearly in tears.

"You have to make your own decision." His voice was soft but firm.

"What choice are you leaving me?" Her voice rose with fright and frustration.

Joshua raised his head now. "I'm not being selfish, Lacey. I'm doing what I think is best."

Lacey sighed heavily.

Micah burst through the back door. "Joshua," he said breathlessly. "Come, quick! There's a baby deer in the meadow."

Joshua glanced at Lacey and stood up. Tousling Micah's hair, he said, "Show me."

Micah tugged on Joshua's hand, unaware of any tension in the room, and Lacey marveled at his innocence, his pure pleasure in simple things. Alone in the kitchen, Lacey put her fingers to her temples and tried to rub away the headache that had overtaken her in the last few minutes. She sat in a stupor for a long time until she heard the weak moan coming from her mother's bedroom. She paused long enough to splash some water on her face before going to see her mother.

"What is it, Mama?" she asked gently as she stroked her mother's hair away from her face.

"H–t," her mother muttered as she thrashed in the tangled bed-clothes.

Lacey stepped to the bedside and tugged on the sheet. Straightening it out, she tucked the end securely under the mattress and folded the top around her mother's waist. But her mother's good arm continued to beat against the bed.

"You're drenched," Lacey said. "You've perspired clear through your nightgown. I'll get you a fresh one."

Lacey selected the lightest nightgown her mother owned. In the weeks since the stroke, she had learned how to manage her mother's life-less weight without losing her own balance. Patiently and carefully, she changed her mother's gown. At last her mother lay back, content.

"Is that better now, Mama?" Lacey asked.

"Bos," she answered.

"The boys are fine, Mama. They went to the meadow with a kite, and Micah found a new deer." She took her mother's hand. "Maybe soon you'll feel up to sitting in a chair near the window." Despite the optimism in Lacey's voice, she did not believe her mother would sit by the window.

"Bos," her mother said again.

"They'll be back soon, I'm sure. I'll send them in to see you," Lacey said as she sat on the edge of the bed.

"Dn–nl," her mother tried.

"Papa took the boat out to go get your medicine. Remember? He said good-bye before he left."

"Gd–gd," her mother echoed as she stared blankly at the ceiling. Then Lacey began to hum a hymn she knew her mother liked. At last the woman's eyes closed, and her breathing steadied.

Lacey gently pulled her hand out of her mother's and returned to the kitchen. She had not been out of the house all day. Soon it would be time to start the stew for supper, and another day would be gone. Suddenly, the back door crashed open.

"I did not!" Jeremiah slammed through the doorway with Joel on his heels.

"You did, too! Don't lie to me!" Joel screamed, yanking on his twin's shirttail.

"Get your hands off of me. It's just a dumb kite."

"It was my kite." Joel shook his fist in Jeremiah's face. "And you crashed into that tree on purpose."

"I have no control over the wind. What did you expect me to do?"

"You didn't have to let it go so high." Joel shoved his twin.

Lacey jumped in. "Boys, boys, quiet! Mama's resting." And, to her amazement, they reduced their argument to pointed looks. "Are Joshua and Micah coming?" Lacey asked, glancing out the window.

"Who cares?" Joel said, stomping out of the room.

Lacey rolled her eyes. "What is going on with you two lately?" she asked Jeremiah. "It seems like you're always scrapping about something."

"It's Joel's fault. Every little thing makes him mad."

Jeremiah was right. Joel was more sensitive than usual. Ever since their mother had fallen ill, he seemed on the verge of panic. A knock at the door interrupted her reflection. Jeremiah pulled it open.

"Hi, Travis," he said, then looked back over his shoulder at Lacey. "It's for you."

She jumped slightly and involuntarily straightened her skirt. "Travis! What are you doing here?"

He gave her a half smile. "Aren't you glad to see me?"

She blushed. "Of course, I am." She met the gaze of his dark eyes.

"I had an errand on this side of the peninsula and thought maybe we could go for a little walk."

"An errand?" she said suspiciously. Unless Gordon Wright was due to arrive, and he was not, Lacey could not imagine an errand that would bring Travis to her.

"All right, so the errand is seeing you. It's a beautiful day."

"Oh, I can see that. And I would love a walk, but I'm here with Mama. Papa's gone for a few hours. I don't think—"

"Oh, go on!" Jeremiah interjected from behind her. "You just said that Mama is resting. I promise to check on her in a few minutes."

"Are you sure, Jeremiah?"

"Don't you trust me?"

"Of course. It's not that—"

Travis chuckled. "Lacey, let's go before you dig yourself a deeper hole."

Lacey sighed. "Well, all right. I don't think we'll be long, Jeremiah. Mama probably won't need anything but some water. The heat's getting to her."

Travis took her hand and pulled her toward the door. To Lacey he seemed lighthearted, and she was acutely aware of the difference between their moods. Her thoughts were a tangle of her mother's illness, Joshua's sudden news, and Joel's erratic behavior. She wanted to concentrate on being with Travis, but she could hardly put together a coherent thought.

"Lacey?" Travis asked.

"Yes?" She realized that she had not been listening to him. "I'm sorry, Travis. Can you say that again?"

"Never mind. It's not important." His eyebrows pushed together in concern. "Are you all right? Is your mother worse?"

Lacey shook her head. "No worse, no better. Just what the doctor said." She sighed and turned toward him. "It's not Mama, it's Joshua."

"Is he ill?"

"No. He's leaving." She recounted her conversation with her brother.

"So you're afraid you can't go back to teaching," Travis said.

"When I came home, I wasn't sure I wanted to go back. But I thought I was going to be able to make the decision. Then Mama got sick, now Joshua's news has come. The choice is being made for me. That's not supposed to happen."

Travis put an arm around her shoulders. "You're in a tough spot."

"It's impossible to make a choice that is best for everyone," Lacey continued. "I have to let the board know before it's too late for them to find a replacement. Gordon will be here any day. I have to send back a letter with him."

Travis stopped walking and steered Lacey around to face the other direction. "Let's go back, Lacey. I'd like to go up in the lighthouse."

"What for?" A moment ago she thought he was offering sympathy for her plight. Now he wanted to do something that made no sense.

"Just indulge me," he begged.

Travis led the way back and opened the small wooden door at the base of the tower. Lacey reached for the shelf just inside the doorway and found a candle. The winding staircase was engulfed in cool, musty air, the day's heat shut out by the thick stone walls of the tower.

"Ready?" she said softly.

"Lead the way," he said, and then she walked ahead of him up the tightly winding wooden stairs. The passageway was dark and dank and nothing like the outside of the lighthouse. The candle was for Travis's benefit; after having spent her childhood climbing these stairs, Lacey knew every step.

Finally, they emerged into the light. Lacey started to go into the room that housed the great yellow light, but Travis touched her elbow. "This way," he said, nodding his head toward the door that would take them out to the narrow deck.

They stepped outside and stood side by side, resting their hands on the red railing. The air seemed cooler higher up, the breeze more refreshing. Lacey squinted into the sunlight that she had been oblivious to all day.

"Tell me what you see," Travis said.

Lacey balked. "The lake, the cliff."

Travis shook his head. "No, not just what you know is there. Take another look. For instance, look over there."

She turned her head to the left. "The meadow. There are so many trees on the peninsula, and in the middle of it all is that beautiful meadow. There's Joshua and Micah—and the deer! It's still there." Micah stroked the neck of the animal with the tender touch of a child.

"Keep going," Travis prodded gently.

"Micah has such a gentle spirit. Joel and Jeremiah don't understand him at all, but Joshua does. I think leaving Micah may be the hardest part of Joshua's departure."

"Now this way." Travis directed her gaze back to the water.

"I can't remember when I've seen the lake so blue," Lacey said. "When it's peaceful like this, it's hard to imagine how treacherous it can be during a storm or how lonely the winters are up here."

"Who made the lake?"

She turned toward Travis. "What are you talking about?"

"Just answer the question."

"God did."

"And who made the cliff this lighthouse is built on?"

"God did."

"And who keeps the cliff from sliding into the lake?"

"I suppose God does."

Travis swept his arm out over the lake. "You have a difficult decision to make, but you are not making it alone. For me, coming up here puts things in a different perspective."

"What do you mean?"

"The lake is treacherous and the winters are lonely. And everything you've ever said about the isolation of living up here is true. But somehow from this viewpoint, it doesn't seem so bad."

Lacey did not respond. Travis was not saying everything that was on his mind. A year ago, she had desperately wanted him to propose and take her away from the peninsula, but he had wisely made her see that getting married was no solution to her inner turmoil. She had come back more mature but still sure she wanted to marry Travis Gates if he would ever propose. What was he waiting for?

She scanned the panorama that seemed to move him profoundly. His time on the peninsula was supposed to be brief, and already he had extended it twice. What was he hinting at—and did it include her?

Chapter 21

The contract that had lain on Lacey's dresser for so many weeks was mailed back to Mr. Duncan, unsigned. With great regret, Lacey had explained that her personal circumstances would not allow her to resume teaching at Tyler Creek. Her careful lesson plans, written for TJ and Sally, Patsy and Maggie, Rebekah and the others, were stacked in a crate and tucked away behind barrels of fuel for the lamp.

Although not uncaring about the circumstances of his family, Joshua nevertheless was determined to go to college, and he left the peninsula during the first week of September, just as the heat of the summer was waning and the winds of winter were beginning to circle the rocks below the cliff. He promised to spend the long Christmas break at home, but Lacey could not think that far ahead. She did not dream of Tyler Creek nor imagine how the routine would be easier when Joshua came home, for her hands were far too full keeping up with the work on the peninsula. She had no energy left to bemoan the fact that she had not returned to teach in a real classroom.

Lacey had picked the vegetables in her mother's meticulous garden and stood in the hot kitchen canning a supply that would last through the winter. Mary Wells ate less and less all the time and showed no pleasure when Lacey put bits of fresh vegetables in her mouth. But the rest of the family would be well nourished because of Mary Wells's forethought.

Lacey's mind constantly contrived ways to keep her younger brothers constructively occupied. Joel and Jeremiah seemed to squabble less if they were expected to do something. Lessons had begun in earnest again, including piano lessons; the boys groaned but eventually cooperated, and for ninety minutes each day, one boy or another was at the keys. After a few weeks of allowing them to adjust to their mother's illness, Lacey continued to keep as much structure in the boys' lives as Mary Wells would have done herself, and they seemed to thrive.

Unfortunately, Daniel Wells retreated into silence much of the time. Robbed of the companionship of his wife of twenty-five years, he spent long hours at the top of the lighthouse, even in the summer when the water was safest. Despite her plans and schedules, Lacey could not imagine how her father would have managed the boys without her, even if Joshua were coming home every few days. Lacey was exhausted keeping up with it all.

Her mother was no better. To Lacey's keen eye, she seemed bonier and more listless with every passing day. Micah would sometimes sit at his mother's bedside, wordless and pale, and Lacey could find no words to comfort him.

Abby's baby had come in the middle of August after a torturous labor. Travis had come running for Lacey at the first sign of Abby's pain, and Lacey had sat with Abby and Mrs. Saget for nearly twenty-four hours. Finally, the baby came. Red-faced, Nathan Andrew squalled his first breath and was clearly afflicted with colic from the start. Abby insisted she enjoyed every moment of motherhood, but she was exhausted, and it was cumbersome for her to visit Lacey with the baby. The two friends saw little of each other, and when they did, Nathan's bellowing made conversation impossible. Abby walked and jiggled him most of the day and deep into the night.

Two men at the camp were gravely injured in a logging accident, proving Joshua's point that the peninsula needed a doctor of its own, and several others had left in search of jobs in the city. With a shorthanded crew, everyone worked harder, including Travis, and Lacey had not seen him in nearly a month. On his first day off in weeks, Travis had borrowed a horse and come to take the boys hiking and promised to stay for supper.

With the boys out of the house for the afternoon, her father up in the light room, and her mother resting comfortably, Lacey had taken advantage of a moment to put her feet up. But it was only a moment, for she soon realized that she ought to be peeling potatoes for supper. Sighing, she pulled herself out of her mother's sagging but favorite chair and scuffled into the kitchen. She took a black iron pot off the wall and went outside to fill it with water.

It was not yet suppertime on a late summer day, yet the sky swirled with impending darkness. Lacey glanced off in the direction Travis had taken the boys, hoping that they were not too far away. She worked the pump until it began to spurt water, then set the pot under the flow. As she thrust her arm up and down, she surveyed the sky. A thick cloud cover had settled in over the lake. When she breathed, she took in the weight of the wet air. Lacey had no doubt that it would soon be raining and that this would be no ordinary rainstorm. Spending her childhood in a lighthouse had made a weather watcher out of her.

Lacey heaved her pot back into the kitchen, lit the stove, and began peeling potatoes. She examined each one, pulling out stray spuds and the squirrelly growths that protruded from them. Potatoes grew plentifully in the yard and kept well in the celler, so the Wells family ate them frequently. As she began to peel them, Lacey speculated about how she might make them less ordinary for this evening. But if she seasoned them creatively the boys would howl in protest, and if she failed to mash them she would have a difficult time feeding them to her mother.

Lacey took two potatoes and set them aside. Her mother would not eat more than a few bites anyway, and there was no point in preparing a full serving of food for her any longer. She was so thin that Lacey had to steel herself to look at her, and her father's eyes hung in sorrow every time he sat with his wife who no longer seemed to know he was there. Micah had finally given up believing that his mother might someday recover.

Lacey checked on the meat, which had been simmering most of the afternoon. Some garden peas, fresh, not yet canned, and baking powder biscuits would round out the meal. Lacey pulled the lid off the flour barrel in the corner of the kitchen and reached deep inside. Gordon Wright was due to come with supplies the next day. If he did not bring flour, there would be no more biscuits for a time.

As she rolled out the biscuits, Lacey made a mental list of the chores for the next day. Micah was not as consistent as he ought to be in feeding the chickens, and the twins should learn to milk the cow without being reminded. Lacey kept hoping a bolt of responsibility would strike Joel and Jeremiah, and she would be spared having to remind them about every little thing. But, after having tromped through the woods all afternoon with Travis, they would be agitated and talkative and not of much use with the chores. Still, she was grateful that Travis was spending his free day with the boys. Lacey herself was focusing so much on structure that she sometimes forgot that the boys needed some fun.

Clapping her hands, Lacey let the flour dust settle into the sink before moving to the back door. The door had been propped open most of the afternoon to let the summer breeze roll through the house, but the breeze had now become a gale. The rain that had begun gently a few minutes ago was now steady enough to drench anyone caught in it. It was a bone-chilling rain, with enormous drops that slithered across every surface they touched.

The boys would be sopping wet by the time they got home, so Lacey went to the hall closet and removed a stack of towels. On her way back to the kitchen, she thought to check on her mother. Abruptly, she stopped as a burst of light flashed three times through the window. She waited a few seconds, and the signal came again. Her father was up in the light room, and he had given the signal for a ship to veer away from a hidden danger. Had he seen a ship, or was he being cautious in the storm?

Lacey began moving through the house again. The shutters rattled furiously in the wind, and she sighed, thinking of the condition that the boys would be in. They ought to have come home by now. But perhaps they had taken shelter somewhere in the forest and would not be home in time for supper at all.

Back in the kitchen, she arranged the towels on a hook near the door. The sky was far too dark now. Instinctively, Lacey went to check on her mother who was awake, her eyes flashing from side to side as the house shook in the wind.

Lacey lowered herself into a chair at the side of the bed and kept perfectly still. *Does Mama hear something besides the wind?* she wondered as her mother's arm jerked awkwardly and she pleaded to Lacey with her eyes.

"Mama, what is it?" Lacey asked. "Is the wind troubling you?"

Still, Mary Wells's eyes flashed.

Then Lacey heard the sound of her father, calling from the tower. His full-throated cry was no match for the storm, but Mary Wells had heard it, and now Lacey heard it, hardly believing that it could sound so distant.

She dashed to the back door, flung a towel over her head, and threw herself out into the storm. With the wind pressing against her, she could do little other than bend her head and follow the side of the house to the tower door. Heaving with every ounce of strength, she pulled it open and hurtled inside. She did not stop to find a candle but pounded up the stairs toward her father's frantic voice.

Chapter 22

S wollen from the dampness, the door at the top of the stairs did not want to open and, in pitch blackness, Lacey beat on it with her open hands. "Papa, the door!" she called, although she knew her father would not leave his post at the light.

Then Lacey heard him calling again very clearly now and, in a frenzied burst, she flung herself against the door as hard as she could. At last it gave way and she tumbled into the light room, where her father was gripping the light and swinging it in great circles. She blinked against the brightness of the four lamps burning brightly, their illumination multiplied in the reflectors behind them.

Lacey lurched over to her father. "I'm sorry I didn't come sooner," she shouted. "I didn't hear you calling."

"It's a large boat," Daniel Wells shouted over the raging storm. "I can't see what's happening. Go to the railing!"

Lacey left the shelter of the dome above the light and, in a few seconds, the towel on her head was drenched. As she scoured the churning waters below, she cast the towel aside and, with the sleeve of her blouse, she wiped the incessant flow of water away from her eyes. Not yet adjusted to the brightness of the light room, her pupils now rebelled against the darkness. Leaning over the railing, she tried to get her bearings. At first she saw no ship for the rain walled off the view in a solid sheath and whatever daylight was left was hidden deep behind the furious clouds, making it seem more like midnight instead of late afternoon.

Lightning split the sky and, in that instant, Lacey saw the craft. Her father was right: It was a large boat, not much bigger than the one Gordon Wright used to shuttle supplies back and forth. No doubt the owners had gone out on a routine errand on calm waters not knowing that the storm would come from nowhere with a ferocious surge that no one could have predicted. In a storm of this magnitude, with the wind blowing straight in toward the dock, there was little hope that such a lightweight boat would succeed in steering away from the rocks. The boat lurched toward the rocks while its crew worked frantically to change the position of the sail.

"Can you see it?" her father called. "Can you tell me which direction to look?"

"To the south!" Lacey shouted, choking on a mouthful of rain.

"The worst of the rocks are to the south," her father said as he simultaneously rotated the lamp southward and pulled on the rope that sounded the foghorn.

"More!" Lacey screamed over her shoulder. In the faint light, she saw three forms scurrying around on the boat's deck as the craft heaved with the motion of the water. Walls of water pounded the cliff and cascaded down over the treacherous rocks as the wooden boat tossed like a weightless piece of cotton.

Daniel Wells had done his job well. No craft had crashed against the peninsula in more than six years, although Lacey remembered many brutal fights against nature.

"Lord, be with those men!" she screamed, hardly hearing her own words. Gasping against the chill that now ran through her from head to toe, she scuttled back into the light room.

"How close are they?" her father demanded.

"Quite close," Lacey responded somberly. "I don't see how they will miss the rocks."

"If that boat hits even one rock, it will splinter into a thousand pieces," Daniel Wells said. "We should prepare to rescue the crew. Someone must go down to the bottom of the ladder and throw out the white life rings with the longest ropes we have."

Lacey's chest heaved with the effort of standing out on the railing; for her to go down the ladder was almost unthinkable.

"Have your brothers come home?" Daniel Wells asked.

Lacey shook her wet head. "No, but I hope they took cover somewhere."

"We have no time to waste." Daniel Wells looked at his daughter. "Do you want to stay here and keep the light burning, or do you want to go down into the water?"

Lacey's heart lurched. She rarely went down the ladder, certainly not in a storm like this. But she would not send her father down, either. Besides, he was more skilled with the light than she was.

"I'll go down," she said, shivering, as she felt her way down the twisting staircase.

At the bottom of the stairs, hanging on hooks embedded in the brick, were two white rings tied to lengths of rope the thickness of Lacey's fist. The yards of rope were far heavier than she could manage comfortably, and so she determined that she would have to take one ring at a time. Grabbing one ring off its hook, Lacey bolted through the doorway and ran to the ladder as the rope unwound behind her. Finding the free end of the rope in darkness was difficult, but at last she had it in her hands. Repeating aloud the instructions for knots that she had learned as a child, she secured it to the crank that they used to haul supplies up the cliff. From the top of the cliff, she squatted and heaved the ringed end of the rope over the edge. It seemed forever before she heard the ring slap the water below.

Should she go for the other ring or clamor down the ladder to throw the secured ring farther out onto the water? Leaning over the edge of the cliff, Lacey peered into the blackness. *The light, Papa,* she pleaded silently, *swing the light.*

The light moved, and she caught a glimpse of the boat that, miraculously, was holding its own; so she scrambled back to the tower for the other ring and repeated the entire procedure.

Now it was time to for her to go down the ladder, but her waterlogged boots were slowing her down. She grabbed at the laces and pulled the boots off. Then she scrambled down the ladder and crashed into the edge of the water. A wave nearly swept her off her feet but she held firm, and when it passed, she fished out the rings and prepared to throw them farther out.

She wished for a light of her own as she wondered if the crew would even see that she was throwing them a lifeline. She heaved the first white ring as hard as she could, and it landed safely beyond the rocks; the second ring followed. She prayed they would catch a glimpse of the gleaming white forms.

Lacey waded back to the bottom of the ladder and with aching arms, clung to its security. Gasping for breath, she raised her eyes to the thrice-flashing light and heard the foghorn. Her father was doing everything he could. Lacey dared not leave her tenacious post until she knew whether she must haul in the ropes.

The hull of the boat heaved up and tilted precariously to one side, but the mast was still up and the sails caught the changing wind. The craft righted itself and veered away from the rocks. The storm continued to pound brutally, but the determined crew persistently moved the boat toward safety, a few inches at a time.

Not much farther, Lacey thought with growing relief. *Only a few more yards, and you'll be clear.*

A few minutes later, confident that the boat would make it safely around the bend, Lacey climbed the ladder. Her father met her at the top with a dry blanket. Huddled together, they dashed toward the house and burst through the back doorway into the kitchen.

"My supper!" Lacey moaned, for she had not thought to dampen the fire in the stove before dashing to answer her father's call. The water had boiled out of the potato pot, and the meat that had simmered and filled the house with its aroma all afternoon was blackened and stuck to the bottom of the pan. The blanket slipped from her shoulders as she let both pans clatter into the sink. Dripping water puddled around her feet.

"Never mind the supper," her father said. "I'll check on your mother. Pray that the boys get back soon." He glanced out the window at the ferocious horizon.

Lacey stumbled across the hall to her own room, peeled off her clothes, and snatched the quilt off her bed. Wrapped in it, she sat on the edge of the bed and shivered, too exhausted to move, too cold to rest. She heard her father's soothing tones telling her mother what had happened, and that all was safe.

Lacey had no idea what time it was, but hours must have passed since she had sat and peeled potatoes and regretted that she would have to mash them. As a vestige of daylight crowned the horizon, she became aware that the storm had abated and that the downpour had dissipated into a drizzle. Gradually, warmth came to her and her shivering slowed, but her aching muscles demanded that she lie down. Still, Lacey was reluctant to shed her quilt and find some dry clothes.

Just then the back door swung open and Travis and the boys thundered into the house. "We got trapped," Joel announced loudly. "You wouldn't believe that storm!"

"Oh, yes, I would," Lacey heard her father answer. "Lacey and I were out in it ourselves."

"Lacey?" Travis asked.

"She was magnificent," Daniel Wells said proudly. "Fortunately the boat got through the passage safely, but Lacey was prepared for whatever might happen."

"She is a remarkable woman," Travis said so tenderly that Lacey almost did not hear the words. "She can always be trusted to do what must be done."

"I'm sorry that she couldn't go back to teaching," her father said in a low, almost sorrowful voice, "but I don't know what I would do without her right now."

Listening from her bedroom, Lacey threw off her quilt and reached for a warm, dry dress. Travis was right. She could do what needed to be done. And what was needed right then was a hot, filling meal for all of them.

Chapter 23

Fall deepened steadily in the weeks after the storm. Gone were the summer showers that within a few minutes would cool the air and then dissipate into a mist. In their place came the graying skies of autumn and the hovering clouds that foretold of winter. Water crashed and swirled at the base of the cliff in the winds. Air blowing in off the cool lake chilled the house.

Lacey chided the boys to make sure they kept the door to the chicken coop closed and did not let the cow wander too far out into the meadow. Now Lacey kept one ear cocked for her father's voice all the time; he seemed in a heightened state of watchfulness, spending hours on end up in the lighthouse. Lacey heard the fog horn blow at every hint of a gray sky, and she knew it would soon be time to batten down for the winter, when crossing the peninsula even with a horse and cart would turn cumbersome.

The Wellses would be on their own for the winter; afternoon visits with Abby would cease; and Travis would have to forego Sunday dinners with them. Lacey sighed as she thought of the loneliness that winter always brought but, in reality, it mattered little to her routine. Keeping up with schooling the boys, nursing her mother, and running the household left her very little time for visiting with a childhood friend or wondering about the intentions of a charming young man. Lacey did not know if her mother had always been so harsh as she had seemed in the last few years, but her own eyes were opened to the consuming reality of forging a life for a family in this place. Even as Mary Wells lay still in her bed, Lacey's appreciation for her mother's tenacity grew every day. Mary Wells had stopped perspiring and started shivering, and now it seemed that Lacey could not keep her warm enough. Every morning and every afternoon, Lacey forced herself to be cheerful as she entered her mother's room and worked the lifeless limbs. She had long ago given up hope that the habit would have any true therapeutic value; Lacey knew her mother would never again move her left side voluntarily. But the forced exercise seemed to help with the bedsores and encouraged her mother to move the right side of her body, even if in protest of the entire procedure.

"She seems no worse today," Daniel Wells had taken up saying. He woke beside his wife in the mornings and spoke to her gently as he readied himself for his day. "I believe she's holding her own now."

Lacey agreed with her father's assessment that her mother did seem to be holding her own. She was not getting worse; but she was not getting better. Her eyes would follow Lacey around the room as she tidied and cracked the window for fresh air but she no longer spoke, and she slept for longer and longer stretches of time.

Even Micah, who had clung to his hope longer than anyone else, had given up believing that his mother would recover. He faithfully visited with her several times each day, and she seemed to appreciate it, but Micah knew his mother would not get better. With his belief had also gone his dedication to his lessons, and Lacey had to nag him almost as much as she did Joel and Jeremiah.

Today was no different. Lacey sat in her mother's easy chair with her head back, listening to Micah read. She dared not close her eyes for fear that she would lose concentration completely and be of no help the next time Micah encountered an intimidating word. As it was, she did not immediately notice when Micah stopped reading. She blinked herself to alertness and urged him on.

"I don't want to read anymore," Micah whined. "The twins have already gone to play."

"They finished their lessons," Lacey reminded him. "You have only a few more paragraphs, and you'll be finished with this chapter."

"But I don't want to finish it. I want to leave it until tomorrow." He slapped the book shut.

Lacey was too weary to argue further. "All right, but you must make up the time tomorrow. Ten extra minutes."

"I'm going out to look for deer." Micah grabbed his jacket and was out the door.

Now Lacey closed her eyes. The clock on the sitting room wall ticked, but otherwise, the house was silent. Mary Wells was sleeping, the boys were all outside, and Daniel Wells was in the tower, polishing the reflecting glasses and the brass trim. Lacey thought of the pile of clothes that needed to be washed, but she lacked the energy to pump enough water to begin the job. It would have to wait another day, even if it meant that Micah wore a dirty shirt tomorrow.

The door creaked open and Lacey heard Micah's footsteps crossing the kitchen. "Did you change your mind?" Lacey called out.

Another set of footsteps followed Micah's.

"Joel? Jeremiah?" Lacey said.

Micah grinned as he appeared under the archway that set off the sitting room. "Look who I found."

Lacey reluctantly opened one eye and then the other more rapidly. Instantly alert, she jumped out of her chair. "Travis! I wasn't expecting you today."

"I know," he said quietly.

Something in his manner struck Lacey odd. His face looked worn out. "What's wrong? Is it Abby?" Lacey asked.

Travis glanced at Micah, and Lacey turned to the eight-year-old. "Did you find a deer, Micah?"

He shook his head. "I just found Travis."

"Then why don't you keep looking," she suggested.

With no further prompting, Micah turned and left the room. When she heard the back door swing closed behind him, Lacey repeated her question to Travis.

"No, Abby is fine and Peter and Nathan are fine."

"Then what is it? You look like you've lost your best friend."

"That just might be the case." His eyes would not meet hers.

Lacey moved around to try to capture his gaze. She put one hand on his arm. "Travis, what are you talking about?"

"I came to say good-bye, Lacey," he said quietly, not raising his eyes.

"Good-bye?" she echoed.

"Yes. I'm leaving the peninsula."

"When?"

"Today. Gordon should be here with his boat in a few minutes."

Lacey withdrew her hand. "Then you must have arranged this weeks ago."

Slowly Travis nodded. "Gordon says I must go now, or I may not have another chance until spring."

"Are you so anxious to go that you cannot wait until spring?" Lacey failed to control the quiver in her voice.

"I have stayed far longer than I expected to already."

"That's true. It's been a year and a half."

"It was only supposed to be a few months."

"Yes, I remember."

"And now I must go."

"But, why? Why now?"

"It is time."

Lacey sat down on the edge of a chair. She had hardly seen Travis in the last few weeks, but knowing that he was only a few miles away on the other side of the peninsula had somehow comforted her.

"Where will you go?" she asked.

"Home," he answered hoarsely.

"I thought the peninsula was your home now."

"To my father's home."

"Is he unwell?"

"Not to my knowledge. But he does want me to return."

Lacey knew very little about Travis's father. Travis rarely spoke of him, and when he did it was in vague terms with little emotion. She found it difficult to believe that such a distant relationship was compelling Travis to leave the peninsula, but she had no right to ask further questions. Travis had never promised her anything, and she was wrong to take anything for granted.

Lacey's eyes moved to the window. Micah roamed the yard beyond the glass. "Micah will be devastated," she said softly. "He has become quite fond of you."

"And I am fond of him," Travis responded, also looking out the window. "I'll try to explain it to him on my way out."

"He's going to have questions."

"I know."

They stood side by side at the window, and Lacey could feel the heat from his body warming the air around her. His breathing seemed weighted and his posture strangely stiff, but he kept his hands in his pocket and his gaze forward.

"Travis, do you. . .will you. . . ?" Lacey tried to speak.

Travis shrugged. "I can't tell you any more, Lacey. I'd better go on down. I promised Gordon I wouldn't keep him waiting when he gets here."

He turned and retraced his steps to the back door. There he picked up a bag before crossing the yard to where Micah played. Micah grinned in greeting, but his expression sobered when Travis lowered himself to Micah's level and spoke earnestly. Lacey watched from the kitchen. Travis had avoided looking her in the eye, but he locked his gaze with Micah's and spoke briefly. Confusion crossed the little boy's face, and he turned and looked over his shoulder toward the cliff.

Lacey saw her brother's mouth move. He was asking a string of questions. She could easily imagine what they were, because she had not had the courage to ask the same questions lurking in her own heart.

Travis pulled himself to his full height, picked up his bag, and began walking toward the rope ladder that would take him down to the water's edge. Before disappearing over the edge, he turned and waved at Micah and turned his eyes to the window where Lacey still stood. And then he was gone.

Micah burst into tears.

On the dock below, Travis greeted the incoming craft of Gordon Wright. "Did you tell the little lady farewell?" Gordon asked in his usual brusque manner. "Won't she even come to see you off?"

Travis threw his bag on the deck and boarded the boat without comment.

"You didn't tell her why you're leaving, did you?" Gordon said.

Travis shook his head.

Gordon scoffed. "She's a smart wench. She just might understand if you told her what you were up to."

Travis still said nothing and, as Gordon pushed off, he stared at the lighthouse and wished he had climbed its tower one last time.

Chapter 24

Two brown-haired heads and one blond one bent over the dining room table. Joel and Jeremiah had each plowed their way, under protest, through a Dickens novel and were now in the throes of the written reports that would prove they had followed the story accurately. The final version must be completed before they could leave the table for the day.

Micah was struggling with his arithmetic. Lacey had written out a page of addition and subtraction that required him to borrow and carry his totals, and Micah did not like it.

Lacey sat at the end of the table, trying to darn a wool sock. She had learned many things from her mother, but she had never mastered darning neatly. She took out her most recent stitches and started again. Winter had set in. The first snow of several inches was already on the ground in mid-November. The boys would need all the wool socks she could salvage.

Joel leaned over and looked at Jeremiah's paper. Jeremiah responded by heaving his shoulder into Joel's chest.

"Hey!" Joel protested.

"Mind your own business," Jeremiah answered.

"I just wanted to see how far you are."

"You're going to steal my ideas."

"We didn't even read the same book."

"Boys, please," Lacey pleaded as she set the sock aside. "He started it!" Jeremiah declared.

"All I did was look," Joel said in his own defense. He had one hand clasped over his injured chest.

"I don't want to hear about it," Lacey said. "I was sitting right here. Just finish your reports and you can go your separate ways."

The twins were twelve years old, but ever since their mother had fallen ill, they behaved as if they were five. In fact, everyone acted differently. Joel and Jeremiah were determined to test the extent of Lacey's new authority over them, even if it meant bringing physical harm to themselves. Micah no longer reveled in every detail of nature and, now when he went outside, he wandered aimlessly around the yard and could report very little when he returned. And her father, never a man of many words, said even less.

Micah slumped back in his chair. "I can't do this," he whined. "I don't understand. How can I take nine from zero."

"Impossible," spouted Joel.

"Can't be done," agreed Jeremiah.

Lacey narrowed her eyes at them. Immediately they turned their heads back to their papers. She turned to Micah. "You're not taking nine from zero," she explained for the fifth time that day. "You're taking nineteen from thirty." Once again she showed him how to borrow and take nine from ten instead of zero. "Now, you try it on the next one." She handed the pen back to him.

Micah took it, but he lowered his hands to his lap instead of the paper. "Another thing I don't understand is why Travis left. Doesn't he love us anymore?"

Lacey picked up the sock and twisted it between her fingers. "I'm sure Travis had a very good reason for going," she said. "He meant to visit the peninsula for only a few months."

"Why did he visit so long, if he didn't like it here?"

"He loved it here," Lacey said quietly. "Back to your figures, please."

Micah did one problem. "It's just not the same without Travis around."

"He was hardly ever here," Jeremiah pointed out, "and he came only to see Lacey, anyway."

Alarmed, Micah turned to his sister. "Is that true?"

Lacey glared at Jeremiah. "Travis is very fond of you, Micah. I know he always looked forward to seeing you."

"Travis wouldn't make me do these dumb sums," Micah muttered.

"Oh, yes, he would! Travis's father is a businessman. I know he made sure Travis could take nineteen from thirty."

"Well, I'm not going to be a businessman. I'm going to operate the lighthouse."

"You still have to be able to figure or you'll never know if Gordon is bringing you the right amount of fuel." She thumped his paper. "Finish, please. I'm going to check on Mama. I'll be right back."

In her parents' bedroom, Lacey found her father sitting at the side of the bed. The curtains were drawn, leaving the room in a dusky shadow. "Papa?" Lacey said quietly.

As if in slow motion, his head turned toward her. He did not speak.

"Papa, are you all right?" she asked.

He nodded, then shook his head.

"Papa, what's wrong?"

"Look at her. I don't think she even knows I'm here today."

Lacey touched her mother's shoulder; her mother's eyes fluttered open and immediately closed.

"She sleeps all the time," her father said. "She's so thin. She doesn't talk."

"I think she knows when you come," Lacey said. "She always seems better after you stop in during the day."

Her father shook his head adamantly. "I used to think that but not anymore."

Lacey did not know what to say.

"You would have liked your mother," he said.

"What do you mean, Papa? You know that I love Mama, despite all our differences."

"It's this place," he said. "If you could have known her somewhere else, when she was young, you would have enjoyed her. When I met her, she was a light. . .a brilliant lamp. I had not known many young women, but I knew that Mary Cooper was miles ahead of the rest. But I brought her here, and she did what she had to do to survive."

"Papa," Lacey said, unsure what she would say next. "It takes a re-markable woman to do what Mama did. I don't think she is sorry about anything."

"She would never let us know," he said. "But what if I had not brought her here. I could have stayed in the city. If she hadn't had such a harsh life. . .if there had been a hospital here. . ."

Lacey sat on the edge of the bed and took her father's hand. Daniel Wells was the last person on earth she would expect to have any doubts about how he had lived his life. Yet, here he was, wondering about how things might have been different.

He looked at the drawn curtains. "Your mother's sister gave us those curtains twelve years ago," he said.

"I remember."

"They have never fit the window properly, and they were faded along the edges when we got them. But your mother never complained."

Lacey said nothing.

"Your mother deserved better than a life of hand-me-down curtains and inadequate supplies of flour. And now look what I've done."

"She's not sorry, Papa. She wanted to be with you."

"She had never been to the peninsula before she agreed to marry me."

He put his head in his hands, and Lacey did not know what more to say. "Can I do something for you, Papa?" she asked.

He shook his head. "I'll just sit here awhile longer, then I'll get you some wood for the stove."

Lacey quietly moved to the kitchen; it was time to start supper. She would make some biscuits to go with the ham and bring up a jar of green beans from the cellar. Taking a mixing bowl with her, she went to the barrel in the corner and measured out enough flour for the biscuits. Outside, flecks of snow swirled through the air, threatening to leave a fresh coat on the ground.

Lacey recalled the previous November. She was two months into her temporary teaching job in Tyler Creek and expected that Travis would propose any day. They could marry when she finished her contract, she had thought, and go to the city to pursue Travis's business interests with his father.

Such speculation had belonged to another person, Lacey now thought. She had returned to the peninsula and might not leave again for a very long time. Travis had sent no word since his abrupt departure, and Lacey was realistic enough to know that she might never hear from him again. But she dared not be as brazen with her feelings as Micah was. She had no time for daydreaming in the meadow or girlish imaginings with a childhood friend. She had her mother to care for and the boys to look after. And now her father. In all her twenty years, Lacey had never seen Daniel Wells in such a frame of mind. Lacey had grown up under the shadow of her father's calling to tend the light. For him, running the lighthouse was not a job, not a responsibility, it was a passion woven into the way he viewed life itself.

When Lacey had entered adolescence, she and her father had begun their occasional talks along the railing. What does it mean to have a calling? How does God call His children? How would Lacey know she was making the right decisions for her future? Lacey still struggled with those questions. But Daniel Wells was her touchstone for finding answers. To hear her father say he regretted bringing his bride to this place was almost more than Lacey could comprehend. What grief, what emptiness would drive him to say something like that?

"Lacey?" Micah called from the dining room.

"Coming." Leaving her bowl of flour on the table, Lacey returned to the dining room. The twins were gone, but their book reports were there.

"Can I go now, too?" Micah asked.

Lacey picked up his paper and scanned over his answers. She circled two of them. "You'll have to do these again," she said.

Micah groaned, and Lacey sighed.

Chapter 25

Lacey shivered and the shivering wrenched its way into uncontrolled quaking. She clenched her jaw and tried to stop, but the shaking welled up inside her, bursting for its freedom through her teeth. Cold air shimmied through her coat and chilled the dress she wore underneath. Her only black dress was a thin one, not at all suitable for a wintery funeral the day after Thanksgiving.

Two days earlier, Daniel Wells had come back from his early morning rounds of stoking the stove and checking on the animals to find his wife oddly still but with her eyes wide open. Her mouth, too, looked as if she had been trying to call out. A few minutes later, Lacey had found her father slumped against the side of the bed, and she knew that her mother was gone.

Micah had shrieked at the news and had wailed his way through the next two days. Lacey held him and rocked him as he trembled. She was twenty years old, Joshua was on his own, the twins were nearly teenagers, and they had all benefitted from the firm but dedicated mothering of Mary Wells. But Micah was an eight-year-old child who needed his mother and would never have her again. As Lacey sought to comfort Micah, she felt as helpless as she had when trying to help TJ Richards and no explanation seemed good enough for what had happened and no alternative for the future would be as good as the past.

The twins had turned quiet, as had Micah. They pushed away their breakfast plates with the news and hardly touched the food Lacey offered to them since then. The pies she had hoarded for Thanksgiving were still on the shelves in the cellar. She had cooked the butchered turkey, but no one wanted any of its meat.

And now they stood gathered around their mother's casket. Lacey was relieved it was not a sunny day. She could not have stood seeing the landscape sparkle on the day she buried her mother. The gray sky supported the mood of the morning. Micah clung to her side with his face buried in her waist. He had not wanted to come to this final farewell, but his father was afraid that Micah would regret his choice later and insisted that Micah attend the funeral. Joshua was missing. They had tried to send word immediately, of course, through a lumberjack who was willing to travel the land route to a place with a telegraph. But they had no way to know if the message had reached Joshua, and it would likely take him two days to get home once he heard the news. Lacey did not expect him before Christmas.

Lacey had trudged over to the lumber camp on Wednesday afternoon to tell Abby's family the news. The path was icy, and Lacey had declined to take the horse and cart because she trusted her own footing more on the uneven path frosted and blanketed by the snow. The trek had taken her nearly three times as long as it did in fair weather, and she was chilled to the bone when she arrived at Abby's tidy little house.

As soon as Abby saw her friend, she knew what had happened. Maternally, she seated Lacey in the chair near the open fireplace and brought her a thick quilt to replace her damp coat. Lacey was vaguely aware that Nathan was fussing in the background.

Abby's mother, the only female friend to Mary Wells on the peninsula in the last twenty-five years, stifled her sobs and went immediately to her kitchen. At points of crisis, cooking was what she did best.

Peter, Abby's husband, returned immediately with Lacey and helped Daniel Wells build a solid casket. He brought his horse and pulled a cart with a selection of fine wood. Abby's father, manager of the lumber camp, insisted that Mary Wells would not be dumped in the ground in a slapped-together pine box. On Thursday Abby's father joined Daniel Wells and Peter to dig a hole in the frozen earth. The icy ground had resisted their efforts, mocking their shovels and splintering beneath their blades only after great effort had been exerted. Mary Wells would be laid to rest next to Daniel Wells's parents, who had also tended the light.

Lacey had not come to the family plot for years. As a child she had played there and wondered about the names and dates she saw etched in the stones. But she had never pictured anyone from her family there.

The gathering at the funeral was small by city standards but overwhelming by the measure of the peninsula. Tom Saget had closed the mill, and many of the men who respected Daniel Wells made their way over to pay their last respects.

No minister came, of course. Daniel stood before the crowd in the black suit he had been married in twenty-five years earlier. He refused to wear an overcoat, and Lacey marveled that the cold seemed not to bother him. As he shuffled and cleared his throat, Micah squeezed Lacey's hand nervously.

"Mary was a woman of faith. She went rejoicing to her Savior. I won't lie to you. I'm sorry she's gone. I'm sorry she was so ill for her last months on earth. I don't know why that happened. But she's with the Lord now, and we must give thanks for that."

A few of the mourners murmured their amens to Daniel Wells's sentiment.

"The boys are going to play," he explained, "and I hope you will all join me in repeating Psalm Twenty-three."

Joel picked up his violin and Jeremiah straddled his cello. Lacey swallowed a sob at the memory of all the music lessons Mary Wells had given the twins. Surely, she had not imagined that they, at the age of twelve, would be playing at her funeral.

After a hesitant start, they played steadily through four verses of "Amazing Grace," and Lacey pictured her mother, keeping time with a knitting needle against the edge of the dining room table. Their last notes drifted into the wind, and Daniel Wells stepped forward again.

" 'The Lord is my shepherd,' " he said quietly, " 'I shall not want.' "

The others joined in and Lacey moved her mouth, but somehow the sounds would not come.

" 'And I will dwell in the house of the Lord for ever,' " Daniel Wells finished. He cleared his throat again. "The women have prepared some food. You are all welcome to come to the house and warm up before going your ways."

Awkwardly, a funeral party dominated by lumberjacks trailed over the ridge and toward the house. The turkey would soon be consumed. Abby and her mother had baked bread and cakes to go with the pies in the cellar. Lacey was not sure how all these people were going to fit in the tiny house at one time. But they must be warmed and fed before crossing the peninsula again.

Once back at the house, Abby promptly handed Nathan to Peter and assumed the role of hostess. She insisted that Lacey situate herself in the sitting room among the guests and let her and her mother take care of serving food and steaming coffee.

Peter roamed the room easily with Nathan on his hip. At three months Nathan was far less fussy than he was as a newborn, and Peter seemed quite comfortable caring for him. Lacey admired that. No matter who Peter was talking to, and he talked to everyone, when Abby flitted through the room with a fresh tray of sandwiches, he raised his eyes to catch her glance. Each time a smile traced Abby's lips.

Lacey had to admit that Abby seemed supremely happy. When she had announced her engagement to Peter, Lacey's spirit had sunk with the conviction that her dear friend was settling for second best. To marry a lumberjack and have a string of babies while trapped on the peninsula had seemed a dismal future to Lacey. But Abby was thriving. Her eyes never lost their shine, a colicky baby had not ruffled her nerves, she embraced a pioneer spirit and built a real house in the midst of a lumber camp. Lacey had to admire her friend. Abby had made a choice that Lacey was sure would mean she was trapped, but Abby did not look trapped now. She looked happy.

Lacey was the one who felt trapped. She had passed up the opportunity to return to Tyler Creek, and not a day had passed that she did not think of TJ and Sally and wonder if there was something more she could have done to help them. And would anyone ever care enough to help them?

Abby's mother drifted by with a tray of small cakes. "Your mother would have been happy with the service, don't you think?" she said.

Lacey nodded. "She would have been proud of the twins."

"She taught them well. I only hope Nathan will have as good a teacher someday." She drifted off again.

Micah appeared at Lacey's side. His eyes drooped, and his shoulders sagged. "Did you have something to eat?" Lacey asked him.

He shook his head.

"If I fix you a plate, will you eat it?"

Again he shook his head.

Lacey sighed and opened her arms. Micah immediately clamored into her lap and snuggled against her chest. Even at eight, he was able to curl into a tight ball and hold very still. His shoulders rose and fell with his breathing. Lacey stroked the top of his head.

Father, she thought, *is this the child You want me to help? Show me what to do.*

Chapter 26

Examining the rag, Lacey determined that she would soon need a fresh one. The brass trim on the glass case enclosing the light had been neglected in the weeks of her mother's illness. Soot had accumulated everywhere, and Lacey had finally decided to tackle the job.

Normally, Daniel Wells was meticulous about this task, and he polished spots that no one else saw. Certainly no one in the waters below could detect the smudges he refused to tolerate. Under his supervision, all of the Wells children had learned to scrub and polish even the parts that already gleamed in the sunlight.

But Daniel Wells had lost his spark; his wife's illness had shaken him enough that he slowed down. In the fall he had been of little help to Lacey in harvesting the garden. Instead, she had conscripted the boys to pick vegetables and help with the canning. With every week that passed, he did less; now he expended effort only for what absolutely could be ignored no longer. Lacey was horrified to think how the family would have fared had she returned to Tyler Creek. Even Joshua might have stayed home had he seen his father in such a state. Joshua would be home in two more weeks for Christmas. He would see for himself.

Daniel Wells made routine visits to the tower throughout the day, but he did not stay long. Lacey was used to her father spending hours in the peaceful tower if there were no other demands on his time. After the funeral, she had expected that he might spend even more time in his private refuge. But the tower did not beckon as it had for all those years. Now he was more likely to sit in a rickety wooden chair in the backyard. In a matter of just a few weeks, he had turned into an old man.

Lacey rubbed harder with the cloth. It was cold in the tower, and she had to keep moving to keep warm. The wind swirled around the tower and whisked through the light room. If she stopped for very long, her fingers might go numb.

At one point she leaned over the railing and surveyed the yard, hoping that the boys were behaving themselves. She had heard no shrieks of terror from Micah. The twins were supposed to be stacking wood near the back door so they would not be caught short if a blizzard struck. Lacey found herself following all the precautionary patterns of her mother. The flour barrel was kept full, jars of vegetables were neatly stacked in the cellar, meat was hung to dry for jerky. If winter assaulted with a full blast, the Wells family would be prepared.

Movement in the water caught Lacey's eyes. A small craft had rounded the jutting land and seemed headed for their dock. Lacey followed her curiosity and peered down at it. It was Gordon Wright's boat. He had come several weeks ago with extra portions of provisions and a stern warning about the need to ration them carefully. She had not expected to see him for several more weeks, until the worst of the winter was over. Lacey thought it remarkable that he had managed to navigate the choppy water, but there he was. Even more remarkable, Gordon was not alone. A second figure now stirred on the deck of the boat. As Gordon wrestled with the sails to turn the boat toward the dock, Lacey's heart thumped faster. The brown hair was longer and the beard was new, but the second figure was too similar to Travis not to be him. Forgetting the cold, Lacey stared down. The figure raised his face to Lacey and then a hand. Yes, it was Travis.

Why did he not send word he was coming? she wondered. But, of course, no one had brought news from the southern part of the state in weeks. Lacey was not even sure if Joshua had received news of their mother's death. A greater question was why Travis was returning at all. Two months ago, on the day of his departure, he had made no promises to return. He had left Micah and Lacey tormented by his departure with no hint that it might be temporary. Why had he come now?

The boys had seen the boat now and were peering over the cliff at the dock. Micah squealed and waved in delight. Lacey winced as she saw him lean farther over the edge than he should have. Jeremiah sensibly pulled him back. Lacey instinctively lurched for the stairs and started her descent. By the time she reached the bottom of the tower and emerged into the sunlight, the boat was docked and Travis was getting off. Gordon waved up at her, and she returned the gesture.

"It's not too wicked a day for a boat ride," he challenged her. "Bring a blanket, and we'll head for the lake."

Lacey rolled her eyes. Gordon was nothing if not persistent. But he was already preparing to leave, having discharged his cargo.

"Have you brought no provisions?" Lacey called down.

Gordon spat and shook his head. "I told you the last time that you'll have to be careful in the winter. Your mother always has been."

Travis turned and gave the boat a shove. Gordon waved his farewell, and Travis began to climb the rope ladder, dragging an overstuffed bag behind him.

"I knew you'd come back! I knew you'd come back!" Micah cried, jumping up and down.

Lacey stood protectively behind Micah, keeping just enough weight on his shoulder to keep him from doing something rash. In another moment, Travis's head appeared at the top of the ladder and her eyes met his gaze over the top of Micah's head. She had both hands pressing quite firmly on Micah's shoulders, but he wriggled for his freedom. As Travis emerged from the ladder and tossed his bag to one side, Micah hurtled toward him and jumped into his arms. Lacey had not seen such liveliness in her little brother since well before their mother's death.

"I just knew you couldn't stay away," Micah exclaimed. "No one believed me, but I knew."

Travis smiled. "And you were right, weren't you?" He smiled at Lacey. "Hello, Lacey."

Jeremiah tugged on Micah's leg. "Come on, let's go."

"Go where?" Micah asked.

Jeremiah glanced at Lacey. "Just come with me. I've got a project for you."

Micah slid down Travis's torso and thumped to the ground. "What is it?" he asked.

Jeremiah rolled his eyes. "Just come with me and find out."

Micah turned to Travis. "You'll be here when I get back?"

Travis smiled and nodded. "You go with Jeremiah. I'll talk to you later."

Lacey threw a grateful and nervous glance at Jeremiah. When the boys were gone, she turned toward Travis.

"Hello, Lacey," he repeated.

"Hello, Travis." Questions pelleted her mind, but she did not ask them.

"You are a sight for sore eyes," he said.

She smiled. "Is that really you behind that beard?"

He chuckled and stroked his hairy chin. "It's me. Do you like it?"

Lacey nodded. "I didn't know you were coming back."

"No one did."

"How did you persuade Gordon to bring you, especially at this time of year?"

"Let's just say I impressed upon him the urgency of my voyage."

"And what was so urgent?"

Travis glanced out over the water. "Unfinished business."

Lacey nodded, even though she did not understand.

"How is your mother?" he asked.

Lacey sucked back a gasp. "I thought Gordon would have told you."

"Told me what?"

"Mama died just before Thanksgiving."

Travis shook his head. "Gordon never said a word."

"Do you want to walk a bit?" she asked.

She took him to the burial plot and knelt to scrape away the ice on the gravestone. Travis knelt beside her in the snow and traced his fingers over the irregular lettering:

MARY COOPER WELLS
WHO KNEW THE SACRIFICE OF LOVE

"I'm so sorry, Lacey," he said.

And she believed he meant it. She swallowed the emotion welling up inside her. "Now I have an idea what it must have been like when you lost your mother."

"And your father?" he asked.

She shook her head. "He's lost without her. He hardly knows what to do with himself. I never knew it would be this way."

"They were together a long time. She was his partner, someone who shared his dream."

Lacey studied his face. The tenderness in his eyes told her that he genuinely shared the grief of the Wells family. But she could not contain her questions any further. "Travis, why are you here?"

"I had to come back."

"Then why did you leave?"

"I had to do that, too."

"You're speaking mysteries, Travis."

"Have you any teaching prospects for next year?" he asked as they began walking back toward the house.

Lacey was annoyed that he had changed the subject. "I haven't let myself think that far ahead. The situation here. . .well, it's too soon. . ."

"So you'll be here?" he said solidly.

She nodded. "I think so."

"Good."

"Why?"

"Because I'll be here. And I'd like it if you were, too."

Lacey's eyes widened. Had Travis really spoken the words she had longed to hear a year ago? "So how long will you be here this time?" she asked cautiously.

"A long time. I'm going to make Peter help me build a small house and have some of my things shipped up."

"A house?" she echoed.

Suddenly his eyes lit up. "Lacey, that lumber camp is going to be a real town. I've spent the last two months with my father telling him about the peninsula. It's more than we ever hoped for."

"What are you talking about?" she asked.

"My father sent me here on a scouting expedition," he explained. "He's not an ordinary businessman. He has quite a bit of money, actually."

Lacey had already figured that out.

"Father is looking for a long-term investment. I've convinced him of the potential of this place—the lumber, the fishing, the hunting—but we'll need to build roads, of course, to make it more accessible. Someday, soon, I think, we'll build a mill right next to the camp. Only it won't be a camp then, it'll be a town, with houses and shops and families."

"Your father is going to pay for all this?" Lacey said faintly.

Travis nodded. "He expects a good return for his money, of course. I've worked hard to prove to him that building a town is a good business venture. But if we put in a branch of our mill and explore the other potential businesses up here, it can be done. We'll create jobs for people who are willing to work hard. Just think, Nathan won't have to grow up alone. There will be friends for Micah, too, and someday, friends for your children."

Lacey blushed. "Let's not get ahead of things. So. . .you're here to oversee this?"

Travis nodded. "I'm here, Lacey. I'm here."

Chapter 27

Surprisingly, the weather cleared. A week after Travis's return, Lacey gave firm instructions that would keep her brothers busy for several hours, and she tromped across the peninsula for a rare winter visit with Abby. There had been no way to send word, of course; she simply could not resist taking advantage of the break in the weather.

Nathan cooed amiably, his colic completely dissipated. He stuck a fist in his mouth and drooled happily. Abby competently balanced him on one hip as she moved about the kitchen, fixing Lacey a cup of hot tea. "Travis didn't tell me you were coming," Abby said, setting the tea in front of Lacey then lowering herself into a chair across the table.

"He didn't know," Lacey answered. "I may look for him before I go home."

"You don't need to look far," Abby said. "He's coming for lunch."

"Here?"

"Yes, he and Peter are going to talk about some plans. Peter is so excited about the idea of building a real town, he can't wait to get started. We were glad to have neighbors when the Stantons moved in, but we need to attract more families to move up here."

"I suppose if you are going to have a town, you have to have people to live in it."

"Maybe someday you'll move over here," Abby mused.

"Oh, I don't know about that."

"But Travis is going to build a big new house. It would be perfect for the two of you."

"I think you're getting the cart before the horse," Lacey said. "Travis and I have no plans to—to. . .no plans for anything."

"Don't be coy, Lacey Wells," Abby said. "He's completely smitten with you, and you are with him."

"You are forgetting that two months ago he left without any

explanation. He never sent a letter, nothing. Then he showed up again out of the blue."

"But now you understand why," Abby insisted. "He couldn't say anything about developing a town until he knew whether his father was willing to finance it."

"Don't forget that last year he practically forced me to leave, even though he was staying here," Lacey countered.

"You're exaggerating. He offered you the opportunity to do something he thought would make you happy. How can you blame him for that?"

Lacey sighed. "I suppose I can't. But I do wish he would speak more plainly. I really have no idea about his intentions."

"And just what are your intentions?" Abby prodded.

"What do you mean?"

"You have to know your own feelings before you concern yourself with figuring out his." Nathan started to fuss. "I'd better feed my son."

"Can I help you get lunch ready?" Lacey offered, glad for the opportunity to change the subject.

An hour later, Peter and Travis burst through the door with rolls of wide paper tucked under their arms. When Lacey heard the door open, she wiped her hands on a dish towel and slowly moved to the front room.

Travis stopped abruptly. "Lacey! Hello! Abby didn't say you would be here."

"Abby did not know. I have imposed myself upon her without an invitation."

"You're always welcome here, you know that," Peter said. "I'm going to go say hello to my son. You two must have a lot to talk about." Peter left the room.

Lacey turned to Travis and smiled. "I wasn't sure if I would see you today."

"I hope you never come all the way over here and don't see me," he replied. "And I hope you'll come often."

Lacey shrugged. "That depends."

"On what?"

"The weather."

Travis nodded. "That's a sensible approach. It's only December. We have a lot of winter yet to go."

"Lunch is ready," Abby announced. She laid Nathan on a quilt on the floor, and he promptly began to inspect his toes.

"Abby," Peter said with his mouth full of ham, "you've got to see these plans Travis has been working on."

"I'd love to."

Without waiting to finish the meal, Peter reached behind him and grabbed the long rolls. Travis hastily pushed aside the dishes and unfurled the plans.

"We'll improve the road we already have," he explained, pointing to a line on the drawing. "We'll make it wider. Down at this end, we'll put in a row of shops. We'll need a general mercantile first of all, and then some specialty shops."

"I'm going to open a furniture shop," Peter declared. He grinned. "I won't have to worry about competition way up here, and there's plenty of wood."

"The mill will need offices," Travis continued. "And we'll want a proper medical clinic. I want to have that ready even before we find a doctor."

Lacey's mind harkened back to her conversation with Joshua, when he had announced his intention to study medicine with the hope of returning to the peninsula some day. Had he known that such a grand plan was in Travis's mind?

"My father wants to put up a hotel," Travis said. "But it might be awhile before a hotel could be profitable."

Peter disagreed. "People will need temporary quarters while they build houses. We must work on the hotel soon."

Lacey chuckled. "You two almost have me believing this place is a bustling metropolis."

"It will be," Abby interjected. "Just wait and see."

"Just where will all these people come from?" Lacey asked.

"Milwaukee, Chicago, Duluth, lots of places," Travis answered. "We'll start by opening a full-service lumber mill right here, instead of floating the logs somewhere else to be milled. That will mean jobs for men willing to work hard."

Lacey looked at the plans. Travis had drawn in a network of streets fanning out from what would be the center of the new town. He was picturing rows of houses, with a central area for shopping and community life. If his plans materialized, the new town would soon outshine the places like Tyler Creek that dotted the map of the state. Travis's eyes shone with a light she had not seen before his departure.

"This is ambitious," she said aloud.

Travis put his finger on the map. "Over here, there will be a church, a real church. And next to it, a school." He raised his eyes and looked at Lacey. "We'll need a teacher."

"What are these?" Abby pointed to a network of thin lines imposed over the whole town.

"Those are the wires for electric lights."

"Electric lights!" Abby and Lacey said together.

"I know that won't happen right away," Travis conceded, "but some of the big cities are thinking about it. The Pillsbury flour mill in Minneapolis is already using water power to make electricity for the mill. Charles Pillsbury has an electric fan in his office! Why shouldn't the whole city have lights?"

"Next you'll be talking about telephones," Lacey said.

"Exactly! It won't be easy to persuade the telephone company to string wires all the way up here, but we won't give up until we have telephones."

Peter reached for the paper and began to roll it up once again. "I hate to eat and dash off, but I have to get back to work." He glanced at Abby. "Your father wants an exact count of the logs we float today."

"You go ahead," Travis said. "I'll be along in a few minutes."

"I should start back, too," Lacey said. "The boys will be threatening each other with bodily harm if I leave them for much longer, and Papa will not be able to manage."

"I'll walk with you part of the way," Travis offered.

Behind him, where only Lacey could see her face, Abby grinned and nodded enthusiastically. "I would be glad for the company," Lacey said politely.

Outside and down the path a few yards, Travis chuckled. "I saw Abby's face in the looking glass."

"Oh, you mean—"

He nodded. "Clearly she was delighted that I was going to walk with you."

"Abby sometimes gets ahead of herself," Lacey said. "She's always been that way."

"And what is she ahead of this time?"

Lacey's steps slowed. "You. Us. She has us married and living in that fine new house you are planning to build with a half dozen children."

"Does that seem so unreasonable to you?" Travis asked.

"Well, I. . ." Lacey did not know what to say.

Travis took Lacey's hand and turned her toward him. "Lacey Wells, you have to know how fond of you I am. But I know how much you have wanted to leave the peninsula. And when your brothers are a little older, or your father recovers from his grief, you'll be free to do that."

"I—"

He put a finger on her lips. "Someday there will be a town here, with children who need a teacher. It's really going to happen. But I know it might not happen soon enough for you. If your dream is somewhere else, I don't want to stand in your way. But God has brought me here, and this is where I belong."

She looked into his eyes and knew he spoke the truth. "I'm fond of you, too," she said hoarsely. "I didn't understand why you sent me away last year, until I went. You were right then; I needed to go. But you don't have to send me away again."

He shook his head. "I'm not sending you away. I just don't want to hold you back."

She searched his eyes. Was he saying everything in his heart this time?

He sighed. "Peter will be looking for me. Will you come to the Christmas party?"

"There's going to be a Christmas party?" she asked.

He grinned and nodded. "A real town celebrates Christmas. Come on Christmas day, that is, if. . ."

"If the weather—"

"Yes, if the weather." He released her hand. "I'll see you next week, Lord willing." And he turned and walked back toward the camp.

In a fog, Lacey turned and continued her trek home. When she came to her clearing, her bootprints from a few hours earlier were the only disturbance of the pristine, sparkling covering. The winter sun, low in the northern sky, was nevertheless strong enough to dazzle the air. Evergreens decades old, perhaps even centuries, stood tall and proud, determined to resist the onslaught of winter with full dignity. Suddenly she wondered why she would ever want to leave this place.

Chapter 28

Is it time yet? Is it time yet?" Micah, already in his coat, pranced around Lacey in the kitchen.

"Just a few more minutes," she said. "Papa's going to make sure the light has plenty of fuel, then we'll go."

"But it's a nice day," Micah protested. "No one will need the light today."

"You can never be sure about the weather, especially in the winter," Joshua replied sternly. He had arrived home only the day before and was already doing his best to help Lacey manage the household. "If we're going to be gone all day, we must leave the light burning."

"We're going to take the cart, aren't we?" Jeremiah asked.

Lacey nodded. "The snow is packed down enough that we can pull the cart. If the three of you want to cram into the back, you may."

"Don't smush me!" Micah warned loudly.

"Shh," Lacey said. "Don't get so excited."

"I don't think we should even be going," Joel said. "We should stay home and have a regular day."

Lacey sighed and glanced at Joshua. Joel had a point. Only a month had passed since their mother's death, and it seemed odd to think about observing any of the family's traditions without her. Christmas Eve dinner was a routine chicken with potatoes rather than the roast duck that Mary Wells would have managed. They had not kept the midnight vigil, waiting for Christmas morn with the house lit up with candles. No one had played a single Christmas carol on the piano. Lacey had made all the boys new shirts. Micah was already wearing his, but the twins had opened their boxes only to quiet Micah's incessant nagging, and they soon set them aside.

For Micah's sake, Lacey had tried to create a festive atmosphere, at least for this one day. Daniel Wells had reluctantly agreed that the whole family could attend the Christmas party at the lumber camp, and the weather had proved no obstacle. He appeared in the dooway and gave Lacey a silent nod. It was time to go.

They arrived at the camp and found it bustling with activity. Abby's mother had conjured up a spread of food reminiscent of Peter and Abby's engagement party. Abby and her neighbor, Lillie Stanton, had surveyed the trees up and down the crude road and designated one as the official Christmas tree. This they had decorated with bows and ribbons miraculously produced from the recesses of their homes.

The boys dispersed, and Daniel Wells settled into a chair next to Tom Saget. Lacey had not expected he would want to be sociable; she was not sure she did herself. But it was a Christmas party, and she could not very well ignore everyone there. Travis had specifically invited her, and he must be around somewhere.

Lacey first went in search of Abby. Scanning the street, she decided that Abby was not likely to have Nathan outside because, although the day was bright for early winter, a brisk breeze chilled the air. Lacey had a fleeting thought that she ought to keep a better eye on Micah. His curiosity might take him too close to some dangerous equipment. She saw his blue coat streak across the dirt road and satisfied herself that he was staying out of trouble.

Abby's house was set back from the main road, and beside it was the small house for the Stantons. At the sight of them, a picture of Travis's meticulously drawn plans flashed through Lacey's mind. Travis was going to build his house a hundred yards beyond the three existing ones, as a token of his hope that the vicinity would one day be filled with homes and families. Lacey could almost imagine what a row of houses would look like, with children bursting out of the front doors on a fine spring day and mothers hanging their wash in the backyards.

She reached Abby's door and knocked firmly. The door flew open almost immediately, and Abby stood before her with bright, excited eyes. "Lacey, I just heard the news! I'm so excited."

Lacey raised an eyebrow. "What news?"

Abby turned away abruptly and began walking toward her kitchen. Lacey followed her in. Nathan smiled up at her from a quilt on the floor.

"I told my mother I would bring these sandwiches down," Abby said, "but I haven't quite got Nathan ready. Would you mind taking them for me?" She handed Lacey a platter.

"What were you talking about a minute ago?" Lacey asked.

"Oh, never mind that," Abby said, turning Lacey around at the shoulders, "just take the sandwiches. Mother's waiting. I'll catch up with you later."

Before she knew it, Lacey found herself standing outside of Abby's house with a platter of sandwiches, the door closed firmly behind her. Puzzled, she trudged down the road toward the common hall to carry out her task. Packed snow crunched under her feet, and the view was so bright she had to squint. Lumberjacks milled around the road, a couple of them raised their eyes to inspect the platter.

"Mrs. Saget knows how to put out a spread," one said. He winked at Lacey. "I expect we'll have another party before long."

Lacey hardly knew this man. What kind of crude suggestion was he making?

Peter passed by on the other side of the road. He waved energetically and called out, "I'm really happy for you," and kept on going.

Lacey turned and stared after him. *What is he talking about? What is everyone talking about? My mother died a month ago, and my father is trapped in a depression. What is there to be happy about?*

Lacey reached the hall. Abby's mother was bustling around organizing the layout of the food, and she nearly snatched the platter from Lacey's hands as she asked, "Where's Abby?"

"She's coming in a few minutes. Nathan wasn't quite ready."

"I'm glad you two had a chance to talk," the older woman said. "I'm sure you've got a lot to tell her these days. She's so pleased, utterly pleased." She turned and was gone, leaving Lacey with a question half-formed on her lips.

Retracing her steps, Lacey saw that many of the men were drifting toward the common hall, no doubt expecting that soon they would be free to fill their gullets with the foods that Abby's mother had spent days preparing. Lacey began to look around for her brothers. With her eyes raised to peer down the street, Lacey did not notice Micah hurtle toward her. He jumped into her arms, nearly knocking her off balance.

"Micah!" she said, startled. "What's gotten into you?"

"Why didn't you tell me?" he demanded.

"Tell you what?"

"You know, what everyone's been saying. Why didn't you tell me first?"

Lacey set Micah down on his feet. "What are you talking about, Micah Wells?"

"You're going to marry Travis!"

Her mouth dropped open. "Where'd you hear such a thing?"

"It's all over the camp. Everyone's talking about it."

Suddenly all the odd looks made sense. "Well, everyone is quite mistaken," Lacey said, lowering her voice and shepherding Micah away from the growing crowd outside the common hall.

"Don't you want to marry Travis?" Micah demanded.

Lacey sighed. "It's more complicated than that. Besides, he hasn't asked me."

A throat-clearing noise behind her made Lacey spin around, and she stared into the eyes of Travis Gates.

"But I meant to," Travis said softly. "That is, I still mean to."

Lacey's mouth dropped open again. "Mean to what?"

"Ask you to marry me, of course."

Lacey glanced around. People were staring at them. "Apparently you are quite confident that I will say yes."

Travis shrugged sheepishly. "I'm sorry about all the fuss. I told only Peter."

Lacey laughed. "And he told Abby, and she told her parents, and her father told a few of the other lumberjacks."

Micah tugged on her arm. "It's true, isn't it?"

"Please make it true," Travis said. "Marry me and build a life with me. . .build a town with me."

"Do it, Lacey!" Micah urged.

Lacey swallowed hard and looked into Travis's eyes. "I think I'll do just that."

A Letter to Our Readers

Dear Readers:

In order that we might better contribute to your reading enjoyment, we would appreciate your taking a few minutes to respond to the following questions. When completed, please return to the following: Fiction Editor, Barbour Publishing, Inc., P.O. Box 719, Uhrichsville, OH 44683.

1. Did you enjoy reading *Great Lakes*?
   □ Very much—I would like to see more books like this.
   □ Moderately—I would have enjoyed it more if _____
   _____
   _____

2. What influenced your decision to purchase this book?
   (Check those that apply.)
   □ Cover   □ Back cover copy   □ Title   □ Price
   □ Friends   □ Publicity   □ Other

3. Which story was your favorite?
   □ An Uncertain Heart   □ An Unexpected Love
   □ Tend the Light

4. Please check your age range:
   □ Under 18   □ 18–24   □ 25–34
   □ 35–45   □ 46–55   □ Over 55

5. How many hours per week do you read? _____

Name _____

Occupation _____

Address _____

City_____ State_____ Zip_____

E-mail_____

$\heartsuit$

HEARTSONG
PRESENTS

If you love Christian romance...

 $10.^{99}$

You'll love Heartsong Presents' inspiring and faith-filled romances by today's very best Christian authors...DiAnn Mills, Wanda E. Brunstetter, and Yvonne Lehman, to mention a few!

When you join Heartsong Presents, you'll enjoy 4 brand-new mass market, 176-page books—two contemporary and two historical—that will build you up in your faith when you discover God's role in every relationship you read about!

Imagine...four new romances every four weeks—with men and women like you who long to meet the one God has chosen as the love of their lives...all for the low price of $10.99 postpaid.

To join, simply visit www.heartsongpresents.com or complete the coupon below and mail it to the address provided.

Mass Market 176 Pages

✂ -

YES! Sign me up for Hearts♥ng!

NEW MEMBERSHIPS WILL BE SHIPPED IMMEDIATELY!

Send no money now. We'll bill you only $10.99 postpaid with your first shipment of four books. Or for faster action, call 1-740-922-7280.

NAME _____

ADDRESS _____

CITY _____ STATE _____ ZIP _____

MAIL TO: HEARTSONG PRESENTS, P.O. Box 721, Uhrichsville, Ohio 44683 or sign up at WWW.HEARTSONGPRESENTS.COM

ADPG05